THE ORPHAN RACE

JENNY JONES

STARDUST BOOKS

THE ORPHAN RACE

Cover Art by Carlos Quevedo

Cover Design by Jenny Jones

Generative AI was not used in the creation or publication of this work.

Published by Stardust Books

https://jennyjonesphd.com

jenny@jennyjonesphd.com
Stardust Books is a registered trademark of Renaissance Femme, LLC.

The Library of Congress Cataloging-in-Publication Data is available upon request.

ISBN 979-8-9880959-3-4 (paperback)

ISBN 979-8-9880959-2-7 (ebook)

Para mi fuego.

PART I

WORMHOLE

CHAPTER ONE

GUILLERMO

A N EARTHY FUNK CLINGS to damp air. The guardian walks down the center aisle with its rows of cryogenic pods stretching from wall to wall. Wind whistles against high windows darkened by rain, sand, and creeping vine. He makes his way to the back. La curiosidad settles in, familiar y tan raro. His footfalls die. The howling wind snarls louder. Moss creeps up a pod beside him and smothers the viewing pane. He can't make out a face through the dust. Guillermo crosses himself and continues deeper into the garden.

There it is. He crouches and wipes dust from the viewing pane with his skinsleeve. Careful, now. Silence folds into him. Long curls tipped with frost are matted against high cheeks, the nape of a neck. Fifty years since he last held estos chinos suaves between his fingers. His throat tightens, salt on his tongue like the alga marina they survived on. Before.

The man in the pod is so much younger than he is now. Guillermo rips a glove off his shaking hand and stares at his own skin, bone and sinew just visible beneath: the cost of immortality. The face beneath the viewing pane holds a youth no GLOW injection could replicate. Could Juan even still love him, old as he is now? For the thousandth time, the guardian resists the urge to shatter the slim plexiglass barrier—all that stands between them.

"A promise is a promise, querido mio." The strangled words break free from the raw flesh of his throat. He spreads his fingers across the cool, damp moss blanketing Juan's pod. "I'll free you from this prison, no matter the cost."

An incoming call blinks in the corner of his eye, distracting him. Órale, why now? He scrambles to his feet and wipes his stinging eyes with the back of his gloved hand. The holographic form of a man materializes, skin shining with decades of GLOW injections. ¡Híjole!—it's Frank Roarke, leader of the entire pinche Coalition. Guillermo swallows, washing away the taste of ocean spray on his lips.

"To what do I owe this honor?" His words barrel down the aisle, pinging off cryo pods and making him cringe. Don't disturb their peace, Memo.

A grim smile twists the hologram's mouth. "I hope I didn't disturb you, Guillermo, but it's urgent. Can you come to the Ring?"

¡Qué extraño! Odd request. Guillermo cocks his head. "For you, Frank? Por supuesto."

"Thank you. Leap if you can, please."

Las sorpresas se multiplican. "Give me thirty minutes. I need to return my moto first." A dozen questions spring to mind, but they'll have to wait.

"Very well. Hurry, please." If the other man is disappointed, he hides it well.

The hologram flickers and fades, leaving Guillermo alone with the frozen bodies. What could Roarke want? Since the Coalition restricts non-essential travel between stations, their leader wouldn't encourage Leaping without a damn good reason. Guillermo turns on his heel, but his gaze lingers on Juan. Sigh. He'd stay until dark if it weren't for the strange call. The earthy musk fades with each stride as he retraces his steps.

Outside the cryo garden, he straddles his hovermoto and twists the throttle. Itza hums to life beneath him, rocking gently as her tires lift away from the ground and fold inward. He leans forward and grips the handlebars, leather creaking. The moto streaks out onto the empty road and arid wind fills the guardian's nostrils. The tension melts away from his shoulders. Whatever this is about, he'll get it done. He always does.

Itza emerges into bright daylight, evoking a flinch from Guillermo. An old reflex. The dome's protection is a small comfort after so many years underground. Cálmate, güey. He strokes the engine of his machine with a gloved hand and wills his heart to slow. Even through the muted orange tint of his visor, her green shine is unmistakable.

A glowing red sign warns of an obstruction ahead. Guillermo narrows his eyes. Why does the guild insist on these relentless safety features? He squeezes the throttle and Itza hums louder. The moto rockets over the debris with room to spare. Bump. With his implants, he selects one of those robotón tunes sweeping the station like a solar storm. A snare drum cracks out a staccato rhythm. Brrrrrrrap-brrrrrrrap-brrap-brrap-brrap. He and Juan would dominate the dance floor to a song like this. His lips part in a small smile.

Once he reaches the outskirts of the station, he kicks his hovermoto into a higher gear. Better not keep Roarke waiting. Dust rises, lashing out at Itza. His loose-fitting skins whip about, but still he rides faster. He presses his body close to his moto and Itza clears the next hill with ease. The hovermoto lands with a satisfying *thump* and he rides on.

SEPTEMBER 28, 3040 | COLOSSI INFINITI, EARTH'S ORBIT

A wave of questions weaves like salsa dancers through Guillermo's thoughts, the rhythm guiding his feet right into his leader's office. Someone clears their throat when he enters and he stumbles in the doorway off-beat. This is Coalition business de seguro, but that doesn't explain why Roarke invited one of his officers. Guillermo breaks into a wide grin despite his mounting confusion.

"Derek! There's a sight." Guillermo strides the length of the room and clasps arms with the officer. Derek returns a limp smile. The guardian steps back, grin fading. The commander is coiled up tighter than copper wire. "Everything alright, 'mano?"

"Everything is fine, my friend."

Guillermo turns as the man from the hologram drifts forward in a high-backed, glossy black chair. A swirling cloud of nanoparticles, equipped with the fastest processing power ever developed, orbits Roarke. Keyed to the unique signature of his implants, the Cerebrum particles expand his capabilities beyond those of standard-issue implants. Guillermo would know: he built them.

He steps forward swiftly. "Evening, sir."

"None of that." Roarke waves away the pleasantries. "Have a seat."

A second hoverchair whizzes toward Guillermo with a soft click of gears. Roarke snares the commander's gaze for one full breath and a look of understanding passes between them. Derek joins Guillermo but remains at attention, his eyes rooted on a point on the far wall.

Ay, nada bien está ocurriendo aquí. Guillermo left Juan's side for this? "Dígame," he demands, crossing one leg over the other and surveying Roarke. "Why am I here?"

The Coalition leader whirs forward. The Cerebrum particles trail behind as if by magnetism. "I've tasked the commander with a mission."

"What mission?" Guillermo folds his hands over his knee and cocks his head. "Nothing has come before the Coalition for approval." Derek's blue eyes avoid his friend's.

"A personal request," Roarke clarifies.

Guillermo's eyebrows shoot up. "Is that wise?"

The Cerebrum cloud crackles like thunder as Roarke's expression darkens. "I don't answer to the Coalition."

"Of course not, Frank." Like Hell he doesn't. Guillermo's clasped hands tighten, but he smothers his outrage and smooths his skins to give his clenched fingers something to do. Roarke obviously wants to keep this in the family.

Guillermo glances in Derek's direction. The commander is a military man, así que he'd never jeopardize his son's missile-like rise to an admiral. Entonces, maybe Jack is already up to speed. It doesn't hurt to ask. "Is Jack part of this, too?"

Derek opens his mouth, but Roarke catches his eye and a strangled grunt, barely audible, escapes his lips. That impassive look returns to his blue eyes and they drop to his boots. Guillermo's heart sinks. This is more painful than watching the commander "dance." Brow pinched, the Coalition leader turns back to Guillermo. "The admiral can't know about this."

Chingados, none of this is above board.

Roarke must have his reasons for ordering covert missions, but Derek is the one who will have to answer to the Coalition, and the guardians might just decide to discharge este cabrón. Guillermo bows his head and grinds his teeth. The whole thing stinks. He slaps his thighs and stands. "Claro. This is neither a Coalition-sponsored mission nor one approved by the admiral? I'll be leaving, now." Roarke watches in silence, but Derek drops his stoic, militant attitude and steps forward.

"Memo, wait. I . . . I need your help. Please." The commander grips Guillermo's shoulder, the officer's desperation betrayed by a tremor in his hand. Now he finds his pinche voice? Still, the guardian can't help but pause. Derek glances at Roarke, then fixes Guillermo with a look more serious than when he asked Guillermo if he could marry his sister. As if reading Guillermo's mind, he explains: "I brought this to Roarke, and I asked to be involved. It's Zomenos."

Guillermo scowls, his sympathy dissolving. "If it's about Zomenos, then Jack should have been the first to know. Adios." He tries to turn away, but Derek's grip on his shoulder tightens.

"It's Terra Nova, Memo."

"Mierda." Guillermo sinks back into his seat.

Roarke inches closer. "You understand why this has to be between us?"

Guillermo rubs his face with his palms. Terra Nova. That's a name he hasn't heard in a long, long time. "No," he answers. "This falls under the purview of the Coalition. Call a meeting and I will be happy to help through that capacity." If Terra Nova is back, fighting them is going to take everything they have. Even Frank Roarke can't do this alone.

The Cerebrum particles glow bright orange, echoing the sudden brightness in the Coalition leader's shining eyes. Roarke's voice tightens. "I need this contained, Guillermo. You are here because Commander Monroe tells me you can help."

"Shit," Guillermo says again as he shakes his head. "What aren't you telling me?"

Derek closes his eyes and takes a shallow sigh. "I've been keeping an eye on the progress of the colony. You know, making sure it all goes smoothly for my boys. Hell, Henry's never even been on an orbiter." He laughs shakily.

Guillermo forces a smile. They all want the colony to succeed. "You raised two good men, 'mano. They'll be fine."

Derek nods, chest heaving with another measured breath. "Well anyway . . . it's the cargo shipments. Freight ships leave for Zomenos every 8-12 weeks, but the last two never made it. Signals snuffed out without a trace."

Terra Nova, targeting the colony? A quick scan through public shipment manifests with the guardian's retinal implants confirms Derek's intel. Doesn't necessarily mean foul play. Guillermo crosses his legs and stares at Roarke. "A lot can go wrong out here. Equipment malfunction, radio wave interference, asteroids."

"I'm a pilot, Memo. I checked for all of that." A nerve works in Derek's temple.

Their leader's reaction is more interesting. The Cerebrum particles still radiate with the man's conviction. Roarke nods. "You're right to be skeptical, Guillermo. The available data place typical operational hazards at a ten percent causal likelihood. The chance of Terra Nova involvement is over 60% and climbing. It would be nothing short of arrogant to ignore this."

Derek's woodenness is making more and more sense. Guillermo sighs and slumps in his seat. "Unmanned ships, I take it? No witnesses."

Roarke nods. "The commander is taking an orbiter out to investigate. The fewer people who know about this, the better. I can't raise the alarm unless I'm sure—that's why I can't involve the Coalition."

The guardian snorts. "Dale. Why am I here, then?"

Roarke exchanges another one of those looks with Derek that Guillermo doesn't like. "I need the commander's coordinates concealed at all times. He tells me you have technology that can help."

Guillermo drums his fingertips on his armrest, not meeting Roarke's gaze. Does he know about Guillermo's xenobot? No, Derek wouldn't betray his confidence. "Technology? Last I checked, my station was downgraded to textiles."

Roarke's eyes narrow. "You've always been capable of more, Guillermo. Prove it."

Unbelievable. Guillermo scowls at Derek. "You told him, didn't you?"

The commander doesn't even flinch. "Diego was made for this, Memo. He can locate the missing freight ships *and* cloak our orbiter. We'll be back before you know it."

A splinter of pain slices across Guillermo's temples. Chingada madre, not now. He closes his eyes and grits his teeth, keeping his voice steady. "This isn't your decision to make."

"It's true, then?" Roarke asks. "You created a living android that can evade trackers?"

Guillermo nods. The damage is done, and his secret is out. He better not live to regret this. "Diego is a xenobot: 78% organic. His power cell is unregistered." He can't help but swell with pride.

Roarke lets out a careful breath, an all-too-familiar hungry look in his eyes. "Can he help us?"

The guardian shrugs. "There's nothing Diego can't do. The real question is: Why should I help?"

"You want this just as badly as we do," Roarke levels evenly, leaning closer.

Guillermo folds his arms. "Oh, I don't know about that."

Derek squats down, blocking Roarke from view, and squeezes Guillermo's shoulder. "Don't be so hasty, Memo. This is what we've always talked about. The whole reason Gabriella and I helped you build Diego. You still dream of opening the gardens up, don't you?"

He knows exactly how Guillermo feels about the gardens, damn it. The vivid memory of sinewy, smoky shiitake is overwhelming. Guillermo closes his eyes and swallows hard. After that meal, Juan announced his cryo assignment. "Yes," he whispers.

His eyes reopen to Roarke's burning gaze. "I know you want to release the frozen. This is your chance, Guillermo. Prove once and for all the true mettle of your station and help us secure the colony on Zomenos from interference. It's the only way forward for Juan."

Guillermo looks from Roarke to Derek. The commander returns to his feet and clasps his hands behind his back again. The Cerebrum particles hovering overhead blaze with reddish-orange fire. Guillermo closes his eyes and breathes in, the earthiness of those mushrooms still in his nostrils.

After all the setbacks? The shuttering of his robotics program? He's waited fifty years for another shot. *Juan.* Could their reunion really be this close?

"Carajo. I'll do it, okay?"

SEPTEMBER 30, 3040 | GUADALAJARA STATION, EARTH'S ORBIT

Nineteen terraformed stations orbiting Earth pulse inside the flickering blue hologram of their Solar System. Specks of space dust, en realidad. Earth shrinks as Mars and Jupiter come into view. Guillermo narrows his eyes and leans closer, rubbing his stubble. He sinks his arms elbow-deep into the hologram and expands it. Mars stretches to the size of a melon. The guardian drops a cone-shaped marker to label the region Derek and Diego would search.

"That seem right to you?" he asks, turning to Diego at his side.

The xenobot shakes his head, pointing. "No, the missing freighters made it farther than that. Coordinates were delivered by the Cerebrum particles this morning." He tugs the hologram and Jupiter lurches toward them. He points again, his green eyes trained on a spot just below the gas giant. "We can track them this far, at least." With his left hand, he expands the cone and it quickly dwarfs the other planets.

"That's gotta be two or three AU!" Guillermo plants his hands on his hips. "That's too much ground to cover. Let's narrow this down to something manageable, no more than a few million kilometers."

Diego glances sidelong at him. "As you wish."

Guillermo steps back, dropping into his chair. He rubs his eyes. It's too early for this, but sleep can wait. If Diego can pull this off, it won't be long before the guardian wakes up next to Juan again. Guillermo can almost feel Juan's curls tickling the back of his neck. He leans back with a crisp grin and rests his elbows on the workbench.

Beside him, Inés leans close, yellow ocular sensors glowing bright. "¿Café?" she prompts.

"¡Por supuesto!" His first robot is nothing so sophisticated as a xenobot, but she knows him well. Inés bobs up and down and rides her hoverboard over the edge of the rail and down to the lower level of their home.

The grinding motor mashing up fresh coffee beans quickens Guillermo's heartbeat. He calls up to the xenobot quietly working in front of the holomap. "Why can't you read my mind like your sister, Diego?"

Back still turned, he answers in a soft voice. "If that was what you wanted, you could have programmed me as such."

Guillermo scowls. His xenobot has his own neural tissue. How can this extension of his own flesh be so uptight? "Relax mijo, era sola una broma." Diego's eyelids flicker. He runs different scenarios through his internal scripts and cross-references them against the holomap. The guardian sips his coffee and watches, an involuntary moan escaping his lips. Citrusy. "This is so good."

Diego turns and scrutinizes the mug. "If you think that's good, you'll be impressed with the beans produced at the colony." He faces the holomap again. "Station coffee is a poor substitute for what it once was on Earth."

Leaning back, Guillermo cocks an eyebrow. "You think so? This beats the stale beans I bartered for in the bunkers."

The search region warps and twists and—slowly—begins to shrink. "The terraformers' guild didn't account for how the artificial climate and altitude on the stations would affect the flavor profile of arabica beans. There is ample terrain on Zomenos for quality coffee."

Sabe. He'll have to ask the boys one of these days. Outside, the sun travels toward its apex. Guillermo winces. Hay que recordar, the bright light is harmless with that dome above the station.

The xenobot's arms fall to his sides as he turns. "It's finished. A search radius of one million kilometers." He wears an expectant gaze.

"You did it, Diego!" Inés trills, head whirling side to side. He ignores her, eyes rooted on his creator.

Guillermo steps close to the holomap. The search region glows softly near Jupiter. There's something else there, something hazy, something frequently discussed among the Coalition: the wormhole. Their ticket off the stations and out of this galaxy. Juan's freedom lies on the other side.

They'll have to get through Terra Nova first.

A crooked smile forms on Guillermo's lips. He's always up for a challenge.

"Bien hecho, Diego. Well done. I'll tell Derek to chart a course." He grips his xenobot's shoulders tight, and Diego lets out his breath, wearing a weak smile.

DECEMBER 8, 3040 | COLOSSI INFINITI, EARTH'S ORBIT

Guillermo steps up to the retinal scanner outside Roarke's office and freezes, just out of range, his gaze trained on the bronze panel concealing the scanner. Seven weeks into the mission, the steady trickle of updates transmitted from orbiter VLT80 back to the Cerebrum particles has come to an abrupt halt. This radio silence must mean that Derek and Diego found something. But what? Guillermo swallows, fingers tingling at his sides. His friend can't fail now, not with Juan's freedom on the line. He thrusts his face into the scanner and violet light washes over him.

It's not too late—it can't be.

The door clicks open, and Frank Roarke waits on the other side. "You're here. Good."

"How many days?" Guillermo asks, seating himself across from the Coalition leader and folding his hands stiffly in his lap.

A muscle twitches in Roarke's temple. "Two."

"That's the second check-in. Something is wrong." Guillermo closes his eyes. ¡Qué obvio! He flattens his palms against his thighs to stop the twitching. "I can try to contact Diego."

"I've tried. The xenobot is unresponsive."

Since orbiter VLT80 is fully dark, the only form of communication open to them is the direct line from Diego to the Cerebrum particles—or so Roarke thinks. Despite the circumstances, a wicked grin spreads across Guillermo's face. "That doesn't matter. Diego and I share neural tissue."

A rare look of genuine surprise strikes Roarke. "That's not standard practice with AI, is it? As I recall, you denied my request to sync the Cerebrum particles with my tissue."

Shrug. He's got plenty to answer for, but this isn't one. "A lot has changed in fifty years, sir. Diego is my first xenobot. He's a bit unconventional in more ways than one."

"How does this help us?" The Cerebrum cloud circling the Coalition leader's head darkens, echoing the man's expression.

The subtle rebuke isn't lost on Guillermo. He rests the palms of his hands on his armrest and leans forward. "You can use me to establish a direct link. It should work, even if Diego is unresponsive."

"Neural tissue is fragile." Roarke taps his forefinger against his chin. "You're already missing some of yours from this ill-advised transplant. We can't risk frying what you've got left."

Guillermo chuckles. "De verdad, but you don't have to worry. My sister performed the biopsy, and I trust her with my life, sir. She preserved some of the tissue from the original procedure to regenerate the tissue taken. I'm completely whole up there," he raps his knuckles against his skull and winks, "and there's more tissue to spare somewhere in that lab of hers." He grows serious. "It's your call, sir. Establishing a direct neural link is a delicate task. With those nanoparticles of yours, you're the only person I would ever trust to pull this off."

"You trust too easily, then," Roarke replies thinly. Yet he's already performing mental calculations, sizing up the task. They both know what's at stake. If Terra Nova has caught up to Derek, the whole mission could be a bust. It would be a fiasco. The Coalition wouldn't allow Jack and the other colonists to leave for Zomenos. Juan would remain asleep in his pod. Guillermo holds his breath as he waits. Roarke owes him this. The Coalition leader spreads his hands and nods. "We need answers and we're out of options. The commander and your xenobot may very well need us. Let's see if this harebrained idea of yours will work."

Spreading out on the cool steel floor, Guillermo facing up. While Roarke works, the guardian stares up at the ceiling. He can't afford to be nervous, not now. Giving in to nerves would flood his body with stress hormones, polluting the connection. He breathes in, letting his skin soak into the depressions in the steel. Above him, Roarke sits, legs tucked underneath and eyes closed. The supercomputer network of swirling nanoparticles that follows him everywhere glows soft blue. Guillermo allows the hypnotic power of the beads to seep through him. His eyelids droop.

With a rush that flips his stomach inside out, he's inside Diego's head. Jupiter and one of her moons loom close. Io, maybe. That'll be helpful for triangulating the orbiter's position later. Hold on . . . where's the viewing pane? He twists around with a grunt. A silent gasp escapes his lips. He's floating in space! The orbiter that Derek and Diego took looks like industrial demolition scrap after ten thousand kilopascals of pressure.

Looking down with Diego's eyes, Guillermo can see his body twirling in zero gravity, his precious organs exposed. Ay no, his xenobot! He wrenches around. Please don't be dead, Derek, please, *please*. The wreckage of the orbiter is everywhere—titanium and Kevlar ripped apart and diffusing into the depths of space. Where is he? Through Diego's eyes, Guillermo tears across the scene.

Without warning, Guillermo is wrested from Diego's body and slammed back into his. This time, when his eyes open, Frank Roarke's eyes stare into his. The guardian rolls onto his stomach and retches.

"You survived," Roarke observes. "Well, that's one less person I've lost today."

Guillermo props himself up with his forearm. "You saw?"

"Everything."

The guardian nods, his shaking body collapsing back onto the floor.

Se acabó: Terra Nova won. He curls away from Roarke, knees tucked into the empty pit of his stomach. Cold, hard, unyielding steel presses into his cheek. He hugs his knees, rocking and shivering. Derek is dead now, and it's *his* fault. How can he face Gabriella? He closes his eyes. It's not just Derek, either. Without Diego, he's just another guardian to Roarke. Guillermo will be long dead before the cryo pods are released. Spit and tears pool under his chin and he shivers uncontrollably. Whether his body is responding to the neural link or to losing his best chance to free Juan, he'll never know.

CHAPTER TWO

MARILINA

"WELCOME TO YOUR first simulation, Dr. Chamorro," a female voice says as Marilina steps into the dome. "Safety equipment awaits you at your seat. We will begin as soon as you are ready." The doctor notes a Finnish accent, light and fresh. Five years with the Meridian have trained her ear well.

She looks down at her own arms clutching her waist. Embarrassing. Dropping them to her sides, she strides forward with her chin high. Her medical training didn't prepare her for this, but she *must* meet the Coalition's flight simulation requirements for civilian colonists. Mami and Papi are counting on her.

"Thank you. Give me a moment." The cramped simulator is webbed in the same slick polymer of her new Coalition skins. Her nostrils flare: rubbing alcohol, sterile yet familiar. She pulls her helmet over her short hair and straps her harness snug against her waist while her visor comes to life with a steady scrawl of technical specifications.

The AI speaks again. "Commencing spaceflight, Doctor."

"Where will this simulation take me?" Her heart flutters inside her chest cavity, but she focuses on the voice.

"I have charted a routine path around planet Earth. There is nothing to fear, Doctor." Marilina smiles humorlessly. Can AI detect nerves?

The dome rumbles. She clenches her seat in a vise grip and straightens. "Your monitor is indicating a rise in heart rate, Dr. Chamorro," the AI says. Her visor confirms: 115 beats per minute.

She closes her eyes. Breathe, Mari. A flight simulator is nothing compared to the early mornings and late nights on call with the Meridian. Just focus on the colony. At once, the gentle smiles of Mami and Papi swim in front of her, cheeks rosy with life after so many years asleep. Her grip on the seat slackens, the number on the visor falling to 90. The rumbling grows to a roar, and Marilina's stomach clenches with the very real lurch of shuttle launch. Beyond the panels of simulated stars, Earth rolls toward her.

Her breath catches. The once blue-and-green hues of the planet's oceans are a murky velvet now. What new species will evolve in its depths, undisturbed by human interference? The sight reminds her forcibly of Quique. She presses her eyes shut and turns away.

"Very good, Dr. Chamorro," the voice says. "All vital signs remain within tolerable limits."

Eyes still pinched closed, Marilina nods to herself. "What's next?" Her words come out high and wafer-thin.

"I will simulate the microgravity environment you will experience for much of your flight. In a real spaceflight, the commander will alert civilians to the appropriate time to remove your harness and roam the flight deck."

Freeing herself from the harness, Marilina stands, her body lighter than usual. Is she expected to adjust to that for months on end? She steps up to the tiny flight deck, unable to pry her eyes away from Earth. Home, technically, but fulfilling her duty will mean leaving this place behind once and for all. She hardly cares. This planet is nothing more than a reminder of what people are capable of at their worst. She turns away. The colony is real. Mami and Papi are real.

Marilina hurries back to her seat. As soon as she's strapped in, her belly rolls with the simulation of downward descent. Earth falls away, out of sight. She purses her lips and digs her fingernails into clenched fists, but she remains cognizant of her heart rate. Failure would only delay her training. Her parents have waited long enough already.

"Congratulations, Doctor. You have completed your first simulation. You may exit the cabin." Marilina leans her head out of the simulator, calculating. A long, darkened corridor stands between her and the civilian side of the Ring, so it's unlikely anyone will recognize her. She steps down from the hatch with a careful sigh.

"That bad?"

Freeze. "Admiral." *Of course* it's the admiral. He stands just beyond the opening to the hatch, out of her direct line of sight. Straight-backed and confident in crisp white skins decorated with colorful emblems of rank and achievement, he is the picture of the Coalition itself. What will he think of his hand-picked physician if she can't even stomach the simulator? She meets his startlingly blue gaze and conjures her most reassuring smile. The Meridian never allow their expressions to betray their own fears and doubts, especially not one tasked with keeping the entire crew alive in the colony. "Good afternoon. I thought the crew was gone for the day."

"It's just us." Admiral Monroe gazes down at her with his brow wrinkled. "Aiming to get a feel for the simulator for the first time without an audience?" The doctor strains to hold a neutral expression. Those unusual eyes of his soften. "It's okay. Most civilians hate the simulator. The real deal is more fun—I promise."

Marilina is taken aback. He's so . . . personable. She sees now why the crew admires this man. It doesn't matter: she's Meridian, and she isn't here to make friends. Her shoulders sag as she smiles wanly. "I'll keep that in mind." She gestures down the long walkway. "I was just leaving. What about you?"

"All done for the day." The admiral falls into step beside her, not at all bothered by her demeanor, it would seem. They pass small viewing portals spaced regularly along the long corridor, each one painting the steel ramparts with the light from stars hundreds or thousands of light-years away. Earth, with its complicated reminders of what they're leaving behind, is out of sight. For that, Marilina is grateful. More simulators appear as they walk, much larger than the one she trained in. Below her feet, she glimpses more long corridors, each one leading to different zones of the Coalition's training program. How strange to be here on the military station instead of responding to emergencies on a civilian station. She'll miss the thrill of the Meridian, but her new role with the colony offers a different adventure, one to cauterize the wounds in her family. For a while, there's nothing but the soft, regular plink of boots on metal as the admiral walks at her side, matching her unhurried stride. He speaks into the silence. "My records have you out for the next couple of days. Are you back on service with the Meridian?"

She smiles at the prospect. If only. "No, I'm just visiting home. It's Our Lady of Guadalupe Day." And her tías insisted.

Monroe nods, business-like. "In that case, enjoy your holiday, Doctor. I hope I'll see you back in the simulator again next week." The admiral waves and turns down another corridor. Marilina finds herself waving back. Odd. She enjoyed his company so much more than expected.

DECEMBER 11, 3040 | GUADALAJARA STATION, EARTH'S ORBIT

Marilina tilts her head back and stares up at the gothic spires of the cathedral. One of her favorite parts of returning home. A stunning red glow lights up the building, a beacon welcoming churchgoers. She closes her eyes, rooted in place by a stern but merry peal that rings out from the bells. Papi loved those bells. A low, crackling boom forces her eyes open. Fireworks. Smoke fills her nose and mouth, like churrasco. Already, dozens of station dwellers are lined up to pay their respects. By the time the day of the Virgin comes, the plaza will be brimming with hundreds of devout patrons. Marilina bows her head and weaves her way out of the crowd.

The wrought-iron gate was left unlatched for her: Tía Fatima's doing. Marilina smiles and steps through the gate toward the modest white home, untouched by the years of her absence. A gentle rush of water grows louder as she nears the fountain. Her steps falter. Abue installed that fountain against Coalition policy, its use forbidden years ago. She's six again, shrieking with laughter and dodging Quique's attempts to splash her. The old pang of regret stirs her. That was long ago. She takes a deep breath, stoops low, and cups her hands to taste the water. Carbonated. The rest falls back to the fountain with a splash. Her fingers touch wet lips. This water was imported from Enceladus, and it's still tightly regulated. Running the fountain again is an unnecessary risk. She pushes the door open.

"I hope you cleaned your room in time, Quique." Tía Pilar doesn't notice her. "Do you want your sister to see the way you live?" Poor Quique, left to answer to their tías all these years while Marilina fulfills her duty. She grimaces and hovers in the doorway.

"Why hide it? Mari knows exactly how I live, Tía." Quique turns and locks eyes with his older sister from across the room. "Are you coming inside or what?" She averts her eyes, sidling into the room behind a stone bust.

"¡Marilina!" Pilar exclaims. "¡Qué maravilla!" The older woman bustles over to her niece's side, kisses her cheek, and heaves her into a tight hug. Quique smirks.

The doctor pats her aunt on the back and smiles. "It's nice to see you, Tía. And you, Quique."

Pilar turns and glares at Quique. "What are you waiting for? Come, give your sister a hug." Pilar turns back to her and beams. "Your mother would be so happy that you are here for el Día de la Virgen." Her words knock the wind out of Marilina. Mami would be here too if she had done a better job. The doctor bites her lip and doesn't reply. "No, no, no," her aunt says. "Don't make that face. This is a celebration." Pilar turns and faces the hallway. "Fatima! Mari is here! Come say hi to your niece, vieja!"

Quique seizes the opportunity to inch closer. "Hey."

Marilina stares at him. "Is that all you have to say to me?" Rolling his eyes, Quique pulls his sister into a tight hug. She stiffens. "Enough!"

"Fine." Quique steps back and appraises her. "How is training going?"

Her belly flips inside itself again at the mere thought of the simulation. "Fine," she echoes, pushing the memory away. "How are those two doing?" She nods toward Pilar, still shouting in the hallway.

"Driving me crazy. Same as always."

They are interrupted by a squeal. Fatima flees down the hall with arms open wide and tackles Marilina in yet another hug. "It's so good to see you, querida," Fatima declares between kisses. The skin around her eyes bears the crease of years of smiling. The family has long since discontinued GLOW injections and the evidence shows.

"I missed you too, Tía," Marilina murmurs into her aunt's sleeve. The older woman smells of papaya.

Fatima takes several steps back and stands beside her sister. The four of them share the same features: dark eyes that sparkle with the freedom of the stars beyond the station dome, brown hair that ripples in waves, and skin that tans to a creamy café con leche. "Have you already gone to receive communion?" Fatima asks Marilina.

Quique barks out a laugh. "She's not going to church, Tía."

Fatima shoots a pained look his way. "Of course she is. She came all the way here for la virgen. Right, Mari?"

Marilina looks away from Quique's smirk and smiles at her aunt. "I've only just arrived, Tía." Quique is right, but Fatima doesn't need to know that. Better to not upset her so soon.

"She has plenty of time for communion, hermana," Pilar interjects, squeezing her sister's hand. "Come. La sopa is almost ready. Mari is starving from all of her important training."

Her aunts lead the way into the kitchen. Marilina pauses at the altar to Our Lady of Guadalupe, where tall candles burn beneath an old, worn painting of the virgin. Roses, hand-picked from the garden, frame the painting. A familiar, faded white cloth lines the altar. Marilina draws the heavy fabric between her forefinger and thumb, rubbing the rough surface between her fingers. A familiar musk wafts toward her, unwelcome. This is temporary. This time next year they'll build a new altar in the colony and maybe then she'll find a reason to worship. She heaves a deep sigh and drops the cloth.

Pilar bustles in front of the stove and calls out orders. Marilina dutifully takes her place beside her brother and sets the table, doing her best to ignore her growing restlessness.

Quique leans close and mutters in a low voice, so the aunts can't hear. "Fatima will never forgive you when she finds out you stopped going to church."

"She won't find out." Marilina raises her voice. "Pilar, you set out the nice cutlery by mistake. Where is the regular silverware?"

"It's not a mistake, querida," Fatima grins. "A visit from our Mari is worthy of fine things." The doctor silently avoids Quique's glare.

DECEMBER 12, 3040 | GUADALAJARA STATION, EARTH'S ORBIT

The entire house is abuzz with preparation for the big celebration. Fatima repeatedly shoos her niece out of the kitchen like a mosquito, so Marilina relents and wanders down the hall to her brother's room. She finds Quique in a virtual reality simulation, his eyes glassy and unfocused, and enters quiet as a nun, seating herself rigidly on the edge of the bed and waiting for him to realize she's there.

"A little rude to interrupt a sim uninvited," Quique says as his eyes focus on her.

"Can you even afford that?" Marilina asks. She regrets her careless words at once.

He sits up and crosses his arms. "Of course I can. You're not the only one supporting this family."

The doctor raises one eyebrow. "The restoration? That can't pay well."

"Says who?" A haughty look flashes in Quique's eyes. "I'm saving lives, same as you."

So competitive. She'll never understand it. "You can't be serious."

"Why not?" He seems keenly interested in her answer.

Marilina folds her hands in her lap and gazes patiently at her brother. "I'm a Meridian, Quique. A front-line emergency responder. How is that the same?"

He leans forward. "Yeah, and you're throwing it away for that colony. When the restoration is finished, Mom and Dad will thank *me*, not you. I'll be a hero."

A hero? His hubris is astonishing. Marilina takes his hands, already weathered from his assignments on Earth. "Quique, I know you think you're doing the right thing, but this restoration isn't going to change anything. Earth is lost to us. We need to move on while we still can. The colony is our future, not Earth."

Quique yanks his hands back. "You don't know that. Radioactivity levels are at record lows."

"What about the ozone levels?" Marilina asks. "The greenhouse effect? The ground crews aren't changing any of that. You should be helping Pilar and Fatima more around here, not wasting time on Earth's surface. You're endangering your life over a pointless project, for Christ's sake."

"Now you believe in Christ?" Quique asks quietly.

Marilina bites her lip. She didn't come all the way here to change her brother's mind. He thinks he's doing his duty, too. Mami wouldn't want her to fight, no matter how foolhardy his ideas are. Tonight is about Pilar and Fatima. Marilina bows her head and closes her eyes. "I'm sorry." She looks up at her brother from beneath her eyebrows and peers closer, noticing a fresh scar beneath his temple for the first time. "When did you get retinal implants?" she breathes.

Quique grins and touches the scar, self-conscious. "Like I said, I work. And it pays, hermana."

"It can't pay that well." Marilina frowns. There's more to this restoration than meets the eye. Maybe she should probe deeper. How well does she know her own brother after all these years away?

No. She tucks her hair neatly behind each ear, avoiding his gaze. She's already doing her duty. How Quique spends his time isn't her concern.

A shadow falls over them. "Are you two coming?" Pilar calls from the doorway. "Dinner is ready."

Marilina pauses just inside the kitchen and rocks back on her heels. "You two have outdone yourselves." Where did all this incredible food come from? A dozen or more candles hiss and sputter in austerity. The simple, round dining table is draped in velvet and heaped in roasted lamb and pork substitutes, ensalada of shredded cabbage and carrots, fried plantains, and gallo pinto. Even the Meridian don't eat this well. The memory of the garden fountain filled with water resurfaces.

Fatima beams and touches her niece's cheek. "You can thank your brother. Only the best for you, mi querida."

"Finally! I'm so hungry." Quique strides past and reaches for a plate, but Pilar swats his hand away.

"Guests first."

Marilina bows her head and squeezes past her aunt and brother to the other side of the kitchen. She grabs a plate inlaid with white sacuanjoche petals from a stack on the table. Her aunts expect her to take her mother's seat at the head of the table, but she hesitates, gripping her plate hard. Mami should be here. Marilina stares at all that food. Is Quique right? Surely he isn't really the only one taking care of this family. That would make her own work merely righteous self-indulgence.

Would it be so wrong if it were?

"What's wrong?" Fatima asks, hurrying to her niece's side and inspecting the table.

Marilina shakes her head and relaxes her grip on the plate. It would be a disgrace to shatter Mami's beautiful dinnerware. She looks into Fatima's eyes and summons a smile. "Everything is perfect, Tía."

Once seated, Pilar takes Marilina's left hand, Quique her right. The doctor closes her eyes respectfully as Fatima begins. "Dios, please bless this feast tonight. Thank you for sending our dear one back to us on this sacred day. May she continue to receive your protection as she begins her most holy mission. Amen."

"Amen," they each chorus. The clinking of forks fills the room. Marilina drives hers into the lamb, somehow tender and fine-grained like real meat is rumored to be. She takes her first bite, eyes popping. The meat is richly seasoned, fatty, and high quality. Oh, how she missed Fatima's cooking.

"When is the big day?" Pilar asks her between mouthfuls.

"The launch is still months away. I have to log enough hours in the simulator before going up on a real shuttle."

Fatima's brow knits together, intensifying her wrinkles. "And you're sure this is safe?"

"Yes, Tía. The admiral himself says so." Marilina smiles at her aunt across from her.

"You met the admiral?" Quique asks with sudden interest.

Marilina nods. "He's leading the first mission personally."

Quique's fork hovers in the air, forgotten. "Wow. Who is in charge of the sector's military without him?"

"I think the vice admiral is the acting admiral while he's gone," Marilina says with a shrug. She bites into a plump plantain and its salty and sweet juices burst on her tongue.

Pilar leans forward wearing a knowing smile and lowers her voice. "I heard that Frank Roarke himself asked the admiral to do it."

"Probably," Marilina agrees. "Roarke meets regularly with the unit leaders. He's invested in the mission."

"Who can blame him?" Fatima's sweet voice is laced in scorn. "Station life isn't what we were promised. Luisa and Rafael have been in cryo for more than ten years now. It's time to move on from here."

"It is," Quique agrees, gaze affixed to his plate. "But why does it have to be Zomenos?"

This again. "You think it should be Earth?" Marilina can't stop the note of contempt that sours her words.

"Your brother is just doing his part to help," Fatima intervenes, patting his hand.

He frowns. "It's more than that. Check the research. With the right efforts, Earth will be habitable again in the next decade."

"I've seen those numbers," Marilina says quietly. How did her brother's mind become so polluted by this rhetoric? "We don't have the resources to pull off that scale of restoration that quickly."

"How would you know?" her brother retorts, his voice rising. "I'm on the ground crew. I've seen it myself: the restoration is working. We could work faster if we had more resources, but the Coalition funnels everything into your precious colony."

Marilina studies him coolly. "You're so confident in Earth that you'd throw away the opportunity at a real home? At seeing Mami and Papi awake?"

"You just don't want to admit that I know better than you about this."

"Ya," Pilar interrupts. "That's enough. What's gotten into you two?"

"Nothing." Quique puts his fork down. "I'm not hungry. Thanks for dinner, Tías."

Breathing hard, Marilina returns her attention to her own plate, but her appetite has also vanished.

Quique doesn't leave his room for the candlelight vigil. Pilar carries on, deftly lighting each wick, but she exchanges a troubled look with Fatima. Marilina ignores them, stepping up to the altar and accepting her candle from Pilar. The weak flame sputters and nearly dies, but Marilina shields it beneath an arched hand until the warmth strokes her skin. The three women kneel before the altar and bow their heads. She can't let Quique get to her. She must endure, like the candle. For Mami.

"Our Lady," Fatima begins. "Protect us until we can be reunited. Guide us so we stray not from our path. Shelter us when we are lost."

Marilina prays in silence. It probably won't make a difference, but she doesn't see the harm in it. She can't bear the distance between her and her family. It just keeps growing, a cancerous lesion stripping its host of life. If you're listening, watch over my brother, please. Just until we reach the colony. It will all be worth it then. Right? The prayers end and she rises gratefully from her knees.

In her room, she removes her mother's cross from her neck and drapes it carefully over the glowing holograph display at her bedside. She lingers beside the photo. It's an old image of her mother, those thick, loose curls of hers parted down the middle. Her hair cupped her cheeks when she smiled. That smile could make Papi do just about anything. Marilina drops her gaze. Mami should be here for the vigil.

"You look just like her now." Quique stands in the doorway watching her.

The doctor smiles. "I'll take that as a compliment."

"She wouldn't appreciate you coming back and putting on a pretense of prayer and devotion if you don't believe anymore."

Marilina frowns. "It's not a pretense. Just because I don't share the same faith you do doesn't mean I don't believe something is out there."

Quique leans against the doorframe. "Is that why you left? What are you searching for, Mari?"

"I'm right here, Quique."

"No, you're not, not really," he presses. Marilina sighs. Why can't he understand? "Even before you signed on to leave the sector behind, you were gone all the time with that Meridian gig you love so much."

She shrugs. The same tired argument, again. "Call it that if you want. The rest of Earth's orphans will follow soon enough."

"Not if the restorationists have anything to do with it." Quique shakes his head with a taunting smile. "Go ahead, leave. I'm headed back to Earth next week, anyway. We'll see soon enough which one of us is right."

Marilina sits back on the bed and purses her lips. Let him think what he wants. Her duty is to her parents, not to him. A blue light flashes in the corner of her field of view—the admiral is calling her through her implants. Marilina stares at the light, stunned.

"I'll let you take that," Quique says while backing out of her room. A holograph of Admiral Monroe flickers to life before her, blocking her from changing her mind and calling back out to her brother.

"Admiral?" Confusion is plain in her voice.

"I'm sorry for the unusual call." Monroe stands at attention, as if briefing one of his officers on Colossi Infiniti rather than calling a civilian in her childhood home. "I know you're on holiday with your family right now, but it's urgent."

Could something have gone wrong with the colony? Nothing about the admiral's calm demeanor suggests anything out of the ordinary. "What's wrong?" Marilina asks, steeling herself.

"There's been an accident on the Johannesburg station."

"Johannesburg?" She blinks. "What does that have to do with us?"

He shakes his head. "It doesn't. Vice Admiral Ono reached out for my support with this, and you're the only Meridian I'm acquainted with." He grins, but his eyebrows pinch together in a grimace—the barest acknowledgment of the bizarre situation unfolding.

"I see." She thought her Meridian days were behind her. Her head spins with the implications. This must be serious if the military division is involved. "Tell me about this accident."

"It was an antimatter explosion."

Marilina grips the bedframe for support. "The particle accelerator is unstable?"

Monroe's calm exterior never cracks. He shakes his head. "I can't explain over comms. If I clear you for an emergency medical transport, can you help? You'll get further instructions on the ground."

She raises an eyebrow. "I'm on personal leave visiting family. Surely someone else can take this."

"This is an all-hands situation." A strained smile crosses his face. "I need someone I can trust on the ground. I know it's a lot to ask, Dr. Chamorro, but I need you out there. What do you say?"

Marilina smiles and bows her head, a wave of excitement dizzying her. One last Meridian assignment to erase any doubt of her in the admiral's mind? The opportunity couldn't be any more perfect, except . . . She steals a glance down the hall, after her brother. Could she really leave now? She planned to mend her relationship with Quique on this trip, but things are worse than ever. She meets Monroe's waiting gaze. If she's already earned the confidence of the admiral, she's not about to turn him down. Quique can wait a little longer. "Of course, Admiral."

"Right." Monroe's fingers fly across the screen of his wristband unit, entering the access codes that will authorize direct travel from the Guadalajara station to the Johannesburg station. Meridian aren't dependent on shuttles or pods in an emergency. He looks at her again. "You're clear. Thank you, Doctor."

Marilina confirms the authorization in her wristband unit. "Received. May I say goodbye to my family? I don't know when I'll see them next."

"Absolutely. Be quick about it."

Snatching the cross from the bedside table, the doctor hurries back out into the kitchen, where Fatima and Pilar sit sipping their coffee and talking softly. The cake they planned to serve after dinner rests on the table between them, untouched. Marilina squeezes Pilar's shoulder.

"Pilar, Fatima—something's happened, a terrible accident."

Tía Pilar understands. "You're leaving? Tonight?" Fatima moans and looks from one to the other, her expression worried.

Nod. "I'm sorry. I wouldn't go if it weren't an emergency."

"It's okay, querida." Fatima rises and pulls the doctor into a warm hug. The doctor breathes in more papaya. "You're always welcome here. You know that."

"I know. Thank you." Marilina gives each of her aunts a quick kiss on the cheek.

"Are you going to tell your brother?" Pilar whispers. Marilina turns toward Quique's room, wavering. A muted tune travels down the hallway toward them. He doesn't want to talk, and maybe they've already said enough. She bites her lip and shakes her head. Duty first.

"I'm sorry. I have to go." Waving, she steps back and disappears.

DECEMBER 12, 3040 | JOHANNESBURG STATION, EARTH'S ORBIT

Marilina freezes as she enters the Meridian and darkness swallows her. Quique's sarcastic smile invades her thoughts. In the next instant, sight and sound return, ushering in a cacophony of insults. Her brother is shoved from her mind. Victims of the antimatter explosion come from all directions, staggering toward a medical tent. She shivers at the chorus of agonized cries. She's never dealt with a crisis of this magnitude. There are nowhere near enough medical personnel on-site, but the blast must have been contained or there would be no one left.

The ground quakes beneath her feet. Marilina drops to a crouch and plants her palms on the ground to either side to stabilize herself. Burned chemicals waft toward her. She wills her heartbeat to slow and assesses the situation. Overhead, an enormous tent secures the perimeter, blotting out the sky above. What could that be for?

The doctor swallows and rises from her crouch, heading towards the medics. Be brave, and whatever happens, don't let the admiral down.

Another aftershock rocks the ground beneath her. Marilina hurries forward. She approaches the first medic she sees, snapping gloves over her hands deftly and surveying the team. "Dr. Chamorro reporting in. What's the status here?

When can we expect an airlift for high priority injuries?" There are just twelve medics floating among the injured, recording patient information and drafting a priority list for the Meridian. Where are the others?

This medic is young, younger even than Quique. "We aren't. The hospital is on the other side of that tent. It's not safe." Marilina follows his gaze, suddenly understanding. The station's dome is compromised, so the tent is maintaining localized air pressure. The medic's voice shakes. "They're saying we're on our own."

"I see." Marilina closes her eyes and nods once. No wonder Monroe was desperate for the Meridian to step in here. She looks around once more. This isn't an ordinary accident, and these medics aren't trained to recognize chemical burns or radiation exposure. She'll have to move quickly. "Okay, you're with me then." Marilina is already rushing forward, but she turns to the medic as he matches her stride and reminds herself what it was like when she first joined the Meridian. "What's your name?"

"Bandile Myburgh."

"Pleasure." He won't be the same after today. Marilina stops in front of a little girl. Her hair is braided neatly down her back and her skins look new, but both are torn. Her wristband unit was wrenched painfully from her, leaving multiple lacerations along her forearm. The child sits quietly, staring at her boots and clutching a teddy in one fist. Marilina glances up. Where is this girl's family?

Myburgh flips open his wristband unit, searching for the child's file, and reads her report out loud. "Aneke, age 8. Minor injuries." He shoots a quizzical look at the doctor.

"Copy," Marilina replies. Myburgh's list of life-threatening injuries fills his screen. He obviously expects her to move on. She'll save lives today if she does, but she squats down beside this girl instead. "Hello, Aneke. My name is Dr. Chamorro. That's a lovely braid. Did your mother do it for you?"

Aneke nods at her feet.

"Do you know where your parents are now?" Eyes glued to the dirt, the girl points beyond the tent toward the heart of the blast zone. They won't be found alive. "Is there anyone here to look after you?" Aneke shakes her head.

Marilina raises an eyebrow at Myburgh. If she abandons this orphan, Aneke will end up in the slums. "Okay. Why don't I take care of that cut while my friend looks for your family?"

Myburgh scowls but lowers his voice. "What about the others, Doctor?"

"Do it." The doctor turns back to the child, who waits obediently. Aneke's injury isn't life-threatening, but the hollow look on her face is all too familiar. Not all wounds are physical. Marilina reaches for the girl's hand and gently turns it, inspecting the lacerations along her arm. They're not deep enough to require stitches. "This will sting a little," she warns, applying a paste to the girl's arm. Aneke sucks in her breath but doesn't squirm. The beads inside the paste stitch the wound together, and moments later, the lacerations are sealed. "All better." The doctor straightens and turns expectantly to Myburgh.

"She has living grandparents." His words are strained. "What would you like me to do?"

"Notify her grandparents of her coordinates. Aneke will remain here until they arrive." Myburgh complies. Marilina drops to her haunches beside the girl once again. "Your grandparents are on their way," she assures Aneke.

To her surprise, the girl drops her teddy, throws open her arms, and hugs the doctor. Marilina hesitates, a lump throbbing in the back of her throat. She hugs the child back, and Aneke hums a song into her skinsleeve. The doctor is startled that she recognizes the lullaby, one her own mother sang to her each night after tucking her in. She closes her eyes. This girl will have her grandparents. They won't replace her parents, but she might still get to have a childhood.

Aneke stops humming. "Why are you helping me?" she whispers into Marilina's hair.

"Little girls need their family," Marilina whispers back. She pulls away and for the first time Aneke snaps to her full height, under 125 centimeters, and smiles, revealing two prominent gaps between her teeth.

"Are you ready for the next patient?" Myburgh asks from behind them.

"Yes." Marilina gives Aneke a small wave and smiles to herself. The former Meridian missed this: the sense of purpose, of changing someone's life with simple acts. "Send them over." She watches the waiting queue of victims from the antimatter explosion shuffle forward. There will be more like Aneke today, so many more. Marilina rubs her forefinger and thumb along the grooves in the cross around her neck while she waits, remembering her last hug from Mami and the promises whispered then.

CHAPTER THREE

JACK

THE RACKET COMING FROM the Coalition's guardians is louder than an entire fleet launching from the hangars at once. No one really knows what's going on, not yet. The reports coming in from Johannesburg are skinny on details, even with Jack's clearance. All he can say for sure is that the particle accelerator bit the dust and a whole bunch of innocent people got hurt.

The air is thick with fear. Jack keeps his own anxiety in check, barely, but he can't blame these guardians for being unable to see reason through that fog. This is just about the worst-case scenario. Admiral Monroe's next mission will rewrite history, but this accident on the Johannesburg station is his own personal supernova, shooting out the cosmic rays that now threaten everything he's built.

The commotion reaches a deafening roar. Has he ever seen all twenty-two guardians of the Coalition together like this? From all the yelling, it sure looks like they're better off apart. He's never seen Lucy raise her voice, but there she is in the thick of argument, waves of indignation rolling off her. Guillermo's there too, a bit less rattled. Only Samkelo Ngcobo is silent, his dark skin ashen.

Jack gives the heated guardians a wide berth, crossing the auditorium and joining the other admirals standing at attention against the far wall. Vice Admiral Ono heads the group, her honey-toned face drawn and pale. She's taking heat for this, and that sucks. Just a few months ago it would've been him. Monroe tips his head and she relaxes just a little, her shoulders dropping and the color returning to her cheeks. Jack is still the admiral of this sector, even if he's stepped back to oversee the colony. He'll do what he can to smooth things over with the guardians, but he doesn't like his odds.

Frank Roarke enters and silence falls. The Coalition leader's sweeping gaze delivers assurances that ordinary words can't. Those glowing red Cerebrum particles fan out above him like a constellation, humming, vibrating, and sapping the tension right out of the room. Peace blankets Jack. He relaxes just a little against the firm steel railing behind him.

Roarke speaks with authority. "Thank you all for answering my summons in force. We must address an unprecedented disaster on our stations: the antimatter explosion in the particle accelerator on the Johannesburg station. Many of you are already forming theories as to what sparked this catastrophic failure. I ask that you hold these theories until after the debriefing."

Jack steals a glance at the assembled guardians. The repercussions of the accident on the Johannesburg station will reverberate across the stations. Antimatter isn't just Johannesburg's main export. It's the lifeblood of the Coalition. Earth's orphans will look to the Coalition to restore order. The response to this accident has got to be quick and decisive. Show the strength of the military and the guardians will fall in line. The admiral puffs his chest out. The colony depends on it—and his own legacy is at risk here. With a signal from Roarke, a man and woman approach the long platform from the back of the room. Jack recognizes Sergeant Arquette, leader of the intelligence division.

As the two head to the front, Roarke speaks again. "Acting Admiral Ono has consented to Admiral Monroe's request to lead the debriefing, as is his right.

I trust that you'll show him the same courtesy you would myself." His words ring with command.

Young as he is for an admiral, Jack doesn't expect the guardians' full support at a time like this. Still, his heart sinks at the mutinous glares that turn on him. He's got no illusion that anything other than Roarke's singular authority is what crushes the temptation to interrupt. Taking a deep breath, Jack runs his hands down the front of his slick, pearly-white skins and smooths out the folds. Earn their respect and the rest will follow. He nods to the other admirals as he joins the sergeant and officer standing at attention.

"Admiral Monroe, it's an honor to work with you," Arquette says in a graveled bass.

Jack bobs his head. "And I, you, Sergeant."

"Detective Wright is head of her unit. She is overseeing the investigation on the Johannesburg station." Jack accepts the detective's outstretched hand, her grip dominating but brief. What in the universe—red eyes! He blinks. Who would want that? Seems flashy, arrogant, and not very practical for an intelligence officer. Not that it's any of his business. He falls into the same easy smile he would offer any other officer. Strange personal choices aside, this detective hopefully has the answers they need, and that's good enough for him. If Wright notices Jack's slip, she doesn't show it.

"You have a reputation for getting results, Detective."

"You could say that." Her glazed eyes hint at how unmistakably boring she finds this. Straight to business, then.

Jack squares his shoulders and folds his hands behind his back. "What can you tell us about the accident, Detective?"

Red Eyes comes to life, those unnatural irises glowing. She turns away from Jack and addresses the Coalition directly, wearing something close to a smirk. Okay, what's her deal? "On December 12th, just after 1700 hours, the particle accelerator on the Johannesburg station went into catastrophic failure, releasing lethal radiation into the surrounding atmosphere. Chemical fire broke out in the facility and quickly spread. The station's dome was compromised. Anyone in the immediate vicinity who was spared from radiation couldn't have survived the rapid change in pressure. Our engineers stabilized the dome, but localized shifts in the atmosphere are taking longer to reverse. Civilians in the surrounding area have been evacuated to Coalition tents built to withstand this sort of scenario. The Meridian are still there, tending to the victims. The body count is still rising, but our estimate at this time is about three hundred casualties.

"My team was dispatched to investigate the cause of the accident as soon as Intelligence received word. We've learned a few things. The first thing you should know, distinguished leaders, is that this was no accident."

Murmuring breaks out at once.

Jack frowns. Wright's report is thorough, but her theater performance is only fanning the anger in their guardians. This is off to a bad start. He adopts a strict tone. "That's a bold allegation, and a serious one, Detective. What evidence can you offer us?"

"Let me explain." Her voice is full of the indulgence of a schoolteacher helping a child work out a painfully simple problem. She points those laser eyes towards the ceiling as if pleading for patience.

He's getting prickly. This isn't math. His own crew's physician is losing precious training hours to this accident, and his engineers are pitching in to restore pressure to the dome. The sooner they reestablish order, the sooner his colonists can return to training.

The detective boulders on. "This particle accelerator is inspected regularly to comply with regulatory standards. The last inspection was only two months ago."

Now we're getting somewhere. "And is the equipment functional?" Jack asks.

Wright nods, evidently pleased that he's following along. It's pretty clear that she thinks she should be running things. "Correct, Admiral. Which means this thing would only have exploded if someone wanted it to." The detective seems oblivious to the agitation brewing in that auditorium. She doesn't understand the guardians like Jack does: if they start doubting each other, order will break down faster than she can say "singularity."

This isn't helping. Time to move this along. "What's your theory, then?" he prods.

If the detective understands Jack's intentions, she ignores them. Obviously enjoying herself, the insolent prick makes a show of pacing the length of the room. "My team investigated every crack of what remained of the facility. No sign of forced entry—the retinal scanners remain intact. In fact, just one individual entered the facility today: the operator himself."

His boots grate into the steel platform beneath them. Get to the point, already. "Where is the operator now, Detective?"

"Deceased." Wright turns away from him and faces the audience just as the muttering peaks. "A victim of his own attack. Don't worry, esteemed guardians. The operator couldn't have acted alone." She clasps her hands behind her back and stands tall. "There had to be an accomplice." With a wicked smile, she continues. "The particle accelerator has over a hundred fail-safes in place to ensure that a catastrophic event is all but impossible. The scale of this explosion means the operator bypassed all the decelerator's safety features. No operator has all those clearances."

"Who has that clearance, then?" Jack asks through gritted teeth.

"I think we'd all like to know the answer to that." Detective Wright actually *winks* at him with those preternatural eyes. Damn her.

If the whispering was bad, this chilled silence is worse. Was Johannesburg's accident really deliberate? What's the point of that? Uneasy, Jack locks eyes with the detective and zeroes in on a sliver of doubt there. For all her swagger, she's just as afraid as he is. Goosebumps prick his skin, but he keeps his cool.

One thing is clear: this is a job for the military. It's time to clean up, and Jack has no intention of dumping this on Ono. The colony will just have to wait a little longer. A small price to pay for humanity's safety. He breaks the silence. "Thank you, Detective. I think we've heard enough." With a final glance in the detective's direction, she's dismissed. He approaches the center of the room again, exchanging a look with Roarke, and the Coalition leader joins him and addresses the assembly.

"Accident or not, now is the time for the Coalition to come together in force. I'd like to hear from our guardians now." Jack stands a little straighter. He couldn't agree more. The whole situation is ugly, but Earth's orphans need their leaders to give them a reason to hope for their futures.

Ngcobo speaks first. "This is one of the lowest moments in the Coalition's history. Hundreds of my people are dead and hundreds more still wait to receive treatment. But the most heinous news of all? The knowledge that this massacre was orchestrated by a common criminal, and that person is still at large." He glares at the others in silence.

Lucy Mérieux stands and leans forward, gripping the seat in front of her. "The perpetrator of this atrocity will be found and tried as the treasonous murderer they are. In the meantime, the Montréal station pledges its funds to the relief of the Johannesburg station. I'm so sorry for your misfortune, Sam." A twinge of pride warms Jack's chest.

"Who would do this?" Another guardian rises while Lucy takes her seat. "Johannesburg isn't the only one that lost something today. That antimatter fuels the Coalition's fleets and maintains the orbit of all our stations. Why would *anyone* target our fuel?" The same question haunts Jack. This attack jeopardizes the stations, the colony, and the entire infrastructure of the Coalition. What's the advantage?

The detective stirs. "Because someone doesn't want us going anywhere."

Roarke holds up his hand. "Thank you, Detective, but let's refrain from further speculation. I'm more interested in charting our path forward." Jack breathes a sigh of relief. Someone needed to muzzle that woman and prevent her from starting a war.

Yet Wright remains standing, determination etched into her dark features. "Speculation is the whole point of intelligence, sir. We're expanding our investigation. The Johannesburg station will see justice done."

She just can't shut her mouth, can she? Jack interrupts. "No need for that, Detective." He glances in Vice Admiral Ono's direction. Earth and all its stations remain under his jurisdiction, and he refuses to leave the safety of those people in Wright's hands. The Johannesburg bomber is still out there, and they'll be looking to finish the job. "Military will dispatch a fleet to the Johannesburg station today to guard against further attack. Thank you for your contribution to this case."

The outraged astonishment that springs to life on the detective's features is worth it. "With all due respect, Admiral," Wright says slowly, "this investigation is far from over."

Jack watches her with indifference. "That's not your decision to make, Detective."

"Thank you both," Roarke cuts in. "I'd like to discuss options with my guardians privately." The Cerebrum particles hum above him, a reminder of who is in charge here.

Jack waits outside with the other members of the military while the meeting concludes. To his satisfaction, the clamoring inside the auditorium is a lot quieter than when the meeting first began. The detective approaches him as the others watch.

"That was out of line, Admiral."

He cocks an eyebrow, tucking his hands into the bomber jacket he wears over his division skins. Wright still thinks she's the one calling the shots here? Well, that'll change. He smiles disarmingly at poor Red Eyes. "You took the words right out of my mouth." He turns to the sergeant. "You'll see that she is disciplined?"

Sergeant Arquette's sour frown drips with disapproval. "Absolutely."

Wright lowers her voice. "This has Terra Nova written all over it, and they never target the same location twice. Send your fleet if you want, but don't cut me out. You need my help." Her red irises are brimming with desperation.

Unbelievable. The smile fades from Jack's lips. How has she come this far without learning her place in the Coalition? There's an order to things here, an unbroken chain of command. He rolls his shoulders and spreads his feet. He doesn't have a shred of patience left for this upstart.

"Listen closely, Detective Wright. From here on out, this case is under the jurisdiction of the military division, so it's no longer your concern. See that it stays that way." The detective opens her mouth, but the auditorium door swings wide and the guardians pour out. Roarke steps up to Jack wearing a scowl that would send any officer with a lick of sense running.

"A word, please."

Flummoxed and still a little hot under the collar, the admiral follows Roarke into one of the many antechambers of the west wing. The door closes and the other man's shoulders slump, the Cerebrum particles wilting along with him. The dim glow of an overhead light casts a harsh shadow on the Coalition leader as he sits on the edge of a steel bench. "Jack, there's something you need to know."

This is beyond out of character. Jack leans against a tall pillar and crosses his arms. "Hit me."

Roarke grips the bench with his jaw set. "A few weeks ago, I sent your father on a classified mission." Blink. What does Dad have to do with any of this? "I needed someone I could trust, and he asked to be sent. The mission's integrity is of the utmost importance, so I couldn't tell you about it."

Shrug. "Okay. No big deal." Since when does Roarke explain himself to his admirals? He calls the shots. But he's still staring at Jack with that weird look on his face. "What's wrong, Frank?"

Roarke closes his eyes. "The mission was compromised."

Blood pounds in Jack's ears. "Wait, what are you saying to me right now?" He rubs his temple with two fingers.

"Your father is MIA." Roarke closes the gap between them and pulls Jack into a stiff hug.

Heart hammering so hard it hurts, the admiral screws up his face and clenches his fists at his sides. Come on, conjure up that classic, easygoing smile. It's no use. His father, the first man to set foot on planet Zomenos, is . . . gone. MIA months before the colonists arrive to claim his legacy. How can they leave him behind? This isn't supposed to happen yet, not now. Jack tugs at the high collar chafing his neck. He can't—*won't*—believe it.

Roarke steps back and clears his throat. "There's one more thing."

A grim smile. "Get on with it." He can't handle any more news.

"Guillermo was working with your father and I on this. I'm . . . worried about him."

The admiral's eyes snap open. "What? Why?" His mind races ahead with fresh fear, but no, his uncle isn't in any danger. Guillermo was with the other guardians just now.

Roarke shakes his head. "The less you know, the better. Just check in with him, will you?"

"Sure, yeah." Maybe Guillermo has something that can help mixed in with his gadgets. The pounding in Jack's ears is so loud that he can't think. He rakes his hands through his hair and loosens his collar again. Why do they make these damned uniforms so tight? He should postpone his crew's mission. Everything is at risk now. He needs to be here, with the Coalition.

Roarke watches him, unblinking. "You need time to process. Take as much as you need."

Jack's racing thoughts click back into the present moment. He catches Roarke's meaning right away. "No way. I'm not stepping down."

Roarke smiles and grips his shoulder. Like a father. "I'm not suggesting that. Just a temporary leave to rest and regroup. Take a few days." It isn't a suggestion.

"I can't." The admiral shrugs the hand away. Roarke doesn't get it. The legendary commander isn't just his dad—the man is his hero. A few days' time is meaningless. Cerebrum particles or not, this man will never understand what Jack's going through. He grunts, resisting the urge to pull out his hair. "I need to monitor the situation on the Johannesburg station." He can't let the investigation fall back to that detective. The Coalition will spiral into chaos. Too much is at stake.

Roarke shakes his head. "Right now, your judgment is clouded, and that doesn't help us. The detective is right: we need to be ready. I'm going to approve Sergeant Arquette's request for more resources for this investigation. Ono can oversee your crew on the ground."

"Come on, you didn't take Wright's conspiracy theories seriously, did you?" Jack laughs. "We're talking about one over-credentialed whack job with an axe to grind. Military can handle this. Intelligence doesn't need to be involved."

Roarke's tone is final as he grips Jack's shoulder again. "You don't have to do everything yourself. Let me help you. Go be with your family. We'll handle Johannesburg."

The smile fades from the admiral's lips. He's been ejected from his own investigation, simple as that, and everything he's worked toward his entire life is suddenly slipping through his fingers.

DECEMBER 13, 3040 | COLOSSI INFINITI, EARTH'S ORBIT

Dismissed, Jack has a lot of time on his hands to plan his next move. He can't back down from the Johannesburg investigation, but Roarke left him no choice. First action on the admiral's list: find his stepmom and tell her the news. She deserves to know what happened to her husband—as much as Jack can tell her, anyway. After that, there's nothing stopping him from learning anything he can about Dad's disappearance. Gabriella will want answers just as much as Jack does.

He marches through the dull halls of the west wing feeling like he's wearing a weighted vest, hardly noticing the officers saluting him on the way. His fists open and close at his sides. This won't be easy. He was too young to remember what it was like to lose Mom. Dad gave a speech at the service. There were flowers. Orchids, maybe. A lot of them. Jack lurches to a stop. Should he bring flowers?

The walkway spills open to a glass cylinder in the south wing with wild views of the surrounding galaxy. His favorite part of the military station. The moon orbits so close he can almost flick it. Jack slows. He is way too young for this. He and Lucy aren't even thinking about kids yet. Don't you have to be a parent to know what to say when you lose one? He presses his hand against cool glass and looks up.

"Where are you, Dad?"

He hurries down the hall, scanning through the double doors to his step-mom's laboratory unit and jogging through a sterile workspace, looking high and low for Gabriella. The hallway leads to an expansive laboratory unit, a living creature. Massive fans hum loudly above and below, keeping a steady flow of fresh air circulating. A magnetic stir bar whistles as it mixes chemicals in a jar. Jack catches a whiff of rotten eggs and wrinkles his nose: sulfur. Gross. In the far corner, a supercomputer crunches data with a purr. How is he going to tell Gabriella that Dad won't be joining them in the colony like they always planned? Jack sighs and continues down the center aisle, scooping up a graduated cylinder and twirling it absently like a baton.

Jack turns at the sound of boots. An android approaches, wearing a lab coat buttoned to his knees. "Welcome, Admiral. The doctor is indisposed. Is there something I can do for you?"

"This is urgent, Bonaccio. Where is she?" He ignores the droid and peers between the shelves. "Gabriella?"

"Back here," she answers in a small voice.

He follows her voice down the aisle and skids to a stop beside the computing station. His stepmom is hunched on her laboratory floor, face buried in her knees, lab coat rumpled beneath her. She wipes away tears and snot with the coat sleeve. Jack falls to her side and pulls her hands gingerly away from her face. Her hair clings to damp cheeks. This is not the impeccable Gabriella Nuñez that raised him.

So much for his speech. "You heard?"

The scientist mops her face with her damp lab coat and croaks out, "Memo called me."

Jack doesn't know what to say, but he definitely should've brought flowers. He pulls Gabriella close. Her head settles into the soft folds of his jacket, the same bomber jacket his father wore and gave him on the day he rose to the rank of admiral.

He rakes his hair between his fingers and thinks through his situation. It's a good sign that Guillermo reached out. The twins have always been close. The admiral ought to take a page out of their book and reach out to his own brother. Either way, his uncle will have answers. What happened to Dad? Jack can't take the burning questions. He needs to know.

Gabriella's long hair tickles his chin, hinting of rain. He looks down. The wetness in her eyes cuts through his heart, but he holds steady. His answers can wait. She needs him.

"Let me take you to my place. You can stay the night." Gabriella nods. He rests his head against steel cabinets. "Tomorrow we'll find Guillermo." And his answers. There's still time to fix this. Jack helps his mom to her feet. He won't fail—he isn't giving up on Dad.

"Ready?"

"Sí."

CHAPTER FOUR

ANNA

THE CROSSROAD AT THE heart of the Ring wriggles with civilians and Coalition officers alike, their pointless chatter echoing in a massive, open walkway. Glass panes stretch from floor to ceiling and blanket the steel platform in starlight. Detective Wright waits just beyond the auditorium in the west wing, leaning against the railing with her ankles crossed. As the guardians spill out into the hallway in groups of twos and threes, they trade fresh theories on the particle accelerator.

Fools.

Anna closes her eyes and breathes deeply, willing patience. Her blood boils at the sight of the admiral—the biggest fool of all. How can he be so blind? The particle accelerator is no "accident," and sending the military to babysit all those poor people on Johannesburg is a waste. Terra Nova is behind this, but they're long gone by now. If she's right, they're working the Coalition from the inside. She crosses her arms. Her window to catch her perp is closing fast. This one is different from all the others. She can feel it. Her nails dig into her biceps. The answers she's been searching for all these years are on the Johannesburg station.

A shadow falls over her. "Inside. We need to talk about the debriefing." Her beefy commanding officer blocks her exit, holding the door to one of the smaller meeting rooms open and wearing one of his signature scowls—or does he reserve that face for her?

There's a lecture coming, but she's not interested in being reprimanded in front of this crowd. Besides, Sergeant Arquette doesn't want the military to take over this case any more than she does. She just needs to come up with the right appeal for the admiral, and her CO will be thanking her on bended knee. "Look, I don't have time for this." She flings her bag over her shoulder and faces the east wing. "If I leave now, I'll get a head start on forgetting that debriefing ever happened." The detective turns on her heel, but he intercepts her, holding the door wide. Now this is pissing her off. "Move."

Her acerbic glare would send most people running, but not the sergeant. He regards her coolly with small dark eyes eclipsed by thick brown eyebrows. "What is the matter with you, Anna?" he asks in his heavy French accent. Charming under different circumstances, maybe. "Even you cannot be foolish enough to antagonize an admiral of the military division. Do you wish to be court-martialed?"

Anna uncrosses her arms and drops them to her sides. Vengeance would be worth it, but she thinks better of saying that out loud. What's the point of confiding in her CO now? He let the admiral humiliate her in front of every guardian in the damn Solar System. But all she says is, "Relax. Monroe is too soft for that." She relents, ducking under his arm and brushing past him to the small room.

"Who says I am speaking of Monroe?" The sergeant narrows his eyes and closes the door, blotting out the stars beyond the Coalition station and the noise coming from its leaders.

The detective bursts into laughter and nearly drops her bag. "You wouldn't. What would you do without me, Sergeant?"

The cool glare on the old boar's face melts. "Enough. I am serious, Anna. You are not telling me everything you know, are you?" Her laughter fades as she shakes her head. "I can't help you if you don't trust me." Her burly CO jerks his head and plants his feet mulishly, but Anna sighs. Trust gets people killed. She crosses the room and drags her fingertips along the dark metal encasing the walls, the thud of her boots muted on these matted floors. Doesn't look like she can worm her way out of this one, and the sergeant just might be able to do what he says. When she's completed her semi-circle, she turns, crosses her arms, and faces Arquette.

"Particle accelerators are pretty damn important, Sergeant. They don't give just anyone the clearance to bypass things like catastrophic fail-safe protocols."

He says, "Of course not. You already know who has those clearances, don't you?"

"Just one person: Guardian Ngcobo."

The sergeant remains deadly silent for several long seconds. "You believe Ngcobo ordered an attack on his own station?" Anna nods and presses her back into the steel wall while he lets out a long breath. "You were right not to share that information with the Coalition."

She smirks. Now he gets it. "No. How do we proceed, Sergeant?"

Arquette draws himself up to his full height. "You will do nothing. The admiral requested that you forward the dossier on the Johannesburg station to his division and destroy your own records. I suggest you redact your theory from the dossier before doing so."

Big surprise there. The detective balls her hands into fists at her side but stays commendably level-headed, if she can say so herself. "You still think this is a job for military? This is an open investigation, sir, and if I'm right, one with serious consequences."

"But you don't know if you're right, do you, Detective?" He shakes his head and adopts a harsh tone. "Accusing a guardian of genocide is a serious matter. I cannot allow you to pursue this."

"Why not?" Anna demands through gritted teeth. The whole point of intelligence is to connect the dots between the known and the unknown.

"Because we don't have any support," Arquette spits in that heavy accent of his, mustache bristling. "That kind of allegation would require the backing of Frank Roarke himself, and we don't have sufficient evidence to come to him, do we?"

She deflates. "No."

"Send the dossier. Destroy everything you have. I'll see what I can do about the admiral. I don't need my best detective at odds with military." That scowl is back.

The detective clenches her jaw so tight her molars ache. So much for his help. "Yes, sir." Fuming, Anna charges past her CO, rips the door open, and marches away. She was *so close.* If she's right, Terra Nova has operatives inside the Coalition, but thanks to the admiral, all that intel is slipping through her fingers. Ma may never get the justice she deserves now. Anna wills her feet to move faster. In the east wing, she can hop a transport pod and leave the sergeant in her stardust.

DECEMBER 13, 3040 | MONTRÉAL STATION, EARTH'S ORBIT

Anna retrieves her Coalition-issue hovercraft from the depot. The vehicle maps its own route, and the station skyline shrinks into the distance. Eventually, the station's dome swallows it. Once the short, blocky mom and pop shops of the east end roll into view, she closes her eyes, kicks her boots up onto the dashboard and rests her head against the window. It feels good to put some distance between her and that fiasco at the Ring. The hovercraft whirs to a stop outside a Zero Gs, this one small and ratty. Detective Wright swings her legs out, boots crunching into fresh snow. She pinches the sleeves of her thin black skins snug at the wrists and hurries inside.

The detective waves at the clerk, heads to the back of the store, and stuffs two packs of jerky into her pockets. Halfway to the counter, she bumps into a kid. "Need something, little man?"

The boy's eyes stretch wide as orbiters. He points at hers. "What's wrong with your eyes?"

Grinning, Anna plants her fists on her hips and leans close. "I took them from the last little boy who asked too many questions."

"Brandon! Get over here, dummy!" The kid's friends intervene in time to stop him from wetting himself. Brandon scoots off, but not without peeking over his shoulder one more time at her. A crew of four or five kids, not yet old enough for trade assignments, peels out of the small mart—they probably shoplifted. They dart across the street, shouting. "That was the detective, spacebrains!"

Every time. Anna cackles under her breath and strolls up to the counter, where she drops her jerky. "Sorry about them, James. I'll pay for whatever they stole."

"Not your fault." The clerk shakes his head. "Wouldn't steal if there wasn't such a chokehold on wages these days."

The detective shrugs. "Meriéux says the colony will change all that, right?"

James looks up at her from under his eyebrows. "You believe that?" She doesn't know for sure, so she holds her tongue. The colony has that too-good-to-be-true stench, and anyway, she can't stomach relying on anyone else to solve her problems, least of all a guardian. Memories of the blast zone resurface: a guardian did that to his own people. Her fingernails scrape the counter as James scans her jerky. "Anything else?"

"Two packs of jimmy." She cocks her head to one side. "A Cotton rye, if you have it."

With a creak, Anna flings the door to her flat wide. At last. She carefully sets the whisky bottle on a bare portion of the coffee table and tosses her new jimmies on top of an empty pack beside the bottle. One pack falls to the floor.

The detective chucks her skinbottoms into a growing pile in the corner of the small studio. She leaps onto the couch, twisting so she lands facing forward.

With one hand, she unscrews the cap on the bottle and lets it fall, then peels back the jerky wrapper with her teeth. Sergeant Arquette's judging eyes stare back at her. She crushes the wrapper with a loud crinkle and tosses it on the table. He's nothing but a spineless yes-man. Kicking her bare feet up onto the cluttered table and munching on jerky, she wiggles her toes contentedly. Time to unwind. Anna pores over the news scroll as she takes a swig from the bottle. Peppery vanilla burns her throat.

"After pledging support to Johannesburg, Guardian Mérieux rejects a two percent wage increase proposed by Montréal council members."

Anna chokes and nearly spits out her whisky. "*That's* her plan?" She rips off another bite of jerky and chews hard and fast. That's how kids like Brandon end up on the street. The detective swallows and forces herself to take a calming breath. Shaking her head, she reaches for the pack on the table and a light, extracting a jimmy with her forefinger and thumb. A skunky pine needle smell wafts from the packaging. They don't roll them all that special at that Zero Gs, but it doesn't matter. She just wants to forget. Tired as she is, one hit is enough to do the trick.

Chuckling, she does another.

The light from the sun fades, and a chill breeze makes its way into the flat. Anna sits up with a groan and crosses the room. The door swings shut with a click. She trips over her skins on her way back and something slides out of one of the inner pockets. She stoops down. It's the dossier on the Johannesburg station.

The one she was supposed to give the admiral before leaving Colossi Infiniti.

Detective Wright stares at the dossier. The admiral will be *pissed* if she doesn't forward her intel, but what's stopping her from holding onto her copy? She returns to the couch, crossing her legs underneath her as she inserts the chip into her wristband unit. The dossier springs to life on the holoscroll in front of her. Forward the evidence and destroy the chip. Those were the sergeant's orders. The Frenchman thinks he's helping, but he's just covering his ass. Why should she do what he says? She knows it all by heart anyway, and she knows the admiral is making a huge mistake—one that might just cost Anna her first real shot at detaining a Terra Nova operative. She rips off another bite of jerky with her teeth as she reads.

DECEMBER 14, 3040 | MONTRÉAL STATION, EARTH'S ORBIT

Sunlight creeps up Anna's chest and face. She groans and sits up. At least it's her day off. Her muscles are cramped and aching and her head throbs, but she feels light. Tomorrow she'll head straight into Arquette's office. If she's better prepared this time, he'll listen. She rubs her temples with the butts of her hands. Stumbling across the flat, she rummages through the scant supplies in the kitchen cabinet, only to curse under her breath. No coffee. The odor of yesterday's sweat and grime still clings to her skin. She opts for a shower.

Refreshed, she confronts her reflection in the mirror. She can't challenge Arquette with that ragged, lopsided knot on top of her head. Anna clips her wristband unit to her forearm and sends a text. It's been too long since the detective has been to Shona.

`Back in town. Can you fit me in? Need a little of your magic.`

A response appears on-screen right away. `My house in an hour?`

`I'll be there.`

Anna swings by the Zero Gs on the way, thanks James, and eats a cinnamon bun on foot. The texture is too much like freeze-dried rations for her liking. The coffee tastes like motor oil, but she drains the cup all the same. When she arrives at Shona's flat, the hairdresser eyes the detective's strands sticking out in every direction, purses her lips, and crosses her arms.

"How long has it been this time?" Shona asks. "Six weeks?"

"Eight."

"Eight!" The woman shakes her head. "Anna Wright, you better sit down and sit still. We've got work to do." Like salon day is more important than a particle accelerator exploding. The detective takes the seat that is offered to her. Shona pulls her hair forward and inspects her strands. "What are you thinking this time?" the hairdresser asks, gently working her fingers through the curls.

Shrug. "Some kind of updo? Or I could go bald."

She might as well have slapped Shona from the indignation streaking her face. "We are *not* chopping this gorgeous hair off. Your mama would rise up from the grave and take us both."

The detective's lip curls. "Ma's grave is empty. I can chop it off if I damn well please."

Shona tut tuts noisily. "I've got an idea. Low maintenance. Even you won't have a problem keeping up with it." Anna shrugs her consent, and Shona beams. "I can't wait for you to see this."

The hairdresser oils Anna's long, kinky locks as the detective settles into the chair, and the room fills with a clean, fresh scent. Anna suddenly remembers the chip still in her wristband unit. She cringes, but there's no way for the admiral to know that the dossier wasn't destroyed.

"You're tense today," Shona says. "What's wrong?"

Anna looks away. "Just stirring up trouble, same as any other day."

"Just like your mama."

The detective frowns, watching the hairdresser weave her hair into thick braids. "Ma was a pushover. I'm nothing like Mae Wright."

"If you say so. She was sweet, but only because she knew how to get what she wanted. She could be tough when she needed to be. Just like you."

Anna shakes her head. "She trusted anyone and everyone. Look where it got her."

Shona finishes and holds up a mirror for Anna. Despite herself, Anna's words catch in her throat. Gold links stud the new, chunky braids coiled into a dramatic, sweeping bun atop her head. Now *this* is a hairstyle for someone who gets what she wants. Slowly, she smiles at her reflection. Mérieux herself doesn't look this good. Shona smirks. "And you wanted to chop it off." The hairdresser doesn't ask for payment, but Anna sends her money.

A blinking light in the corner of her eye announces a call from the sergeant just as the detective arrives at her front door, and she accepts. It's about time to make the old boar see reason. Arquette flickers into view as she enters her flat.

"What can I do for you, boss?"

"Something has come up. Can you come to the Ring?"

Anna smirks. He's finally come to his senses. "Be there in twenty."

DECEMBER 14, 3040 | COLOSSI INFINITI, EARTH'S ORBIT

The sergeant's office is shrouded in darkness. Anna marches forward at a brisk stride. She's in enough trouble without appearing to stall. Her eyes adjust quickly thanks to the surgeon who gave them to her all those years ago, but the unusual surroundings slow her, nonetheless. Arquette sits at his desk with his hands folded tight, and he isn't alone. The detective can't believe it. That sly dog managed to wrangle Frank Roarke *and* Guardian Nuñez. The Coalition is taking Terra Nova head on, and this is her chance. Good thing she paid that trip to Shona. She could kiss the sergeant.

Those vermin are going to pay for what they did to you, Ma.

With Anna stunned into speechlessness, Roarke speaks first. "I understand that today is your day off, so I must apologize for asking you to join us, Detective." The Coalition's leader is just another skinny white man with dark eyes—like most of the other men from the west end of Montréal—but there's no mistaking Frank Roarke in his grunt skins, old-school bunker boy beret, and that famous luster to his skin tone that gave the GLOW injections their nickname. Anna should say something, but she's having trouble forming words. An indistinct warble comes from the back of her throat instead. Roarke exchanges a glance with Sergeant Arquette. "Have a seat. We have a lot to discuss."

A chair whizzes around Arquette's desk and comes to a stop behind her, and Anna drops into it, never taking her eyes off Roarke. She's quaking with energy.

Standing beside the sergeant, the Coalition leader leans against the desk and spreads his hands. "Let me begin by commending your handling of the Johannesburg investigation yesterday."

"Thank you for the opportunity, sir," Anna blurts. "With your resources, I'm confident we can zero in on our bomber and get justice for the people of Johannesburg." Roarke pitches his head back and frowns, his lips parted with some unspoken thought.

From the corner of the office, Guardian Nuñez leans forward with his palms planted on his thighs and smiling bitterly. "We're not here to talk about Johannesburg, Detective. We're here to offer you a case."

"Oh!" Anna's mouth falls open. What could be more important than the particle accelerator? Her gaze darts to Sergeant Arquette, but she can't read his beady little eyes. She focuses on Nuñez. Why is he here? He's obviously got the ear of their wise and noble leader, but he doesn't have jurisdiction over her. The detective taps the heel of her boot, thinking. Play this out. "I'm all ears."

Nuñez exchanges a look with the sergeant. "Bueno, pero, I can't say anything more until you've deactivated your implants and your unit."

Her eyebrows almost disappear into her bun. "Why would I do that?"

The sergeant leans forward with his shoulders hiked up to his ears. "This isn't a typical assignment, Wright. If you accept this case, you won't have a team. You will work alone and report directly to the guardian. Discretion is essential to your safety. I have already deactivated my implants."

Anna chews on this new revelation. She's never disabled her implants in all the years she's had them. Reluctantly, she does as she is instructed. "Okay, I've gone dark." She wiggles her fingers. "What's this case?"

That bitter smile crosses Nuñez's face again. "We need your help to retrieve a missing orbiter."

Her face falls into a scowl. A missing orbiter? How trivial. "What about the particle accelerator?"

Nuñez exchanges another glance with Arquette. Mustache bristling, her CO puffs his chest out and matches her scowl with one of his own. "The Coalition has graciously permitted additional resources for Intelligence to proceed in that arena, but that's not why you're here."

"Bullshit." Her fists clench at her side. "That's *my* investigation. I should be taking point."

"We know about your theory," Roarke puts in. "Guardian Ngcobo, committing genocide on his own people?"

So much for trust. Anna turns her acid glare on the sergeant. "I thought you were going to help, not spread my theories around the galaxy."

"Your theory is sound, Detective, but it misses the mark." Nuñez steamrolls her as if she hadn't spoken. He shakes his head. "Sam isn't our man, but someone else in the Coalition must have authorized the deceleration." The detective is skeptical, but now isn't the time for a debate. They wouldn't be sitting in the literal and figurative shadows over just any ship. This guardian must have something big in mind. Nuñez leans forward. "This runs a lot deeper than Johannesburg. If you're serious about catching your perp, then there's something on that orbiter for you, too."

"That so?" Anna narrows her eyes. Has he made the connection to Terra Nova yet? She won't know unless she plays along. "Retrieve, or rescue?"

Something flashes across the guardian's face—regret? "We don't expect there to be survivors." Anna cocks an eyebrow. What fresh hell is she being dragged into? Nuñez bulls forward. "There were two passengers onboard the orbiter: Commander Derek Monroe, and a robot named Diego. You'll find their last known coordinates already in your inbox when you reactivate your implants."

Sure enough, her wristband unit blinks out of the corner of her eye, but she keeps her gaze trained on Nuñez. She leans back in her chair and crosses her arms. "Monroe, eh? The officer that discovered planet Zomenos?" A veritable celebrity, that one.

Nuñez straightens. "La neta, sí—the one and only. He was investigating missing shuttles traveling through that region. I need to know what happened to Monroe, Detective, and to . . ." His voice cracks as he drops his gaze. ". . . to return his body to his family for burial, if possible."

The detective sighs and tilts her head to stare at the low ceiling, but her focus is razor sharp. "Why me? Any intelligence officer could do this. What aren't you telling me?"

"Like I said, this runs deeper than Johannesburg. We believe Terra Nova is active again."

Her neck snaps straight and lets out a long, controlled breath. So, they're in sync after all. She'd give anything for another shot at these bastards. "That's quite the theory, Guardian."

"You know I'm right. You've been thinking it too, haven't you?"

Anna shrugs noncommittally. "It fits their profile." Why share her suspicions so soon?

An enthusiastic gleam flashes through Nuñez's eyes. "Here's the thing about Diego: he isn't just any robot. Terra Nova is his expertise. Finding and preserving him is critical to the mission."

This could very well be her lucky break. Is the guardian willing to trade? The detective rests her elbows on her seatback, crosses her ankles, and cocks her head. "Let's say that's true. What does this case have to do with Terra Nova?"

"We don't know yet," Nuñez admits. "Monroe's mission was to investigate transport shuttles to Zomenos that went missing. We suspect Terra Nova is involved."

"It's consistent with past activity," Anna agrees. "Why would Terra Nova target transport shuttles?"

Roarke's gaze settles on her. "I would have thought that much would be obvious to someone with your talents."

She crosses her arms. "Maybe I want to hear you say the words."

"You said it yourself yesterday. Terra Nova doesn't want us going anywhere. The logical conclusion is that they seek a return to Earth."

Or they just want us all dead. "Maybe." The detective springs to her feet and paces to the other side of the small office and then spins to face the men. She's not prepared to walk away from her investigation into the particle accelerator, but she's already connecting the dots between these events. Her fist clenches and unclenches at her side. Choking off the antimatter puts pressure on the Coalition to choose between the restoration and the colony. There's plenty of idle grumbling over that on bar stools all over her station. Is Terra Nova choosing a side in the debate? Why?

Nuñez settles back comfortably, crosses his legs, and folds his hands over his knee. "If you do this, you'll have full consent to use Diego to help find your Terra Nova sympathizer."

Bingo.

A dark bot with the full download on Terra Nova activity might just be the lynchpin in her entire investigation. Her own resources for this are embarrassingly limited, even at the top of Intelligence. "Alright. I'll track down your missing orbiter, but only if I'm allowed to use whatever intel I gather as part of my investigation."

The sergeant stands and positions himself between his detective and his superiors. "Be careful, Anna. We may have already lost good officers to this cause." She can't believe it. The old boar actually looks worried.

Detective Wright flashes a wicked grin and winks. "Don't worry, Sergeant. I'm not getting myself killed. You'll be putting up with me for a long time."

Terra Nova is going down.

CHAPTER FIVE

GUILLERMO

N O SOUND ESCAPES GUILLERMO's lungs when he shouts. Blood pumps in his ears as his eyes pop open. Surrounded by pinche space dust. Shrapnel floats past, unaffected by his silent screams. He heaves into a roll, craning his neck, and ojos azules fall into view. Vacant, hollow eyes. Derek's eyes. He can't be . . . Guillermo lunges forward, arms stretched wide, and snatches at the commander's collar, his wrist—anything.

The guardian wakes in a cold pool of sweat, arms still outstretched in front of him. Heart racing and breathing hard, he drops his arms and lies in bed. Diego twirls in a vacuum, the same as every other morning this week. The xenobot was Guillermo's fulcrum: the centerpiece around which everything else pivots. Juan believed in the bots even when Guillermo himself didn't, even throughout the setbacks, acaso cuando el inventor tenía miedo. Grunting, he twitches the damp sheets aside and hauls himself, swaying, to his feet. Entonces, Juan was wrong. The guardian's promises are sand-blasted and blown to the far corners of the galaxy along with Diego's guts. And Derek.

Poor Derek. Perched on the edge of the bed, Guillermo checks his wristband unit on the stand. 0727. He groans. Elli and the boys will be here within an hour. It's past time he faces them.

In the kitchen, he pours drip coffee and chooses an old record with his implants. The syncopated rhythms of gg del mar fill the house. No escuchaba esta guitarra hace tiempo. The music takes him back to wrenching on Coalition tanks, long before he ever suspected he would be a part of the organization. The doorbell chimes behind him, and a menu of response options appears in his field of view.

`Unlock front door.`

He holds his mug to his nose and breathes in. The tension disperses from his shoulders as the shuffling of boots fills the small dwelling. Nothing he says to his familia will make this right, but he must own his mistake. Turning, he locks eyes with Gabriella. Derek is his fault. Guillermo sent the love of Elli's life to his death. The look in those honey-brown eyes of hers, mirror to his, strips down the sliver of resolve he's built in the last week. She steps forward hesitantly and he closes the gap between them in two quick strides, pulling her into his arms. The scent of her long, dark curls overwhelms him. She hugs him tight, but he's rigid. It's too much. Stepping back and searching her eyes for the outrage, the hate that should be there, he finds only wordless understanding carved into her features.

A nervous grating of boots pulls Guillermo back into the present. Looking up, he catches sight of Jack and Henry waiting in the doorway. Henry flashes a sheepish smile, but Jack wears dark circles under his eyes. Gently, the guardian extracts himself from Gabriella's arms and steps forward.

"Hi boys. Come in, come in."

"Hi Tío," they chorus, crossing the threshold. Lucy Mérieux brings up the rear in a long, black trench coat. Guillermo blinks as she unravels a glittering black scarf and hangs up her coat with the others, wishing his nephew hadn't brought another guardian into his home. This is family business, and he doesn't know the Montréal station's young new leader well enough to trust her with his xenobot. He glances irritably at Derek's oldest son, but he knows better than to protest. Jack is a man now, and a man in love.

Chairs scrape the floor as his guests take seats at the dark steel dining table. Guillermo downs the rest of his coffee and joins them, sitting across from Jack with a long sigh. It's time. What did he want to hear when Juan entered cryo? The admiral's piercing blue eyes, so close to the ones haunting Guillermo's daily nightmares, unnerve the guardian, yet he forces himself to meet them.

"I'm sorry for what happened to Derek and for my part in his mission. Your father loved you two. You didn't deserve to lose him so soon." A nervous jitter settles into his left hand. Chingada madre—too much coffee, güey.

Henry's face warms to a bright pink before he buries it in his mug of cocoa.

Derek's eldest frowns and leans forward, his own mug untouched. "Did we really lose him? The nature of his mission . . . How can we know for sure?"

"Jack is right, Memo. Derek could still be alive." Cheeks rosy, Gabriella breathlessly seizes her son's hand, her eyes burning into Guillermo's.

Guillermo tucks his twitching hand under the table, unable to meet his twin's hopeful gaze. He's thought of nothing else for days. "Frank has the Coalition's best detective looking into it. We'll have a full report soon, but mijo—I saw the wreckage. He couldn't have survived."

His words only provoke more questions. Jack rests a loose fist on the table in front of him. "See, that's what I mean. There are protocols for this. What detective? Was his body cam retrieved, or are we talking about footage from the orbiter? Roarke needs to release the mission details to the Coalition. This is the way it works. When one of our own goes MIA, the military is always involved. Military, not intelligence. Always." The knuckles in his fist turn white. "I should be there," he says finally. Guillermo suppresses a smile. So much like Derek, that one.

Still staring into the foam, Henry speaks up abruptly. "Listen to Tío, Jack. He's working directly with Roarke."

Guillermo shakes his head. "Your brother's reaction is understandable. I wish I had better answers, but the mission remains classified. You have to trust me when I say that we're doing our best to get all the information."

Jack glares at him. "No offense, Memo, but this isn't your jurisdiction. I am duty-bound to the officers of the terrestrial fleet."

This earns the admiral a scornful look from Gabriella. "Don't speak to him that way."

Guillermo covers Gabriella's hand with his own. "It's okay, Elli. He has every right to be angry with me." He meets Jack's gaze. "Derek took this on to protect you, all of you. Don't let his sacrifice be in vain."

Lucy touches the admiral's shoulder lightly, and he uncoils. "What is your involvement with the commander's mission, Guillermo?"

"That's classified," he repeats irritably. Jack might already view this woman as part of the family, but she's still a guardian, and a newcomer at that. Diego's role in Derek's mission is between him and Roarke. They can't risk word spreading about the xenobot. "Mira. This mission is aboveboard. Trust me on that. It'll only take the detective a few days to reach the orbiter's coordinates, and then we'll know more."

Jack plants his elbows on the table and runs his hands through his hair. "Fine. You'll keep me informed?"

A careful sigh of relief. He might just accept Guillermo's answers, after all. "Yes, mijo. Of course."

The admiral nods. "Good. I still want a copy of the footage."

A bitter smile quirks Guillermo's lips. Te doy la mano y te tomas el codo. "I'll run it by Roarke." Jack leans back, pacified at last. It's as good a time as any for the old guardian to show his face to the Coalition leader. Truth be told, he's been dodging Roarke's summons for days.

DECEMBER 14, 3040 | MONTRÉAL STATION, EARTH'S ORBIT

Guillermo arrives in the antechamber to Roarke's office, but hesitates at the door. There's only one reason the man would be this desperate to see him: the Coalition leader wants assurances that Diego isn't Guillermo's only xenobot, that their plan will still work. He closes his eyes. Juan's cells are safe in his shop. Can he admit to Roarke that he has another bot in the works? Even in the privacy of his own home, he's never said the words out loud.

"Come in, Guillermo."

Wincing, the guardian steps up to a biometric scanner. The doors open with a flash of blue. The bright sunlight that streams in through floor-to-ceiling windows forces Guillermo to shield his eyes. The civilian stations started as big rocks, asteroids terraformed and then protected from the harsh rays of the Sun with domes, but Colossi Infiniti is a military station, man-made without any dome. He's come a long way since the bunkers, but this is too much.

"¡Órale! How can you stand that light?" he demands, protocol forgotten.

In his high-backed seat, like chiseled obsidian, Roarke turns away from the window as Guillermo approaches a wide desk. "Better to acclimate now, while we still live under the protective domes of the stations. Once we transition to the colony, there will be no such protection."

Un problema para el futuro. "Doesn't it sting?"

Roarke spreads his hands. "I've been acclimating for months, a little at a time." The man glides toward the desk in that formidable chair of his as the light nonetheless dims. "This orphan race is weaker than its predecessors," he remarks with a subtly bitter smile.

"And yet we're the first to live among the stars," Guillermo says shortly. He swivels away from Roarke on his heel, faces the double doors, and steels himself. "Dale. You know what I came to talk to you about."

"I do. How is the admiral?"

"He's asking questions." Turning, he notices the nanoparticle cloud hovering above Roarke glows bright red.

"Sit, Guillermo. He'll have his answers soon enough. The detective's orbiter is cleared for sub-light speed travel."

The guardian scoffs, but he accepts the chair across from Roarke. "You know how the Coalition runs. Turf wars can get ugly, and this is the second time you've pushed back against the military."

"I *am* the Coalition, Guillermo." A nerve works in Roarke's temple. He folds his hands on the smooth steel slab between them, maintaining eye contact. "Jack will exercise patience, or I suggest you remind him how. You know what's at stake." Guillermo grinds his teeth, but Roarke is right: his technology is at risk. The detective needs time to intercept Diego. Roarke unfolds his hands and flexes his fingers over and over. "We have to assume the worst. You understand that, don't you?" Unbidden, dreams of the splintered orbiter resurface. Guillermo shuts his eyes against esa pesadilla and nods. "Even if the detective retrieves your xenobot, we may not recover sufficient intelligence to close in on Terra Nova. The colony might be compromised."

And Juan will remain asleep. A rattling sigh shakes Guillermo's chest. "We need to regain the upper hand."

Pulsing fiercely, the Cerebrum particles emit a low hum as Roarke blinks. "It is imperative. You have a suggestion?"

Guillermo nods. "De seguro. I'll share it if you grant Jack access to the footage from Derek's orbiter."

Roarke jerks his hand flippantly. "I calculate minimal exposure risk in releasing the footage itself. If it keeps the admiral in check, fine. Now, tell me your idea."

Not so fast. Guillermo shakes his head. "Our original agreement still stands?"

A strained smile crosses the Coalition leader's face. "Of course, Guillermo. The cryo pods will be on the next freighter to Zomenos. You'll be reunited with Juan."

"Thank you, sir." Guillermo returns a lopsided grin. "The thing is, Diego might be lost to us, but he isn't my only xenobot."

"The technology is reproducible?" Roarke glides around the desk, closer to his guardian. His nose is inches from Guillermo's face. What will he say when he learns the whole story? Will he demand the bot for himself or simply destroy it? Eyes narrowing, he leans back in his seat. "That's good. I suggest you make that your primary focus while we wait for more news. Anything we can use to gain an edge over Terra Nova is critical right now. It's the only thing that matters."

Guillermo bows his head. "Consider it done." He's committed now, so que será, será.

DECEMBER 14, 3040 | GUADALAJARA STATION, EARTH'S ORBIT

Inés's yellow eyes follow Guillermo in silence as he paces the upper shop level of his home, boots echoing along the platform. He looks out of his broad, two-story windows from time to time. The plan behind his second xenobot was just a theory until now, an idea to calm his nerves whenever he thought of Juan's frozen, useless body in the gardens. As long as he never acts on it, it can stay that way.

Comforting.

Harmless.

Should he really go through with it?

"¿Papá?" Inés stands at his feet, her steel face rotated upwards toward him.

"Yes?"

"You look scared."

Nervous laughter escapes his lips. He sinks to the ground beside Inés. Guácala, he's sweating. "I guess I am."

The bot's optical sensors shrink and expand, like irises struggling to adjust to an overload of white light. "Why?"

He sips café and gazes out the window. Sunrise on the stations looks like peeling back the skin of a mango: vibrant reds and greens meet bright orange at the center. He never expected to live long enough to witness it, but now it's just a part of his daily ritual. Another sip. If Juan could see this, he would be up early every morning to paint it. Guillermo suddenly grips his mug tight, scalding his hand, but he doesn't let go. Juan isn't going to see this, he remembers, but if he succeeds, Juan will see the colony. The question is: Can Juan forgive him for what he has to do to get there?

The guardian pats his bot on the shoulders, but his eyes are on his workbench. Inside a small incubator rests a petri dish full of stem cells. Every week, those cells grow and multiply, slowly taking on three-dimensional form. That ball of cells is just visible under a light microscope.

Juan's cells.

Quizás, he could try another way. His success with Diego relied on nada más que his own biopsied nervous tissue. That's it. Guillermo could deliver a second xenobot to Roarke without ever touching Juan's cells. And yet . . .

"I miss his smile." The guardian squats beside his first bot. "Do you remember that crooked tooth of his? Juan's, I mean."

Inés bobs up and down. "Yes, Papá. You told him Mamá could fix it, but he refused."

"He always said, 'Art is in the little imperfections'." Guillermo straightens and sets his mug on the bench. "Now he hasn't said a word in fifty years." He pulls on a pair of gloves. He won't see that crooked smile again for at least another year, maybe more. He has to go through with it. "¡A la mierda con eso, Inés! We're finally going to hear his voice again."

CHAPTER SIX

MARILINA

CIVILIANS IN TRAINING FOR mission Z1 are expected to be on site in uniform and at attention each morning at 0600 hours. Part of the discipline they're expected to master, and supposedly less rigorous than what officers go through. Marilina usually looks forward to basic training about as much as a child anticipates a 22-gauge hypodermic needle, but today a peculiar eagerness settles in as she enters the locker room and disrobes alongside the others. After Johannesburg, she welcomes a bit of routine.

"It's nice to see you again, Dr. Chamorro," her unit leader, Dr. Nuñez, whispers beside her.

"Brilliant work on the Johannesburg station," the lab technician, Keshi Okumu, adds as they line up, the rubber soles of their training sneakers squeaking on the court. All three of them wear the fitted navy-blue polymerized skins of the crew's medical unit. "We're lucky to have you on this mission."

Memories of her last assignment resurface. Marilina smiles and bows her head rigidly. "Thank you." Lucky?–hardly. She presses shaking hands into her thighs to still them. Her career as a Meridian ended a disgrace to her family and to her station. Sore and weary, she closes her eyes, swallows, and focuses on little Aneke's braids. Don't think like that. This isn't the first time the Meridian have encountered such casualties. She performed the best she could, given the circumstances, and her crew understands that. Her family must accept it, too.

Officer Kamal marches into the gymnasium in the crisp white skins of the military and stops at the front of the group. Silence descends. Marilina stands at attention, following him with her eyes. The drill sergeant pauses, and whatever eagerness she felt before dies. Her absence, however warranted, would not go unpunished. She holds her head level and waits to be called upon, pushing the Meridian from her mind. This is what matters now: her crew, their mission, and the colony.

"Valencia, step forward." Marilina blinks, surprised to be spared. A tall, red-haired woman in the green skins of the agricultural unit steps out of her position in line and faces the crew. "Marcus," Kamal barks. "What's wrong with Valencia's uniform?"

Without hesitation, a voice answers from the back of the group. "Sir, those boots are not fit for training."

Kamal tucks his hands behind his back and dips his chin. "Correct." He turns to the woman as her complexion reddens. "Are you aware that those boots are caked in mud, Valencia?"

"Yes, sir," she answers in a small voice, her shoulders drooping as she hangs her head. Marilina grimaces silently and stares at her boots. Failing the morning inspection is unbearable.

"Excuse me?" Kamal asks.

Valencia belatedly snaps to attention. "Yes, sir!" she repeats clearly.

The drill sergeant nods. "Get changed. Meet us on the track." Valencia hurries away. Kamal turns back to the rest of the crew. "Remember, it doesn't matter who you are when you're off-station. In here, you are representatives of the Coalition. What does the Coalition embody, Chamorro?"

Marilina stands straighter. "Courtesy, discipline, and readiness," she answers in a loud, clear voice.

"Correct," Kamal says again. "The rest of you, on the track. Forty-meter sprints. Go!"

The crewmembers queue up on the track, five across. Marilina falls into step beside Okumu and makes sure to "hustle." She's three weeks into basic training now and can predict how the officer will respond to the undisciplined. At the screech of the whistle, Marilina darts forward with the others in her pack, focusing on lifting her knees all the way up and driving her heels. The Meridian maintain a daily fitness regimen not unlike this, but the doctor isn't accustomed to someone humiliating her for poor form. By the end of the morning session, sweat beads on her forehead and trickles down her spine. She must smell worse than a culture of *C. diff*.

"Well done today," Kamal says, coming up beside Marilina while the others wait in line for water. "There's someone here to see you." He nods towards the exit, where a woman loiters. She's rather conspicuous, and not just because she's the only one not outfitted in polished, fitted military skins. Marilina turns back to him, questioning silently. "She's with medical," he says with a shrug. "I assumed you knew her." He inclines his head. "Go on. We're done here for the day."

The doctor crosses the lacquered court to the other side of the gymnasium and approaches the stranger, her sneakers squeaking the whole way there. Up close, the shapeless smock-like skins brand the newcomer as a nurse-android from the Ring. Her confusion escalates. The Meridian seldom have anything to do with the Coalition hospital.

"Marilina Chamorro?" The doctor nods, averting her eyes. Colossi Infiniti has the best androids in the Coalition, and this one could almost pass for human. The best indicator is the iris: the synthetic ones don't respond to light as naturally as human irises do. "They only just told me I'd be able to find you here. I've been trying to get ahold of you for the last hour, Doctor," the nurse complains with real human irritation.

"Sorry for your trouble. What can I do for you?"

The nurse huffs through her nose. "I'm with admissions." Her tone suggests that this should clear things up. "We've found a room in the ICU for your brother. Room eleven, ground floor. I can take you there."

Marilina must have misheard. "My brother? Are you sure you have the right person?" Quique can't be here—he's on Earth, with the other restorationists.

"Enrique Chamorro." The android blinks and enunciates each syllable, her irises dilating distractingly. "He is your brother, right?" Marilina nods, still not following, but the nurse bobs its head and turns on its heel. "The specialist will be in to see him soon, so if you want to speak with him, we should really be going." The hairs on the doctor's arm prickle, yet she freezes. The nurse registers her confusion and deflates. "No one's told you yet, have they?" she asks in a considerably gentler tone. Marilina shakes her head, straining to keep her escalating heart rate in check. The android squeezes her upper arm. "I apologize for the lack of communication, Dr. Chamorro. Here's what we know: Enrique's equipment malfunctioned on Earth's surface, leaving him exposed. He is suffering from severe radiation sickness." She beckons, hand outstretched. "Come with me."

The doctor remains rooted in place. Quique was safe at home with his VR simulation and their tías when she left. If he had just waited patiently for her, he would still be there, ready for a new life in the colony, but he had to prove a point instead. Pain jolts her back to the present: her grip on the cross around her neck is so tight that the grooves have carved a mark on her palm. She swallows and stares at that waiting hand. This android must think her out of control.

"Everything okay here, Dr. Chamorro?"

The admiral stands at Marilina's side. She blinks several times and clears her vision. Where did he come from? "Hello, Admiral," she murmurs. "Yes, everything is fine." Her words sound gritty and unnatural, even to her. Monroe tilts his head disbelievingly, taking in the nurse beside his crew's physician. The doctor hesitates, but she shakes her head and starts over. "No, everything isn't fine. It seems that my brother is in the ICU."

"We should hurry," the nurse presses again, her curious gaze lingering on the admiral.

Monroe's confident posture droops. He closes his eyes and nods. "I'm so sorry to hear that, Doctor. Please go with the nurse. I'll speak with Kamal."

"The officer assured me that training is complete for the day," the nurse interrupts. Her voice softens. "I know that this is upsetting, Dr. Chamorro, but there are other patients waiting for me, too."

"I know my way around the hospital. I'll go with her," Monroe breaks in. Both women turn and stare at him. "Go ahead. Take care of your other patients. We'll find our way."

The android opens its mouth to argue but concedes without argument. "Thank you, Admiral."

Marilina turns and looks up at him as the nurse walks away. "You didn't have to do that," she says. She hardly deserves favors from him now, not after Johannesburg.

"Yes, I did," Monroe counters placidly. He gestures in the direction the nurse is heading, tucking his hands into hidden pockets inside his ivory skins. They exit the gymnasium and enter the corridor together. He glances down at her. "I came down here to check in with my crew and found my lead physician obviously upset."

"I don't know what I am." Marilina gazes sidelong at him. Her heart rate has slowed since he arrived, but her fears won't be silenced until she sees Quique. She grips her cross again, remembering the look her brother wore when she set the necklace on her bedside table. How did things go so wrong between them? She quickens her pace. "You don't have to come with me. You must have better things to do than escort me through the halls of the Ring."

"It's the least I can do after sending you into the heart of a terrorist attack. Thank you, by the way. I read your report. You saved at least a dozen lives."

Marilina casts her gaze downward. "You shouldn't be thanking me, Admiral. The report also says I lost dozens more."

He regards her in silence, but his gaze softens. "It's Jack." The doctor stares at him, too surprised to answer. They fall into a comfortable silence as they traverse long hallways and head for the main antechamber. They approach a lift encased in glass. The admiral steps in front of a biometric scanner, and two glass panes part with his credentials. He extends his arm, holding the doors open for her. "This lift will take you to the ICU. You should be able to find your way from there. I'll leave you to your privacy, but I'll check in with you later. Is there someone I can call for you in the meantime?"

A pang of guilt twists Marilina's stomach. "My aunts need to be informed."

"Done."

Marilina faces the lift. "Jack?" she calls, testing the name hesitantly. The admiral nods. "Thank you. The Meridian is a solitary trade. No one has ever been there for me like this before. Like a . . . friend."

A smile twitches at the corners of the admiral's lips. "One thing you'll learn about being on a crew is that we're not friends. We're family, and families look out for each other." Marilina considers this in silence as she steps into the lift and Monroe backs away. "Okay, one last question before I leave you to your brother."

"Yes?"

"Do you like rocket dogs?"

DECEMBER 18, 3040 | COLOSSI INFINITI, EARTH'S ORBIT

Marilina scans a holographic scroll at the entrance to the ICU for room eleven and follows the signs to Quique's room. Rounding a corner, her whole body stiffens as if she's nailed to plywood. Her brother is in a bed against a far wall, alone save for the nurse-droids that come and go checking vital signs. A monitor beeps softly beside his bed. Sheets rustle as a nurse inspects a line carrying life-saving nutrients to his patient's veins. Oh, Quique.

The doctor edges closer, and with a hammering heart, stares down at her younger brother. Quique is unresponsive. His complexion, normally the amber brown of iodine in solution, is showing signs of jaundice, and his skin is dried and cracked. Compared with a week ago, he looks frail. An involuntary rasp escapes Marilina's dry throat as she grips the sheets between useless fingers. She is much, much too late.

"Good morning. You must be Enrique's sister." A steady voice pulls her back into the present moment. She turns and looks up into eyes darker than the very hollows of the Meridian. "My name is Alejandro Martinho."

Her eyes widen at the familiar name. "You mean *Guardian* Martinho."

"You may call me that if you wish." Pale lips curl into a smile. "What should I call you?"

"Dr. Marilina Chamorro." Her gaze wanders back to her brother. What is a guardian doing in Quique's room? Only one explanation makes sense. "You're the specialist treating my brother?"

Martinho bows his head, hair dark enough to match his eyes. "If you consent to transfer him to my care, I will be."

Marilina bites her lip. She knows nothing about the guardian's qualifications. His glossy skins that catch the light don't exactly suggest a member of the medical unit. "You're a guardian, not a medical practitioner. Why would I consent to that transfer?"

The guardian laughs cheerlessly as a nurse wordlessly replaces the medication pumping into Quique's line. "You have every reason to be skeptical of me, but you have nothing to fear, Dr. Chamorro. I'm a former Meridian, like you."

This revelation makes her head reel. Another Meridian, here? Her trade is exceptionally rare, almost as rare as guardians themselves. More questions spring to her lips, but she suppresses them. Quique is no ordinary patient, and a Meridian may be able to help. Marilina cocks her head and smiles through her surprise. "Accepting that incredible statement for now, I have to ask: why would a Meridian-turned-guardian take my brother into his care?"

Martinho steps closer to her brother's bedside. His dark eyes soften as his hand hovers over Quique's. "I feel personally responsible for Enrique's condition." The guardian's voice wavers, but he regains control. "I oversee the restoration and its ground crews on Earth. I accept the blame for Enrique's accident." The dots connect in a rush: the surprising wealth that her brother has come into, and his blind devotion to this cause, all stem from this man. Now that she's met Martinho herself, Marilina can't fault her brother for choosing his cause over hers. The guardian turns and faces her. They're standing suddenly much closer than she remembered. He takes Marilina's hand in his. "Enrique stands the best chance of survival with me, Dr. Chamorro. Please allow me to make this right."

Marilina nods. "You're welcome to try." Martinho wastes no time, spinning towards the bed and bending close over Quique. Another android appears, deposits a scanner at the foot of the bed, and exits. The scanner springs to life, hovering over the bed and washing Quique in blue light while Martinho assesses his patient's vital signs. Marilina takes a seat and observes the examination with hands folded stiffly in her lap. "His symptoms are quite advanced." Now that she's here, her hopes of her brother making it through this are dwindling fast.

"That's to be expected," the guardian murmurs without looking up. "He was lost, abandoned for dead by his team. It was a stroke of luck that he was found at all. He was without gear for two days."

With a vigor that surprises her, Marilina surges to her feet. "Two days? Then, he *should* be dead."

Martinho looks up, and his lip curls again. "Exactly. That Enrique Chamorro is here with us now, alive, is proof of the success of the radioactivity cleanup." He straightens and turns to the scanner at the foot of the bed. Images of Quique's organs are displayed in holographic form. There's damage to his heart, liver, and kidneys. "I will order tests. I'll return with the results."

Marilina approaches the bed in small, stiff steps and gazes down at Quique. She has so much to say to her brother, but something holds her back. He's in an induced coma, so the conversation would be entirely one-sided. He looks so pale and weak. Her stomach twists in knots. This might be her last chance to say *something*. Did her determination to reunite her family destroy their relationship permanently? She never imagined that it would drive such a wedge between her and her brother. She brushes Quique's thick, long hair out of his eyes.

"I'm sorry, Quique."

DECEMBER 18, 3040 | COLOSSI INFINITI, EARTH'S ORBIT

Marilina has, in fact, never heard of rocket dogs before, and the admiral delivers enough for her and both of her aunts. The spicy sausage of Montréal is a bit like the chorizo of her home station. If only the sauce weren't so messy. Twice, she almost spills down the front of her Coalition skins, cringing at the thought of explaining such a stain to Kamal.

Noisy bustling carries down the hall—Pilar and Fatima. Setting aside her empty wrapper, Marilina stands and meets them in the doorway. Pilar pulls her into a tight hug, but Fatima rushes past to the patient's side.

"¡Quique!" Fatima cries, tears streaming down her cheeks. "Mari, what happened? ¡Dios, salva a mi sobrino, por favor!"

Marilina meets Pilar's troubled eyes. "I met with the doctor. Quique was in an accident on Earth. He's experiencing radiation sickness."

A shuddering breath rises and falls in her aunt's chest. "Thank you for making arrangements for us to travel here."

"It wasn't me." Marilina shakes her head. "That was the admiral's doing." Remembering the food, she turns and scoops up the extra rocket dogs. "He brought these for you two."

Pilar smiles and grips her shoulders. "I should have known. We're so proud of you, querida mía." She accepts both sausages and turns to the bed, where

Fatima sits gripping her nephew's hands with her head resting in his lap. Pilar sets one rocket dog beside Fatima and whispers in her ear, then turns back to her niece. "Isn't this your specialty, Mari? There must be something you can do for him."

The doctor's stomach clenches. "He's in the best possible care, Tía. Another Meridian. Guardian Martinho."

"A guardian?" Pilar's frown deepens. "This is your brother. Shouldn't you be in charge?"

Marilina smiles through the twisting shame in her stomach. The beeping monitor suddenly feels impossibly loud, the sound waves crushing her ears. She and Quique have never been as close as Pilar, Fatima, and Mami, but she's here now, isn't she? She swallows and holds her chin high. "You don't have to worry. I researched him. Martinho was one of the best of his time, and he's continued to study radiation sickness even after his appointment to a guardianship. Quique is in the best possible care." Pilar raises an eyebrow and plants her hands on her hips, but Martinho returns and they lapse into silence.

"I have Enrique's test results," the former Meridian informs them, his gaze lingering on Fatima. "Is this a good time to go over them?"

"Please yes, Doctor," Pilar answers.

"These are my aunts," Marilina explains.

He nods and clicks his heels together. "You should know that the damage is extensive. Enrique is experiencing multi-system failure."

Pilar's lips tighten into white strips as Fatima clasps her hands together and bursts into fervent, muttered prayer. Marilina straightens and nods once. Quique doesn't need his sister or even God right now. He needs a Meridian. "I'm not surprised. What treatment are you recommending?"

"The attending physician had him on IV fluids, morphine. Hardly effective." Martinho frowns with bitter remorse. He cares deeply for Quique. That's obvious.

"Routine end-of-life care," Marilina agrees. She steps closer to the guardian and lowers her voice. Her aunts don't need to hear this. "The attending didn't expect Quique to live through the night." Not an unfair assumption, given her brother's condition.

Martinho's eyes of bottled night flash. "I'd like to try something more experimental."

"Go on." Marilina straightens, frowning.

Martinho is sizing her up now—for what, she can't guess. "My colleagues and I have been developing a treatment for severe injuries like these."

"For radiation sickness? What treatment is this?"

"Your brother received a powerful dose of radiation, but not quite a lethal one. We've developed a potent chelator that should allow your brother to pass the toxins and survive."

What colleagues? Marilina's throat tightens. "That's not possible. Pentetic acid chelation isn't effective at high REM or at end of life."

Martinho's smile widens. "I told you, this drug is experimental, and it's highly potent."

Marilina clenches her hand tightly over Mami's cross. She knows better than to let this guardian get her hopes up. Quique is nearer to death's door than most of the patients she's lost over the years. His chances of survival are less than 1%. When their parents are finally awakened from cryo, he won't be there to greet them.

Fatima rubs Quique's knuckles between firm fingers. Marilina hesitates. This is her baby brother. A young man now, maybe, but one she's only just beginning to get to know again.

Quique.

This could be her last chance to repair their relationship, and she'll never forgive herself if she doesn't try. She looks up and nods. "Do it." Two nurses appear with fresh medication almost as soon as the words leave her lips.

"You're making the right decision. We can save him, together." Martinho surprises her by gripping her shoulder. The guardian flips open his wristband unit and enters the codes for Quique's new treatment.

Marilina backs away and drops into a chair, drained from the magnitude of the decision. Soon, the women are alone in the ICU room again. The young physician leans forward and rests her elbows on the soft bedding, musing about the colony. They'll get through this, all of them, and maybe then her brother will recognize how dangerous this restoration is and decide to join her and the rest of the family on Zomenos.

CHAPTER SEVEN

JACK

L INEN PILLOWS CRADLE JACK's head while he stares up at the ceiling and contemplates the day ahead. Over a thousand guests are expected at Dad's service today, and they'll be looking to Jack to see if he has what it takes to fill the commander's boots. The admiral rolls his shoulders, loosening his muscles. He must be ready. Beside him, Lucy stretches, cat-like, and rests her head in the crook of his arm. They lay in silence. As the sun rises over the sleeping station, she props her chin on his chest and studies him.

"You're worried about the service, aren't you?"

Jack's eyes find hers. He nods, returning his gaze to the ceiling. "This memorial has to be worthy of Dad's legacy. I have to play my part, even if the whole thing is for show."

"You'll be outstanding." She uses her guardian voice, authoritative and final. The intensity in her probing brown eyes sears him. "Is that all?"

The admiral sighs and musses his hair with his free hand. "It's all so rushed. Roarke should've stepped in to delay the proceedings. The wreckage from Dad's ship hasn't even been retrieved yet. He could still be . . ."

Soft lips brush his shoulder. "It didn't look like he could have survived from the footage we saw."

"Right." He leans on his elbow. "And where exactly did that footage come from?"

"You heard Guillermo." Lucy folds her hands across her bare stomach. "It was recovered from the ship."

Jack shakes his head and runs dark, velvety sheets between his forefinger and thumb. "When? By who? Something doesn't add up here. Roarke is keeping me in the dark on purpose."

"What makes you say that?"

He pummels his pillow with a fist, startling her. "Sorry," he says quickly. "It's just that Roarke doesn't have unilateral jurisdiction to dispatch Coalition officers on missions without prior approval from the division. The whole thing stinks of overreach."

"True. A guardian wouldn't get away with that." She frowns and gazes at the ceiling. "Want me to look into it?"

"No, it's okay." A grimace. "You've got a lot on your plate already." If word gets out that an admiral is using guardians to fight his battles, he'll lose the respect of the entire Coalition. With a kiss on her forehead, he unravels from the sheets. "What is Roarke up to?" Jack mutters as Lucy heads into the washroom.

Daisies waft into the closet from the washroom as the admiral rummages through his scant wardrobe. Floating orbs light his path as he shuffles all the way to the back. All eyes will be on him at the memorial. Farce or not, he has to live up to Dad's long reputation with the Coalition, and that includes looking the part. He pushes Lucy's formalwear aside, sliding stiffly into a debonair set of black skins with gold trim along a high collar. Smiling, Lucy steps out of the washroom and leans against the doorframe as he pins the admiral's insignia to his breast.

"And you were worried about doing him justice."

He turns. "There's more to this than appearances," he explains, preparing a defensive speech, but Lucy steps forward on her toes and plants her lips on his cheek, and he promptly forgets what he's saying.

DECEMBER 19, 3040 | MONTRÉAL STATION, EARTH'S ORBIT

In the distance, thousands of lights wink in the dim glow of early dawn, like so many stars in faraway galaxies. The station dwellers are only just beginning their day. Jack crunches through fresh snow to the podium alone and waits for the service to begin. Dad's casket is there. Empty, but wrapped in a red and white flag and topped with a wreath of white flowers. The Coalition ensured a proper military burial for Commander Monroe, even if its leadership failed him when he needed it most.

When the service begins, he steps forward and faces an assembly of two thousand waiting faces. They have their questions, but they'll accept whatever answers their admiral offers. A planetary body doesn't object to the star it orbits, after all. It will remain tethered, however uncertain its future. Endless questions without answers. It's up to Jack to hold them all together.

"Dad was a Coalition officer all his life," the admiral begins. "When people ask what it was like to be raised by the man that discovered Zomenos, I usually say that he's just Dad. But he's more than that and always will be. Dad never belonged to his family. His heart was always out there, in space. Wandering. Exploring. Serving." He still is—somewhere. Jack's gaze sweeps the audience, and he recognizes many officers of the Coalition, stark in black skins rather than the military's white. Frank Roarke stands at the front of the assembly,

Cerebrum particles swirling around his artificially youthful face in a neutral gray cloud, same as always. Jack will deal with him later. He sets his jaw. "The real test of a man's measure isn't who he is or what he has. It's what he leaves behind. Derek Monroe left us with as long a legacy as anyone. Zomenos will forever be his legacy, and he will always be remembered as one of the most consequential of Earth's orphans to have ever lived."

The admiral steps down from the podium. Five officers join him beside the casket and bear it down the steps toward the cemetery for burial. At the very front of the crowd, Lucy wears a small smile, her eyes shining. Jack takes a deep breath and winks back at her. He made it through.

His energy spent, he just wants to get his answers and leave, but a throng of well-wishers comes between the admiral and his leader. The charade isn't over yet. A group of Coalition officers mills about nearby, several members of his new crew among them. Screw it—he's the man of the hour, isn't he? May as well blow off a little steam while he waits for his opportunity. With a diplomatic nod, he maneuvers away from an approaching web of guardians and sidles up to his pilot wearing a grin.

"Colter! I was wondering when you would turn up."

Colter Pruitt steps forward and shakes hands with Jack, slipping a mickey into the admiral's hand. "Sorry about your dad," he says in an uncharacteristically somber tone.

Jack sniffs the opening of the flask. Whiskey. Nice. "Thanks." His eyes linger on the officer standing at a respectable distance from the admiral with hands clasped behind his back and shoulders squared. He recognizes the closely shorn dark hair. "It's Kamal, isn't it?"

A nod. "Sorry for your loss, Admiral."

"I appreciate that," Jack answers. "You didn't have to come all this way, Officer. How did my crew do in basic training today?"

"They're not awful, for civilians." Kamal grins self-consciously and shakes his head. "The doctor missed training today. I don't mean to pry, but we've all heard about Dr. Chamorro's brother. You wouldn't know anything about that, would you?"

The admiral's jaw tightens, but he finally spots his true target near the drink counter. About time. "No, I don't." A mental note to investigate later. He'll need to move fast. Roarke is slipperier than a Jovian jet stream. Jack returns his gaze to the drill sergeant. "Would you excuse me?" Kamal salutes and Pruitt slaps Jack on the back as the admiral shoots back his whiskey and peels away from the group, doing his best to appear unhurried.

He's finally going to get some answers.

"I'm glad I caught up with you, Jack. I didn't think I would have a chance to offer my condolences."

Feeling anything but cheery, the admiral adopts an easy smile. "Thanks, Frank." Roarke hands him a silver medal affixed to a red, black, and white ribbon. The smile fades. "The Sacrifice Medal? Dad is MIA, not dead." He presses the medal back into Roarke's hands, but Roarke pushes it firmly back.

"I know. That's why I'm giving this to you privately. The commander deserves more recognition for his service."

No, he deserves a search party. "Thank you." The admiral positions himself between Roarke and the rest of the attendees, blocking the Coalition leader's escape. "I want to know everything about Dad's mission. You owe me that."

Roarke lowers his voice so far that Jack strains to hear him. "Not now, and not here." He grips the admiral's arm, and the loud drone of all those guests claps out, like being hurled out of an airlock. Jack scans over Roarke's shoulder, but they're suddenly alone somewhere else in the cemetery. He shivers. Leaping gives him the willies. "What are you thinking, approaching me like this at a public event?"

"It's not public anymore now, is it?" He shrugs his arm and Roarke releases him. Jack smooths the fabric of his skins and grudgingly tucks the medallion into his breast pocket. "Answer me. I'm asking you as an admiral of your Coalition—the very Coalition you pledged honor and transparency to."

"Those were simpler times."

His unusually loose formal skins pull tight across Jack's chest as he steps forward. "That's where you're wrong. Time runs out for all of us, even you. Do you want to be remembered as a liar and a dictator?"

"Nothing is so black-and-white." The Cerebrum particles thrum loudly. "Your father understood discretion. You could learn from him." Jack squares his shoulders and ignores the rebuke. Roarke has got to be running out of excuses. Sure enough, the tension falls away from Roarke's shoulders and his voice loses some of its edge. A breezy wind whistles lightly through sparse trees, unburdening their branches of last night's snow. "The colony is in danger, Admiral. Terra Nova is back, and they've been disrupting shipments." And he actually tells the admiral everything: the delays to the colony's vivarium, the missing freighters, and Guillermo's role in setting the flight path for the commander's last mission.

Jack crosses his arms and spreads his feet, his boots sinking deeper into the snow. He suspected something big, but not Big with a capital 'B.' Unwilling to relinquish dominance over this confrontation, he smothers his surprise. "Okay. Why am I just now hearing about this?"

"I couldn't risk you jetting away half-cocked in an unauthorized orbiter with the full force of the military, could I?" A strained smile stretches across Roarke's face. "You're too important to the colony."

Arms falling to his sides, Jack arches an eyebrow. "Don't give me that. Any pilot worth his stars could fly a few civilians to Zomenos. You withheld this from me so I wouldn't stop Dad from agreeing to your suicide mission."

"No, I didn't." Roarke shakes his head. "It's always been you, Jack. From the moment I learned of your father's discovery, I knew you would be the one to lead our people to the colony. He knew it too."

"I was a kid, Frank."

"You were born to it, and you've never disappointed me. Don't start today."

Flattery isn't going to work. "So, what? You sent Dad to his death in my place?"

Roarke's gaze drops, and snowflakes land on dark lashes and reddened cheeks. So, he has enough decency to pretend shame. "Your father volunteered to lead this investigation to keep you alive."

A nerve works in Jack's temple. This isn't helping. Dad is still out there, somewhere. "Great plan, Frank. What do we do now?"

"You will do nothing." The Cerebrum particles crackle like thunder as Roarke's eyes snap to attention. Jack takes a reluctant step backward. Maybe he's pushed too far. "Guillermo and I are handling this investigation. The colony must be your focus. After the commander . . ." His voice splinters, and he clears his throat. "I won't risk your life over this."

But he'll put Guillermo in the line of fire? Jack grinds his teeth, but there's nothing to gain from provoking the Coalition leader further. He's got enough on his plate with this news of delays to the vivarium. "Fine. Message received. Do me a favor and take me back, will you?"

Roarke obliges with visible relief painted on his shiny face. Wordlessly, Jack stalks away from the most powerful man alive, working hard to keep his pace light and unhurried as the wind picks up. Inside, he's fuming. Frank Roarke has him strung up like a puppet—Dad too, and maybe even Guillermo—but as long as Guillermo is involved, he can show some patience. His trust in Roarke is thinning with each passing day, but Tío won't let Dad down.

The sun is fully overhead now, its sharp rays filtering through the station's protective dome and peppering the guests harmlessly. Kamal's questioning concern surges to the forefront of his thoughts. Roarke is right about one thing: the colony is at risk, and so is everything Dad worked for. There's no margin for error. The doctor has been through a lot in a short period. Terra Nova doesn't need to sabotage the colony if it self-destructs. Jack runs his hands through his hair. He can't afford that loose end. Spotting Lucy consoling Gabriella in a quiet corner, he catches her eye. Lucy excuses herself expertly and steers through the crowd to his side.

"Can I get a lift?" He flushes at the pleading note in his own voice.

Lucy studies him over the rim of her glass. "You know I'm not supposed to do that."

Jack raises an eyebrow. "You guardians Leap everywhere. I need to get out of here, check on a crewmember at the Ring."

"The doctor?" He nods, and Lucy sets her glass down. "That's a noble reason to leave early." She stretches out her hand, and he takes it. He feels guilty about ducking out of the service, but Dad, of all people, would understand. Nothing is coming between Jack and the colony—not even Terra Nova.

DECEMBER 19, 3040 | COLOSSI INFINITI, EARTH'S ORBIT

The breezy winds of the cemetery on the Montréal station vanish, replaced by the still, cool air of the ICU on Colossi Infiniti. More goosebumps. Jack looks around, but the unit is quiet. At the far end of the hall, a muted conversation is going on between a doctor and two nurses. A woman quietly reads last rites to a patient in a room nearby. Jack lets out a breath—Chamorro's brother is across the hall.

"Is this it?" Lucy asks, and he nods. "Go on," she says in a low voice. "I've barely met the doctor. It wouldn't be appropriate for me to go in there with you. I'll come back for you after the service is over."

"Agreed." Now that he's here, he's not exactly sure what he plans on doing, but the least he can do is offer the doctor his support. Chamorro will follow through on this mission. He's sure of it. He can't say how he knows that, but she's got the look: she's all in on the colony. He squares his shoulders and marches down the hall.

Not much has changed since yesterday. Nurses shuffle right past like he's no one important (typical androids), a waste disposal clicks and whooshes at regular intervals, monitors beep. Only the brother himself has changed. Poor kid—not yet twenty, by the look of him—is withering. His yellowed skin, cracked raw and peeling, sags and pulls away from his bones. Thick tufts of hair fall away from his head and form a crown on his pillow. There's *less* of him in that bed today than there was yesterday. Jack swallows and steps forward.

"That's embarrassing," the doctor says between fits of laughter. "What did you do?" Staggering to a halt, he hovers just inside the door. Laughter, here?

A man's voice answers. "I was left without reasonable options." The admiral strains to hear over a group of hospital staff passing behind him. "I told the patient that the rare cancerous lesion he demanded my services for was nothing more than a boil." Women bubble with more laughter.

Jack doesn't see another option, so he tramps into the room wearing a questioning smile. "Howdy. I came to check in on the patient."

Dr. Chamorro turns from her brother's bedside, eyes brightening. "Good morning, Admiral. That's kind of you. He's responding well to treatment thanks to Guardian Martinho." Jack recognizes the guardian at once, standing near the head of the bed in distracting satin skins fit for a production at an opera house. Beside the doctor, two women sit beaming—these must be the aunts.

"Glad to hear it." Jack focuses on the doctor, who still wears yesterday's Coalition skins. "I hope I'm not interrupting. I heard you weren't at basic training today."

Dr. Chamorro bows her head. "I feel terrible about that. Officer Kamal must be worried, but I needed to be with my brother." She gently cradles the patient's hand in her own.

Martinho finishes administering a series of shots and removes his gloves. "Enrique's progress is encouraging, and nothing short of revolutionary." His gaze lingers on Jack's breast pocket, where the silver medal shines visibly against the admiral's dark formalwear. "It's quite thoughtful of you to stop by, Admiral, today of all days. Isn't this the day of Commander Monroe's memorial?"

Wrong-footed by the guardian's attention, Jack hesitates and tucks the medal deeper into his pocket. "It is, but I have a duty to my crew too. I couldn't rest without checking in on our head physician's well-being."

"You don't need to worry about us, Admiral. Alejandro is a wonderful doctor," one of the aunts puts in, leaning forward. "He's done such a good job with our poor Quique."

Jack meets Martinho's dark eyes, and the guardian shrugs. "The admiral and I share a sense of responsibility to our own. Enrique is an important part of

Earth's restoration. He is worthy of every minute." The older women's eyes shine, and Jack notices a small smile on Dr. Chamorro's lips too.

These restoration fanatics are hardly the same as the colonists, but Jack smiles easily. "That's honorable, Guardian. I hope my own crew never feels like they must risk their own lives for our mission."

Martinho tilts his head and narrows his eyes, regarding the admiral like one of his patients. "A life worth living is worth dying for."

Yikes. This fanatic is keeping Chamorro's brother alive?

Dr. Chamorro rises and steps between the admiral and guardian. "Can we talk outside?"

"Gladly." Jack follows her out of the room and into the hallway, his gaze lingering on the guardian.

The doctor faces him. "I never had the chance to thank you for the food. It meant a lot to all of us."

"Don't mention it. Happy to help any way I can."

She inches closer and lowers her voice. "I had no idea that your father's service was today. Are *you* okay?"

"Yes," Jack insists, a little too forcefully. The doctor raises an eyebrow. He sighs, running his hands through his hair. "It's been a long day, I guess." He removes the medal from his pocket and turns it over and over. **SACRIFICE** sears into his mind.

"I really appreciate you checking in, but you don't have to stay." Jack looks up at the doctor watching him and pockets the medal again. "Pilar is telling the truth: Alejandro really is an excellent physician." The zealot can't be *that* useful, but it's not his place to comment. "People are expecting you, aren't they?"

"They are," he admits. "I didn't mean to intrude here, but I had to make sure you were okay."

The doctor smiles radiantly. "I am thanks to you. We're a family, isn't that right?"

Jack grins. "You've got that right." One problem at a time. Chamorro's in a much better mood than yesterday, and that's what matters. Today, it's the doctor. Tomorrow, he'll find a solution to the colony's vivarium problem.

CHAPTER EIGHT

ANNA

Almost one entire week without a jimmy. Anna kicks her boots up on the empty pilot's seat beside her, which creaks in protest against her rubber soles dragging against it, and replays Guardian Nuñez's recorded neural link with his bot. If it isn't salvageable, this holiday on Jupiter will be a colossal waste of time. She rubs the spot between her shoulder blades in circles just to give her restless, tingling fingers something to do.

There it is. Bending forward with hands splayed over the console, she peers into the holo display. A rare assignment sometimes takes her outside Earth's orbit to the fuel depot on Mars, but this is brand new. Her orbiter was cleared to zip on at 0.5% light speed, yet Jupiter is another day away. She pinches the gas giant between a forefinger and thumb, smirks, and leans back, unable to tear her eyes away from those smooth stripes. The view does make up for the lack of certain comforts.

She'll never admit *that* to the sergeant.

Beneath the striped planet, the display projects reams of classified information on failed cargo shipments through this region. All unmanned except her target. Nothing good can come of locating the commander himself among the wreckage of his ship at this point. Interstellar forensics is hardly her specialty, but the radiation waves coming off Jupiter's magnetic field will probably mummify the corpse. The thought sets the hairs on her arm on end.

Bot or not, this is the closest she's come to vengeance. She settles deeper into her chair and closes her eyes. Terra Nova targeted the supply chain when Ma died, too. Sabotaging cargo shipments now makes sense if they really don't want the colony to proceed, but what *do* they want, then? What's any of it got to do with Johannesburg? The detective can't see the angle yet. She drifts into sleep and wanders blithely through space on another unfamiliar ship, Saturn's rings angled toward her from above. A burning flash of light takes Ma, and the detective's eyes, with it.

The ship's AI interrupts. "We are within 5 million kilometers of Jupiter, Detective Wright. Given the calculated threat levels in the region, I recommend full shields for the rest of this journey."

Anna blinks, wiping fresh tears from her cheeks. Jupiter has swollen to the size of a watermelon, but those rings are nowhere in sight. Another nightmare. "No argument here." Odds are good that more hostile ships will be waiting at the wreckage. Her eyes narrow. Terra Nova better finish the job this time, or they'll need more than a set of new eyes when she's done with them. In the cramped middeck, she shuffles through her rations, rips open a packet with her teeth, and sucks down warm oatmeal. Left hand loose on her hip, she stares at the security footage.

"I'm coming for you, bastards." Anna downs the rest of the oatmeal and crushes the packet in her fist.

DECEMBER 20, 3040 | JUPITER'S ORBIT

"Good morning, Detective. We have arrived."

Anna jerks upright, then sucks her breath in and digs her nails into the fibrous console. Debris from orbiter VLT80 stretches in every direction for hundreds of kilometers, Jupiter's massive bulk lurking just beyond. Just like the exploded freighter above Enceladus all those years ago.

Focus, Anna.

"Right." She cracks her knuckles. "Establish a perimeter, Contessa. We'll start broad." The bot is here somewhere, and she's going to find it.

"Preparing systems for launch." A simulated face appears and runs diagnostics on equipment stowed in the auxiliary payload. "The probe is online and operational. Ready to deploy."

The detective grips the console, leaning forward. "What did you find out here, Monroe?" A probe deploys below deck, and the ship rumbles. A camera feed transmits its winding progress. "What's that?" The probe slows, its feed sharpening. A body. Not the commander—it's wearing civilian skins.

A bemused Contessa tilts its head. "It has an organic signature. It may be an assailant."

The ache in Anna's fingers returns. "There's no sign of a second ship. Must be the robot."

The probe approaches. There's no question now: this is her target. One leg is ripped from its torso, exposing cables and wiring where a femur should be. A real man would have bled out and shriveled under Jupiter's radiation, but the robot is barely affected. Good. Maybe this little excursion isn't a waste of time after all.

"How unusual," Contessa remarks.

"Agreed." The detective leans back, rests her chin on her knuckles, and wiggles her fingers. "Bring it onboard."

"And the commander?"

Anna shrugs. "Might be pulverized by now. Might not even be out here. The robot has information. I want it."

The sophistication of Nuñez's illicit bot is admittedly impressive. Contessa's analysis confirms that the machine has human skin and even organs. When the bot first came aboard, it looked very much like the raisin a human would have withered into, yet unlike any human the detective has ever met, it begins regenerating in the confines of the ship. Hopefully, this ingenuity extends to the robot's familiarity with Terra Nova. Whatever it is, it's so far from a typical bot that Contessa has trouble locating its processor.

"What are you?" Anna breathes.

Another hour stretches on, but the surgery continues without success. She groans and rolls her skinsleeves up past her elbows. Wrist-deep in the robot's intestinal tract, she searches for the microprocessor storing the robot's data. Preserving the machine looks out of the question (Frankenbot's damage is beyond Contessa's skills), but if the detective can get its chip out safely, she'll get some answers. She grips hard, yanking on messy entrails, but the bot's eyes shoot open.

"What are you doing to me?"

Anna yelps and tumbles backward onto the shuttle floor.

"Where am I? Where's Derek?" The robot's eyes dart all over the place, taking in the shuttle, its missing leg, and the shoddy surgery.

Tasting iron, the detective rubs her throbbing tailbone and glares at the stammering machine. "You're on my ship." She rolls her tongue over her swollen lip. "As for the commander—can't say. I'm investigating his disappearance."

The robot calms down, focusing. "Then who are you?" Uneasy, like it doesn't trust her.

Anna plops down on a bench across from the robot and crosses her legs underneath her. "Relax, Guardian Nuñez sent me. I'm Detective Wright." Unresponsive, the machine stares glumly at the floor, so she grabs its shoulders. Firm shake. "Get a grip," she growls, planting her palms on her thighs and squaring her shoulders. "Did Nuñez deliberately program you to be worthless, or is it just my luck? I need access to your CPU. I need to know what happened to your ship, robot."

It stills and looks up from its misery. Now, that's a bright green. "My name is Diego."

"Sure." Who cares what this thing calls itself? "Well, Diego, did you record anything useful in that processor you call a brain?" The bot doesn't answer. Its face bends into a . . . sullen look. The detective drives her itching fingers into her braids. Lord, she sure could go for a jimmy. If "Diego's" chip was fried, this machine is a useless hunk of metal to her. She hops down from the bench and paces the cramped orbiter. "Forget it. Nuñez will know what to do with you." Not a promising start, but maybe a reboot will fix the glitches. Anna halts in her tracks. Great, it's smiling now. "I thought Coalition bots were supposed to be good at emotion."

The bot grins wider and shakes a full head of thick, curly locks. "I think you're a bit misinformed about my kind, Detective."

Eyes narrow: that's real human hair. "How so?" She leans against the console and crosses her arms.

"I have no CPU, for one."

Anna cocks an eyebrow. "You're saying you're *not* an android?" This isn't helping. The sooner the probe completes its search, the sooner she can get this machine back to Nuñez for a full diagnostic and repair. "Contessa, this is obviously a waste of time. Close this thing up, will you? I need to get washed up."

The ship comes to life. Mechanical arms repair the gaping incision in the bot's abdomen made during the detective's careless surgery. Ignoring this, the bot replies, "I'm a xenobot." Still smiling—damn it. "A humanoid. Unlike Contessa, I am very much alive. My neural circuitry is similar to the Cerebrum particles, meaning 'that processor I call a brain' is beyond any CPU you've ever seen."

Down the hall, Anna removes her soiled skins and scrubs the machine's innards from her arms. She's going to smell like raw meat for weeks. Smirking, she calls out. "So, you're what . . . almost human?"

The skin around those arresting eyes wrinkles when this bot laughs (definitely more human than android), but the smile vanishes. "Could a human survive Jupiter's magnetosphere unshielded?"

"Touché."

The machine watches her intently. "What have you learned from your investigation so far?"

"Not much, yet." Returning, the detective crosses her arms and bends forward. "I was hoping you could tell me what happened here."

The bot stares up at the holo projecting the footage captured by the probe. "I can't remember. Radiation-induced cognitive impairment is not uncommon. Attention, verbal and spatial memory, and novel problem-solving ability can all be affected. As I said before, my brain is very real, and I am not immune to such effects. Don't worry. My symptoms should abate once my cells regenerate. You'll have your answers then." Sarcasm—great. What good is a "xenobot" to her if it doesn't regenerate? Anna sighs and chews her fingertips, grateful that they taste nothing like raw meat. "Why did Guillermo send you, Detective?"

Stalking into the middeck, the detective pokes her hand into a ration bin and pauses. She rehydrates two packets of tomato soup and tosses one to her new companion. "You can have that, if you even eat. I already told you. Nuñez sent me to retrieve whatever was left of you, the commander, and your ship's logs."

It looks down at its leg for the first time. Do xenobots feel, or is there just a command-line interface throwing an error code for missing tissue? Is that any different from the way retinal implants expand her mind, or bionic eyes replace her lost eyesight? Anna pinches the bridge of her nose. She was never a fan of philosophy. Hopping back up on the bench beside the bot, she crosses her ankles and slurps her soup. The machine peels back the wrapper and eats. Anna stares, fascinated.

"I'm sorry there isn't much to return," the bot mutters bitterly. "Did you know what you were flying into when you agreed to this investigation?"

The detective waffles her hand. "More or less. You were MIA. The obvious explanation is that you got too close to whoever is targeting the supply ships to Zomenos."

"And you agreed anyway? This could be a trap. Somehow, my preparations failed. You're in danger here." The bot falls silent, staring at shiny white flooring.

Anna hesitates, feeling strangely sympathetic. "Look, this thing with Monroe wasn't your fault, and I'm not anyone else's responsibility." Wait, why is she consoling a robot? No, a xenobot. She glares at the machine. "We're seeing this through, and then I'm going to help you get your memories back. Just don't fail *me*, okay?"

DECEMBER 21, 3040 | JUPITER'S ORBIT

Adamant about making up for its failures, the xenobot joins the detective on the command deck, and they resume the search for the missing officer. Time to find out just how deep these maddening cognitive defects run. Reluctant to concede full control, Anna claims the command seat, but she grants full access of the probe and its camera feed to the bot at her right. To her immense relief, the probe is online in seconds.

"Your coverage is low," the bot says. "I'm expanding the search perimeter."

One eyebrow quirks upward. "We got distracted when we found you. I don't actually know much about operating a probe. Contessa sets the coordinates."

"That's perfectly fine, because I do," the bot responds brightly. It eases back, maneuvering with its good leg. Anna crosses her arms and glares, prompting a smile from the bot. "Relax. I'll let Contessa run the show unless there's good reason not to."

Contessa deploys the probe, and they wait. The xenobot's limited brainpower still comes in handy: the new search region is broader, but more accurate, and that suits the detective. It's dark and eerie and infinite out here, and the wreckage makes this corner of the universe feel like an open grave she might fall into if she's careless.

The bot orders the ship AI to stop the probe in its path, and Anna glances at the machine beside her. "What's up?"

"That debris is not from my ship."

She zooms in on the footage. "Contessa, any survivors?"

"No organic signatures detected, Detective."

Anna zeroes in on an emblem just visible on a singed flank. The name of the second orbiter is just visible: VLT60, not VLT80. A glance at the bot. "Good eyes. That's one hell of a coincidence." Fingers drum on the console. Only one reason the orbiter would look so similar to Monroe's. "It's Coalition-issue."

The machine closes its eyes and presses its back into its seat with its eyelids fluttering. She's gotten used to it: it's that bot brain in overdrive. Seconds later, those bright green eyes snap open. "There's no record of this ship with the Coalition."

The detective rests her elbow on the back of her seat and tucks one leg under the other, flattening her twitching fingers as she considers. "A black ship? Only two ways to explain that."

"Either this orbiter was stolen and scrubbed from the record, or it's a copycat."

Anna cocks her head. "Exactly. Which is it?"

"Coalition shuttles use antimatter. A civilian shuttle wouldn't have access. It would be limited to methane. If the fuel reserves are intact and can be located, we might be able to determine which."

A rush of excitement leaves the detective heady. Plenty of civvies can get methane, but the list of people with access to antimatter is much shorter. This could be the biggest clue in history to identifying a Terra Nova operative. Anna punches in new directives for the probe before the xenobot finishes its sentence. "Copy that. Operation needle-in-a-space-stack is a go." She turns and smiles. Maybe she'll keep the machine around.

Callisto is nearer to them at their current coordinates than Jupiter itself, the moon's jagged, ice-capped surface so much like Earth. "This could take a while. I'm hungry." Anna springs up and heads for the mess hall. "You coming?"

She shovels down a lettuce wrap hungrily. The bot eats, but not much, filling the time by excising the dead tissue from its amputated leg and re-sealing the wound with goo from the dispensary. Xenobots can apparently regrow whole arms and legs, and this one is making way for a new limb. The detective wrinkles her nose and keeps crunching, but she doesn't look away. If it can do *that*, it can get its memories back—no question.

The probe completes its search of the second ship several hours later. Anna drops into the command seat and leans forward with her elbows on her knees. The composition of the fuel reserve appears in a holo—anti-matter—and she whistles, long and low.

"Do you know what this means?"

The bot nods. "If I understand your theories correctly, it suggests that Terra Nova has infiltrated the Coalition." It folds its hands in its lap. "How do we proceed, Detective?"

She chews a fingernail, staring at the holo. There could be more evidence on this ship. A lot more. Her hunch is that they won't get lucky twice, though, and every moment that they spend here exposed is an opportunity for Terra Nova to gun them down. "Right. Let's collect as much evidence as we can before we recall the probe. We need to resume our search of your ship's wreckage. Monroe must have gathered more information than what was transmitted to Roarke. If we can salvage the black box, we might find out what Monroe was after that made him a target. Tomorrow, we return." The bot updates the probe's directives. An impulse surges. "Hey, good work today. Seriously. You're an alright detective."

"For a robot, you mean?"

She rolls her eyes and shoves him, not hard. Robots sass now, too? "For anyone."

The xenobot grins. "Thanks, Detective."

DECEMBER 22, 3040 | JUPITER'S ORBIT

Locating the black box turns out to be easier than finding an open port to dock in at the Ring. Even though the box has "standard Coalition circuitry," the xenobot finds nothing inside. No evidence, no leads, and no officer.

Anna's gaze flits past the xenobot to the camera feed. "What is the likelihood that the commander's body drifted beyond our search radius?"

"The probability of finding Derek Monroe within the defined coordinates is greater than 99.5%."

"Right." She nods to herself. "Then we have two ships and no bodies. You won't like what I'm about to say, but . . . I think the commander was taken captive."

"I agree. He's out there still, and he needs my help." The xenobot drops its hands to its sides, looking suddenly ashamed. "I failed him, and now I'm useless to him without my memories."

"You feel powerless."

The bot freezes. "You could say that. I'm not used to failure, much less the kind that might have cost a man his life. It feels like I should have been able to do more." It laughs, high-pitched and strained. "I know. That's a silly thing to say."

"It's not silly." She would do anything to bring Ma's murderers to justice. She slams her fist down on her own console. "Shit!"

The bot breaks the silence. "What do we do now, Detective?"

Anna meets its questioning gaze with a shrug. "You said it yourself. Your memory will return once you're healed. There's nothing left for us to do here. Time to go home."

"Recalling the probe," Contessa informs them in a crisp voice, as if it's been waiting all along for them to reach this conclusion. "Please review the flight path charted for your return."

Anna narrows her eyes at the long silence from the xenobot. "What's the matter?"

It scratches an itch near where its new leg is growing in. It's been doing that a lot over the last couple of days. Noticing her looking, it jerks its hand away. "I don't have a home."

After approving the flight path, Anna pulls her feet up, resting the heels of her boots against her thighs, and cocks her head. "What were you doing before this?"

"Androids aren't allocated living space the way humans are, and I couldn't live with Guillermo forever. So, I stay in the slums with other androids."

She settles deep into her chair and hugs her knees to her chest. "A lot of humans end up there too. If you're *really* useless, you go into cryo. But you're not an android, and you're not useless. You're coming with me—if that's alright with you, Diego." The bot is stunned into speechlessness, and that's a compliment, coming from a supercomputer.

The engines fire back up, making the whole orbiter rumble. Anna lapses into brooding silence. She didn't find all the answers she wanted here, but finding Diego made it all worth it. With the xenobot at her side, she stands a chance of closing in on a Terra Nova operative. Beside her, the humanoid parses the probe's footage with its eyelashes fluttering. Once it gets those memories back, she'll be unstoppable. Relying on someone else for something this important makes her fingers itch all over again, but it's not a someone. It's a bot. She closes her eyes and focuses on this as they leave Jupiter's graveyard behind.

CHAPTER NINE

ALEJANDRO

S UNLIGHT FILTERS THROUGH THE station's dome and lights up the stencils along a golden horn. Alejandro's eyes follow, the harsh sharpness of the white glare contrasting the soft, plying notes of an acoustic guitar strumming a warm bossa nova. He turns and looks out the broad window up at that dome. Freedom or cage? His gaze settles on the gramophone, housed in a cabinet inlaid with shelves of vinyl records and leather bound books. Selecting a well-worn book, he crosses the study to his preferred armchair, footsteps muted by thick walnut flooring. He thumbs to his saved page and begins to read.

"Good morning, sir. I didn't hear you return."

Alejandro looks up at his personal assistant. "Yes, it was late, and I didn't see reason to disturb you. Guests will arrive soon. You'll see that they are appropriately welcomed?"

"Of course, sir." Luiz's thoughts about this, whatever they may be, remain concealed from his human-like face. "I wasn't aware of any guests. Are you hosting the other guardians?"

A shake of the head. "Members of the Chamorro family. With Enrique under my care, his loved ones have no choice but to sleep at Colossi Infiniti." They deserve better after the loyalty and dedication Enrique demonstrated on Earth. "We will host them here. Please show them the same care you would myself."

The android's eyes widen, an unnaturally delighted smile penetrating his cheeks. "Consider it done. Will you be taking coffee this morning?" He eyes the book in Alejandro's lap. "Your meeting starts in fifteen minutes."

"Yes. A cafezinho, please." Alejandro lowers his gaze back to the book, a rags-to-riches tale of an ordinary man caught in a plutocracy. He absorbs each word with interest, well and truly lost in the story. Faux lamb's hide slippers hovering above the rim of the book pluck him back into the present moment. Marking his place in the book again, he accepts a small cup of coffee from his assistant. He closes his eyes and breathes in a bold, smoky aroma. "Thank you, Luiz. You may go." A sip. Rich and balanced, with hints of toasted nut and cedar, this dark roast isn't too sweet. Perfection.

Alejandro stands. Though his patient has consumed his attention these past days, he's not forgotten who is responsible. His immense respect for Maggie won't absolve her: she must answer for Enrique's condition. If she can't, well—a pity, for her. Trust is hard-earned and too easily lost, especially his own. He crosses the room to the gramophone, lifts the thick stylus from the record, and returns it to its standby position beside the plinth. Silence follows.

In quick succession, three holoforms fill the room. Leaders of the restoration, each one. Still wearing her respirator and heavy radiation suit, Magadaline Barasa arrives first. The ground crew must be working late. She peels away her mask, exposing a dark bald head beneath, but doesn't meet Alejandro's gaze. João Alves materializes second in a hard hat and the customary lightweight skins of guild engineers. His usually warm smile is absent. Edward Langlands arrives last, his thick hair askew and his stubble unshaven. He nods curtly at

Alejandro, adjusting his glasses, and he, too, averts his gaze. The guardian sips from his china and waits.

The geologist breaks the silence. "Good morning, sir. I would have called in sooner, but we're short-handed down here right now."

"You're exactly on time, Maggie." A wave of his hand. "How is the cleanup going?"

The geologist snaps straighter. "Rather well, sir, all things considered. Our newest site will be up and running by the end of the month and should speed up the work."

"Excellent." Their future on Earth is still mired in plutonium contamination, but the new site will rekindle confidence in the restoration. "And yet, speed isn't the only metric of success." Alejandro runs his thumb along the edge of his china and holds Maggie frozen with an arresting stare. "What has your investigation revealed regarding the injuries sustained by Enrique Chamorro?"

Maggie's response spills out in a rush. "An anomaly, sir. Nothing like this has ever happened in the decade since I was appointed, and nothing like it ever will again."

"Is that all? I need not remind you that our recent failures will be heavily scrutinized."

Her voice drops to a whisper. "How long have you and I worked together, Guardian Martinho? Have I ever broken my word?"

"Time is irrelevant, Maggie." Alejandro's grip on his china tightens. He can't show leniency here—not now, when Enrique Chamorro lies in a filthy hospital bed in multi-system failure. Word of his condition already spreads throughout Colossi Infiniti, a poison to Alejandro's cause. "With the explosion on the Johannesburg station, Earth's orphans need reassurances. This accident only deepens the fear that holds us back from a return to Earth. The next I see you, your answer must be sufficient. There will be no more chances. I cannot allow mankind to turn its back on Earth for good."

Edward stirs beside Maggie. "I may have something useful to add, sir."

Alejandro turns a cool glare to the mathematician. "Speak."

"We haven't looked at all the variables impacting public perception of the cleanup." Edward adjusts his glasses once more. "It's true that the new site will accelerate the pace of the cleanup efforts. By about 12%, in fact, but that's not what's significant. That site will also be the primary base of operations for the xenophyophore production facility."

Alejandro relaxes, understanding the connection Edward seeks at once. His shoulders settle comfortably. "Yes. The protist shows considerable promise in accelerating the cleanup."

"And mitigating the danger to the ground crews," Edward adds, smiling.

Turning away, Alejandro steps close to the high window. Edward is clearly doing the geologist a kindness in drawing the attention away from her failure. The guardian closes his eyes and lets the sun warm his face. He means to stand his ground, to restate his position. Soft steps interrupt his thoughts, and there's only one person it could be. He turns, opening his eyes and smiling at the remarkable Marilina Chamorro. The physician smiles back, her eyes roving over the many distractions of the study as she makes her way to his side. Alejandro steps forward and kisses her cheek in greeting and then returns his attention to his team. The mathematician came to Maggie's defense. If Alejandro is unyielding now, he risks losing Edward's commitment. Radical change demands radical action, but not at the expense of his team. He turns to his engineer. "What about you, João? Anything to comment?"

João clears his throat and loosens his collar, nodding. The man spent a lot of time with Enrique on the ground crew. All the more reason to trust his commentary. "Ed is right to be optimistic, sir. In field tests, isotopic labeling confirms the uptake and breakdown of organic compounds and heavy metals. We haven't tested plutonium uptake yet, but nearly every species of xenophyophore consumes radioactive nuclides. Ground-crew safety will definitely improve with the rollout of the xenophyophore biotech." The engineer tilts his olive-toned head down.

The unicellular organism is just what Alejandro needs to persuade the Coalition to grant more resources for the restoration. This radioactive waste spill might indeed soon be regarded as a small hiccup. "How soon can you be certain about the plutonium uptake?"

João glances sidelong at Maggie, who clears her throat. "We'll begin testing at once. We can have preliminary results at next week's meeting." He could have answered, but the geologist is the one under pressure. For the team's sake, a modicum of trust in Maggie is warranted, however reluctant the guardian feels to grant it.

"See that you do. Definitive evidence that the xenophyophores can safely recycle plutonium waste is precisely what is needed to eliminate reservations about the eventual habitability of Earth."

"Yes, sir," they chorus, and Alejandro ends the call.

DECEMBER 22, 3040 | SÃO PAULO STATION, EARTH'S ORBIT

A hand on his shoulder stirs him out of his reverie. Dr. Chamorro stands at his side. "Luiz said it was alright to enter. You think these xenophyophores are really the answer?"

He sets his empty china tinkling on a small round table and regards her. The physician is a colonist, yet she's far from obtuse. Could she be convinced of his plan? "I do. For years, the twin dilemmas of inhospitable temperature and lethal radiation have kept us off Earth's surface. The answer has been at the bottom of the ocean this entire time. Or perhaps more likely, the xenophyophore is just the first solution to emerge. So much marine life was lost to those wars, after all."

The physician tucks her hands behind her back and watches him like he's a patient recounting his symptoms. "But where will they go? Won't the plutonium contaminate the water?"

"Any plutonium released back into the water will be inert."

"What about infection prevention?" She fires back. "Xenophyophores are like amoebas, aren't they? Exposure could be deadly. I don't have to tell you that. Will the water still be safe for drinking and swimming with those floating around at high density?"

Remarkable, indeed. A smile crosses the guardian's face. "I asked all the same questions myself. You have nothing to fear from the protists, Doctor. Xenophyophores thrive at deep-sea and will be released back into the ocean at safe distances from human drinking sources. As for swimming, well." Alejandro catches her hands in his. "I'm pleased that you're already imagining a world where humanity is orphaned no more and can swim in their own oceans again. When that day comes, the xenophyophores will have returned to their natural habitat on the ocean floor, far from all but the most adventurous divers."

The skepticism behind her eyes recedes, her expression softening into cautious acquiescence. "I hope you're right," she says. "For Quique's sake." She turns away and approaches the cabinet. Although she may not share her brother's passion for the restoration, she remains open-minded. A rare and valuable trait. Her eyes are wide as she points up at the shelves. "Where did you find these?"

"A relic of my predecessor." Alejandro joins her in gaping up at the immodest collection of music and literature. He dismisses it with a wave. "Sebastián Cruz held power and influence well before the wars. Presumably, that is how he managed to preserve so much." Even if he accomplished so little.

The physician picks up the book that Alejandro set down just before the meeting and rifles through its pages. "There must be so much history tucked inside these walls."

"History won't save us now. We must make our own future." He takes the book from her and replaces it in its proper home.

Her smile warms his chest pleasantly. "Never mind. Thank you for your hospitality, Alejandro. My family isn't a burden on you?"

He shakes his head. "It is nothing. Are the accommodations to your aunts' liking?"

An embarrassed smile tarnishes the physician's features. "Fatima insisted on one more night at Quique's side, but they both agreed to follow tomorrow morning. They're afraid of being so far from my brother during his recovery."

"I understand completely. Luiz will see to their travel. But Dr. Chamorro, Enrique's recovery could take days. Weeks, even. I can Leap to his side at a moment's notice. There's no need for you or your aunts to wait in that ICU the entire time."

She falls silent. Probably choosing the politest way to excuse herself and return to Enrique's bedside. Alejandro waits for her to continue, dread suddenly and inexplicably polluting his tense body. Some part of him hoped she might stay awhile, perhaps visit more of his station while her brother's health improves. He's grown used to her company. So alike, the two of them. Haltingly, she answers. "They will love it here."

A pleasant surprise. He relaxes, and a strange impulse overwhelms him, yet a rare indecision holds him back. Radical change can take many forms. Perhaps there's room for the physician in his plans. "That's enough talk of world-terraforming for one day. You are interested in music. Have you ever held an instrument?"

"Not since my last stay with a guardian."

An involuntary grin stings his cheeks. "Come with me, then."

To his delight, the physician follows him out of the study and down the antiquated spiral staircase to the main floor, where the instruments are stored. Alejandro reaches into the glass cabinet and retrieves a small metal cylinder. He hands it to the physician, who stares at it quizzically.

"I'm not a musician," she tells him, pressing the instrument back into his hands. "What is this?"

"It's a ganzá. Give it a shake." Her expression doubtful, she shakes the cylinder. Seeds inside rustle. "Music is that simple."

She laughs, continuing to shake. "This isn't music."

"That's a matter of perspective." Feeling a bit foolish, Alejandro reaches into the cabinet again. "This is a cavaquinho." He strums a few simple chords, matching the rhythm of the ganzá.

The physician's face brightens. "That's lovely."

"See?" He smiles. So, he hasn't yet spoiled this. "Perspective."

"How do you know about all of this?" The ganzá stills.

Alejandro shrugs, his idle strumming taking on a traditional samba. "All of that history upstairs."

She raises her eyebrows. "Isn't it difficult to learn an instrument?"

"It requires time and patience, yes." He sets the cavaquinho down. "To be frank, I rarely entertain company here. I am used to solitude, and that affords certain opportunities."

"Solitude is something the Meridian know well." The physician relaxes, tension easing out of her shoulders. "Thank you for sharing this with me." She averts her gaze, evidently ashamed. "I'm a Meridian now, but I'm not used to any of this."

Something else they have in common, then. "I wasn't always a guardian with the clout and wealth of an entire station at my fingertips."

Her gaze is suddenly piercing with intensity. "No? Who were you then, before?"

Isn't that the question? His gaze falls. "A topic for another day, perhaps." He's enjoying the young physician's company more than he thought possible. He won't ruin that.

Their conversation is punctuated by voices filling the main floor. The Chamorro aunts. Just as well. In the span of a day, the physician has come closer than any other. "Luiz will see that you return to Colossi Infiniti on time for basic training tomorrow morning." Curiosity gets the better of him. "Will it be the same for you after everything you've learned about the restoration today?"

The physician smiles. "I don't know if anything will be the same after today." Her fingers brush the cavaquinho. "I never knew how much scientific rigor went into the restoration. It makes me wonder what else is possible."

"One day, the atmosphere on Earth will be conducive to life again. You'll see then just exactly how remarkable the xenophyophores are."

She returns the ganzá to the cabinet. "I really hope so, Alejandro."

They lapse into a comfortable silence, and he senses it will come to an end soon. It's the first time in his memory that he's felt as comfortable in the presence of another as he is alone.

CHAPTER TEN

GUILLERMO

G UILLERMO RAPS HIS fingertips on his workbench to the rhythm in "Oye cómo va" and inspects Juan's rapidly dividing cells under a microscope. The guardian reaches for a frothy mug of café, pero nothing cures insomnia like the rush of a new project. The multicellular growth in the petri dish is visible to the naked eye now. Slurp. It'll need a larger vessel soon. When the time is right, a humanoid will emerge. He sets the mug carefully on a coaster, away from his machines and his soaring wall of well-organized tools, and wipes foam from his upper lip with the back of his hand. The blow of losing his best friend and his first xenobot still haunts him, but this xenobot has come the farthest since Diego, and that plasters a grin on his tired face.

"Perfecto! It's time, Inés."

Returning the dish to its incubator, Guillermo pushes away from the workbench and high-fives the robot sitting across from him. The disorganized cluster of stem cells is ready for insertion of the power cell that will program it into a humanoid with all the same knowledge Diego started with. Without Diego, this new xenobot must be the one to stop Terra Nova.

Dale—who better to free Juan than Juan himself?

"Gracias, Papá." Inés bobs her silver head up and down. Unlike the ball of cells in the petri dish, she's completely abiotic, fully machine. Guillermo's very first build after he returned home from the robotics guild. "Will Mamá be visiting soon?" The robot asks hopefully. "We couldn't have done it without her."

His hand freezes over his mug. His sister was the one who taught him to culture living stem cells into tissues that he could equip with his power cell, but her habit of letting things like "ethics" dictate her life has a way of holding her back. Guillermo drops his hand onto the metal slab in front of him, feeling every nick and warp his tools have made over the years. Inés is right: this is a collaboration. It's not just about Juan. Xenobots will change the Guadalajara station forever and free Guillermo's people from the cryo gardens, and Gabriella deserves to see it as much as he does. He sighs and sends a message to his twin through his implants.

`Elli, ¿cómo te vas? Can you talk? Got something for ya.`

`In mission prep. Call you after.`

Guillermo eyes Inés. "Tienes razón. Elli will call soon." She'll understand. Won't she?

`Incoming transmission. Sender, Anna Wright.`

The guardian's stomach turns over faster than an engine. So, the detective has reached Jupiter. Maybe she'll be able to return Derek's body to Elli and find Diego before Terra Nova does. Another slurp. Guillermo plays the recording out loud so Inés can hear too.

"Hello Nuñez. I've got your bot."

Glance at Inés, stunned. "She did it! Wright found them!"

Inés coos demurely, her optical sensors warming to a dark orange. "That's wonderful. I miss Diego."

He rubs his stubble. What did they find out there?

The transmission continues. "Your bot is in bad shape. Got a case of amnesia." He quirks an eyebrow at Inés. Eso está tan mal. Without Diego, Juanito will be starting from scratch. "We made some surprising discoveries. I won't say too much here, in case this transmission is intercepted. There were two orbiters, but no sign of life. The second orbiter could belong to our target, but without a body I can't rule out capture. We're on course to return to your sector. Should be back in a couple of days. Wright out."

Hand shaking, the guardian sets his mug down on the bench and buries his face in his hands. Derek, a hostage? That doesn't make any sense. Either way, the commander is lost to them. Now that the Monroes have returned to Colossi Infiniti, Guillermo will have to break this news at Christmas. It's face-to-face news. Cold metal touches his elbow, and he jumps, but it's only Inés.

Get it together, pendejo. The timestamp on the detective's transmission reads 0930, only thirty minutes ago. "Okay, Inés. Unless I'm mistaken, your brother will be back in just a couple of days."

The robot paws at her auditory sensors. "But he has amnesia! What does that mean? Will he even remember us?"

The guardian shakes his head, looking down at the petri dish. "I don't know." Drastic favors from Elli might be needed to restore the xenobot, and Diego may never be the same again. Guillermo has to be realistic. He opens the cabinet overhead and retrieves a case the size of a tack. Inside, it holds a shining new copper power cell. The time for doubt is over. With a turn of the latch on the incubator door, he reaches inside, picks up the dish, and sets it inside a biosafety cabinet. Juanito's got to be ready to fill Diego's boots. Anything to secure the safety of the colony for the release of the pods.

A blinking light in the upper right corner of his vision announces an incoming call from his twin. Guillermo cuts the music as her blue hologram materializes. Her big smile is a relief, even if it delivers one sucker punch of guilt. She won't be smiling when she learns what the detective's investigation revealed.

Just a few more days, Elli. Then everyone will know.

"What's so important that it can't wait until Noche Buena, Memo?"

A strained smile crosses his face. So many things. He turns on his microscope and transmits the video feed to her implants, nerves fraying. "Remember when I asked you if a xenobot could be made in someone else's image?" It's now or never. Hopefully she'll accept his decision.

She laughs. "I remember telling you it would be more like a leaf cutting. Why?"

A nervous grin. "Elli, I did it. I cultured Juan's cells, just like you showed me."

The laughter dies on her lips. She watches Guillermo place the petri dish on the stage and focus the lens, then inspects the footage in complete silence for a long minute. A lead ball settles in the pit of his stomach. If his own twin can't accept Juanito, how will Juan react? Straightening, Elli plants her hands on her hips and glares at him. "Guillermo, what are you trying to accomplish here?"

"Exactly what I said before. Building a xenobot in Juan's image."

An exasperated sigh. "No. Vas a reemplazarlo." She paces, a trail of blue light following in her wake. Words can't explain what it's been like all these years, alone, fighting for something he can't have. Reaching the opposite wall, she spins, eyes wide. "What about Derek? Are you going to replace him, too?"

The lead ball wrenches Guillermo's gut. Don't tell her, not yet. "This is different. Elli, I miss him."

She returns to the center of the room. "You're playing God. Promise me you'll stop."

This was a mistake. He shuts off the feed. "I'm sorry. You're right. It was selfish of me. I'll see you at Christmas, okay?" After the call, he glances at the petri dish. It isn't selfish. He's doing the right thing here. Elli just can't see the whole picture. When all is said and done, she'll see things differently, and so will Juan. Guillermo picks up a syringe and inserts the needle into the sterile packaging containing his power cell. Inés's silent, glowing eyes drill into him. He ignores her. With a steadying breath and sure hands, he lowers the needle below the pink liquid media. Under the microscope, the power cell embeds successfully into the ball of cells. He withdraws the needle and returns the dish safely to its home.

A veces, the end *does* justify the means.

DECEMBER 22, 3040 | MONTRÉAL STATION, EARTH'S ORBIT

If anyone will understand, it's Frank Roarke. Later that afternoon, Guillermo arrives in the Coalition leader's expansive entryway still wearing shop skins blackened with welding burns. Gone is his well-lit—if cramped—shop, replaced by a dimly lit room. Aquí y allá, the sun intrudes through thin, rust-colored curtains, adding a texture to the curtains like copper shavings on a lathe. The Coalition leader stands in the shadows, the nanoparticles that orbit his head appearing dark, overcast and gloomy. The echo of Guillermo's boots on his tiled floors makes him turn his head, his down-turned mouth matching the particles.

"What's this about, Guillermo?"

The guardian strides forward with a grin. "I figured you'd like to know that my current xenobot is progressing ahead of schedule." For once, he gets to be the one to surprise Roarke.

"Now, that *is* good news." His leader visibly relaxes, the dark cloud above him softening to a dull gray. "What about the detective?"

The grin slides off Guillermo's face. "On her way back with Diego. She thinks Derek was taken hostage."

"The attacker took the commander but left the xenobot?" Roarke steps into the light, and his voice cracks like a whip. All those GLOW injections can't hide the weary shuffle in his step or the gravel in his tone. "No, that's illogical. Terra Nova doesn't take prisoners, and they wouldn't have left without your xenobot."

Shrug. "De acuerdo, but that's all I have to go on right now." Following Roarke into an ascetic living room painted the color of iron ore, Guillermo drops onto an unyielding modular sofa facing a bare wall.

"Let me know when the detective arrives. I want to be there for the debrief." Roarke wipes his line-free, gleaming face and joins the guardian on the couch. "You have good timing."

Guillermo crosses his legs and frowns. Something is definitely off about Roarke today. "Good timing for what?"

"New information has come to light. I think you'll agree that this makes the motivations of Terra Nova a lot clearer and, for once, more predictable."

How cryptic. Predictable sounds good, but it also sounds too good to be true. Guillermo rests one fist loosely at his hip. "Dígame."

Fingers steepled, Roarke fixes a piercing gaze on his guardian as the Cerebrum particles intensify to match the rust color of the room. "Remember the disagreement between military and intelligence over whether establishing a military presence on Johannesburg would protect from further attack by Terra Nova?"

A bitter chuckle. "I remember you putting Jack in his place." Guillermo grows serious. "Was there another attack?"

The Cerebrum particles ripple when Roarke shakes his head. "No. Ever since the commander left to investigate the missing cargo shipments, I've been looking for ways to recoup the fuel shortfall this will cost us. That's when I stumbled onto it. Detective Wright's assessment was correct. Terra Nova has abandoned Johannesburg in favor of a new target. Mars."

Cold all over, Guillermo shivers and rubs his arms. "The methane." He takes a deep breath when Roarke nods and lets it out slowly. This is not good. Mars is the stations' primary source of methane, the fuel that powers everything from the agricultural units to the cryo gardens. His fist clenches in his lap. The detective was right all along: Terra Nova played them, and Jack fell right into their trap when he ordered that military maneuver. "The Johannesburg station was a diversion."

Roarke drops his gaze, and the particles overhead return to their muted gray. "Seems so. The civilians of Johannesburg were never the true target."

Guillermo glares at him. "No, but they were slaughtered all the same." Resting his elbows on his seatback, he leans back and closes his eyes. Roarke isn't the one he's angry with. "Why now? We fought Terra Nova back years ago. Now we're seeing attacks on civilians and our most important resources." He rubs his eyes. "What's changed?"

"You're right. Things are escalating fast. Something must be done." His leader's shoulders sag with the weight of his next words. "I have a favor to ask of you."

Another favor, eh? Maldita sea, those are stacking up quickly. Guillermo settles deeper into the stiff couch and stares at the grooves in the blank wall in front of him. "What can I do for you, Frank?"

Roarke launches into what sure as hell sounds like a pre-planned speech. "These attacks have gone on too long, and they're only getting worse. In times like these, the people look to their leaders. Jack might have been wrong about Terra Nova's true target, but he was right to show strength. Two strikes against the stations transpired under my watch. I allowed myself to focus only on tactical maneuvers when I should have denounced Terra Nova from the very beginning. In that regard, I have failed Earth's orphans." The nanoparticles droop as his soft brown eyes drill into Guillermo's. "It's time for a change in leadership. Once the colony is settled, I'll announce my plans to step down. I want you to be my successor."

Uff! This is unexpected. Guillermo twists, drives his knee into the cushion, and sits up. "Sir, I can't allow you to do that."

His leader stares straight ahead at that plain wall. "Earth's orphans deserve a leader who can keep them safe. On Earth, I was able to be that person, but out here . . ." He leans forward, elbows on his knees, and buries his face in his hands. "I thought the Cerebrum particles would make me immune to mistakes, but the truth is that no amount of augmentation will ever give me what I saw the first moment I laid eyes on you: unflinching determination and ingenuity."

"Am I blushing?" Guillermo crosses his arms and scowls. "A lot of people might disagree with you, sir." Roarke has his shortcomings, but he still wears the Cerebrum particles, and he's kept mankind united for decades. There's no telling what the other guardians will do if they think Guillermo is seizing power. He could have a civil war on his hands, and that'll tank the colony. Standing, he grips the Coalition leader's shoulders until Roarke meets his gaze. He won't jeopardize Juan's release for this. "Let's not get carried away. Focus on the methane. Just like the attack on the Johannesburg station, infiltrating the operations on Mars would have required the help of a guardian. It's time we start seriously investigating the Coalition. If we're going to make it to the colony in one piece, we're going to need you, Frank." A nerve works in Roarke's temple, but he doesn't challenge his guardian. Guillermo seizes the opportunity to continue. "Wright is on her way back from the wreckage site. I'll put her on this right away." The detective will be more than happy to tackle Terra Nova again—no doubt about that.

"I promised my station that the cryo gardens were temporary, and that means facing La Tierra Nueva head-on and getting off the stations. We can do this, Frank. Usted y yo, just like old times. With the xenobots, we can track down these terrorists. Have faith."

The stakes have never been higher. Elli, Jack, and Henry are all headed for the colony on Zomenos. If Roarke caves to Terra Nova, they'll be stranded. Xenobots or not, Guillermo can't stand against the other guardians and win. For his plan to work, he needs Frank Roarke.

A slow smile takes shape on Roarke's weary lips for the first time that day. His nanoparticles take on a vibrant mango glow, making him look like the Lord and Savior himself, resurrected. "Very well. We have a lot to discuss with the detective on her return." Roarke allows himself to be pulled to his feet and stares at the guardian, his smile souring. "There was a time when you never would have dared defy me, Guillermo."

"You were more intimidating on Earth." Wink. "Give us more of that guy."

CHAPTER ELEVEN

MARILINA

DECEMBER 23, 3040 | COLOSSI INFINITI, EARTH'S ORBIT

THE SMALL CONFERENCE ROOM hums with excitement. Standing at the center of a semicircle of the doctors, researchers, and nurses that comprise the colony's medical unit, Dr. Nuñez wears a radiant smile. "It was confirmed this morning. Construction is complete. The colony is ready for us." Grinning like children, the others break into applause.

The unit leader enters a series of commands into her wristband unit, and a holograph displaying the colony materializes. Drones have been laying the foundation for the first manned mission to Zomenos for months. The feed shimmers and reforms, unveiling a kitchen, bathrooms, and gymnasium. The circle tightens as the others lean in. Marilina's shoulders brush Okumu's, and she smiles at the technician, making a mental note to thank Luiz for ensuring she didn't miss this needed respite from worrying about her brother.

Nuñez waves for the group to follow. "Come, come. They're expecting us."

Bemused, Marilina follows her unit leader up one level to a room three times the size of the one they usually meet in, more lecture hall than conference room. Is the entire crew here? The doctor creeps to the third row and squeezes into a hovering seat between Nuñez and Okumu.

The door closest to the stage opens and snaps shut. A hush falls. Marilina blinks, sitting taller. Frank Roarke? The Coalition's leader doesn't do appearances. She exchanges a glance with an awestruck Okumu. Roarke seems perfectly ordinary, but there's nothing ordinary about the mist of nanoparticles that pulses with the full spectrum of colored light above him. Fatima is fond of saying that he works brujería, that those particles allow him to speak with spirits, and that's how he always knows what will come to Earth's orphans before it happens. Marilina suppresses a smile. Science and technology are far less sorcerous than that.

Admiral Monroe appears onstage beside Roarke, rubbing his hands together and bouncing on his heels. "Welcome! Today marks the first official day of Phase II of mission prep, and that makes you the first civilian crew to pass basic training." Applause drowns his words and draws a grin to his face. "I know you're all wondering why Frank Roarke is sharing the stage with me. We'll get to that.

"The emphasis in Phase II will be mission-readiness. Your unit leads have spent a long time planning this, and now it's more important than ever that we come together as a crew. Your units each have their own goals, but we must put our mission and community above that. Now, let's hear from our leader himself!"

More applause thunders as Frank Roarke steps forward, but he commands silence with a single wave. His eyes snap up, and Marilina feels those gentle brown eyes bear into hers. "It is an honor," he intones, "to meet the crew working to bring mankind home." He cups his hands together, and the mist over his head softens to a white haze. "I came here to share my deepest desire for your success in person. Each of you is a renown leader in your chosen trade, but each of you has sacrificed for this colony." Quique's cracked lips and brittle hair flash before Marilina's eyes. She swallows a lump forming in her throat. How does Roarke do that? She holds her chin high. "These sacrifices will be worth it. There's nothing more important to me than your mission. If there's anything the Coalition can do to make this mission smoother, you need only communicate those needs to the admiral or Guardian Mérieux."

After the enormous hall rent even larger by Roarke's presence, the medical unit's usual conference room feels small and insignificant. The usual views of Earth just beyond portal windows have never been less interesting. Nuñez pulls up the holograph of the colony again and zooms in on a structure. The others crowd around her, all smiles and eager chatter. "This is the infirmary. It has capacity for inpatient, outpatient, and emergency care; laboratory testing; and routine physicals." Like a VR sim, the holograph flickers and displays each section of the infirmary. "Dr. Chamorro, you'll need to arrange a transfer of medical records for the crew from the Ring before our departure."

"Of course. I'll schedule physicals for flight clearance, too." Marilina glances down at her fitted navy skins, still new to her after the flowing turquoise skins of the Meridian. After all these months of training, shuttle launch is suddenly approaching fast. The thought fills her with a rush of adrenaline, but it's bittersweet. This is it. Quique will surely be on his feet in time for the launch and well enough to congratulate her himself, in person. Alejandro's quick fingers flying across the strings of the cavaquinho flood her thoughts.

Her face warms. The time to fulfill her duty to her parents—Quique, too—is now. Alejandro is charming, but he's also a restorationist. He'd never join her on the colony . . . would he? She tugs the collar and wrists of her skins, smoothing each wrinkle flat, and refocuses on the discussion at hand. No regrets, Mari.

A biologist named David leans in, looking anxious. "Why aren't the living quarters safe inside a dome like the vivarium?"

Nuñez pauses the virtual tour of the laboratory unit. "The planet supports human life, so the development unit deemed it unnecessary."

David licks his lips. "We could expose ourselves to lethal microbes."

Marilina snaps to attention. Extraterrestrial infection would introduce an entirely new field of medicine. Far more interesting than routine physicals and GLOW injections.

"I see. Is there anything in the labs to justify added caution?"

His neck reddens. "Our tests were inconclusive."

Marilina steps forward. "David has a point. Just because we didn't find anything in a few liters of water doesn't mean there's nothing there."

Outnumbered, Nuñez holds up her hands. "¡Basta! Okay. It's not up to me, but I'll pass along your concerns to the development unit again." She turns to the others. "Let's discuss the research expedition."

The holograph zooms out, far above the colony. The site hugs the bank of an enormous river and nestles against a forest. Marilina's heartbeat quickens, and she hungers to see this planet in full color. Even the most well-traveled among the Meridian, with experience on all twenty-one stations, would envy this.

"We will verify the footage transmitted by the drones. Even though we've cataloged everything within ten kilometers of the colony, a lot can change in a few short years."

The doctor files away the details of Dr. Nuñez's plans for later, worry over her brother once again splintering her focus. She checks her wrist-band unit discreetly, but there are no new messages. She relaxes. Pilar would call right away if anything changes. When the meeting ends, she's relieved nonetheless. The others head toward the exit, but Nuñez touches Marilina's arm as she passes.

"Dr. Chamorro, the other unit leads are meeting for dinner at Guardian Mérieux's house. You've been at your brother's bedside for days. Enjoy a nice meal before you return."

Marilina clams up. The Meridian aren't accustomed to indulgence. One of Lucy Mérieux's extravagant dinner parties would serve the best meal the doctor has eaten in weeks. For a moment, she's tempted, but what if something happens to Quique while she's gone? She can't take the risk.

"I appreciate the invitation, Dr. Nuñez, but I want to be there for my brother."

To her surprise, her unit leader stoops down and hugs her. "Of course," Nuñez murmurs in her ear. "I would feel the same way if it were my brother."

Stiffly, Marilina hugs the older woman back. Nuñez straightens and smooths her hair. "Cualquier cosa para familia. Isn't that right?"

The doctor's throat tightens. "Anything for family," she repeats.

DECEMBER 23, 3040 | COLOSSI INFINITI, EARTH'S ORBIT

Anxious as to the condition she will find Quique in, Marilina steps rigidly back into the ICU. The regular beeping of the heart monitor relaxes her. She draws close. A small dialyzer sits on the table across from her. Gears whir in circles, cleansing Quique's blood of the toxins exiting his body and returning his blood back to him. Her brother will need a kidney transplant if he survives this, but the dialyzer is keeping him stable while he's on Alejandro's therapy. Marilina closes her eyes and sighs deeply as she sinks into a chair, the tension releasing from her shoulders.

"You've returned." Alejandro stands from a corner and joins her at Quique's side, looking rather refreshed, considering how early he left for the ICU that morning. The sight of this relative stranger is surprisingly comforting after just one afternoon together.

Marilina returns her gaze to Quique, who sleeps peacefully. "How is he?"

Crossing his legs, the guardian locks his hands over his knee and leans forward. He wears cologne, light and crisp. "He's stable. Dialysis is helping speed up his recovery."

"And his heart?" Her eyes are glued to the BP monitor.

Alejandro reaches across and squeezes her hand. "All is well so far. He should begin showing signs of progress in the next day or two."

"That's good news." Marilina rubs her eyes and cushions her temples between her knuckles. Her brother might just recover. He has no idea how lucky he is to be under this guardian's care, and Alejandro's generosity extends far beyond Quique. "I hope my aunts haven't taken over your estate already."

The guardian smiles. "I'm delighted to host them. They're asleep, for now. Luiz is having a meal prepared for when they awaken. How was training?"

She drops her hands into her lap. The sight of her brother made her nearly forget. "Frank Roarke was there, in person. He delivered a big announcement to the entire crew: the Coalition is ready for the units to submit their plans for the colony."

"Inspirational." He leans back in his chair and tucks his chin between his knuckles. Marilina smiles, amused. The leader of Earth's restoration, pleased with the colony's progress? He notes her disbelief. "Truly. Your mission interests the Coalition a great deal."

Her smile fades. "Why do you care if the colony succeeds?"

Alejandro returns her amused smile. "Your mission is about more than just that colony."

"What do you mean? The colony *is* the mission."

He shakes his head and leans forward. "What do you know about the mineral deposits there?"

Surprised, her brow furrows. "Not much. Drones found evidence of mineral deposits below ground, I think. The researchers were excited that they were carbon-based."

"Have you considered what those mineral deposits could mean for the stations? For Earth? What if the value of your mission isn't in colonization, but in accelerating Earth's revival?"

So, this is about the restoration after all. She sits back and looks at Quique. Mineral deposits or not, this restoration almost killed her brother. Her voice takes on a hard edge. "None of us are in a hurry to mine that planet, if that's what you're thinking."

"Of course not." Alejandro looks impressed rather than ashamed. "You have an uncommon affinity for finding connections between ideas with ease." He slides to the edge of his seat and gathers her hands in his. "Big changes are difficult and frightening, but I don't have to tell you that. You're a colonist.

What if your colony were Earth's salvation? Would that be any less noble a cause?" Marilina looks away, stroking her mother's cross with her thumb. Everything she's learned about the restoration over the past few days is inspiring, but Quique still lies unconscious in front of her. She's not ready to think of a future on Earth. A squeeze of her palm makes her look up into Alejandro's eyes. "Think about it: you and your brother reunited, a restorationist and a colonist working together in harmony, like it was always meant to be."

She *has* thought about it over and over again. It's not possible. "That's a nice idea," she allows. It'll never come to pass. This guardian is full of grandiose ideas, but her duty is to her family and to her crew, not the restoration. When Quique awakens, they'll have a long talk about his work, and he'll agree that Earth isn't worth risking his life over any further. Still, the gentle pressure of Alejandro's thumb rolling in circles over her knuckles is soothing in a way she can't name.

DECEMBER 24, 3040 | COLOSSI INFINITI, EARTH'S ORBIT

After a scant few hours of sleep, Marilina returns the next morning to an ICU screeching with activity. Nurses prep for a big procedure. The doctor's alarmed gaze rakes up and down the floor. She exchanges a glance with Pilar and, with a brief squeeze of her aunt's hand, hurries into Quique's room.

It's been mere hours since she left his side, but her brother now fares considerably worse. Face drawn and hands feebly at his sides, his breath comes in shallow gasps from lips dry and cracked. Heavily lidded eyes follow his sister as she swallows and rushes forward.

With unusual austerity, Alejandro steps forward, places his hand on Marilina's back, and steers her aside with his head bowed. "There's an anomaly in his vitals," he explains. "Hypertension. It could be nothing—"

"—or it could be the onset of acute cardiac distress," Marilina interjects, "or a dozen other possibilities."

The guardian nods. "We'll know more in a moment. I've arranged for the OR to be prepped, in case." He circles the bed and surveys the monitor while a nurse injects antihypertensives into a catheter line. The tension in the air chokes off yesterday's hopeful delusions of Quique's recovery. Marilina brushes what remains of Quique's long hair, matted with sweat, away from his eyes. She blinks, and heavy lashes stick together.

"Enrique, you're experiencing acute hypertension," Alejandro announces in a loud, clear voice. "Please try to remain calm. I've given you medication to restore your blood pressure. Now, I'm going to examine you. Just relax." Quique closes his eyes. Marilina watches the guardian's impassive examination. She had believed that if her brother ever awoke again, it wouldn't be in this ICU, but his treatment clearly hasn't worked quickly enough. Reaching into a drawer on a cart, Alejandro retrieves a handheld ultrasound. Electrical activity of Quique's heart appears in a holograph above the bed.

"Mari." Her brother lifts a trembling hand centimeters above his sheets.

"No, Quique." Fatima shushes him as Marilina takes his hand. "Please save your strength. Dr. Martinho is here. He's going to help you." Eyes still closed, her brother murmurs something that Marilina takes for assent. She kisses his cheek and whirls toward Alejandro, blurry eyes questioning.

"Do you feel any pain?" he asks. Quique nods, placing one shaking hand on his chest. The guardian's face tightens. At the press of a button, he calls for a nurse.

"Yes, Dr. Martinho?"

"My patient is heading to the OR. I'll oversee the procedure myself." He discards the trash from the ECG and returns the ultrasound to the cart, turning at Marilina's light step. "His heart is ischemic."

She holds her head high. "I saw. You're scheduling a bypass?"

"Yes." Alejandro surprises her with a gentle hand on her shoulder. He gazes at his unmoving patient. "Enrique, your heart isn't getting enough oxygen. We need to get you into surgery to clear the blockage." Quique nods again.

Nurses spill into the room and cart him into the hallway. Alejandro and Marilina follow beside them, Pilar and Fatima trailing close behind. They're outside the OR in minutes. The guardian pauses, looking at Marilina.

"I can't prohibit a Meridian from entering."

She goes rigid. Nothing is coming between her and her brother. "No, you can't. Quique is my responsibility. Let me assist with the procedure."

"Dr. Chamorro," Alejandro speaks her title softly, "it would be best if you waited outside. You know that." She opens her mouth, but Pilar's voice interrupts from behind.

"Let's have a seat, Mari."

Alejandro nods. "Wait with your family. Please," he adds, applying emphasis to the last word. Defeated, Marilina stands rooted in place as he hurries into the operating room. The energy she'd felt earlier evaporates watching the doors slide shut. An arm wraps around her shoulders, and she looks up into Pilar's worried eyes.

"It's just a bypass surgery," the doctor murmurs. "A perfectly routine procedure."

Her aunt smiles, her eyes hinting at her own misgivings.

Marilina waits in silence between her aunts, grateful that, for once, they don't intrude on her thoughts. This is the worst-case scenario for Quique. Alejandro's therapy must not have worked fast enough to spare her brother's most vital organs. Did she really believe that she deserved a second chance with her brother after all these years? She takes a shuddering breath and unsticks her hair from her cheeks, running her fingers through the short strands to smooth them flat again. It's up to Alejandro now. The thought steadies her.

The doors to the OR swish aside two hours later. Marilina tears her eyes away from a scratch on the floor and leaps unsteadily to her feet. Still in surgical skins, Alejandro strides forward urgently. Hollow eyes search the waiting room and light on Marilina. The firm set of his jaw slices through her heart. She raises her hands and covers her mouth, head whipping side to side.

"No," she whispers. "No, no, no." Beside her, Fatima gasps and clutches her arm.

Alejandro blinks. A single tear escapes, rolling onto his cheekbone and catching the air, scattering into dozens of microdroplets. Marilina hurls herself at him, beating her fists on his chest. She should have been there, shouldn't have let this guardian convince her to wait outside. He catches her reflexively and holds her against his chest. Hot tears run down her cheeks and through her nose. She can't breathe. Her fists fall, yet Alejandro holds her firm, her tears soaking his surgical skins. She grips her cross and closes her eyes. It's over, Mami.

It's over.

CHAPTER TWELVE

JACK

JACK CLAPS ALONG TO one of those robotón tunes that Guillermo likes. The walls of the lounge in his uncle's small house thump with bass. Guillermo grips his sister's waist and launches her into the air, and she shrieks with laughter. Beside Jack, his brother erupts into a cheer. His uncle twirls Gabriella, her long curls fanning out. The admiral catches his stepmom's arm and steers her away from the coffee table, laughing along with them despite the impatience gnawing at him. Guillermo assured them that there would be news about Dad after dinner, but now that the dancing has begun, it'll probably continue until midnight.

Lucy leans in and whispers in Jack's ear. "I can't believe you almost let me miss this."

Distracted, he grins. "Nochebuena rules." Celebrating the night before Christmas is a tradition Dad and Gabriella started when the boys were still in school. They have to keep the ritual alive until he's found. The admiral prods his brother in the rib cage. "Show Lucy the twanger." To her, he explains,

"Tradition is the youngest puts baby Christ in his crib." Henry jumps to his feet a little too quickly and throws his arm wide.

Lucy catches him. "Easy."

He smiles sheepishly. "Sorry, Lucy. That ponche is *strong*." He stumbles toward the dining table as the song ends, pulls out a bin full of decorations and, grinning, whips baby Jesus out.

Jack rolls his eyes. "Just do it already!" His brother laughs and plants the figurine in the manger, and the lights click into a soft yellow.

The twins join them. "Thank you, Henry," Gabriella murmurs, planting a breathless kiss on her younger son's head.

"Drink up!" Guillermo calls, ladling more punch into his mug.

The admiral follows his uncle to the table, where the guardian helps himself to more red chile enchiladas. Now is his chance. He intercepts Guillermo with one of his best smiles. "Slow down, Memo. You promised news."

The guardian scowls. "Patience, mijo. Enjoy yourself for once."

Crossing his arms and leaning against the table, Jack holds his smile. "I am. Tell me."

While Inés lowers the volume, Guillermo waves everyone closer with a two-armed sweeping gesture. "Dale. Get closer, all of you. This is serious."

Henry drops into a squat on the floor. "What's up, Tío?"

Guillermo drops his gaze to his boots. "You know I keep my promises. Remember the investigation into Derek's disappearance?"

Jack's mouth is drier than the surface of Mars. He knew it. They found him. "Hard to forget. Why?"

"The detective located his orbiter." His uncle avoids eye contact with Gabriella. "Two ships, actually. No survivors."

Then Dad's really gone. The admiral's chest feels crushed. He can't believe it.

Beside him, Lucy squeezes his hand. "Did the detective return with the body?"

"There wasn't one."

The sound cuts out like a switch turned. Jack's head snaps up, and he searches his uncle's shifty eyes. "He's a captive, then."

His mind races, the details of an extraction taking shape in his mind: location, personnel, gear, timing. The Coalition needs to be brought up to speed. Does Roarke know already? He's the last person Jack wants involved in Dad's rescue, but the military could use whatever haphazard intelligence this detective wrangled to coordinate an offensive. And then there's the colony. How bad are the setbacks? He doesn't have an answer yet. The crew needs to be notified.

But Guillermo shakes his head firmly. "We don't know that for sure, Jack."

The admiral stands, fists clenched. "What *do* we know, then? What's the plan, Memo?"

His uncle stares up at him from the couch. "You probably don't want to hear this, Jack, but Roarke was right to be cautious. That second orbiter we found with your father's ship? It belongs to the Coalition."

Jack falters. "This is an inside hit?" Guillermo nods. That changes everything. "That's it. I'm coming off the bench. Dad is out there, and we have to find him."

"Mira." Guillermo steps forward and grips the admiral's shoulders. "You want answers? So do I, but we need to play this smart. Don't let your anger cloud your judgment. You have an important role in this." His gaze sweeps the others. "All of you do. Those of us willing to stand up against Terra Nova are counting on the colony being there when this is over. What's the shortfall from the shipments that never made it? How will the Coalition make up for it? That needs to be your focus."

Hands running through his hair, Jack nods. "You're right, Tío." His uncle is a guardian, and the best placed among them to find Dad's assailants and whoever they work for. The admiral has no choice but to rely on Guillermo here. It's time to do what he does best. He's got to pull his crew together and get this mission back on course. Dad would want him to see the colony through. The Monroe name rides on it. He lets out a long breath and locks eyes with Gabriella, and he can tell she agrees. "We have a lot of ground to cover."

DECEMBER 26, 3040 | MONTRÉAL STATION, EARTH'S ORBIT

Squinting against the sunlight flooding his living room, the admiral tugs milky white drapes closed. "I wanted those shut," he snaps. Lucy stares at him, and his anger fades. "Sorry. I'm a little tense. Gabriella and Darnell view the doctor as a liability to the mission." This isn't the meeting with his unit leads that Jack had in mind. The matter of the missing cargo needs to be addressed, but this request comes on the heels of the death of Dr. Chamorro's brother, and he can't refuse. He sweeps his hair back with short fingernails, remembering the frail young man in the ICU.

Some holiday.

Lucy places her hand over Jack's. "This is your decision. No one will defy your order."

Doesn't mean it won't be a bloody battle. The others will expect him to revoke Chamorro's clearances. He checks his retinal display—0650 hours—and marches back and forth across the steel floors of the long rectangular room, ignoring the androids that avert their eyes and avoid his smoking slipstream as they go about their duties to Lucy. The help isn't Jack's concern right now. The entire debate is a nonstarter. Chamorro is dedicated to the mission, and she already feels integral to the crew. Cutting her now will only delay the mission. He can't let that happen.

Early morning sunlight still peeps through the curtains as Jack and Lucy call in to the meeting. Gabriella appears first, her image taking shape in a wavering blue smoke. It's hard to tell from a holo, but his stepmom looks pretty refreshed for a woman who's lost her husband. Phase II is good for morale, hers included.

"Let's get right into it, shall we?" Lucy suggests.

Darnell Brown's shimmering holo speaks first. "Dr. Chamorro comes highly qualified, but she's not the only doctor on the stations. It can't be that hard to replace her." He punctuates his words with two claps.

"Chamorro isn't just any doctor," Lucy says. "The Meridian are seasoned professionals used to treating patients in unfamiliar territory, and usually under duress. That's exactly the kind of person we want at the helm of the colony." She shakes her head. "It won't be easy to recruit another one."

Gabriella's mouth forms a thin line. "Chamorro is qualified—I have no doubt about this." She taps her foot with arms crossed. "However, I'm not as confident as Lucy that the crew is best served by her in this condition." The look she gives Jack is pleading. "She's the head physician. It's too big of a risk."

Everyone turns to the admiral. "What did the psych eval show?"

Gabriella throws up her hands. "She passed with flying colors. No hint that she might be underperforming." She shoots a sour look at the others. "Why is she missing training and meetings, then?"

"Chamorro has come through before. She will again." Jack locks his hands behind his back. There's no margin for personnel replacements in Phase II, because there are no shortcuts to getting them trained up on time. A new head physician would set back the mission timeline for the entire crew. "I hear your concerns, Gabriella, but I've made my decision. Dr. Chamorro will remain on the crew." His stepmom doesn't conceal her look of betrayal. Go easy on her. "Call the doctor in for a performance review, Gabriella. I'll gladly join you. Lucy and Darnell are right. We're not replacing her this close to launch." He turns his attention to Dr. Brown. "If no one has anything else to add, let's talk about the shipping setbacks. Mind filling the rest of us in?" Gabriella's mouth falls open, her eyes darting from Dr. Brown to to the admiral.

Wrong-footed, the unit leader raises his eyebrows. "Well, well, well. They told you. Good. We lost two of our six scheduled shipments over the last year, and that's going to strain the vivarium when we arrive."

Were the guardians in on this? Jack glances in Lucy's direction. She shakes her head—big surprise. "Sorry. I don't know anything about that." Another one of Roarke's unilateral indiscretions, then.

Brown plants his hands on his hips. "The fact is, the vivarium is behind schedule. We need to make up the difference."

"What happens if we don't?" Lucy asks sharply.

"The primary crops were seeded." Brown shrugs. "We might have to get creative." Lucy wears a mutinous expression.

Jack has heard enough. "Thank you, Darnell. Put in a request for additional shipments to close the gap. Let me know if you get any pushback for it. I'm happy to step in and push it through. Let's follow up separately so we can go over the shortfalls together and come up with solutions." It'll take a lot more than this to put a stop to the colony.

DECEMBER 27, 3040 | COLOSSI INFINITI, EARTH'S ORBIT

The admiral's orbiter docks at the Ring as the sun sets behind Earth, casting a cherry red glow over the interlocking rings that give Colossi Infiniti its nickname. Ordinarily, a rare sunset like this would call for a cold brew, but in his distracted state, the view is spoiled. This meeting isn't on the books, and that probably means leadership will be there. Jack exits through the airlock and takes a lift to the training facilities. Better now than later: in Phase II, he'll be logging 60 hours or more every week in the command seat and on EVAs.

In the west wing, he falls into line behind the Coalition's guardians filing into a conference room and takes a seat in a row circling a small platform. From the front, Frank Roarke steps onto the platform. He faces the others, his fleet of nanoparticles circling grimly.

"Several of you have voiced complaints about mission Z1 to me in private, and I am taking those seriously." Jack swallows. What complaints? He turns his head discreetly and catches Lucy's eye, but she shakes her head. She's just as in the dark as he is. Great. He leans back in his seat and faces Roarke. "The stakes have never been higher. Earth's orphans look to you, their trusted leaders, to guide them. Your faith in the colonization is important to me, and that's why I've invited Admiral Monroe to speak to these concerns. Join us, Admiral." Keeping his expression neutral as he rises is tough for Jack, but he strides up the floating platform and stops at Roarke's left side. Dim lights surround the podium. A spotlight. "Please share your own opinion of the state of your crew with us."

Jack squares his shoulders and meets the gaze of Guardian Kapadia in the first row, speaking clearly and confidently. "Everything is well in hand. If you're concerned about our head physician, I've already met with my unit leads about her. I am personally seeing to it that Dr. Chamorro remains on track with her training and other duties for this mission." He clasps his hands behind his back, feeling self-assured.

Roarke shakes his head. "You misunderstand. The Coalition believes that you, Admiral, are showing signs of unchecked trauma. You were last seen in public abandoning your father's memorial early. How do you respond?"

A roaring whoosh thumps in Jack's ears. He blinks, disoriented. "I left to check on a crewmember in the ICU here at the Ring. Guardian Martinho can confirm."

From a few rows back, Martinho rises and nods. "The admiral visited my patient, Enrique Chamorro."

The Coalition's leader bows his head. "There is also your previous motion to establish a military presence on the Johannesburg station."

"I had my reasons." Jack grinds his teeth. Why are they dredging all of this up? And is that damned spotlight necessary? "There's nothing wrong with changing tactics. Every admiral does it."

Guardian Ngcobo speaks from his seat at the back of the small room, his low voice ringing. "What is up for debate is whether your overall judgment is impaired. Your approach was rash and did nothing to dissuade further attack on the Mars depot. We all endure the consequences of your actions, Admiral." Jack is at a loss. What happened to the Mars depot?

"Everything Admiral Monroe does is in service of the Coalition," Guillermo puts in. "Who here hasn't made a bad call?"

Ignoring him, Martinho steps up onto the platform, nods at Jack, and addresses the other guardians. "A full psychological evaluation would remedy these concerns." Murmurs of consent echo along the walls. He lowers his voice. "I'm truly sorry, Admiral. This is for the protection of Dr. Chamorro and the other members of your crew." The thumping in Jack's ears returns. Martinho isn't the only one looking out for the doctor. The admiral stuck his neck out for Chamorro.

Roarke steps closer and grips Martinho's shoulder. "Thank you, Alejandro. Let's put this to a vote." Several hands go up. Jack closes his eyes. This isn't happening.

Lucy leaps to her feet in the front row, spreading her hands on the table, tossing her hair over her shoulder and narrowing her eyes. "This is outrageous. I trust Jack with my life."

Ngcobo's voice booms out again from the back of the room. "You have your own biases, Lucy. The Coalition is obligated to investigate these claims."

Roarke's gaze sweeps the room, landing on Jack. "Very well. Admiral Monroe, you are temporarily grounded, pending your evaluation and internal review by the Coalition." Jack swallows and stares back at Roarke. A cold sweat arrests him as he nods. How can Roarke do this on the eve of Phase II? This will absolutely delay mission launch, and for what? Unfounded accusations of mental instability? His bitter smile lands on each of the guardians as they exit the way they came. How many of them would happily suspend him long enough to eliminate the colony as a viable alternative to Earth?

CHAPTER THIRTEEN

ANNA

THE ORBITER KISSES THE dock and sways. Anna closes her eyes and inhales, then wrinkles her nose. The cabin reeks of fish. Diego's leg must be infected, but when she told him so, he denied it. "Xenobots don't get infections." She's no scientist and doesn't care, really, but that smell is nasty. This isn't exactly what she had in mind when she took on the brooding xenobot. Amnesia or not, she fulfilled her end of the bargain with Guardian Nuñez, and now it's his turn to fix his rotting robot so they can be on their way. Bagging Terra Nova will be oh, so sweet.

Beside her, Diego frets. "I don't want to see him."

A muscle twitches in Anna's jaw, but her eyes remain closed. "I know." Against her better judgment, she faces him. "It won't be that bad. He can't blame you for the amnesia."

He stares at his hands. "I should have been able to protect us—him." He looks up. So much angst in those green eyes. "Whatever happens to Derek next is my fault. Worse, I failed Juan."

Anna crosses her arms. "Who is Juan?"

"Guillermo's partner. He's been in cryo for the last fifty years."

Well, this is news. "How did you fail a guy who is frozen solid?"

Diego laughs with a bitterness so deep that Anna quirks her eyebrow and leans closer. "The whole reason I exist is to help Juan. The first androids were supposed to ease the needs of your kind and make it possible to end the cryo program." He drops his gaze. "Guillermo had higher hopes for me. A safeguard for the colony. But I failed too."

The detective settles back in her seat and whistles. "That's some real human guilt." Mm-hmm. The holo above signals that they've been approved to unload. She turns back to Diego, her gaze hardening. Any fool can see he is doing his best for that creator of his. For some reason. "Juan isn't your fault. Understand? Now, help me with the equipment." Therapy is over. They've got work to do.

Nuñez waits for them just beyond the hatch, staring expectantly at her with an unusual scowl and looking grouchier than Sergeant Arquette did that time Anna crashed a Coalition hovercraft chasing a lead through the station square. Is the guardian that upset over Diego? Or is it the commander he's worried about?

"You look like hell, Nuñez." She hops down lightly and springs upright on the balls of her feet. Her joints still work after a week in captivity. Thank you, GLOW.

Diego appears beside her, fidgeting with his skins. Nuñez cries out, running forward, and pulls the xenobot into a fierce hug. So, the guardian cares at least a little. Anna plants her hands on her hips and hangs back. Nuñez peels away, dropping to his knees and inspecting his xenobot's leg. It's come a long way in a week. The bright red new flesh cracks and peels and stinks, but it's whole.

"The detective didn't mention this," Nuñez grumbles while he inspects the tender flesh. "Elli's waiting for us at home. She'll take a look."

So chatty onboard the shuttle, Diego suddenly clams up. "It's nothing," he mutters, and twitches his leg away. It sure looks like all that agonizing earlier was unjustified.

As if reading Anna's mind, the guardian sits back on his haunches. "Derek?" he whispers. When the bot shakes his head, Nuñez swallows, nodding, and turns away.

"I'm sorry," Diego says in a strangled voice. He sinks to the ground beside his maker and reaches shyly for the guardian's hands. "We'll think of something else. The colony will succeed, and Juan will be restored."

Nuñez scoffs. "I don't even want to discuss that right now."

Can't he see how hard Diego's trying? The detective drops her hands to her sides and rolls her eyes. All this sappy crap is too much. Terra Nova is waiting. "Touching reunion. I'll be back for the bot." She sidesteps Nuñez and heads for the locker rooms.

"Not yet, Detective." The authority in the guardian's tone, so unusual coming from him, stops her in her tracks. "We have a lot to discuss. Join us on Guadalajara while my sister tends to Diego's injuries."

Sigh. Nuñez's over-sized role in her life has ended. If the xenobot's memories can be retrieved, he might still be useful to her, but she's never relied on anyone else before—anyone *human*, anyway—and she's not about to start. "What do I look like, your personal errand girl? I have a job to do. Find someone else to do your bidding."

The guardian shakes his head. "Trust me, Detective. You'll want to hear what I have to say."

She doubts that, but his conviction piques her interest. What now? "Let me collect my things and we can get out of here." Anna retrieves a blessed pack of jimmies, a change of skins, and a lighter from her locker. Coalition skins pool at her ankles as she shrugs a black jacket over a fresh outfit that'll blend in with the civvies, slides a jimmy out of a pack, and lights it. Skunky smoke unfurls in winding tendrils around her face. Grinning, she returns to the steel platform outside. "Let's get on with this, yeah?"

Nuñez grips their shoulders, and the locker room disappears.

DECEMBER 27, 3040 | GUADALAJARA STATION, EARTH'S ORBIT

The jimmy almost falls out of the detective's mouth. What in the name of hell? They're not on Colossi Infiniti anymore. Is this a living room? Through a window to the left there's a plant, and beyond that, tall buildings in the distance. This must be the Guadalajara station. She's seen guardians Leap before, but the shock of experiencing it herself is unmatched. With a downward glance, she notes that the smoke cloud coming from her jimmy is static, like she hasn't just traveled 10,000 kilometers in the space of an instant. She cocks an eyebrow at Nuñez.

"The transport pods at the Ring work just fine, you know."

He shakes his head. "Too visible."

Anna flops down onto a couch across from him and rests her elbow on a plush cushion. "Is this where you off me?"

A woman appears behind him—the aforementioned sister, judging by their matching caramel eyes and high cheekbones. "Thanks for coming, Elli. Detective Wright, this is my sister, Dr. Nuñez."

The detective gives the stranger a once-over. Attractive, like her brother, and the same height. The kind of woman who takes herself seriously. Anna nods once. "Pleasure. So, can you fix the bot?" Diego needs his memories back if he's going to be any help.

Doc glances at the xenobot. "I'll do my best. What caused the amnesia?"

Anna shrugs. "He says it's the radiation."

The guardian heads into the bathroom, apparently looking for supplies. "See what you can do for his leg," he calls. "That smell is increíble."

The doctor props Diego's leg on the low table across from Anna and inspects it with an eagle eye. "Judging from the odor, the new growth didn't take." She looks into his eyes. "We might have to start over. Your wounds weren't properly disinfected."

Diego is crestfallen. "I did what I could with the supplies on that orbiter."

Anna leans forward and plants her elbows on her knees, bun swaying. "I thought xenobots couldn't get infections."

Nuñez steps in front of her, blocking her view of the makeshift operating room unfolding in his living room. "Your transmission was light on details, Detective. Did you learn anything useful from this mission?"

"Oh, I'm learning loads." She peels her eyes away from the doc and meets the guardian's glare. "Like I said, your bot took significant damage." She jerks her thumb towards Diego. "Far as I can tell, his marble is roasted."

Whipping around to his sister, who has finished sterilizing the room and is now rolling up the patient's skins, Nuñez says, "Can you do anything about that?"

Doc purses her lips and applies alcohol to the wound. "I don't think so. He might recover his memories as he heals, but there's nothing I can do to speed that up."

"What about the flight recorder?" Nuñez presses, fists clenched at his sides. "Did you find it?"

The detective nods. "We got the black box."

"And?" He steps close, his whole body rigid with anticipation.

Anna frowns up at him. "It was no use. The thing's fried."

"How?" he demands. "Flight recorders are insulated against heat and protected by titanium and Kevlar."

Feeling prickly, Anna raises an eyebrow. She did not endure two weeks of solitary confinement on that orbiter to be treated like a damn fool. Catching her eye, Diego shakes his head and then looks up at his maker. "Radiation, same as myself. That wreckage was in Jupiter's magnetosphere for days, unprotected. By the time we recovered the recorder, it had suffered complete memory failure."

With a sigh, the guardian shakes his head and plants his hands on his hips. "I had hoped that you would have something more concrete for me, Detective, pero I've got something for you. Something has happened. On Mars."

Anna perks up. "Mars?"

Nuñez nods. "The fuel depot there is in jeopardy. We could run out of power before we ever get to the colony."

"Terra Nova?"

"Not just that. You remember your hunch about a guardian being responsible for the Johannesburg station?"

The detective nods slowly. She thought of little else during her holiday in Jupiter's shadow. "What about it?"

His grim smile fills her with dread. "We think the same thing is happening on Mars."

"Holy shit, Nuñez. Why didn't you lead with that?" Anna crosses her arms and leans back. It adds up: someone powerful is standing between Earth's orphans and that colony. The question is, who?

Diego grunts, and all eyes turn towards him. "We have to stop them." He looks down at his shiny new leg with detached despondency as the doc makes her first incision, cutting away the new growth. Anna pulls her skins up over her nose.

Nuñez folds his arms over his chest. "Not so fast, pendejo. You need to heal. Your eyewitness account is the biggest advantage we have right now." His eyes darken. "If medical intervention can't help us, maybe robotics can." The detective laces her fingers together and tucks her chin beneath them. What the hell does that mean?

The doc applies a fresh paste of greenish goo to Diego's exposed leg. He looks away. "Please, Guillermo."

The guardian crouches beside the xenobot and squeezes his shoulder. "Think about it. It could be a surgical investigation. Human brains are bad at recall. If you allow me to access your neural circuitry, I might find information that's locked away and inaccessible to you."

Now, this is unexpected. Anna sits up straighter.

Diego jerks away from Nuñez like he's been jolted with electricity. Doc lurches forward, hastily pinning his leg down, and exchanges a warning look with her brother. "A surgical investigation?" Diego repeats. "You think you'll find something I can't?"

"It's possible," the guardian insists, his gaze souring. "If you won't do it for me, do it for Juan."

A crooked smile parts Diego's lips. "Would you perform this surgery on him?"

Nuñez barks a laugh and shakes his head. "Of course not. It's too dangerous for a human, but you would be fine."

Looking more like a caged animal than a humanoid, Diego recoils. "You don't know that. You might rewire my brain. How do you know that I'll still be *me* after this surgery?"

The siblings exchange a confused look, and the guardian says, "Relax. You'll be 'you' in every way that counts."

The angst returns to those green eyes. The detective sighs. This isn't heading anywhere good. "Aren't we missing the bigger picture here?" she interrupts. "We know Terra Nova has access to Coalition ships. That narrows down our suspects—at least enough for the working parts of Diego's brain to sort through. Is it worth risking his remaining abilities with this surgery?"

Nuñez glares at her. "I built him. I know what I'm doing."

"You're winging it." Rising, she holds out a hand to the xenobot. "Hurry up, Diego. This is your specialty." Her tone softens as she addresses the scowling guardian. "He'll be plenty useful to me on Mars while he's recovering. When we get back, I'll have my suspect in custody and you'll get your answers. Deal?"

"Are you sure about this, Detective? If Terra Nova is working with guardians, they're more powerful—and more dangerous—than we ever thought possible."

Anna winks at Diego. "They're not the only ones with an ace up their sleeve." Smirking at Nuñez, she says, "Terra Nova is about to learn that *they* should be scared of *me*."

DECEMBER 27, 3040 | MONTRÉAL STATION, EARTH'S ORBIT

Once the doc issues a clean bill of health for Diego, the detective brings him to her flat. After all that tension between him and the guardian, it's a relief to be alone with the bot again. With a sweep of her arm, she throws the door wide and ushers her guest inside. Walking past the pile of clothing on the floor and into the kitchenette, she yanks open the fridge, but there's nothing inside but a bottle of ketchup. She closes the door and pulls two packets of beef jerky from a cabinet instead, tossing one to Diego.

"Good thing you don't eat much."

Still standing in the doorway, he catches his packet and frowns. "This is how you live?"

"You were expecting one of those guardian manors?" Anna drops onto the couch and crosses her legs underneath her.

"You're a senior detective in the Coalition. Why do you live in such poor conditions?"

Cackling, Anna pats the empty seat beside her. "Don't be rude. Sit down. You won't catch anything, I promise." Diego looks skeptical, but he joins her on the couch.

The detective flips open her wristband unit. "We don't have time to waste. Without that methane, the stations will go into deep survival mode. Fuel will be restricted, and that'll only make travel more difficult for us. I have a contact on MS275 that owes me a favor, but he'll only meet in person. I'll arrange a meet and we can get out of Dodge at first light." After dictating her message, she enters a series of codes, and a holo pops up in the middle of the room with specs of MS275, the mining outpost that orbits Mars.

"Okay, Robot. What are we thinking?" Silence falls. After a pause, Anna rolls her eyes and turns to him. So moody. "I'm kidding. I know you've already processed the data on MS275. Who is our suspect?"

Relaxing, he glances at the specs. "Your theory regarding the guardian is plausible." His green irises flicker, and a new holo appears beside Anna's in teal. Cool. "These records show exports to and from the civilian stations here in Earth's orbit."

"Right. And?"

Diego's gaze refocuses on her. "Those freighters are unmanned. The ground crews on MS275 lack the credentials to operate them."

Anna bites her fingernails, tasting the remnants of her last jimmy. "Who has those credentials?" Those eyes flicker again, and the holo shimmers, a short list of names replacing the export data. She commits each one to memory, pointing at the name at the top. "Is this our man?"

A nod. "Kojo Osei, guardian of MS275." A holo of the man appears alongside a list of personal facts. Diego recites them aloud: "Age: fifty two. Birthplace: Lagos station. Trade: geologist. Assignment to restoration in 3008. Reassignment to MS275 in 3018."

Ripping off a piece of jerky between her teeth, Anna chews and reads Osei's background. Her eyes narrow. "Geologist, huh? How did you land a guardianship, Kojo?" she mutters under her breath. Her gaze returns to his picture, lingering on a set of fat, jeweled rings on his meaty fingers. "Send me profiles of the others, but Osei is the primary suspect unless I say otherwise. We need to get to know our target better. Mars's exports aren't just disappearing. They must be going somewhere, but where? And why? What does the guardian get out of it?"

Diego nods. "Human psychology can reveal a great deal about criminal motivation." He looks down at his jerky, untouched. "What about your motivations, Detective? You have a fondness for food. Why is there none in your home?"

Shrug. "Full refrigerators are for people who have time to use them."

He hunches forward, unconvinced. "You don't have to take assignments in other sectors, or even other stations if you don't want to. What are you chasing after?"

Anna looks away. What's this got to do with Osei? "I have my reasons."

Standing up, Diego walks around the pile of clothing to the other side of the room. Curiosity getting the better of her, she follows. He stops at a small table lit by a floating orb and rifles through the photos in the display. The detective looks over his shoulder in silence. Stopping, Diego hands the display to her, and her chest tightens. Her grip turns to iron. It's Ma. "I know that Mae Wright died on a freight ship importing water from the Saturn sector," Diego says gently. "Terra Nova was suspected, but there was never a trial. You were thirteen."

Heart hammering, Anna slams the block back down onto the table and glares at the floor. "Who are you investigating, me or Osei?"

Warm fingers slip around hers. She looks up into eyes full of sympathy. "I'm not investigating you, Detective. I'm just trying to understand my new partner."

Her eyes burn as she stares at Ma's dimpled cheeks. "Everyone always says I look just like her, but I never had her smile—even before the accident." She touches her cheek. "That smile made her a lot of friends, but it didn't do her any good on that freighter."

Those green eyes hold hers unflinchingly. "You want justice for what happened to your mother, don't you?"

Anna tears her eyes away. "I don't want justice. I want revenge."

CHAPTER FOURTEEN

GUILLERMO

DECEMBER 27, 3040 | GUADALAJARA STATION, EARTH'S ORBIT

Beneath the Guardian, his moto hums along at a steady pace, cutting a path through dense fog and humid rain. Guillermo pats Itza reassuringly and grips her handlebars tighter. Juan would say it's better to take it slow on these slick roads. Besides, there's no sense in rushing. This may very well be his last visit to the gardens for a long time.

Up ahead, a group of tradesmen hurry out of the textile mill and into the rain. A civilian shoves away from the group, and someone pushes back. Guillermo slows on the moto as he approaches.

The one who started it glares. "Don't push me!"

"Back up, puto. We're all just trying to get home." The other man rejoins the others and tucks the brim of his hat low against the rain.

Twisting, the instigator wraps his arms around his opponent's neck. "I need to be on the first shuttle. I missed rations yesterday." He shoves the man onto the ground and hurries forward. After more yelling, a riot breaks out.

A Coalition hovercraft descends on the tradesmen. "Everyone inside the shuttle now! Curfew is in two hours."

"Hold on, Officer." Guillermo hops down from Itza and opens his visor. This isn't his Guadalajara. Some of the tradesmen recognize him at once and shrink away from the fight. "You're angry. You have every right to be. I'll extend ration distribution so everyone gets their share. Just be patient. The Coalition is working on solutions. We can't fall apart now, not after all this time." He receives a few weak nods and murmured agreement, but the core rioters stare back at him in naked defiance. Even though the workers file meekly onto the shuttle, their guardian's got no illusions about who they'll blame while they nurse their bruises. They want retribution, and they're coming for Roarke's Coalition. It's like this on every station now.

Rainwater clings to his eyebrows as Guillermo arrives at the cryo gardens. Hopping off his moto and stroking her leather, he can see the gardens remain unchanged from his last visit. Here, supply chain disruptions mean little. It's a cool, dark and damp place. Long, thick vines creep lovingly along a glass dome encasing the gardens. Through a set of double doors, ivy covers nearly every surface. The guardian flicks raindrops from his skins and steps inside.

The living tomb embraces its newcomer. He strides down the familiar long rows of cryogenic pods, passing hundreds of faces with closed eyes and elbows tucked at their sides. He breathes in familiar moss and exhales fog. For many, that earthy smell stirs memories of loved ones. To him, it brings memories of home, of Juan. Not for the first time, he wonders how many of the frozen still have loved ones to return to.

Shivering, he hurries to his partner's side and, crouching, wipes frost from the viewing pane with a gloved hand. Juan's eyes, so brooding and mysterious when awake, are closed. Guillermo envies his peaceful sleep—or is it waking madness?

A hushed quiver of anticipation radiates from the gardens. Maybe he's crazy, but the garden seems invested too. His words come in a whisper. "I come with news, amor." Guillermo rests the palm of his hand on cool plexiglass. Around him, life support machines hum in a chorus, like a church choir. God hasn't forsaken the gardens, and neither will he. "I've found an excellent detective to keep the colony safe. She wants to take down La Tierra Nueva even more than we do, and she's taken poor Diego under her wing." Wet laughter escapes his throat. "The bad news is that todo se va a la mierda. Derek is missing, and Diego is pretty much useless right now. We can thank Terra Nova for that too—maldita sea." His gloved hand clenches over plexiglass. "They're choking off our resources to force us into submission, and Roarke is starting to crack, so I guess it's working." Guillermo laughs again, a mirthless sound that echoes down the aisle, and lowers his voice further. "The Coalition might withdraw from Zomenos. I need you here, Juan. Everything's falling apart without you." He hesitates, his words sticking to the roof of his mouth. "You're going to have to trust me on this. My new xenobot has your cells. He's *you*, Juan, and he's perfect. He's the answer to our prayers."

La paz is violated by a bright red hologram projection. Guillermo stiffens and checks his retinal implants, but there's no incoming transmission from the detective, and no one alive can broadcast through someone else's implants. Ducking low behind Juan's pod, the guardian narrows his eyes and looks all around, but he's alone.

The hologram projection looms large, dwarfing the cryo pods beneath it. Guillermo stares up at images broadcasting rapid-fire. Earth—pre-war Earth, that is—spins like a top. Mushroom clouds of smoke pop up, first over Europe, then the USA, then Asia. It's footage of the deployment of the nuclear warheads over Russia, China, and North Korea. He swallows, tasting bile. Bunkers were their salvation back then, and their prison. Earth spins faster, smoke unfurling and enveloping the planet. It dissipates, and the oceans darken to a sickly purple-orange, the atmosphere gone.

A voice speaks, low and garbled. "Fifty years since Earth's orphans fled its surface. What were we promised then? What do we have to show now for fifty years in space?"

Guillermo's expression turns to stone. Terra Nova.

The voice rumbles on, joined by others. "Frank Roarke is vision-less and controlling, a puppet master stringing us along on marionettes toward a future that doesn't exist on a planet that will never be ours. Join us, and Terra Nova will set you free. Free to reclaim what should never have been taken from us in the first place. We call on Earth's orphans to choose a new leader to step forward and set the record straight. Join us, or fade into history like the surface dwellers that condemned us to space. The choice is yours.

"Rejoice in the pale blue dot."

The voices dissipate as the planet reverses direction. The oceans return to blue, the atmosphere rich once more. Guillermo rolls his eyes as the hologram fades, leaving a bright red afterglow burning in his retinas. These evangelists weave a powerful story, but that's all it is —a fairytale. They know nothing about life in the bunkers. Shaking fingers reach for his temple, and he remembers the lux goggles he wore over his eyes all too well. These pinche terrorists will antagonize the Coalition until escape from this solar system isn't possible. The past will swallow their future. His gaze drops to the pod beside him. A future without Juan.

Guillermo sits down with a groan. Who else watched this broadcast? Odds are good that anyone with implants got the transmission, although he can't figure out how Terra Nova pulled that off. He turns his back to the cold pod and closes his eyes.

"I won't let them do this, Juan. We just have to wait a little longer, amorcito. I'll get us through this, just like I always do. La Tierra Nueva is no match for your double."

DECEMBER 30, 3040 | COLOSSI INFINITI, EARTH'S ORBIT

Three days pass without a word from Frank Roarke.

Guillermo attempts contact with the Coalition leader through every means at his disposal, first sending direct messages through his implants, then, when no reply comes, Leaping directly to the Montréal station. To his amazement, Roarke's estate is empty. Confused and growing increasingly troubled all the while, he retreats to the Guadalajara station and focuses on Juanito. If the most powerful man alive has lost his nerve—or fallen into Terra Nova's hands—it will fall to his new xenobot to restore the power balance. Only Juanito can challenge the Cerebrum particles and survive.

A brief message finally arrives. `Coalition meeting today at 1600 hours. My estate.` The terse order is almost as unsettling as the silence that preceded it, but Guillermo saunters into Roarke's upstairs office with a grin splashed on his face, anyway. Whatever transpired with the Coalition leader is none of his business, so long as Roarke is finally taking action against Terra Nova. Guillermo steps over the threshold and, finding his leader facing the window behind his desk, strides forward quickly.

"¡Mil gracias! It's a relief to see your face, Frank. What's going on? I've been trying to reach you for days."

Roarke turns slowly, but he isn't alone. Standing in the corner of the office in a classy set of shiny black skins is Guardian Alejandro Martinho. Caught off guard, Guillermo's mouth hangs open. Their leader speaks into the silence.

"I'm glad you're early. There are some things we should discuss. Have a seat." Against his better judgment, Guillermo obeys. Roarke steps around the desk, joining Alejandro's side. "The orphans are restless, and the atmosphere is ripe with insurrection. Terra Nova is just capitalizing on what's already playing out on the stations. My days leading this Coalition are numbered, and I need my position to go to someone I can trust, a proven leader that Terra Nova wouldn't dare challenge. Alejandro is that man."

Guillermo's jaw nearly falls into his lap. "Excuse me?" His gaze flits from Roarke to Alejandro. "Frank, I can't believe my ears. You're *stepping down?*" They'd talked about it, of course, but he assumed the matter settled after he turned Roarke down.

Roarke's jaw is set firm. "I've always said that the day Earth's orphans stopped believing in my leadership would be the day for someone else to take the reins. Alejandro and I have different methods, but we share the same goal: to reach a permanent home. My orphans are enthusiastic about his restoration. He can unite us again."

"Terra Nova is the one calling for your replacement, not us."

Alejandro interjects. "To be clear, I don't oppose Roarke's leadership. Given the ultimatum of these terrorists, however, this path will prevent widespread panic and ensure the Coalition retains power in the days ahead."

Guillermo shakes his head. "I'm sorry, Alejandro, but no." He turns a hard look on Roarke. "How can you give in to those extremists? I built those Cerebrum particles for *you*, Frank, not Alejandro. Use them! There must be another way."

Roarke draws himself up to his full height. "The Cerebrum particles are precisely the reason I know this to be the *only* way to defeat Terra Nova. To oppose them now, after everything that's happened, only ensures the collapse of the Coalition—maybe even all of humanity." The Cerebrum particles pulse with a ferocity Guillermo's never seen before. "With Alejandro at the helm, we stand a chance. It must be done."

Slumping back, Guillermo says, "We worked so hard for that colony."

Roarke's would-be successor wears a mollifying smile. "Under my leadership, the missions to Zomenos will proceed. You have my absolute assurance of this."

Debatable. Alejandro can say whatever he likes, but he's a restorationist, not a colonist. A vote for him is a vote against the colony. Against everything that Gabriella, Jack and Henry have worked for. Against Juan. Guillermo buries his face in his hands.

"I'm sorry. I can't support you in this, Frank."

"That's okay, my friend. This is for the people to decide, not us." Behind them, the rest of the Coalition can be heard queuing up outside the office. Roarke fills them in on the plans for the vote, but Guillermo hardly listens. What will Alejandro do with the Cerebrum particles once he gains control? Does he mean what he says about continuing the colonization of Zomenos? Why would he bother if he simply wants to return to Earth? Guillermo settles deeper in his chair, studying Alejandro Martinho.

Inevitably, the meeting evolves from a debate over whether Terra Nova can be stopped in some other fashion to an in-depth examination of Martinho's claims for Earth. The decision may be in the hands of the orphans, but the support of the Coalition will hinge on whether Alejandro can convince them he can keep them alive.

"This group once believed in the restoration," Alejandro reminds them. "I understand that the failures of the past have made you reluctant to invest in a future on Earth. I want to prove to you that our return home is not only possible, but the right decision for our failing stations." He steps back as a hologram of their home world appears in the center of the room, the planet twirling slowly on an axis. It looks like hot salsa slathered on a bean burrito—if a burrito were coated in deadly radiation. "This is the Earth of today, the one you are familiar with. My crews on the ground have slashed radiation by over 75%, putting the planet on a trajectory toward habitability for the first time in decades. Look at what we're projecting the planet will look like in one year's time if the Coalition were to sign off on expanding xenophyophore production." Earth spins, the murky orange-violet color of the ocean cooling to a more palatable greenish-blue. The atmosphere thickens. A few of the guardians are smiling, but Guillermo feels nothing but skepticism. So easily reassured. Does Roarke really believe in this path, or is he just caving to pressure?

Samkelo Ngcobo waits for him outside the office. They fall into step, a brooding silence growing between them. Their footsteps fall hard and even, echoing off the walls of the long hallway. Only once Roarke's office is out of sight does Samkelo turn to him.

"Do you believe we can salvage Earth?"

Closing his eyes, Guillermo leans against the wall and remembers the dark, damp, and cool bunkers. He's one of the few orphans still alive that remembers life below that burned burrito's surface. That hologram made it look inviting, but it's anything but. He shudders and shakes his head.

"No. Not right now, at least. Maybe with the nanoparticles . . ." But if the solution exists, Roarke would have thought of it by now. This vote is the best plan the Cerebrum particles gave him. Guillermo shakes his head again. "It doesn't matter. We have to go along with this vote."

Samkelo wears a knowing look. "You have another plan, don't you?"

"I'm gathering contingencies." Guillermo pauses. He and Samkelo have a long history, but they've never discussed Terra Nova. Samkelo's no fool, and he's lost people to Terra Nova, too. Can he count on the other guardians?

Hands tucked behind his back, Samkelo bows his head. "If there's anything I can do to be of service, name it. The time has come to choose sides, old friend."

A trickle of sweat runs down the back of Guillermo's neck. The second shuttle that the detective found near Derek's wreckage was Coalition-issue, he remembers. *Someone* in their midst orchestrated the abduction of his best friend, but who? A muscle twitches in Guillermo's hand. No one is above suspicion right now, not even Samkelo. He can't risk exposing the detective or Diego. If they successfully identify the Coalition's double agent, it could turn the tide in Roarke's favor. He nods at the waiting guardian.

"I will. Be safe, amigo."

DECEMBER 30, 3040 | GUADALAJARA STATION, EARTH'S ORBIT

Guillermo sinks down at his workbench and drops his head into his hands. How can things be unraveling so quickly? A few short months ago, the Coalition had been optimistic about the colony. Now it clamors for the upheaval of all its carefully laid plans. All because of Terra Nova.

They need answers, so the guardian dictates a message to the detective. `Any luck with the methane?`

Wright's response is reassuringly fast, but light on details. `Negative. K dodging a meet. Informant wants more time.` Guillermo sighs into his hands.

He trusts the detective to get the job done, but he can't afford another failure. What if Diego can't come through after the damage he sustained? The guardian decides to record a message for Wright looping her in on the vote, but thinks better of sending it directly through his implants since those are apparently compromised.

"What's wrong, Papá?" Inés moans on the bench across from him. "You haven't smiled once today." Guillermo looks up. The robot's ocular sensors are round with worry, her ears tucked low. He forces a grim smile.

"I have a lot on my mind, Inés."

He takes a deep breath, gaze settling on the small vivarium, roughly the size of a tool chest. Juanito sleeps peacefully inside it. Terra Nova wants Roarke's power, but they don't know about the xenobots. From the very beginning, his xenobots were the antithesis of the Cerebrum particles—humanized machines to outmatch the artificially enhanced intelligence of the wearer of the nanoparticles. With any luck, Juan's stem cells will impart some of the artist's creativity into the xenobot, but transplantation of Guillermo's own cerebral tissue led to his first success. He has no guarantee that Juan's stem cells will work, and with the Cerebrum particles on the line, he needs to be sure, to replicate the success of his first transplantation. Juanito, a Guillermo/Juan lovebot? He swallows back a wet laugh. No matter who Terra Nova places in charge, they'll be no match.

Reaching into a cabinet and retrieving a needle and syringe, he glances in Inés's direction. "It's time, mi querida. Will you do it?" He has to be asleep for this.

Her ocular sensors widen and constrict as she stares at the syringe. She looks up at him. "This is what Juan wants?"

Guillermo squeezes the little bot's hand. "Of course it is." When he built Diego, one of the final steps was transplantation, and Gabriella had done the procedure—against her own protests. Inés is more than up to the task, but she's nervous.

"And my new brother needs your cells?"

A nod. "You don't have to worry," he lies. "I won't feel a thing."

"Lie down then, please." Her creator drops to the floor and rolls up his skinsleeves. She grows still, focusing on her task. The bot's torso pitches toward Guillermo, holding a needle high as she draws up a sedative. "I'm going to poke you," she announces unnecessarily. A swift insertion smoothly delivers the drug that will put him to sleep—except it doesn't. Goosebumps prickle down his spine. Something's wrong. He can't move, but he can see, hear and feel, and he is powerless to tell Inés to stop.

Carajo.

Inés retrieves a second needle. This one will pierce the base of Guillermo's skull and take a biopsy. He stares at the needle, long and powerfully strong. It will drill right through his skull sin problema. He shouts, but no words come. He waves his arms, but he's paralyzed. Inés bends close to his face.

"I'm sorry, Papá. I can't let you do this."

The robot whirls away, inching toward his chest instead. A wave of panicked confusion overtakes his fear. What is she doing? Inés places the second needle into his arm, but the syringe isn't empty. There's another fluid inside.

This isn't right. What is Inés doing to him? Guillermo struggles with all his might to move anything, even his pinky finger. As the needle breaks his skin, he regains a sliver of muscle control and his whole body jerks. The needle slips, and fluid squirts harmlessly onto his skins. The robot spins backwards with a yelp, and the syringe falls. Shock and fear mingling in her crazed ocular sensors, Inés rocks herself upright and flees on her hoverboard. Energy spent, he finally falls asleep.

CHAPTER FIFTEEN

MARILINA

DECEMBER 30, 3040 | COLOSSI INFINITI, EARTH'S ORBIT

DARK STEEL RATTLES BENEATH Marilina's feet, making her wince as she crosses the long hallways of Colossi Infiniti. Her unit lead made it clear that she should be grateful to even be on the military station after all the time she's taken off from training. She rounds a bend and wheels to a stop, heart catching in her throat. A small viewing pane offers a peek of the solar system beyond, Earth just visible.

Marilina swallows and steps closer, pressing a shaking hand to cool glass. This is what Quique gave his life for. Her heartbeat quickens. Looking at it now, she notices that the atmosphere of her home world is richer than it was in her girlhood, and the ocean has regained some of its color. The restoration is working. Earth isn't empty after all, and it might still have something to offer. Alejandro's proudest achievement.

Guilt arrests her, frozen before the viewing pane. She's avoided him over the last week, but how can she face him when she still isn't over Quique? Yet the unread messages are piling up, and he deserves a response after everything he did for her.

Marilina pulls herself away from the portal. Dwelling on all of this isn't doing her any good. She closes her eyes and draws in a deep breath, willing tension out of her shoulders and neck. Rumors are flying left and right about what the methane deficit means for the stations, but she's certain that more civilians will go into cryo—maybe even Pilar or Fatima. Squaring her shoulders, she continues down the hallway. She couldn't save Quique, but there are people alive who are counting on that colony. Her family needs her to succeed now more than ever.

The crew has only just been notified of the accelerated timeline to launch, and there's a lot of ground to cover to be ready. On her first day back, she's only just started working on medical clearances. A small exam room is up ahead and to the right. She steps up to the door and stands in front of a biometric scanner. A status light turns green, and the door clicks open. Marilina steps inside, pleased that this space remains stocked despite the uptick in her patient load. New orders came through during her break to evaluate the admiral. She hasn't seen him since, well, before, but he's obviously behind her continued appointment as head physician, and she must thank him for allowing her to see her duty through.

A holograph of him forms between her and the sink, the smoldering rage in his scowl startling her. "All crewmembers report to meeting room 7B. There's been an urgent development impacting our mission." The holograph repeats its pre-recorded message.

The meeting room is packed. Marilina has no idea what this is about, but the crewmembers at the front of the room wait stiffly, white-faced and silent. She spots Dr. Nuñez with a handful of the others from medical. Marilina catches her eye with a questioning look, but her unit lead simply shakes her head. Eyebrows raised, she joins the lab technician, Keshi Okumu, whose own eyes are wide and anxious.

"Sorry about all of this." The admiral enters, skipping hastily up a set of steps to a stage at the front of the room. "Earlier today, Terra Nova released its first public broadcast. Anyone equipped with retinal implants or who happened to be in proximity to one of our holographic screens saw it firsthand, but I know most of you haven't. Although I'd rather not breathe any more life into this, I will replay the broadcast now so we're all on the same page."

A holograph flickers to life beside the admiral as he falls silent. Keshi squeezes Marilina's hand hard. The doctor knows next to nothing of the terrorists, but when she was young, Terra Nova had been a name whispered between children when the nuns were out of earshot. Eyes widening, Marilina stands at attention throughout the broadcast, her Meridian training holding her steadfast against her rising fears.

The broadcast ends, and the admiral steps forward. "There will be a vote soon to decide the new leader of the Coalition. Frank Roarke himself has backed Alejandro Martinho, and the unit leads have already met with Coalition leadership to discuss what this means for the colony. This is a rapidly evolving situation, but as of now, I ask that you please don't panic and continue with mission preparation." Alejandro, the new leader of the Coalition? Stunned, Marilina backs into another crewmember and murmurs an embarrassed apology. "Rapidly evolving" doesn't begin to describe the pace of these changes.

An officer in white skins rises near the front of the room. "Shouldn't we take this threat more seriously? I don't want to piss off Terra Nova."

The admiral's demeanor is unchanged as his gaze falls on the officer. "We *are* taking this seriously. The Coalition decides the fate of our mission, not Terra Nova."

The officer pales to a sickly blue, but he doesn't back down. "And if crewmembers are targeted directly?"

"If you encounter a Terra Nova operative, report it to the Coalition immediately. Do not engage on your own. Remember why we're doing this. The colony is our future, our legacy. Are we going to let Terra Nova take it from us?" Silence follows, and the admiral nods. "You're all dismissed."

Thoughts splintering, Marilina follows the others out of the meeting room. The Coalition can't disband the crew over this, but she would hardly blame them if they did. None of them wants the attention of these extremists.

And what about Alejandro? It's not safe for him to take Roarke's position. A door opens to her left, and the crew is joined by members of the Coalition. Preoccupied, Marilina steps woodenly to the right, giving the newcomers room. But then he's there, standing in front of her wearing that rare smile of his. Warm relief floods through her.

"So, you've returned to your mission, Doctor. I'm glad."

The guilt returns. "Thank you." She lowers her voice. "Are you worried?"

"You heard." Alejandro shakes his head. "There is nothing for you to fear." His eyes sweep the crowd surrounding them, noting the watchful eyes of her crewmates. "I would be happy to share more with you in a less crowded locale. Allow me to take you to dinner." His dark eyes soften. "It's the least I can do."

She has no more appointments, but she hesitates. "Curfew is in an hour, and we're under orders to remain on Colossi Infiniti." With fuel reserves so low, inter-station travel is heavily discouraged now. Marilina wouldn't even be cleared to use a transport pod to visit her aunts. Alejandro, however, remains undeterred.

"I'll have you back on time, I assure you. I am still permitted to Leap, and travel to my own station is never off limits."

Nervous about this suggestion, Marilina rubs her cross. "My crew already doubts my commitment."

Alejandro smiles. "Then surely they don't understand you half as well as I do." He holds his hand out. "Just an hour to ease my worries. I know how hard Enrique's loss was for you."

She does want to hear his reasons for feeling so assured in the face of Terra Nova's threats. More than anything, she realizes how much she's missed his company. His confidence is infectious. Without him, she's felt cold, alone, and uncertain. She takes his hand. "One hour, then."

DECEMBER 30, 3040 | SÃO PAULO STATION, EARTH'S ORBIT

They arrive at a spacious food park lined with ten food trucks and several picnic tables for those not in a hurry. The tables are empty, and the few people in line request their food to go. Some trucks are already cleaning up and taking down their signs. Like everywhere else, the streets of São Paulo will soon be deserted for curfew.

Unruffled by these details, Alejandro leads Marilina into the center of the park. He points. "The arboretum is around that bend. We can order takeout and eat in privacy."

"What kind of food do they serve?"

"Anything you can imagine. I'm getting the beef stew from the Ethiopian truck."

Marilina raises an eyebrow. "We don't have Ethiopian food on Guadalajara." There are no Ethiopian stations. If their cuisine survived the wars, their refugees must have found sanctuary elsewhere, like her grandparents did.

Alejandro smiles. "Well, then you must try it."

Following his lead, she orders sega wat, and they carry their food past the empty tables to the arboretum. If the park was sparse, the arboretum is abandoned. Alejandro finds a short park bench where they sit. He hands her a bowl, and she digs in.

"You haven't answered my messages," he observes without judgment. "How have you been?"

The memory of Quique, gaunt and weak, comes to mind, and her stomach tightens. "Sorry I've been distant. I'm better than I was." She meets his gaze. "It was easier that way."

He touches her hand. "I understand. Sometimes just having something else to do, to focus on, makes the pain of a loss more manageable. It seems that the mission keeps you very busy right now."

She nods. "Our timetable for launch was accelerated in response to the fuel shortfalls. The Coalition wants as much time as possible to get people off these stations." She flushes. "But you already knew that, didn't you?"

"I know some of what goes on with your mission, yes, but the Coalition doesn't consult its guardians on everything. Do you feel prepared?"

Setting her fork down, Marilina tilts her head back. That depends. Will the admiral be receptive to a psychological evaluation? "We will be." They have no choice. She folds her hands in her lap and studies the guardian. "Do you?"

"I do." Alejandro sets his fork down too. "There will be a vote, and if Earth's orphans choose me to lead, I intend to see us safely back to Earth."

"How did all of this happen?"

"Roarke asked me. Terra Nova will stand down with a restorationist running the Coalition. The enemy you know." He smiles.

Marilina grips her cross skeptically. "But what will they do to you once they've removed Roarke from power?"

He sets his bowl on the bench beside him and takes her hand. "They won't threaten me. These terrorists do want the restoration to succeed."

"And after?" Her voice quavers, and she looks away. "I can't lose you too."

A touch on her chin prompts her to look up into eyes hardened with assuredness. "You're forgetting that when I am leader, I will have access to all the considerable processing power of the Cerebrum particles. Terra Nova is no match."

"Frank Roarke surely said the same words."

This only earns a smile. "Roarke grew complacent after all those years in power. He became too dependent on his Coalition to make the hard decisions a true leader must. I won't repeat his mistakes."

She laughs. "Don't underestimate them, Alejandro."

The guardian reaches forward, brushing her short hair away from her eyes. "I won't. I won't let any harm come to you or your crew either. You have nothing to fear from Terra Nova."

"I'll hold you to that." With a sigh, she rests her head against his shoulder and gazes up at the stars. "One way or another, extremists or not, the stations are coming to an end, aren't they?"

"I'm a firm believer that endings are but a necessary step for new beginnings."

She sits up and raises an eyebrow. "I didn't take you for someone who would use a cliché."

He grins. "We all have our weaknesses. You, being chief among mine."

Scoff. "Another cliché."

"And yet, you're smiling." Alejandro bends close and kisses her softly, their lips just touching. Wet electricity courses through her spine, down her fingertips and up the hairs on her arms. She grips his skins and pulls him toward her, kissing him again, longer. A light burns the back of her eyelids, forcing them open. A Coalition officer in navy blue skins approaches from further up the path. With his hand on her back, Alejandro straightens. She eyes a baton at the officer's waist warily. Since when does the Coalition send armed officers to enforce curfew?

"Good evening," the officer says. "Curfew is in fifteen minutes. You don't want to be here when I make my rounds again."

Alejandro stands and approaches. "Please excuse us, Officer. This woman is here as my guest. I accept responsibility for her presence here."

Two floating orbs rise higher on the path, casting the guardian's face in sharp relief. The officer's jaw drops. "Excuse me, Guardian Martinho, but I didn't recognize you. I meant no offense."

"Absolutely none taken."

The officer hesitates. "I don't want to cause any trouble, but you'll be leaving soon, right?"

"As soon as we collect our belongings." With a nod, the officer disappears back down the path. Alejandro turns back to Marilina. "I apologize for that. I hope I didn't embarrass you."

She smiles, gathering her bowl and utensils and joining him. The man very well might lead the entire Coalition soon. However improbable this thing is between them, she knows only that it must continue, and if anyone can find a way, it's him. "You, embarrass me? I can't imagine how you could ever pull that off."

CHAPTER SIXTEEN

JACK

Two MONTHS. THAT'S ALL that stands between the crew and shuttle launch. A short timetable under the best circumstances, complicated needlessly by the admiral's pending review. Jack leans forward, his skins tightening against flesh, and rests his elbows on a smooth table. This is it. Everything he's accomplished led him to this. He should relish this. Instead, his abdominal muscles are spun up so badly he can hardly think. How in the universe are they going to be prepared in time?

"Admiral Monroe? What do you think?"

The question drags Jack away from his spiraling thoughts and back to the present. Across the short table, Dr. Brown waits expectantly. Resisting the urge to stand up and pace, the admiral folds his hands on the table and holds Brown's gaze.

"Sorry, Darnell. A lot on my mind." Rubbing his hands together, Jack shifts his gaze to a holo projection between them. He'll just have to do his best to keep the mission moving forward. Three cylindrical dewars are suspended in space, their proposed contents listed to the right. If he understood the primer correctly, the embryos inside those tubes will grow into the livestock for the colony's farm. Nuts. He barely spares a glance at the list, shaking his head. "Those dewars weigh a lot, Doctor, and we need to keep the payload light. Do we really need to transport live embryos if we have the stem cells to make them?"

Brown taps his foot beneath the table. Confrontation makes him squirm. "We do. Embryogenesis technology has come a long way, but it's slow and imperfect. Livestock is essential to the colony. We have to give this the best chance of success."

Great. Another "critical" item to bring aboard the shuttle. Civilians, especially these scientists, don't understand the complexity the added weight creates for his engineers. Jack turns to his stepmom, sitting beside Brown. "Gabriella?"

She clicks her tongue. "Those stem cells were frozen during the wars, and they're decades old. I'm sorry, but even at -196°C, I'd expect low cell viability."

Jack grimaces and turns to his left, where Roarke and Martinho monitor the unit leads. The reason behind their presence doesn't need to be stated: the results from the psych eval put the admiral's performance under a microscope.

"We must consider the consequences of failure in light of the fuel crisis, Admiral." Roarke's eyes turn to Jack without moving his head. The Coalition leader has become more stoic than ever in the last few weeks. A vibrant green glow emanates from the Cerebrum particles orbiting his head. "Bring both."

No surprise there. The admiral's jaw tightens. Choose your battles. "Understood." He shifts his gaze to Dr. Brown, whose dark cheeks brighten. "Could we pare the tubes down to one dewar, then?"

"I'd have to run the numbers." Brown's hands open and close, his brow furrowed.

Martinho says, "It's not possible, Admiral, but two dewars would keep the odds of success within acceptable limits." A compromise is sealed under a hefty silence.

From Jack's right, Lucy ventures, "If we're in agreement, we should discuss cryo."

His head snaps in her direction. "That's not up for debate."

"Lucy raises a good point, Admiral." Jack turns his glare on Roarke, but the sudden warmth in the man's voice surprises him. There's still a man in there, after all. "Cryo can preserve resources and speed up the timeline for the second mission."

Voice turning to steel, Jack says, "These missions are about preserving life. I can't ask my officers to go to sleep after we land. If we're doing this, we're *all* doing it."

Martinho leans in. "Cryo needs only last until Earth is ready for repopulation."

Another glare. "Our mission is colonization. Earth doesn't factor into our objectives."

Outside the small meeting room, Lucy gives Jack a meaningful look. "Alejandro Martinho might very well be leading the Coalition soon. Don't antagonize him."

Jack waves her ahead of him. "He won't win. Frank Roarke has led the Coalition since before either of us were born." Their boots thud evenly on the steel platform guiding them through the long halls of the west wing.

"A lot of people like what Alejandro has to say, Roarke most of all."

"He's just lost his nerve." He clenches his fists. Shortcomings aside, Roarke is still the colony's biggest proponent. What does a change in leadership now mean for the mission? And for all his smooth talk, Martinho has said absolutely nothing about how he'll handle Terra Nova. The Coalition needs to show strength now more than ever. Martinho just doesn't have what it takes to fill their leader's boots. There's no point in saying any of that out loud, though. Lucy is a bureaucrat, not an officer, and she thinks like one. Up ahead, the crossroads bisecting the Coalition station is visible. He stops. "My appointment is in ten."

Her gaze flits to the south wing, basking in the sun, then back to Jack. "Speaking of people who like what Alejandro has to say. Will you behave this time?" He looks away, but her hand on his shoulder makes him face her. "Jack, Chamorro has to clear you for the flight."

He brushes her hand away, his voice hardening. "I'm the commander of this mission, not the doctor. She wants this as much as I do. She'll clear me." Jack strides into bright sunlight, ending the argument. He loves the woman, but he's not going to take a lecture. The doctor's recommendation for continued observation is absurd and offensive. He marches into the central nexus of the Ring, the narrow walkway widening into an open atrium with viewing panes the size of freight ships. In the south wing, he hops a lift up to the medical unit. If it weren't for him, Gabriella would have replaced Chamorro with some other physician, and the doctor would have gone back to the Meridian. She'll return the favor. He's sure of it.

The admiral pushes against the door to the exam room, but it doesn't budge. He falls back a few paces and knocks. Let's get this over with. Muffled laughter bleeds into the hall. The doctor must have another patient ahead of him. A moment later, boots scuff the floor, and a tall, red-haired woman dressed in the green skins of the ag unit opens the door and steps into the hallway with a big grin splashed across her face. Recognizing Jack, she turns the color of cherry pie.

"Sorry, Admiral."

Cooling off, Jack shakes his head. "Don't mention it."

Behind his crewmate, the doctor calls. "Come in, Jack." The exam room is unchanged from his first session. He crosses to a table, scooting onto a short metal seat, and Dr. Chamorro turns to him with a pleasant smile.

He points at a silver tray beside her. "Is that GLOW?"

Inside, amber gold liquid swishes. "It is. The rest of the crew is receiving their first doses this week. I know you've received treatment before, but flight protocol requires me to administer a fresh dose."

"That's fine."

She makes quick work of washing up and sterilizing his shoulder. A whiff of perfume distracts him from the prick of a needle and the ice-cold liquid it delivers. That signature crushed lavender fills his mouth, and involuntary swallowing does nothing to kill the acidic flavor that persists.

Chamorro smiles. "Sorry about the taste."

"Could be worse." He settles in. "What are we going to talk about this time?"

The doctor retraces her steps to the other side of the small room and perches on a hard stool, her smile fading and her tone growing measured. "That depends. Have you thought about what we discussed last week?"

"Sure." He rolls his shoulders. It's been a long enough day without rehashing this.

"And?" She prompts. "How do you feel about your father's MIA status?"

Jack crosses his arms. "How do *you* feel about all of this? You're fine with Terra Nova endangering our mission?"

A cautious frown bends the doctor's brow. "Frank Roarke believes in Alejandro, and so do I. He's said publicly that the colony will proceed under his leadership."

The admiral can't help but raise an eyebrow. "I'd be more worried if I were you. If Terra Nova can rip the Coalition right out of Roarke's hands, they can destroy Alejandro Martinho."

"This isn't about me, Jack. We're here to talk through your emotions."

Groaning, he swings his feet. "With all due respect, Marilina, I just don't see how 'dealing with my emotions' is going to move the needle. The Coalition needs to locate Terra Nova and extract my dad. Therapy doesn't change that."

"That could take a long time. Therapy can help you process your feelings in the meantime. Make it manageable." The warmth in her voice cools. "Think about the mission. You're not the only one who's lost someone."

"The mission is the whole reason I shouldn't waste time with these pointless sessions," he snaps. An icy pause stretches between them. The doctor raps on her wristband unit with quick fingers. Jack cocks his head. "What are you doing?"

"Your unwillingness to work with me leaves me no choice. I'm recommending a leave of absence from Colossi Infiniti of no less than one week."

His lips part in stunned silence. No officer would presume to order him to do anything. He leans forward, gripping the steel bench until its sharp edge digs into his palms. "Dr. Chamorro, I am your commanding officer."

"And I am your doctor. One week. If you improve, you may return to your post."

Blood pounds in his ears. There's no time for this. Voice frying, he croaks, "Shuttle launch is two months away. The crew needs me."

She stands and turns away from him, busying herself with her stack of syringes. "Right now, your duty is to yourself. Everyone else can wait."

JANUARY 9, 3041 | MONTRÉAL STATION, EARTH'S ORBIT

Jack rolls onto his back. After weeks of sleeping on the firm cots of the Ring, the silken sheets cushioning his sore muscles feel like heaven.

House arrest isn't without its perks.

Staring up at the ceiling in darkness, Jack is consumed by thoughts of Terra Nova: which stations are most vulnerable, tactics that would offer the most protection, and how to pinpoint the bastards' location and extract Dad. Vice Admiral Ono would want to hear his ideas. He holds his wristband unit up to his eyes and squints through the low light, but it's pointless. His comms are restricted to his emergency contact and his physician.

Lucy sits up in bed beside him, her sharp eyes lingering on his lit wristband unit as he tucks his arm back under the sheet. "Still thinking of reaching out to Ono?" A sideways glance and a nod. She props her head up on one hand with a sigh, her curtain of dark hair falling over her shoulder. "You're almost through the week." Jack closes his eyes and doesn't answer. Easy enough for her to say, free to come and go as she pleases. "You're following the doctor's orders, right? Daily recordings uploaded to the server?"

"Yes." He holds his wristband unit up so she can read the time stamps on his entries, but opens his eyes to her disbelieving frown under the wan light. "What?"

"We need you back in mission prep, Jack."

Rolling onto his side, he looks up at her. "I've sent in feedback on everything the unit leads have given me."

"That's not enough. Time is everything right now. You don't want the launch postponed, do you?"

"Of course not." Like he needs a reminder. This whole therapy business is one giant distraction from the mission.

She leans forward and kisses his cheek. "Just do what the doctor says and get back to the Ring." He rolls back over while she gets up. Once she's ready, she returns to his side for a goodbye kiss and then Leaps to the Ring. Jack envies her ability to travel with ease right now. He's not allowed to go anywhere until Chamorro signs off. Sighing, he throws back the covers. Might as well get this over with.

Heading into his study with a mug of warm coffee, Jack flops onto his favorite armchair. Its brown faux leather creaks in response to his weight. Warm pink light falls on him from the orbs floating above. He drums his fingers. There must be something acceptable he can deliver the doctor. He hasn't been phoning it in—well, not exactly—but he has nothing to say on this subject, either. Yes, his father is missing, but more importantly, an officer of the Coalition was taken hostage, and it's the admiral's responsibility to extract him. But the doctor is stubbornly holding her line, so if he wants the suspension lifted, he has to play ball.

How do you feel about your father's MIA status?

Just one week of this. He closes his eyes, searching for words. "Bad, okay? I feel like crap. I didn't even know about his mission. The Coalition never would've approved it. Dad deployed right into a known hot zone without backup, and now he's MIA." Once Jack gets going, he can't stop. "But the worst of it? I look like an idiot. The whole goddamn Coalition is laughing at me while I sit here writing in my diary instead of doing something about it.

We're about to make history, but I'm sitting on the sidelines while my crew prepares without me."

Yowza.

He blinks and lets out one long breath. She wanted to know his feelings, and boy, is she going to get them.

CHAPTER SEVENTEEN

ANNA

JANUARY 9, 3041 | MS275, MARS'S ORBIT

I N A DARK, DAMP apartment unit in the lower east quadrant, Anna faces a window thick with dirt. All this waiting makes her fingers itch. The stations need answers to the fuel crisis, and the detective intends to find them. Luckily, her informant finally feels up for a meet. Beside her, Diego wears a grin that matches how she feels inside. Mm-hmm. She closes her eyes and holds a jimmy to her lips, her lungs filling with a gritty texture. Beyond the window, a heavy wind kicks up fresh dust. It's good to get the case moving again. Too many of her leads have gone cold, but she's struck a chord here, on this sandy rock. She takes another hit. Vengeance is near.

Tracks outside trace miners' boots to a shuttle that operates on a circuit to the mines below Mars. Out and back, pairs of tracks weave a trail without variation. Anna turns at the scrape of heavy boots behind her and flicks the butt of her jimmy into a waste receptacle. Her time is now.

A steel chair with stains on it catches her eye, but it wobbles at her touch. She remains standing. An official statement released by MS275's guardian calls the fuel crisis a "devastating mining shortfall," but from what Diego pieced together, it's a load of crap, and her informant says he knows what's really happening to the fuel reserves on Mars. This miner's statement needs to be on record. Zeke's information is trustworthy—if he'll talk. The long flight with that xenobot picking at his leg the whole time better be worth the intel. She turns to her host, a short, balding man.

"What can you tell us about Guardian Osei, Zeke?"

The miner studies the detective in silence. "Did you bring it?" he asks in a rasping, low baritone.

"Oh, I brought it," she mutters under her breath. Searching official Coalition filings through her retinal implants, she projects Zeke's file to the room. The miner steps close, eyes pausing with aching precision on every letter.

The detective leans against peeling orange wallpaper. "It's all there, Zeke. Your daughter will be assigned to the medical trade when she comes of age next year."

He looks up sharply. "What's this about the food service division?"

Shrug. "Doctors and nurses have to eat?" She called in a lot of favors just to get this request considered.

Diego stirs. "You're lucky they changed it at all, Ezekiel."

The miner glares at him, then fixes Anna with a flat look. "You said you could get Sarah into the academy."

"And I did." This is boring. Sarah is one girl, but Anna has the entire orphan race to worry about. "What's it going to be, Zeke? Do you want your daughter in a factory for the rest of her life?"

A vein purples at the man's bare temple, but he must be thinking of Sarah, because he closes his eyes and answers. "Osei likes nice things like the rest of 'em. Must not come from money like guardians usually do, else why would he be here?"

The detective's boots scrape dirt as she crosses her ankles. "Were you here when he took over MS275?" Nod. Inside the can where her spent jimmy rests, a weak reed of smoke curls and breaks against heavy, warm air. "What was that like?"

Zeke shrugs. "Think he thought it was going to be like guarding any other station." He shakes his head. "It ain't like that here."

Always so damn curious, the xenobot steps closer. "What do you mean?"

"We're just a labor force." Zeke's expression turns hard. "Ain't much of a community to guard."

Diego's eyes gleam in the low light. "You're treated like servants."

An awkward pause follows, but mercifully, Zeke ignores the xenobot's odd remark. "Something like that. After Osei showed up, our shifts went from ten to twelve hours. New instructions: need more wellhead gas coming off the pipelines for the stations. Next thing we know, our operations are way up."

Anna frowns. "How do you explain the dip in methane exports, then?"

Zeke stumbles backwards. Her crimson red irises unnerve the bravest men, but this one maintains composure. "The fuel is there. It just ain't reaching the stations. I know where it's going, though."

Surprising for a miner. "Don't make me guess."

His reply comes soft but clear. "Earth."

She snorts. "Don't waste my time, Ezekiel. Can you pin that on Osei or not?"

He nods, slow. Serious.

If Zeke's not bullshitting her, that means Osei—and Terra Nova—isn't just in favor of Earth's restoration. He's siphoning all of MS275's resources into speeding up the timeline. Monroe's disappearance, Ma's death: all of it was for this.

The question is why?

Her heartbeat quickening, she turns toward Diego. From the gleam in those green eyes of his, the significance of all this isn't lost on him. She can't see how the pieces are connected yet, but this is her strongest lead on Terra Nova in years. Mustering practiced coolness, she leans back and waves at her informant. "Go on."

"Some of the men are gone missing. Then, one of the men in my unit starts bragging about a new assignment, so I followed him to the south quadrant.

Found all the missing miners, and they aren't too upset about it if you ask me. If you want answers, look up Kirk Dawson."

The bot handily extracts the available information on their new target and forwards the coordinates of Dawson's last known location to Anna. She straightens. "Thanks, Zeke. If any of this checks out, I'll see what I can do about Sarah. That's a promise." If the miner believes her, he doesn't show it.

The detective leads the way down to Dawson's apartment, her head wrapped in a scarf. Thanks to her unfeeling, bionic eyes, she hardly notices the dust, but she does notice that Diego protects his head and eyes, too.

"Does the sand bother you?"

The bot shrugs. "Not normally, but with this wind, it can do some damage. If I can avoid having to grow back my skin, I will."

They find the unit unlocked. With a glance at Diego, Anna pushes the door open and steps inside. From the look of things, Dawson hasn't been here in a while. She watches the window out of the corner of her eye. If he was taken by force, the perps could return.

"You take the kitchen," she calls over her shoulder, heading into the only bedroom and scanning for signs of a struggle. Enhanced eyes shine UV light onto the sheets, the floor, and the walls in search of bloodstains. Drawers yank open. Lifting the mattress, she scrutinizes the other side. Finding nothing, she drops the mattress back onto its frame. Something clinks, and she freezes. Dropping to her hands and knees, she scans the area around the bed and loudly sucks in her teeth.

Gaze steeped in concern, Diego pokes his head in. "Find something?" The detective squats down on hands and knees and retrieves a wristband unit. Either Dawson's or his assailant's. Brushing off dirt, she squints at the screen and holds it up for Diego, who snatches it and punches in a series of codes, wearing an intense frown.

Anna sinks onto a stool. "What are you doing?"

The xenobot grins up at her. "I'm going to see what it says."

She looks on in silence. Wristband units are heavily encrypted, but this one suddenly glows to life. Raising her eyebrow, she crosses her arms. "Useful trick. I'll never use one of those again."

Diego climbs to his feet with a chuckle. "Wristband encryption is very secure in the hands of a human."

"Tell that to Dawson."

"Wait, I think I found something. A recorded message."

A holo of a bald man in fine skins abruptly fills the small room, speaking in a booming voice. "Welcome to the team, Dawson. I need someone to lead a new drill site in the south quadrant, and I'm hoping that's you. The methane you collect will be processed and transported to Earth. Drones will handle most of the hard labor, as always. Discretion is not optional. Under no circumstances will you share information about this project with anyone. Failure to adhere to this directive will have fatal repercussions. If, however, you prove to be the man I know you can be, you will be rewarded generously by our mutual friends.

"I look forward to working with you. Detailed blueprints await you at the coordinates in my next recording. Yours, Kojo."

Stunned, Anna rocks back onto her heels. "It's all here."

The shock on Diego's face mirrors her own. "We have Osei on record declaring intent to violate the Fuel Expediency Agreement."

"Do you know what this means?" A tinny laugh escapes her throat. "We've got him. A guardian committing treason against the Coalition."

Diego looks frustrated. "He doesn't directly implicate Terra Nova in his message. Are they the 'mutual friends'?"

"That's a job for the tribunal. All we have to do is bring in Osei and we'll be that much closer to nailing those bastards."

JANUARY 11, 3041 | MS275, MARS'S ORBIT

Wrinkling her nose, Anna steps into a shower pod. Beneath her feet, years of soap scum and suspicious copper-colored stains threaten to claim her life. She closes her eyes, curls her toes inside her shower shoes, and turns the nozzle. Lukewarm water blasts her in the face. Fast as she can, she showers and hops out into the washroom.

"We're moving out," she announces as she closes the door behind her. Dropping her bath skins, she pulls on a brightly colored set of loose skins that cinch at the wrists and ankles in the style of the miners.

"Why?" The xenobot withholds his usual protests at her nudity and simply stares at her.

The detective adjusts her hair wrap. "Got a message from Nuñez, but this place isn't secure." With any luck, the guardian will come through with their arrest warrant. This room is one of thousands of short-term rentals for temp miners on MS275, and there's no telling how many Terra Nova operatives there are in this shithole. If Anna and Diego are going to confront Kojo Osei, they don't need prying eyes and ears tipping him off.

From the edge of a bed quilted in dark stains that hint at darker secrets, Diego looks up from his daily routine of fussing over his injuries. "Everything we passed on our way here looked about the same."

Shrug. "Then we do it outside."

"You think huddling together at the mercy of that wind is less obvious?" He shakes his head. "It'll draw too much attention."

With a scowl, the detective slips into her jacket, wraps her head protectively, and beckons the xenobot. "Come on. We'll do it down in the empty lot behind the shuttles. No one goes there."

A fleet of empty shuttles is lined up outside. The miners are already back from the day's shift, but none linger. That's good. Anna and Diego skirt the loading platform and head for the empty lot. The wind turns out to be mercifully tame, but that also means their voices will carry farther. Drawing her scarf closer around her face, the detective shields her conspicuous red eyes from onlookers. The xenobot glances repeatedly over his shoulder.

"Stop that," she hisses, pulling her scarf down just enough to speak. Sand peppers her nose and cheeks. "If you want to draw less attention, don't look like you have something to hide." She unlocks the message from Nuñez—double-encrypted, interestingly—and his holoform flickers into view, those bright honey eyes of his looking uncharacteristically severe. She exchanges a glance with the xenobot. "What's gotten into him?"

"I don't know." Diego's green irises widen and constrict in rapid succession. "He looks . . . worried."

Nuñez runs his hand over his stubble. "Things have changed, Detective. Maybe you already know that Terra Nova has made moves since your departure. Listen to me. Things are upside down right now. Roarke folded and agreed to a vote for the next Coalition leader, but the Coalition might not protect you if he's replaced. Whatever you're going to do, you need to do it muy rápido—fast. Understand? The one man who can bring down Terra Nova is right under your noses. You know what you need to do."

The holoform vanishes.

Anna yanks her scarf low. "What the hell was that?"

Diego shakes his head. "It must be the Cerebrum particles. He's *always* been worried about abuse of his nanoparticles."

"Oh, really? By the time we're through with these clowns, the particles will be the last thing on Terra Nova's mind."

JANUARY 11, 3041 | MS275, MARS'S ORBIT

Sitting in the sole chair in the room she shares with Diego, Anna plants her elbows on her knees and rests her chin on her knuckles. Cross-legged on his bed, the xenobot strategizes lamely with her, but all of their ideas are dead ends. There's no way to get to Osei unnoticed. They sit in silence for a long time, but eventually Diego stands. In a rotten mood, the detective watches him collect their belongings.

"What are you doing?" she growls.

He turns, holding a stack of neatly folded skins. "I need to be prepared. In case Guillermo needs me. Something's not right. I can feel it."

Great. The ace up her sleeve is getting cold feet. "You're running away? We're on a case."

"I know." Diego drops the pile of skins on the bed and cocks his head. "It's not like we're going to confront Osei head-on without the Coalition's backing, are we?"

"Intelligence is about a series of leaps of faith. We'll land on our feet. Trust me." Anna springs up. She ought to take her own advice. Snatching her jacket off a hook, she turns back to the xenobot. "It's still early. If we leave now, we can catch Osei in his office."

Diego crosses the room and bars her way. "And do what, Detective?" She doesn't like the look he's wearing, like she's some fool child throwing a tantrum.

"Arrest him." She reaches for the doorknob, but he holds the door closed.

"We don't have a warrant," he reminds her. "Please be rational. Guillermo isn't protecting us anymore. We need a plan."

"I don't need protection, and I've heard enough of your plans," she snarls. "I'm a detective. I can detain anyone I want for twenty-four hours. That's more than enough time for the sergeant to review the case and grant us that warrant." Coalition be damned. Her window to connect Osei to Terra Nova and bring down those murderous zealots is closing.

The xenobot steps out of her way with his hands in the air. "Fine. Do it your way."

Finally. She sidesteps him and yanks the door open.

Anna slams the door behind her and storms out of the building. Belatedly, she remembers her scarf upstairs. Wind blasts her face with punishing force, but she won't turn back. She's tired of all these spineless cowards burying her leads and letting Terra Nova string up the orphan race like marionettes. Ma never let anyone stop her from closing in on a suspect.

Then again, Ma is dead.

She needs a vehicle to get out of the east quadrant and reach the guardian's headquarters. The detective stomps down to the lot and stops in front of a shuttle. It's an older model, probably recently decommissioned. Her Coalition credentials reverse the lock, and she boards.

Inside, the shuttle is huge. At least fifty workers could easily ride it down to Mars, maybe a hundred. Seating is limited, but there are plenty of handrails to hold on to. The detective turns her attention to the shuttle's AI. It wakes up for her, but the pigheaded computer refuses to do as she asks.

"Just take me to the guardian's headquarters," she repeats.

"Request denied. I am only cleared for one destination, and I'm not authorized to leave the lot." Anna's hands ball into fists, but she wills herself not to smash the computer.

"Need help?"

Turning, she sees Diego grinning up at her from the doorway. "No."

The xenobot makes short work of overriding the AI's programming, and within minutes, they're on their way. Anna stares out a window down at the bleak surface of MS275. With so little terraforming completed, the station still resembles its predecessor asteroid, just with the perk of an internal gravitational force. Unwilling to meet Diego's watchful gaze, Anna stares intently at the rocky surface.

"Thank you," she mutters in the direction of the escarpment ahead. The bot turns away, and she sneaks a glance. He's taking in the mines below, back arched, a wound spring ready for action. Not a coward after all, maybe. Anna smiles and quickly averts her gaze.

JANUARY 11, 3041 | MS275, MARS'S ORBIT

The detective takes care to avoid the word "arrest" with Osei's aides. Technically she isn't doing anything wrong, but the fewer witnesses, the better. An official statement released by the guardian's office blames MS275's fuel shortfall on insufficient methane output. When news of his arrest breaks, it'll be a bombshell. Better to have Osei safely in the Coalition's hands first.

After an unbearably long wait, an aide leads Anna and Diego into an expansive office with panoramic views of the Martian surface. At the press of a button, two plush armchairs in jam red swirl down from the ceiling in a graceful arc. Eyeing the seats, the detective recalls the sad state of the furnishing everywhere else on this station. This trumped-up pawn of Terra Nova is quickly rising to the top of her scum list.

"Refreshments?"

Three stemmed glasses appear on a tray at her elbow. Cognac. That's a disappointment. With her pack of jimmies still in her room, she'd rather have something like oolong tea to soothe her nerves. She knows better than to decline. Cognac is a traditional choice for a business meeting on the Lagos station, where Kojo Osei is from. She accepts, and the aide pours three glasses.

"Greetings, Detective." Anna recognizes Osei's booming voice from the recording on Dawson's wristband unit. A hefty man with an obvious taste for fine things, he wears skins of rich satin dyed burgundy, and jeweled rings decorate meaty fingers. "How can I be of service? You certainly made an impression on me with that summons."

"But not a powerful one, or you would have granted us an audience." A dangerous smile plays on her lips. She sips cognac, notes of honey and caramel filling her nose.

Osei ignores her naked insolence. "And yet, here you are." The smile that he returns is thick with venom. "We will need our shuttle returned to its proper lot. Our station has such limited resources, Detective. You understand that."

That's her cue to drop the pleasantries. "Your resources are what we're here to discuss, Guardian Osei. I don't need to remind you that two-thirds of the stations' fuel is produced here in the Mars sector. This fuel deficit is nothing short of a devastating loss. Can you account for your drop in output?"

Surprisingly, Osei bows his head. A picture of penitence. "I'm well aware of the shortfall. My men are working around the clock to bridge the gap for the stations."

"Have you stopped to wonder where all that missing fuel went in the first place?" Anna sips her cognac breezily. She's enjoying the stuff.

A trembling hand grips his glass. "Am I being accused of something, Detective?"

"What my partner is trying to say," Diego cuts in with a warning look in Anna's direction, "is that we'd like to bring you in to Colossi Infiniti for further questioning."

Booming laughter erupts from the guardian's broad chest. "Would you? So you're asking me to return to Earth's orbit with you. Now? When my workers need guidance most?"

"It's not a request." With a swish, Anna finishes her cognac and sets down her glass. She and Diego stand, looming over the guardian's oversized steel desk.

Bejeweled hands fold together as Osei glares up at them. "Very well. Do as you must, but know this, Detective. This could very well be the biggest mistake of your career." She doubts that very much. This is big, and they both know it. Bagging a Terra Nova operative inside the Coalition? Ma is finally going to get the justice she deserves.

CHAPTER EIGHTEEN

ALEJANDRO

JANUARY 12, 3041 | SÃO PAULO STATION, EARTH'S ORBIT

BENEATH THE HIGH WINDOWS of the study, sunlight filters through the station's dome and warms Alejandro's back. The tension eases out of his stiff shoulders, making his lip curl. Ever since the vote was announced, the preparations have been ceaseless. With the careful discipline afforded him over many years of practice, he stands straight-backed and attentive to the speech Luiz crafts. It must be both ruthlessly logical and relentlessly persuasive. Earth's orphans must follow the guardian willingly back home, and with the reveal of the xenophyophores, they'll have no reason to oppose him.

Alejandro folds his arms. "The facts are accurate and the argument is convincing, but the flow spoils it." He will lose this vote if he fumbles his opportunity to connect with every orphan. "I can't be seen as leaning on numbers and diagrams. The spark of emotion must grip them and never let go. That's how we win."

"Beginning again, then."

Enviable, this android's seemingly effortless ability to weave human language into a persuasive monologue. What are the limits of these machines, imbued with all the wit and guile of the cleverest of men? What are the limits of man, with access to such processing power? The Cerebrum particles must sustain his vision if they fall to him.

Luiz wears an expectant look after the seventh iteration. Alejandro waves him away. "Yes, I think we have it. You may leave. Maggie is joining me shortly." The android leaves the guardian alone in the study, surrounded by what remains of man's recorded intellect. An empty slot in the wall of books catches his eye, and he gazes up at the shelves, undecided as to whether these trinkets will follow him to Earth. Picking up a leather-bound edition of *The Republic*—*real* leather, how maudlin!—he marks his page and returns it carefully to its place beside *The Iliad* and *The Oresteia*. He's grown fond of these thorough collections of philosophy and literature, despite how abhorrent the notion of a collection is.

Maggie's report will be welcome, a crucial thread to layer into his speech. Since Enrique Chamorro's accident, she has worked tirelessly to restore faith in the restoration. The introduction of the xenophyophore colony produced overwhelmingly positive results, and only the most willfully blind among them would deny Earth's rapid, sweeping transformation anymore. However painful the loss of Enrique, Alejandro owes the success of the restoration in large part to her. With the vote ahead, he can afford to exercise gratitude.

A blinking light in his periphery announces her call. He accepts, and Maggie's holoform fills the study with a cerulean haze. Standing in the loose-fitting, breathable skins of the ground crew, her hazmat suit nowhere in sight, she must be indoors. Her naked head shines radiantly in the sunlight pouring into the study.

"Welcome, Maggie. What news do you have of the cleanup efforts?"

"All is in hand, sir. My crew is an eager proponent of your biotech. With the xenophyophores, risks are all but nonexistent, and the speed of the cleanup surprises even me."

A nod. "Excellent news. Do you have the latest projections?"

"Sent." Out of the corner of his eye, a notification confirms secure delivery of the message. A holograph of a long table of calculations materializes between them.

Alejandro pores over the numbers. "This is more than adequate. Thank you." The Coalition already supports him, so all that's left is to win over Earth's orphans. With these numbers, he will. "Do you know what this means, my dear Maggie?"

The geologist shakes her head. "No, sir."

A winsome smile spreads across his cheeks. "It means that this election victory is all but assured. It means that we're going home. Thanks to you, Maggie."

Her face shines timidly. "Just wait until you see it with your own eyes, sir. Good luck with your presentation."

Facing the window once more, Alejandro watches the sun disappear behind Earth's bulk. Home. For the first time in his memory, that word feels real. Tilting his head back, he yearns for raw sunlight to heat his untested skin. Eyes closed, he imagines the Cerebrum particles writhing in twisting concentric circles outward from his own body. With that power, his wish is all but granted. To control his own destiny rather than be carried towards it.

A notification in his implants breaks the spell. The sender's name prompts his eyes to snap open. With the presentation coming up, he'd forgotten his dinner reservation with Dr. Chamorro. It was no small matter to convince the physician to leave Colossi Infiniti again. She remains devoted to the colony, as is her right, and she is entrenched in her own work. He could cancel. The physician would understand. Yet it is her face that he sees last each night when he closes his eyes for sleep, and he would very much like to see that face in person again. Sitting in a comfortable faux leather armchair, he sends a short reply to the physician amending their plans. Dinner in. He needs a distraction from all this preparation. It won't do to dwell on the presentation, after all.

"Luiz."

The android appears with reassuring speed. "Yes, sir?"

"Dr. Chamorro is visiting again this evening. Will you prepare a second plate?"

"Of course, sir. I'll have a stew ready within the hour."

Another notification arrives, and Alejandro straightens. Victoria Bernard wouldn't contact him if it weren't urgent. What could she want? He accepts the call, and Victoria's holograph fills the study. Like so many guardians, she fashions herself in opulent, flowing skins that harken back to the rule of monarchs. He stares blankly at the woman.

"Victoria, to what do I owe the pleasure?"

She smiles demurely, but beneath the façade he detects trepidation. The golden bracelet on her wrist clinks as shaking fingers touch her cheek. "Alejandro, it's simply awful. Kojo's been detained by the Coalition over this mess with Mars."

The floor lurches beneath him. A guardian, arrested? "Surely not. On what grounds?" This is unprecedented. Did Roarke know about it, and if he did, did he hide it from Alejandro intentionally?

Victoria shakes her head tearfully. "No official statement has been released."

"An act of desperation, perhaps." Loyalists to Roarke, undoubtedly. Alejandro turns on his heel, facing the window where all that remains of the Sun is a vermillion disc. Kojo's fate was sealed the moment Terra Nova ousted the Mars depot, but the Coalition can't vilify MS275's guardian. Alejandro runs his palm across his smooth chin. The public grows more sympathetic toward the restoration with each day, but this could sow fresh unrest. More than ever, the orphans require a stable base of power. He turns back to Victoria, who waits with fear in her eyes. "You must be there for the tribunal. The orphans need to see a guardian speak in Kojo's favor."

Her nose wrinkles. "Must I? Guillermo will surely lead the tribunal. How will it look if I support a criminal?"

"I'll deal with Guillermo." The eccentric guardian of Guadalajara enjoys a special closeness with the Coalition's leader, but that's about to change. From the ground floor, the doorbell chimes, and Luiz answers. Marilina. For the second time today, she's slipped his mind. He closes his eyes, forehead knotting with consternation over his own distractibility. To Victoria, he says, "Find out when the tribunal will convene. It is essential that we maintain support for the restoration."

"Of course."

JANUARY 12, 3041 | SÃO PAULO STATION, EARTH'S ORBIT

Seated across a long table made of Brazilian hardwood, Alejandro faces Marilina. For the first time since he's met her, the physician wears something other than the strictly professional skins he's grown used to, opting instead for a set of flowing turquoise skins that taper at her waist.

"You look lovely. Those skins bring out your eyes." Privately, he chides himself once again for forgetting such a commanding woman.

She smiles, loose curls bending with her cheeks. "Thank you. I feel a little overdressed now. I thought we were dining out."

"My mistake. A lot has happened today, and the reservation completely slipped my mind, but that's no excuse. Please allow me to make it up to you."

Marilina shakes her head. "I understand. You must be under so much pressure." He is reminded once again of how uncommonly easy it is to speak freely with her. She reaches across the table and squeezes his hand. "It helps that Luiz is such an incredible cook."

Savory aromatics waft into the room from the kitchen beyond the wall. Alejandro breathes in, the familiar smells comforting. How is it that a man of his standing is suddenly nervous? Under the table, he wipes his palms. "Have you had bobó de camarão before? It's a popular dish here. Traditionally, it contained seafood, but this is obviously vegan."

"I can't wait to try it." Marilina settles comfortably into her seat. "The colony will have livestock, you know. I may live long enough to eat real meat."

"Lucky you." Earth's repopulation could begin within the year, but the physician's shuttle will reach Zomenos long before then. If the crew gains approval to leave. Alejandro would never ask her to stay, but he's not sorry about the present delays. He studies the woman currently in control of the timeline. "Is the admiral still on a leave of absence?"

A frown. "Word gets out quickly, doesn't it? It's only for a week."

"His evaluation is a topic of interest to the Coalition." Alejandro notes the sudden shift in her posture, the idle way she rubs her throat and neck. Placing the admiral on leave was undoubtedly difficult for her. "A week is rather brief for a change of heart, isn't it?"

"He just needs time and space to reevaluate his priorities. It's a gift. It can't be easy with how much pressure he faces. He did the same for me after Quique." The napkin beside her plate crumples under her fist.

"Hopefully, the admiral views it that way."

"I can't control how Jack feels." The physician looks up at him with a frown. Definitely a sore point. The food arrives, a momentary distraction from the sudden tension between them. Alejandro stands and takes the casserole dish from Luiz, serving Marilina himself. He spoons white rice onto her plate beside a creamy stew, then returns to his own seat and does the same. Marilina digs her spoon into the stew and looks up, surprise erasing her earlier disdain. "Is this shaved yuca?"

An impressed smile bends his lips. "You know of yuca?"

"It was a staple where my family came from."

"I didn't think Guadalajara had yuca."

Those dark curls bounce with her headshake. "Not Mexico. Nicaragua." This is new information. He studies the softer arch in her cheekbones, the rounder curve of her nose, the broader taper to her neckline, as she takes her first bite. Yes, her features are rather different from the others on her station. Fuller. He should have seen it before. "This is delicious, Alejandro." They both turn their attention to the stew in silence. Luiz has perfected the spice blend, and it leaves just a hint of sweet coconut lingering on the tongue. Marilina sets her spoon down, her gaze refocusing on him with more of that earlier concern. "What is it about this restoration that drives you?"

Alejandro follows suit and sets his own spoon down. He dabs his napkin to his lips, holding her gaze. "I am eager to see Earth repopulated. To reclaim our planet. To eat meat."

The physician leans in. "The colony offers everything Earth does and more. What is it about that planet specifically that calls to you?"

Memories long buried ripple just beneath the surface, clamoring for release. He closes his eyes and forces them back down. Years of self-discipline taught him not to be so reactionary. Adrenaline courses through his veins, a primal warning to turn away from this path, but he ignores this too. Something about this woman makes him want to answer, and answer truthfully. "I wasn't always a man of good fortune and expensive skins. When I was a boy, I was an orphan." He reopens his eyes. The physician's chin is propped up in both hands, elbows on the table and eyes full of surprise.

"I'm sorry to hear that. I never would have guessed."

Straightening, he smooths the front of his skins. "It's not something I advertise. But I've seen humanity's lowest moments."

"Do you mean The Last War?"

A mirthless smile strains his cheeks. "I'm not so old as that. I'm talking about this, right here, on these stations. Look around. These guardians talk of fairytale lives on faraway planets while they fatten themselves on rich dishes. When I escaped the orphanage, I swore not to buy into the empty promises. I didn't become a guardian for the power. I did it to see these systems of inequity dismantled. To return Earth's orphans to their true home." Speaking the words out loud after so many years of silently repeating the promise to himself feels strange.

"You feel a sense of duty." Marilina reaches forward, taking both of his hands in hers. "What about Terra Nova? You're not afraid of what they can do?"

Alejandro grips her hands tighter. "No. Once I have the Cerebrum particles, no one need fear Terra Nova again." That familiar look of doubt mars her features again. "The Cerebrum particles offer incredible power, Marilina. With them, I can't fail."

"You can't know that. We'll never really be safe with Terra Nova out there."

He shakes his head. "Terra Nova operates through scare tactics and violence, but at their core, they want the same things I do. They will come to heel." Laughter ripples up from his chest. What is he doing discussing terrorists over dinner with a beautiful woman?

"That's enough talk of politics for one night, I believe. Please tell me more about Nicaragua. What happened to it? I've discovered precious little about your home in my predecessor's study."

Marilina sits back in her chair and releases a breath loaded with questions. With her thumb, she traces the outline of the cross she wears always around her neck. She clearly wants to probe this subject deeper, but, surprisingly, she submits to his curiosity. "Nicaragua was dealing with its own challenges long before the wars. My grandparents fled to Mexico. Others went north or south. You may even have a few Nicas on your station." She sighs and smiles, finally meeting his gaze. "I guess I can understand your aversion to guardians."

Power corrupts. Alejandro rubs her knuckles with his thumb. "We're both orphans, then." So alike, the two of them. She may not see it yet, but she will. He raises his glass. "May we make our own futures in a place we can call home."

The physician's skins rustle as she lifts her glass to meet his. "To home."

CHAPTER NINETEEN

GUILLERMO

S PLASH.

Freezing water douses the guardian's eyes, nose, mouth, ears. Guillermo sputters, choking, and strains into a half-upright position. ¡Qué chingados! Collapsing back onto cold steel, he gasps and rolls, shivering, to his left, but something soft on either side of his head restricts his movements.

"Woah. Easy, Nuñez. It's me, Detective Wright."

Blinking, he opens his eyes to a blurred inferno. He scuttles instinctively backwards, pressing deeper into the pillows. Vision sharpens, and the flames split into the scarlet demon eyes of the detective. His racing heart makes him dizzy. "Hijueputa, it's you alright." Diego's head appears to his right. "Ah, mijo. Bien, bien. Where am I? What's going on?"

The xenobot recaps a needle and sets it aside. "Guillermo, thank goodness." He scoots close, green eyes wide and round. "You're at home, in your shop. I think you were drugged with one of your neuromuscular blocking agents. The drawers up here are all open. I can't find Inés. What do you remember?"

Inés.

Images flash through Guillermo's mind: the surgery, his bot's betrayal, the ensuing paralysis. Shaking worse than a hovermoto in a high-speed death wobble, he lurches upright and slumps into Diego's waiting arms. He has to find Inés.

The xenobot's eyes flit to the detective. "I asked you to keep him still."

Wright rolls her eyes, rocks backward on her heels, and stands. "He's not exactly cooperating." She moves away, and Guillermo glimpses the disaster inside his shop. Sidestepping a shattered syringe at his side, she makes an idle circuit of the workbench and lingers before the vivarium. His breath catches. Between its flaking wafers, the translucent chrysalis holds a fully grown clone of Juan hugging his knees. Damn. It's too late for that pinche transplant. Maybe that was Inés's plan all along. The detective says, "Well, Nuñez? There's no sign of a break-in."

A sigh rattles Guillermo's tender ribcage. Rubbing his chest, he answers, "It was Inés. She injected me with that." He points a weak finger at the syringe, laying on the floor in a pool of congealed liquid.

Those green eyes trace a line from Guillermo's fist to the floor. "Inés drugged you? She wouldn't do that."

Guillermo's mouth goes dry. "She was helping me perform a biopsy."

"Some help," the detective mutters from beside the bench.

The xenobot's eyes turn to steel. "Another neural biopsy? Are you *trying* to kill yourself?"

"Sorry to interrupt, but your—pet—is awake." The detective bends at the waist, resting her elbows on the workbench and studying the chrysalis.

Guillermo and Diego turn as the newborn's eyes open.

Diego whips back around. "You didn't. Guillermo, how could you?" His voice quakes with restraint.

"I did what I had to." The guardian tests his legs. Nada tostada. He can barely wiggle his toes, let alone stand. "Help me up, will you?"

Diego obediently wraps both arms around Guillermo's torso and heaves him upright. "Anna, take his feet, please." The detective shoots a withering glare at the xenobot, but, with a lingering gaze at the chrysalis, she straightens and helps carry the guardian into the lift and down to a couch.

"I need to see my bot," Guillermo protests.

In the kitchen, Diego pulls containers out of the fridge and mashes everything into the same bowl. "You need rest." Wright drops onto the other couch across from Guillermo.

"Don't even think about propping those boots on my table, Detective."

"Copy that." With one eyebrow raised, she appraises him. "I'm sorry about your rogue bot, Nuñez, but we need to talk about the reason we're here. We've got Osei."

His eyes widen. In the aftermath of Inés's betrayal, he forgot all about the investigation into MS275's guardian. "You got an arrest warrant?"

"No thanks to you."

Guillermo collapses deeper into the cushions. Another failure, this one of Roarke's making. "I'm sorry about that. I couldn't risk it. Not after Terra Nova released that broadcast."

"A warrant would have exposed the investigation," Wright completes his thought for him. "I know. That doesn't matter anymore. With the vote only a week away—"

"What? One week?" He bolts upright, ignoring the shake in his legs.

Those unnatural eyes narrow. "Eight days, actually." She leans forward, elbows on her knees. "You knew that already, didn't you?"

Headshake. "Last I heard, the date wasn't set."

The detective leans back and studies him with detached curiosity. "What's today's date, Nuñez?"

"December thirtieth? Thirty-first?"

A lopsided smile spreads across her face. "How much tranquilizer did your bot pump into you? It's the thirteenth."

Guillermo runs a shaking hand over his eyes. "Of January? My God, I've been out for two weeks." If Inés hasn't returned on her own, she either can't or won't. He has to locate her and find out what went wrong.

"Appears so." Folding her hands over her belly, Wright settles into the couch. "Right. With the vote only a week away, the sergeant has arranged for Guardian Osei to go on trial the day beforehand. We need you to lead the prosecution."

He laughs weakly. "I don't know the first thing about prosecution."

Shrug. "The fact stands. It has to be you."

There's no denying that. Only another guardian would be taken seriously by a tribunal. No guardian has ever been charged before, let alone for a crime as big as this. Kojo is accused of diverting essential resources for his own purposes, at the expense of every station, así que another member of the Coalition must take the lead.

"I understand. I'll do it."

Diego hands a bowl and a spoon to Guillermo. "Not until you eat." The brown mush smells wonderfully like a burrito bowl, but the first bite sticks to his tongue like wet sand.

"Guácala. The beans are dry."

"That's all I could find." Diego sits on the edge of the table and watches Guillermo take a few more reluctant bites. "We have to find Inés."

"Dale. I'll go with you."

The xenobot stiffens. "You're in no condition for that, and I don't think she wants to see you. Detective Wright and I will look for her."

"Excuse me?" the detective calls from behind him. "Aren't there enough bots running around this place? Detective Wright is going home and taking a real shower." A look from Diego quiets her protests.

Turning back to Guillermo, the xenobot continues. "Whatever you're doing here needs to stop."

Since when does Diego call the shots? "You have no idea what I'm doing."

"Exactly." His first xenobot paces the length of the room, reaches the kitchen, and turns. "You hid this from me, didn't you? You didn't want me to know that you were duplicating Juan because you knew I'd put a stop to it."

"It's too late for that, mijo. Juanito is here."

Brow knotted in desperation, Diego rests his hands on the arms of the couch and leans close. "It's not too late. His programming has only just begun. Tell me you aren't giving him Juan's memories."

"Hard-coded into the power cell." It wasn't strictly necessary, and maybe he shouldn't have done it, but why stop at imitation flesh and bone when he can have the real Juan back?

Arms falling to his sides, Diego steps back and nearly topples the table. "If you do this, you can't go back. Juanito is a person now, and he's walking around with a living human's face. What's he supposed to do when Juan wakes up? What will he say?"

"Done is done. Juan wouldn't lecture me like this. Juanito is just a bot. He'll be fine."

"I can't believe you would say that to me." Diego studies Guillermo. "I don't even recognize you anymore." He turns to the detective. "Let's go find our missing robot, Anna." Diego holds the door open for the detective, shutting it with so much care that Guillermo wishes sourly that the xenobot had just slammed it instead.

JANUARY 13, 3041 | GUADALAJARA STATION, EARTH'S ORBIT

"Screw him." Nonetheless energized by his pathetic meal, Guillermo sits up from the couch. This time, his legs support his weight, if weakly. It doesn't matter what Diego says. Juanito is here, and there's work to do. Despite what Diego thinks, this new xenobot isn't some selfish indulgence. He's the antidote to Terra Nova, and he needs training.

The guardian shuffles into the lift like an abuelo. The doors slide open to Juanito, watching him with the same pensive frown that Juan wore whenever he was working on a new tattoo design. Guillermo's heart booms in his ears, unprepared for the way this xenobot's surprised mouth curves in a perfect mirror to Juan's. The shake in his knees returns. The newborn makes slow work of peeling away from the chrysalis. A thick mixture of clear hemolymph and darker fecal matter (chrysalis caca) oozes over the edges. The guardian snaps on gloves and offers his hand.

Juanito stares at the proffered hand. "You're Guillermo. The inventor."

Grin. "That's right. Take my hand. I'll help you out of there."

The xenobot shakes his head. "I overheard your argument downstairs. You are injured." His eyes screw up in concentration. "Inés. She betrayed you. And later too, Diego walked out on you. Your creations, both of them." His gaze snaps to his creator. "Why have your robots turned on you?"

Deflating, Guillermo perches on the edge of a stool with his hands loosely at his sides. The time for denial and deception is long past. "Because of you."

Whatever Juanito understands of the two robots, this answer visibly surprises him. "Me. How? I haven't done anything yet."

A sigh escapes the guardian's lips. "That doesn't matter. You were built in the image of my partner."

The young xenobot nods. "Juan. Why does this make them angry? Isn't Diego built in your image?"

"Not exactly. My tissue was implanted into Diego after he was built. You were grown directly from Juan's cells. You . . . look just like him."

Juanito grows silent, staring at the viscous fluid pooling inside his vivarium. "If it was wrong, why did you do it? The truth."

Again, Guillermo shrinks. "I missed him, and I was desperate. But I always planned for your build, and you have your own purpose in this world. Your likeness doesn't change that."

"No. I get it now. Diego is angry because you've robbed me of a chance at my own life."

This is ridiculous. How many orphans are still waiting for their chance to live? Guillermo laughs bitterly and offers his hand a second time. "We're getting ahead of ourselves, aren't we? It's your first day of life. We should celebrate. Let's get you washed up. I have so much to share with you, Juanito."

The xenobot tucks his elbows into his sides and shakes his head. "Don't call me that. I don't want anything from you. I don't know who I am yet, but I'm not Juan, and I'm not here for you. Only I can decide who I'll be. I'll escape from this perverse sac on my own and decide how to navigate this curse alone."

"You don't mean that. Let me help you."

"I hate you."

Guillermo's cheeks burn like he's been slapped. He drops his hand and closes his eyes, taking a steadying breath. This xenobot has Juan's face, but he's not Juan. Was all of this a huge mistake? Well, no matter. Terra Nova won't care whose face he has. Juanito—or whatever he wishes to be called—just needs to accept the mission. "Fine. See yourself out of the chrysalis. Try not to damage my tools on your way out of there. I'll be downstairs." He swipes a syringe of liquid gold from a drawer. GLOW will restore him in no time. If he's going to put up with a surly teenage xenobot living in his home, he's going to need his strength.

Hours later, the lift floats down to the ground floor with not-Juanito inside, fully clothed in a set of skins as black as tattoo ink. Guillermo looks up from the dining table, and his lip curls. For a bot so determined to live his own life, not-Juanito can't help but dress just like Juan. The xenobot's head swivels in the direction of the kitchen, nose upturned at the sweet smell warming the house.

"There's pozole on the stove if you're hungry."

The xenobot dips a ladle into the pot and sniffs, then spoons dark red liquid into a bowl and joins Guillermo at the table without making eye contact. He lifts his spoon experimentally to his lips, then shovels three more spoonfuls.

"This is good," he says, gaze focused on his bowl. Pozole rojo is Juan's favorite soup, but Guillermo doesn't say that. The xenobot clears his bowl and sets it aside, and finally looks up. "I'm going by Carlos." Guillermo suppresses the involuntary grunt of disgust that wells up in him. That name doesn't suit the xenobot at all, but he doesn't say so. Carlos continues in a monotone. "I don't like it, but I will always share Juan's face. There are worse problems to have. I may as well serve some purpose in this lifetime. You had ideas for me beyond serving as Juan's substitute. How do we stop Terra Nova?"

Guillermo breaks into a grin. "I thought you'd never ask." He waves his hand, and a hologram materializes. A massive, domed amphitheater rotates between them. "The Hall of Orphans."

Carlos leans close to the hologram, lighting his smooth olive features in a pale glow. "I recognize it. It's reserved for the most serious crimes, isn't it?"

"¡Exactamente! We've got the most serious crime of the space age on our hands. A guardian named Kojo Osei was arrested today in connection with Terra Nova. He abused his authority, diverting shipments to Earth that were supposed to go to the stations. It was confirmed by Intelligence."

Carlos's brow furrows. "If he's already been caught, what do you need me for?"

"Slow down, jefe. The tribunal could dismiss his case. In fact, I'd count on it. Kojo didn't make it to where he is without friends." Guillermo raps the table with his knuckles. "Our priority right now is preparing an airtight prosecution. It's not just about jailing Kojo. If we do this right, we can get him to reveal Commander Monroe's location and name other operatives. Help me prepare, Carlos."

"Yes, of course. This is obviously important work." He scoots closer, pulling Juan's scrumptious curls away from his eyes and tucking them in a bun. Noticing Guillermo's attention, he adds, "This doesn't mean I've forgiven you." Guillermo swallows the hard lump in his throat. The fruit of his labor is nothing like he'd hoped for, nothing like Juan. Juan's likeness dies in those cold, indifferent eyes. Maybe Carlos will never be the man that the guardian loves, but he's still a walking supercomputer, and he owes his life to his creator.

It's better this way, with Carlos hating him. This xenobot will confront the Cerebrum particles very soon, and he might not walk away from that. Guillermo steeples his fingers and stares into the twirling blue hologram. Whatever it takes, Juan.

CHAPTER TWENTY

MARILINA

JANUARY 16, 3041 | COLOSSI INFINITI, EARTH'S ORBIT

WARM WATER SPRAYS SOAP bubbles down the doctor's arms and legs, spiraling down her fingertips and pooling at her feet. She never imagined that she'd one day run two miles every morning before breakfast, but the mandatory schedule for all crewmembers has become a daily ritual. Units will pair up after lunch for payload procedures, but for now, she looks forward to a few hours' reprieve of catching up on prep. Seven minutes in, the water cuts out, and Marilina steps out and towels off.

"Good morning, Keshi." The doctor shields her eyes from the bright sunlight overhead, falling into step beside the lab technician. They pass rows of cubicles, each one occupied by their crewmates. Muffled conversations happen behind a privacy shield of warm light.

Okumu smiles, with radiant white teeth. "Hi, Dr. Chamorro. Excited for this?"

Marilina returns a rueful smile. "Not especially."

Stepping into a cubicle, she loses sight of the others in a papaya-colored blur. A cool breeze flows. Chatter from their crewmates dies, blocked out by the shield. The technician pulls up a shimmering blue holograph of a medication list. With less than seven weeks until shuttle launch, every medication brought onboard must be carefully reviewed and routed to the military for approval. She says, "Vitamin D is missing. These antiemetics need to be updated to match the approved list." Okumu's hands fly through the air, amending the record. "Don't forget to add insulin for our two diabetics."

"Done." Okumu glances sidelong at Marilina as she works. "Are you going to watch the trial?"

The doctor steps to the right, cross-referencing the approved medication list with those of the crew. "Maybe. I'm on leave tomorrow, so it depends how far behind I am when I get back." Dr. Nuñez is obviously displeased that her head physician is taking another leave of absence.

Wearing a conspiratorial smile, Okumu bows her head of dozens of closely wound knots. "That's right. Visiting home?"

Marilina wears a rigid smile. "Something like that." This will be the last time she sees her family now that Pilar and Fatima have decided to join her parents.

"Lucky you! I put in a request to be present for the birth of my goddaughter, but they denied me. Anyway, I hope they lock that guardian up tight. No one can play with our fuel and get away with it."

"Definitely." Marilina idly reminds herself not to get on Okumu's bad side.

They keep at it for the rest of the morning. Again and again, Marilina's thoughts return to her aunts. Their decision is completely unexpected, confusing, and a little insulting. Families of the colonists are eligible for mission Z2, so they could have opted out of the cryo program entirely. They understand the risks perfectly well. The only explanation is that her aunts don't believe she'll succeed. Otherwise, they'd never consent to cryogenic sleep. Instead, Marilina herself will perform the vitrification, and she'll be completely alone afterward. She rubs her cross and sets her jaw.

Alejandro: `Lunch in 15?`

Lips part in surprise. She didn't know the guardian would be on station today. Above his message, her wristband unit reads 1145. Office hours end soon either way. She turns to Okumu. "Alright if I head out now?"

The technician pauses. "You're skipping lunch? It's rocket day." Rocket dogs were on the menu the day the admiral returned to training, and rocket day became an instant tradition.

"I'm meeting someone."

The doctor backs out of the cubicle before Okumu can protest, feeling a twinge of guilt. Rocket day really is quite fun, but she hasn't seen Alejandro in days.

She spots him in the hall just outside the cafeteria. "What are you doing here?"

His messages hint at long days and nights of preparation, but he looks as refreshed as he always does in a set of dark emerald skins cut at sharp angles that highlight his straight jawline and broad shoulders.

That rare smile of his bends his lips. "It's good to see you too." He waves her ahead, and they step into a line where, indeed, rows of steaming rocket dogs wait invitingly. "The Coalition brings me to the Ring quite often." The line inches forward.

Marilina raises an eyebrow, yet she smiles back. "And the vote?"

"I'm polling rather well for a contender as young as I am."

"No one is as young as they appear."

"That's hurtful." She doesn't answer, so he adds, "I'm only forty. Don't look so relieved."

The doctor whirls away, staring unseeingly at the rocket dogs in front of her. She *is* relieved. Some guardians are well into their eighties and nineties, and with GLOW, age loses its meaning.

Stepping up to the counter, she places her order, this time feeling bold enough to try the firedog that has her crewmates so impressed. Behind her, Alejandro orders a spaceduster with hot sauce. They make their way to a corner table, tucked under a low steel beam and a high portal window facing an open galaxy. She takes a bite of vegan sausage, dripping chipotle sauce on her tray.

Alejandro follows suit, watching her as he digs into his dog. "You're worried, aren't you?"

She pauses and wipes her mouth. Clearly, he can tell that she's avoiding bringing up her aunts. "No, I'm just confused. Frustrated, even. Why didn't they ask me?"

He lowers his dog. "They would have done it, anyway. The difficulty is in accepting the decision, I think." He studies her over a bun topped with chopped onion. "I can come with you if you'd like to help with the vitrification. You shouldn't have to do this alone."

"Thank you. I'd really like that." She blinks tears out of the corners of her eyes. Why is she crying?

The guardian reaches across with his own untouched napkin and dabs her cheek below the temple. "Careful—you don't want serrano in your eyes."

She grips his wrist. "Are you sure about this? The vote . . ."

"I'm sure." He withdraws his hand and cocks his head. "You know that you aren't alone in this, don't you? Call me anytime."

Marilina settles back in the stiff metal chair. "Well, yes. For a few more weeks, at least. What then, Alejandro?" They've never talked about this. A future. She exhales carefully, heart railing against the walls of her chest.

He leans forward and smiles. "I have an idea. A method to use on your ship, the colony, anywhere. That way we can be together even while we're apart."

Her laugh is light and airy. "Don't be ridiculous. Implants, holographs—they all have their limits. Once I board that shuttle, you won't see me outside of recorded messages and quarterly calls. If you still want to, that is."

"Of course I do. Isn't it obvious how much I care about you, Marilina?" The expression he wears is unusually severe. "Leaping exists, doesn't it? We can't know the bounds of such technology without testing them. It's a matter of ingenuity and courage. That's what the Cerebrum particles can do. For me. For you."

Marilina blinks and bites her lip. "Maybe, but it would be a fuel sink."

"Let me worry about that. Trust that when the time comes, you'll know how to contact me."

JANUARY 17, 3041 | GUADALAJARA STATION, EARTH'S ORBIT

Closing time nears. A woman wearing colorfully striped skins pushes roughly past Marilina in search of whatever last-minute item is missing from her pantry, muttering a hasty apology. Enthusiasm for the coming vote has gone a long way to ease the tension in her fellow station-dwellers, but rations are still restricted. Marilina bows her head, focusing on the basket of plantains one aisle to her left. Gladly paying for her produce, she escapes the cramped market out onto cobbled stone pavement. Passing the cathedral, she turns into a plaza beneath a pair of old Gothic spires. The solitude is welcome, even if splintered by guilt.

A band of children circles behind the cathedral to where the old sandpits still stand. Marilina gasps, swallowing back a painful lump in her throat. When she and her brother were children, they used to play there before Mass. The doctor sits on her feet and leans her back against cool stone, taking calming breaths and running her thumb along her mother's cross. Once, she kicked sand into Quique's eyes and sent him howling. Papi was stern with her. She must learn discipline, he said. Her brother had been allowed to remain a child, but Marilina had prepared to lead the family. Now, Mami, Papi, and Quique are all gone, and Fatima and Pilar will follow soon. Was it ever worth it? Her eyes squeeze shut.

Laughter pulls her back to the present. Two children take turns on the swings. The rocking reminds her of the Coalition recordings of the oceans of Zomenos: huge rippling bodies of untamed violet water that splash onto beaches with a ferocity unlike anything she's ever seen. The doctor relaxes against stiff, unyielding stone. Yes, it will be worth it. Quique was lost to her the day her childhood ended, but duty led her to Alejandro and the colony. While the sun sets over the station, she imagines water tickling her bare feet.

"I'm back," Marilina calls as she steps inside. A bouquet of roses sits on the table beside the door. It wasn't there when she left. "Sorry I took so long. I stopped by the—oh."

In the living room, Alejandro is deep in conversation with a flushed Fatima. He turns, locking eyes with Marilina and smiling. Her heart jolts. The bag of groceries falls to the floor beside her, and a single brown yuca rolls two feet away and sways back and forth.

Alejandro crosses the short distance between them. He stoops, retrieves the yuca, and returns it to the bag at her feet.

"You're early," she says.

"I wouldn't miss it." He bends and kisses her cheek lightly. A surge of warmth swims through her.

Fatima plods to Marilina's side and plants her hands on her hips. "Don't just stand there, mija. Ven, both of you, come inside! Mi papi built this house himself, Guardian Martinho. It's just like our casa on Earth, in Nicaragua."

Marilina touches her aunt's shoulder gently. "Tía, Alejandro is used to much better than we are."

"Don't be ridiculous," Fatima says, chest swelling.

The guardian's lip curls. "It's a charming home, mi cariño."

Her aunt beams. "You speak Spanish?" She rounds on Marilina. "You didn't tell me he speaks Spanish."

"São Paulo took in many refugees during the Last Winter, the same as Guadalajara. Many of us speak fluent Spanish and Portuguese."

The three of them enter the kitchen, where Pilar is preparing dinner. Marilina sets the bag of groceries on the counter, and Pilar immediately sets to peeling and chopping vegetables. Two more bouquets wait on the dining table, filled with vibrant freshly cut white flowers accented in yellow. Stunned, Marilina approaches the table and stiffly picks up the bouquet. An island breeze wafts from its petals. She whirls around and looks up at Alejandro.

"Sacuanjoche. My favorite." Behind Alejandro, Fatima grins devilishly. Marilina closes her eyes and nods to herself. "You told him."

"I appealed to your aunt for suggestions," he amends, setting the bouquet on the table again and taking her hands. Pilar finishes piling yuca into a deep pot, then wipes her hands on a rag and carries a stack of bowls to the small, round dining table. Alejandro steps forward, lifts the heavy pot from Pilar's trembling hands, and sets it gently on the stove.

Overwhelmed, Fatima rushes forward and cups the guardian's cheeks in her hands, pulling his face low. "Thank you, thank you, *thank you*, for finding our girl. We were worried we were leaving her too soon, but she's different with you in her life."

Marilina tucks her arms behind her back and averts her gaze. This might be her aunts' last opportunity to embarrass her before the future leader of the Coalition and the man she can't stop thinking about.

"Trust me when I say that it is she who has found me." He listens raptly to Fatima's stories about Nicaragua and the Guadalajara station while the stew simmers. "I look forward to seeing the cryo gardens. My station's cryo program is nothing like the famous Guadalajara gardens."

"The orphan race's heroes all rest in our gardens," Fatima proclaims, beaming.

Pilar carries the pot into the dining room and rolls her eyes. "Yes vieja, but these days the gardens are bloated with the underprivileged. It's rare for any of us to be assigned to a trade half as prestigious as the Meridian. But you two are changing all of that. We're both so proud of you." She makes a shooing gesture with her hands, ushering them all to the dinner table. "Go on, eat!"

"It's a shame that Nuñez has done so little to change things," Alejandro remarks as he dips a ladle into the pot. "I thought he promised to end the cryo program when he joined the Coalition."

"Guardian Nuñez faced many setbacks, but no one wants the cryo gardens emptied more than he does." Pilar counters.

Alejandro bows his head. "We all do. When I take the lead, we won't have any further need of the gardens."

After dinner, Marilina walks the familiar path to where Mami and Papi lie dormant. How many times has she visited this place, whispering promises of a future where they're all together? She shivers in the cold air and takes a deep breath. At her side, Alejandro's head turns constantly. Her aunts lag behind, whispering quietly to each other.

Fatima stops at Mami's pod. "We kept our promise, Luisa," she whispers, crouching beside the pod and pressing one hand to the viewing pane. A lovely vine cups the base of the pod, far from what little light breaks through the shrouded glass overhead. "Little Mari is ready. She doesn't need us anymore. We've come to join you." Marilina crouches beside Fatima and puts her arm around her aunt's shoulders. Pilar joins them, and they sit in silence.

Usually, an escort would accompany her aunts to their pods, but Alejandro's Coalition credentials buy their privacy. Instead, Marilina leads the company to their resting place, parallel to those of Marilina's parents. Gently, she wipes dirt away with a rag and opens the pods with her wristband unit. Fatima exchanges a look with her youngest sister.

"Don't you dare let them separate us," Fatima admonishes her.

"Separate us?" Pilar laughs, eyes shining. "I wouldn't force poor Mari to deal with you all by herself, viejita."

Marilina helps Fatima into her pod. Across from her, Alejandro offers his hand to Pilar. Lying comfortably on her back, Fatima grips Marilina's hand. "Don't worry about us," she chides. "We've waited for this day for a long time. Just focus on your work, and we'll all be together again soon."

An urge soars through Marilina to throw her arms around Fatima's neck and tell her just how much she means to her. In so many ways, the squat older woman is the mother she never had. The one whose bed she crawled into at night after Mami went into cryo. The one who saved the last piece of tres leches for her on Nochebuena. The one who screamed with pride from the front row of the Meridian ceremony. Marilina grips the rim of the pod tight, but only nods.

"Rest well," she answers softly.

She reaches into her bag and retrieves a syringe. With practiced hands, she injects anesthetic into Fatima's left arm. Alejandro does the same for Pilar. Once Fatima's eyes start drooping, Marilina inserts a breathing tube down her aunt's airway. She is grateful that her hands remain steady throughout the vitrification. Standing, she watches the lids seal. Alejandro takes her hand as the pods fill with the ice-cold liquid preservative.

"That was brave of you."

"I don't feel brave."

Alejandro steps closer. "It would have been hard for anyone."

"Thank you," she whispers. "It was a lot easier with you here."

He runs a hand through her short curls. "I'll always be here. You should know that."

She swallows. "I do." It's strange to hear such tender words spoken to her. She's never imagined caring for someone this way, never cared for anyone besides family. Ever since that day in the sandpit, duty has consumed her life, but Alejandro has never asked anything of her. Instinctively, she reaches up and tugs his shirtskins. He bends forward, and unspoken emotion pours into their kiss.

"Allow me to take us somewhere private," he suggests, his voice nearly a whisper. The chilled gardens are replaced by her empty bedroom. They sink onto her bed. Alejandro reaches for the zipper at the back of Marilina's neck. "May I?"

She sits up as his mouth covers hers. "Never alone?"

He pauses. His dark eyes penetrate hers with the intensity of the ocean itself. Again, the image of the Zomenian shoreline resurfaces in Marilina's mind.

"Never."

CHAPTER TWENTY ONE

JACK

Now this is more like it.

The admiral kicks his boots up onto an empty steel auditorium chair in front of him and burrows his head into his jacket, folded underneath him. Orbs light the room in cool colors. Beside him, Lucy wears an eager smile. He downs his first lager with a smack of his lips, then cranes his neck. Fanning out behind them, the rest of the crew sticks mostly to their units. Bonds don't form overnight, not in a crew of this size, but four months aboard a shuttle ought to change that.

An enormous holo swallows the central platform of the auditorium, and a hush falls over the crew. The Hall of Orphans. The projection flickers, and a hooded figure steps up to a bench. This must be the judge tasked with sentencing Kojo Osei. Behind Jack, someone whistles.

"To the Coalition," the judge intones in an artificially scrambled voice, neither male nor female. Tiered stands behind the judge fill with the holographic projections of the members of the tribunal, randomly selected orphans from every station in Earth's orbit. Holos inside a holo. Jack scratches his head and chugs another beer while he chews on that concept. Looking like a cornered rat, Guardian Osei shuffles into the room, escorted by two military officers. The auditorium quivers with the crew's anticipation. After his own turn under the Coalition's microscope, the admiral doesn't envy the guardian.

Guillermo appears, hair swept to one side, his shining blue holoform swaggering across the platform. He calls Ezekiel Grainger as his first witness, an MS275 miner that testifies to the extracurricular activities of his guardian's men. His statement does well with the tribunal. Osei stares mutely ahead, hands clenched into fists.

Lucy leans close, smelling like daisies. "This is good. Osei is under pressure. We might get some answers today." Jack's grip on his lager tightens, but he only nods. His uncle shot him a message before it all began, giving the admiral a heads-up about his plans to wring Dad's location out of the guardian during the trial. Do they really have enough to get him to take a plea deal? After all this time, it feels like a long shot.

"How does the defense respond?"

"Thank you, Your Honor. The defense calls Guardian Bernard." A woman takes the stand, festooned in sweeping sapphire skins and a heavily powdered nose.

Jack leans to his right and mutters into Lucy's ear. "Do you know her?"

Setting her beer on the ground, she turns her head and checks on the crew discreetly. "Yes. She guards the Marseille station. Don't underestimate her." He leans back and rests his chin on his knuckles. This better not take the pressure off. Osei needs to take that plea deal.

Bernard settles onto the stiff witness bench and adjusts her skirtskins, a lioness observing her kingdom. She smiles adoringly at the tribunal. "My dear, sweet orphans," she purrs. "I assure you that Kojo is a fine guardian. Whatever the cause of these aberrations in the reports, he is above blame. Please don't be frightened by the words of a simple miner. The miners of MS275 are well-known, low-class criminals." She goes on like this for a while, but her testimony doesn't hit its mark. Whispered objections rise in the stands until several members of the tribunal stand and boo her off the bench.

"How do you like that? Selfish guardian." Turning his head, Jack glimpses his younger brother's hands cupped around his mouth. Henry catches his eye and grimaces. "Oh, no offense, Lucy." Lucy only smiles, all armor, and returns her attention to the trial.

Guillermo calls his next witness. "Kirk Dawson, you're a tough man to track down. Dígame, what is an MS275 miner doing running a distillery on the beaches of the Mumbai station?"

Dawson looks worse than Osei. Hair standing in three different directions, he's twitchy, spooked, and checking the exits like he's the one on trial. "I retired," he answers lamely. "Got my sentence on MS275 reduced for good behavior and wanted to make something of myself. Don't got family to go back to. Mumbai seemed as good a place as any to start over."

"Tell us about that good behavior, Kirk."

The miner stares at the floor, his gears cranking audibly. "Worked hard, that's all."

"On what, Kirk?"

Dawson swallows and scratches his arm, rocking back and forth. "Guardian wanted more wellhead gas. I helped get it." He scratches harder.

"More wellhead gas," Guillermo thunders. "Oh. You're referring to Osei's response to reports of declining methane exports. He needed to boost his supply. The stations were counting on that fuel."

"No, sir." The miner's arm is bleeding, but he can't seem to stop. "This was before that. Exports were through the roof. We just needed more. For Earth." Murmuring breaks out among the tribunal again. The admiral glances at Lucy, the hand holding his lager sweating. This is it: Guillermo's chance to seal the deal.

The judge stands and spreads their gloved hands across the bench. "Thank you. The court will adjourn while the tribunal deliberates. We will resume with the casting of the vote in one hour."

"Send that crook to prison!"

Confused, Jack hops up and stretches his legs while the rest of the crew lines up for another round. The keg is soon tapped. He's not sure how to feel. The evidence against Osei is pretty damning, so he'll probably go away for a long time, but the prosecution accomplished little else. Osei didn't give up anything, let alone Dad's location.

A message from Roarke comes through his implants. `Meet in room 076 in 10. Top Secret.` The admiral stares at it for a long minute. Is this a joke? Coalition officers aren't cleared for Top Secret meetings. That kind of thing is reserved for guardians and Frank Roarke himself, but the message came directly from him. Jack returns to his seat and grabs his jacket.

"Something's come up. Gotta go."

Lucy's head whips around. "You're leaving now? The tribunal is about to make its decision."

"Let me know how it goes." He kisses the top of her head and shrugs Dad's bomber jacket over his skins, making his exit as quickly as he can without drawing the attention of his crew. Luckily, they're all pretty buzzed and placing bets on the sentencing. Outside, he takes the steps back up to the main lobby two at a time and rides a lift down to 0. Reinforced glass gives a 360° view of the solar system and a staggering up-close lens of the moon. The admiral trains his eyes on his boots. Dad's still out there somewhere, captive to Terra Nova. Did they miss their shot at finding him?

Room seventy six is small, crowded, and noticeably dimmer. Jack takes in the motley crew: Frank Roarke, Guillermo, Sergeant Arquette, Red Eyes, Diego, and a stranger. A little underwhelming for a Top Secret meeting. In just three steps, he crosses the room.

"What is this, a meeting of the vampires?" It's warm in here, so he tosses his coat on the back of an empty chair. "Hey there, nice to meet you. Admiral Monroe." He holds his hand out to the stranger, but freezes. Juan? But that's impossible. The admiral shoots a questioning look toward Guillermo, who doesn't meet his gaze.

The stranger steps closer and takes his hand in a firm handshake. "Carlos." Jack relaxes into one of his easy smiles. He's had one too many lagers if he's seeing Juan's face in the shadows.

"Thanks for coming, Jack." Roarke steps into the light and—yowza!—the coming vote is seriously straining him. The Coalition leader looks like he's missed a few GLOW injections, the skin on his face sallow and hanging on like debris in a slipstream. The admiral hates what Terra Nova has reduced his leader to. If Alejandro Martinho wins that vote, he's screwed. "You watched the trial?" A nod. "That'll make this faster, then. As you may have guessed, what was released to the public was heavily redacted."

Jack crosses his arms and arches his back. "Fill me in, then."

Guillermo clears his throat. "I promised you Derek's location. Jack, we got it."

Arms fall to the admiral's sides as his jaw bottoms out. "You're kidding." His uncle shakes his head, a slow, tired grin touching his lips. Jack closes his eyes and laughs. "You're the man, Guillermo!" No one else is smiling. He cocks his head. "What's wrong?"

"There are complications, Admiral." Detective Wright steps forward as Guillermo falls back, like a well-choreographed offensive maneuver. She opens her fist, and a holo appears beside her. "This is footage from VLT60."

Jack squares his feet and leans in. "The black ship at Dad's last known location? I thought the flight recorder was damaged."

Guillermo shakes his head. "Wiped, it turns out. Kojo turned over the unedited footage in exchange for a reduced sentence. Just watch."

The admiral falls silent as a *third* orbiter appears on the scene. Squinting, he can just make out the pilot. "Can you zoom in?" Wright freezes the frame on the incoming ship. The pixelated footage re-samples automatically, and the features of the pilot sharpen. Jack crosses his arms. "That's just a kid."

The detective nods. "Look at her eyes."

Bending at the waist, the admiral notices now that the girl's irises are streaked in purple, like two orchids. He shoots a harsh look at Red Eyes.

"Friend of yours?"

She glares back, her own eyes glowing like two taillights in the dim room. "There's no club membership for bionic eyes."

The sergeant steps between them. "Enough, Anna. Admiral Monroe, we've run this child's image through every database we have. There's no record of her."

An impatient snort. "You checked medical? Those implants would be registered."

"Yes," Sergeant Arquette growls in his low register. "Her procedure was off the record." The admiral raises his eyebrows. This girl's parents must be either desperate or stupid to sign off on an unlicensed surgery. He rubs his face. How are they going to find Dad when they can't even identify this child?

"Keep watching," Red Eyes prompts. "There's more." The footage resumes. A probe deploys from the girl's ship, winding its way into the wreckage. Jack sucks in his breath. There he is—Dad (alive!)—his outer skinsuit still intact, but unconscious. Raking his fingers through his hair, the admiral watches the probe collect Commander Monroe unceremoniously from the wreckage and return to its ship. The orbiter whirls around, arcs around the planet, and is swallowed up by a wormhole.

The same wormhole the colonists are taking to Zomenos.

Silence falls as the holo cuts out. Roarke steps forward once again, and the intelligence officers fall back. "Her orbiter never returned. Admiral Monroe, we believe this child is operating independently of the Coalition and Terra Nova. The colony must be her destination."

Fist clenched at his side, Jack keeps his voice level. "That doesn't make a lick of sense, Frank."

"None of this does, but she has nowhere else to go. Zomenos is the only planet in that system that can support human life. Your father is there, Jack, and you're headed right for him." Roarke opens a new holo displaying a flight readiness report for the *Rebirth*. The admiral stares at the dizzyingly long list of columns, all marked green: flight path safety, range safety, licensing, security, ground support, even payload review. He looks up at Roarke.

"You cleared mission Z1 for launch."

The Coalition leader nods. "The only step that remains is to notify the crew."

Jack steps back and runs his hands through his hair. This is insane. His navigators prepared a flight plan for six weeks from now, not today. The civilians think they have another month before they say their goodbyes to friends and family. How can he tell them all to pack up their lives and board the next ship out of the solar system tonight?

But Dad might be there. The pit of his stomach hollows out. It's a big "might." They're chasing an unidentified minor flying a stolen ship to an alien planet. The commander might not even be there when the *Rebirth* lands. Yet Jack's been waiting for this evidence for over a month, been asking for a chance to do something. He can't turn away. Not now. Dad needs him.

"Okay. Let's do this."

JANUARY 20, 3041 | COLOSSI INFINITI, EARTH'S ORBIT

Roarke makes the announcement himself, sparing the admiral from the anger of the colonists with his usual stoicism. For once, Jack is appreciative. A mutinous crew would have been hell to contend with for the next four months. Staring up at the ship that will finally bring him home, his heart sputters faster. His whole life has led to this day. The long years in training. The trivial assignments out to Enceladus and Mars. The pinning of the fourth star to his lapel. Just so that one day, he would earn the honor of leading the first mission to the colony, the home he dreamed of so often but had never known. This is his legacy.

"She's a beauty, isn't she?"

Turning, the admiral salutes an approaching officer. "Come to admire your work, Chandra?" The Coalition's top engineer joins his commanding officer and peers up at the starship. "That's the weirdest-looking shuttle I've ever seen." Where most orbiters and single-crew shuttles are sleek, lightweight, ivory discs that slip in and out of light speed with ease, the *Rebirth* is an inky black arrowhead.

Chandra nods. "It was a challenge. A human payload of eighty-five crewmembers and their associated provisions. The *Rebirth* will probably remain a one-off." He glances sideways at Jack. "None of us expected to depart in the shadow of the Sun."

"Neither did I," the admiral responds truthfully. He hasn't briefed his officers on the real reason behind the accelerated launch, and he doesn't intend to until they're well on their way. This zippy departure gives them an advantage over Terra Nova, and he won't risk that. He pats Chandra on the back, which the officer obviously dislikes. "Glad to have you aboard."

Excited chatter buzzes loudly. The men turn. A group of people heads their way. Jack glances at Chandra. "My uncle will be in that group. I should say my goodbyes."

Chandra bows from the waist. "See you onboard, Admiral."

The metal platform rings with every thud of his boots as Jack hurries into the crowd. There isn't much time. The ground technicians are already running launch procedures. He spots Guillermo, saying his farewells to Gabriella and Henry. The youngest of the Monroes looks sharp in the olive-green skins of the ag unit.

"You look good, Henry," Jack observes.

Henry's eyes brighten, his chest swelling. "You're not the only one who can pull off the officer look."

"Derek will be so proud to see you both like this," Guillermo says. Voice cracking, he covers his mouth with his fist. Jack winces at his uncle's slip, but the others don't notice.

"Come here," Henry says. He swats Guillermo's fist away and hugs his uncle.

"Your father would have loved to command this ship," Gabriella says quietly, "but I always knew it would be you, Jack."

The admiral looks up at the *Rebirth*. His stepmom doesn't know about Dad yet, but there's no time to bring her or Henry up to speed. "I hope I can do him justice." He puts his arm around Guillermo and speaks low and fast. "Are you going to be okay here? The Coalition is going to change if the vote goes Martinho's way."

"I'll be fine. I've been dancing the tango with the Coalition a lot longer than you." Guillermo winks. "I'm older than I look, mijo, and wiser."

Jack grins. "At least one of those things is true." His smile fades. "Just be careful, okay? I don't like the look in that detective's eyes, like she can smell blood in the water."

Guillermo pulls him into a bear hug. "I'll be careful. Just bring Derek home."

It's time. The admiral signals his officers and climbs through the main hatch, stumbling to a halt inside. He's floored. No amount of time in the flight simulator could prepare his civilian crewmembers for this. Lighting from a domed ceiling casts a warm glow over the flight deck. Floor lights lead straight to the tip of the arrowhead. Encased in thick windows, a centralized cockpit promises an incredible view. Behind the officers, the other passengers shuffle forward, seeking their designated seats.

In short order, the airlock is sealed off. The crew fastens their harnesses while Jack speaks with Mission Control. "Copy that, Colossi Infiniti. Beginning launch sequence now. Take-off in nine minutes." The admiral pushes a series of buttons on the panel before him, and two large holos project his face to the entire crew. It's beyond weird to see his own face magnified like that. "Welcome, everyone." The hair on his arms tingles with anticipation. "Shuttle launch is in just eight minutes. Take the time now to review your harnesses." He pauses and scans the system report for malfunction alarms, then looks up. "This is my first time flying with civilians." He flashes a winning smile. "Relax. I think you'll enjoy the ride." A smattering of applause answers.

Sealed off from the rest of Colossi Infiniti, the engines roar to life. Beneath the shuttle, the hangar floor parts and the bottom of the ellipsoid structure of the military station peels away, revealing a limitless universe. The restraints supporting the shuttle are released, and it sways. Jack imagines Lucy's eyes wide with her first spaceflight. The rocket boosters ignite, and the whole starship shudders.

All at once, they shoot forth into the stars. The admiral maneuvers the ship into a roll, then pitches upside down. Audible gasps reach his ears from beyond his helmet. The rocket boosters are released, freeing the *Rebirth* for its flight out of its home system. He grins and settles comfortably into his seat. Nothing beats flying through space.

We're coming for you, Dad.

CHAPTER TWENTY TWO

ANNA

JANUARY 21, 3041 | MONTRÉAL STATION, EARTH'S ORBIT

THE COALITION CRUISER GLIDES to a stop outside the detective's flat, and Anna's boots sink into fresh snow. The door clicks shut behind her, but she doesn't follow Diego up to the flat. Not yet. Leaning against the slick white door, the detective pulls a fresh jimmy out of her lucky pack. She's been saving this one for the right time. The Coalition went up against Terra Nova and won. Strike, light, inhale. Mmmm. Feels good.

Upstairs, she's immediately wrong-footed.

The front door creaks open to tinny, hollow singing. Worse, the living room is . . . spotless. Gone are the open bottles of rye whisky on the living room table, the half-filled ashtrays, the piles of skins on the floor—wait, where are her skins, then? Anna trudges past the stumpy robot called Inés and into her room, flinging open the top drawer of her dresser. Sure enough, her skins are sorted and folded inside. She rips the top pair out and huffs.

They're clean.

The robot washed and folded her skins.

Fantastic. Anna rescued one lost little robot from the streets and became its lord and savior. The detective lets out a breath and strides through the doorway. Inés waits across the room, hovering anxiously just outside the kitchen.

"Is everything okay, Detective Wright? I tried my best to follow your system, but it was really hard. Espero que todo esté bien."

A bark of laughter. "Thank you, Inés, but I don't have a system." Anna unzips her skins and tosses them in the corner of the room, noting a disapproving glower coming from the robot. What does she have to do to get this bot to stop cleaning up after her?

Inés wrestles with some internal indecision, then whirls around and returns to the kitchen. "Diego, will you help set the table?" Frowning, the detective follows. Aromas of warm ham and cheese waft toward her, making her mouth water. Something crackles on the stove, so she pokes her head in. Inés tops a pair of sandwiches with fried eggs. Still playing nanny, then.

Stomach rumbling, Anna follows Diego and Inés, still trilling and singing something in Spanish, to the dining table she never eats at. Diego cuts into his sandwich, and runny yolk dribbles down the sides. Something white and creamy oozes out.

She can't stand it anymore. "What's all this?"

"Croque madame," Inés warbles, her robotic eyes widening and constricting rather distractingly.

"And what is that?"

The bot deflates. Glancing uncertainly in Diego's direction for support, she says, "It's French. I researched your station. I read that it's very popular here, isn't it?"

"Ah." Anna tilts her head back. "Inés, my parents are from Baltimore. The USA. Montreal is just where I rest my bones at night."

The robot absorbs this information with rapidly spiraling eyes. "Oh. Well, do you like it?"

"I do." Diego wipes yolk from his chin and wags his fork. "Try it, Anna. It's really good."

Relenting, the detective slices into the monstrous sandwich and crunches into warm toast. Inside, egg meets creamy, salty, ham and cheese. It's quite possibly the most decadent thing she's ever eaten.

After dinner, she nudges Diego between the ribs. "We need to talk." The xenobot stirs from a food coma and follows her into her bedroom. She closes the door and turns to him, arms crossed. "It's been a week. It's time for Inés to go home."

He laughs. "Why? Is her ham and cheese too rich for you?"

Anna glares at him. "It is, but that's not the reason. You know what is."

His smile slides off his face. "She doesn't want to go, and neither do I."

"Come on. If this boring domestic dispute wasn't consuming your attention, you'd wonder what Osei thought was worth risking everything for. Who was he working for? Whoever it is, their hold on him is powerful enough to keep him from ratting. Nuñez is holding more cards than he showed us today. Aren't you curious what else he knows about Terra Nova?"

"No."

Storming across the room, the detective lifts the mattress halfway into the air, but thinks better of flipping it. She turns and glares at the xenobot instead. "This isn't a halfway house for robots with grudges against their makers. Inés doesn't belong here. I'm tired of her cooking and cleaning and singing. You and I still have work to do." The door creaks open, and two glowing yellow eyes peek inside, round and sad.

"You don't like my singing?"

Diego falls to his knees and scoops up the half-pint. "I love your singing, Inés." Back on his feet, he turns a cold look on Anna. "We'll go. Sorry that a little gratitude ruined your bleak existence."

Great, there goes her xenobot. Anna has no use for Inés, but she can't let Diego walk out of her life. Even with amnesia, his processing power is unmatched. And he's grown on her, a little. Eyes rolling back into her head, the detective groans. "I don't mean that. The sandwich was really good, Inés. Thank you." She meets Diego's dubious gaze. Merciful Lord, he's not letting her off that easy. She takes a steadying breath and continues. "And your singing is fine. Look, I know you both want an apology from Nuñez more than anything." The xenobot's abruptly shifty demeanor proves that she's struck on the truth here. She seizes it. "You won't get it by hanging around my flat. If you want him to treat you right, you're going to have to demand it from him."

Diego sets Inés down and sits on the edge of the sagging bed. "It's not just about me or Inés. Did you see the way Carlos looked at us during the trial?" Hard to forget. The other xenobot is cold, calculating, and cynical—the opposite of these two knuckleheads. "Something's not right about him, but Guillermo is so consumed by his own machinations that he's blind to it."

Anna joins Diego on the bed. "Fair enough. Let's take off his blinders, then."

JANUARY 21, 3041 | GUADALAJARA STATION, EARTH'S ORBIT

"Remember," the detective says as she approaches the guardian of Guadalajara's estate with two surly robots in tow, "this isn't about Carlos. It's about opening Nuñez's eyes to the truth." Diego doesn't answer. Stepping up to the front door, she bangs until it opens.

Trap music blasts the porch. Anna and Diego slap their hands over their ears in unison.

"Turn it down!" the detective shouts, unsure whether the guardian can even hear her.

Nuñez turns his head and yells something inside, and the volume cuts in half. His smile is bitter. "Sorry about Carlos. I don't think he even likes it all that much, to be honest. He just does it to piss me off." Honeyed eyes fall on the squat robot between Anna and Diego. "Inés!" He drops to the ground and hugs her. "I was so worried about you. Thank you, Detective."

"She's all yours," Anna mutters, but the uncharacteristically dangerous look in Diego's green eyes silences her.

The guardian only has eyes for Inés. "What happened? One minute, you were helping me perform the biopsy, and the next you attacked!" He spins her around, inspecting her paneling with narrowed eyes. "Was it Terra Nova?"

"No. I injected you all on my own."

He stills. "I was out cold for two weeks, Inés. If it weren't for Diego, I would've died." Not Anna, she notices irritably. Crouching low, Nuñez studies his bot with fresh suspicion. "Or was that the point?"

"I didn't mean to hurt you, Papá!" The robot makes a curious, wiping motion across her faceplate, like a bashful child caught in trouble. This guardian builds the most interesting toys. "I only meant to stop you."

"Well, you succeeded." He glares at his bot. "Why did you do it?"

For all the trouble she's caused, Inés still gazes up at her creator with nothing but repentant adoration in her big yellow eyes. "I did it for Juan. He wouldn't want this."

A shallow sigh wells up from the guardian like a wounded beast. "He wouldn't want me dead, either."

While Anna's happy the pair are making amends and that Inés can go home instead of annoying her with French sandwiches and Spanish lyrics, that's not why she's here. "Why don't we take this inside? I have questions for you and the new bot."

Nuñez searches Diego's eyes urgently, no doubt looking for forgiveness. He nods. Inside, the music still blares, but the volume is at a tolerable level. The upside is that this house smells nothing like the barrage of cleaning products they left behind at the flat. The detective scans the lower level, but the Carlos bot is nowhere to be seen.

"Where is he, then?"

With a shrug, the guardian drops onto the couch against the far wall. "Upstairs. Says he won't live down here with me."

"He's taken over the shop?" Diego interrupts, alarmed. "That's a little disrespectful, isn't it?" He doesn't wait for Nuñez to answer, crossing the room and boarding the lift and beckoning Anna like some dog. Vexed, but curious, she follows. A giant privacy shield blurs their view of most of the shop. Four large speakers point at the downstairs lounge. She now sees where the loud music is coming from. Striding across the shop, she hacks into the sound system using a trick Diego taught her. The music cuts out.

"What the hell?" The privacy shield separating Carlos's "room" from the rest of the shop dissolves, and Carlos bumps right into Diego as he strides out. The two xenobots spring back and circle each other, Diego studying the young new bot with the concern of a schoolteacher, Carlos prowling like an apex predator searching for weakness. Diego must be worthy, because Carlos straightens and offers his hand like a civilized human. "Hi. We met yesterday."

"Diego." Catching a glimpse inside the bedroom, Diego peers with wide eyes. "What's all this?" Wall-to-wall holos portray Earth, the broadcast from Terra Nova, profiles of several suspected operatives and every guardian, and reams of information on Alejandro Martinho.

The shield seals. "My room, my business. Can I help you with something?"

Diego won't let it go. "You're training to take on Alejandro Martinho, aren't you?"

Anna perks up. "The soon-to-be new leader of the Coalition? That's bold."

"Boldness is a thing of humans," Carlos replies indifferently. "I have work to do. Excuse me."

"Wait." Diego grips his arm. "Are you feeling alright?"

Carlos pulls away. "I try my best not to feel anything." He stalks back into his room, the privacy shield sealing behind him.

"So, that's Carlos," Nuñez declares with false cheeriness as Diego and Anna step out of the lift. "Es un gran pesado, don't you think?" Inés passes out glasses of water.

Diego answers, "I think his chip is faulty. Your latest xenobot feels no emotions."

"Ah, that's where you're wrong, young one." Nuñez waves his glass at Diego, sloshing water. "Carlos is *so* emotional that he must play the part of the robot just to survive. Don't let him fool you. He cares more than any of us."

Dryly, Diego says, "Just not about you."

"None of you do anymore. Isn't that why Inés tried to kill me?"

"I didn't, Papá!"

The detective leans against the wall and closes her eyes. "Great. She's hysterical now." Her head lolls toward the guardian. "Is it true that your baby xeno is investigating Martinho?"

"You saw that?" Nuñez slumps back against the couch. "Yes."

She crosses her arms. "Why?"

"Don't tell me you haven't connected Terra Nova to the restoration yet."

"That's obvious. Why would Martinho work with them? He's already a guardian, and he's about to get everything he wants."

Nuñez laughs bitterly. "Not everything. You can study the guardians as much as you like, but that's no substitute for being one of us. I know Alejandro, Detective. He wants to return to Earth, and he's going to get it, but what he really wants is the Cerebrum particles."

Anna quirks an eyebrow. "Really? Martinho said all this to you?"

"I know the look. He's as radical as they come, and power-hungry, no matter how much he denies it."

"That's just speculation."

"No, it's intuition." Intuition is a poor substitute for evidence. She exhales noisily and reaches for a pack of jimmies. "Don't you dare light that inside my house, Detective."

"Fine. Listen, I get it. Our big baddie is still at large, and you figure Osei has to be working with another guardian, but your argument for Martinho is thin at best. What about Bernard?"

Nuñez rolls his eyes. "Victoria? Oh, I wouldn't waste my time on her. She's just an opportunist, if you ask me."

Hands on her hips, Anna bends at the waist. "She testified on Osei's behalf. What's a woman of her standing doing befriending someone like him?"

Nuñez clutches his stomach and hoots. "Ese pendejo isn't her friend. Victoria must need something from him, or else she wouldn't waste her time."

"Or someone else needs him. Someone Bernard respects more. Fears, even." She springs up onto the balls of her feet. "You're in luck, Nuñez. With Osei in jail, I'm free to look into our mystery ringleader. I'll work this angle with you."

Diego rounds on her. "You're investigating Martinho now, too?"

"Relax. I'm just shaking trees. The thing about me is, I'm a people-person, and it looks like those are in short supply."

He snorts. "I'll go with you."

The detective grips his shoulder lightly and steers him into a back room, away from the guardian. "If your daddy is right, my job isn't done. *Your* job is right here, keeping an eye on him. Stay here, Diego. See if Carlos comes up with anything useful against Martinho. If anything Nuñez says holds water, I'll let you know." The xenobot obviously wants more than anything to go with her. It's really kind of sweet, the way he tries so hard to keep her safe. Anna can take care of herself, though, and Diego is just loyal enough to let her.

CHAPTER TWENTY THREE

GUILLERMO

THIS IS ABSOLUTAMENTE ONE of the nicest conference rooms in the west wing. Sitting inside the arc of one of the station's titanium helices, the room curves into a bowl. Outside these spacious windows, Earth hovers near, with a focal point of lights concentrated inside the habitat of the ground crews. Due east, the moon reflects off Earth's oceans. A rainbow of light forms a halo over the planet's rapidly rejuvenating atmosphere, the crown to Alejandro's new kingdom. Se imagina que debe ser espectacular. It's a gathering of the guardians, after all.

To Guillermo's left and right, more guardians Leap into the room. All but Kojo and Lucy arrive within seconds of each other. Even Lei Du has come all the way from the mining outpost near Enceladus. Everyone wants to witness the first election of the space era.

"Guillermo, it's wonderful to see you. Mind if we chat?"

The man of the hour himself stands just behind him, dressed sharply in white skins that shrink at his chest, his arms, and his thighs. Guillermo wears his finest today, a dark set of navy skins that brings out his eyes, and still Alejandro outshines him. The guardian of Guadalajara shrugs and whisks a martini glass from a passing android. He's going to need a drink to face Roarke's challenger looking like that. Alejandro leads him into a dimly lit closet along the far wall with just one orb emitting weak pink light in a corner. If Guillermo didn't know any better, he'd think the young guardian is about to make a move on him.

"What can I do for you?"

Alejandro grips Guillermo's shoulder warmly, but the smile on his face doesn't match his touch. "It's past time I thank you for all the work you've done. We all know that Roarke considers you his right-hand man, and why shouldn't he? You're a man of great talent."

A chuckle. So, he *is* making a move—a political one. "De nada, amigo. Frank and I go way, way back."

"Yes, all the way back to the bunkers. Isn't that right?"

"Bingo." Guillermo sips a gin martini.

"You were responsible for his Cerebrum particles, weren't you? But you weren't always devoted to his cause. You're a man with your own goals. Opening the cryo gardens. Have you ever considered that your people might sooner prefer a return to Earth?"

There it is. Up close, the corners of Alejandro's eyes sprout little wings when he smiles. This eager stallion is so young he hasn't even had his first shot of GLOW. He's got a long way to go before he can step up to Guillermo, yet here he is, all bravado.

Guillermo spears an olive and crushes it between his teeth. "De vez en cuando, sí. There was a time when it might have made sense. Are you asking me to join your cause, Alejandro?"

"The Coalition is evolving, Guillermo. I'm only asking you to change with us. Wouldn't you rather see the gardens open now, on Earth, rather than in some unpredictable future on Zomenos?" Alejandro crosses the small closet, basking in faint pink light. "Work with me, and we'll accomplish the unprecedented."

Guillermo sips his martini. "What about the colonists?"

Alejandro flicks his wrist in annoyance. "What about them? The colony has its role to play, but our future is on Earth." He turns, his young cheeks lit with a pale glow, skins bright in the semi-darkness. "Look at the mess we're in. We can't afford to be paralyzed by indecision any longer. The orphans are growing restless, Guillermo, and they require a firm hand to guide them. We can't respond to terrorism with ineffective half-measures. My leadership will require an obedience you're not used to, but it's a necessary step to achieve the stability we all want."

Half-measures? Guillermo coughs into his glass. Derek risked his life to ensure the success of the colony. What does the young stallion know about leading? Straightening, he smooths his skins. "Be careful, Alejandro. Frank once thought he could curb the threat of Terra Nova, too. You'll need the Coalition's support if you're going to survive."

The stallion steps close, so close Guillermo can taste the man's powerful cologne. "I already have it. You should concern yourself with your own future."

Alejandro passes him, opening the door and stepping back into the light. Guillermo follows to a raucous cheer. Guardian Kapadia steps between them, slipping her arm around Alejandro's waist and handing him a glass of champagne.

"There he is. You did it, Alejandro! You won the vote!"

Ever a consummate professional, Roarke approaches Alejandro with swift, sure feet. Kapadia falls back with her head bowed. "Congratulations on the vote. I concede your victory." He takes Alejandro's hand and raises it as he faces the other guardians. His guardians. His Coalition.

The Cerebrum particles slither away from his head, snaking around Alejandro's wrists. They undergo a metamorphosis, radiating with golden light. Guillermo shields his eyes. Alejandro's own eyes burn golden white, and he hovers inches above the floor. With the transfer of power complete, he returns to the ground, and the goldenrod leaves his irises, replaced by his natural inky black.

"To the new leader of the Coalition. May your rule be just."

Guillermo raises his glass with the others. Time to meet his future, then.

JANUARY 22, 3041 | GUADALAJARA STATION, EARTH'S ORBIT

Boots fly into a corner. Collapsing onto his couch, Guillermo drops his head into his hands. The house is silent, so Carlos must be asleep. It's late, and the guardian's ears still ring with revelry. Every time he closes his own eyes, Alejandro's gilded ones burst with light. Roarke never did anything like that. The stallion is mastering the Cerebrum particles with worrisome speed. ¡Maldita sea!

"That bad?" Diego hovers over him holding two beers. "I saw the results of the vote." Guillermo accepts a can and scoots down, letting the xenobot in. Diego sits. A chorus of popped aluminum precedes sizzling foam. The guardian slurps down half his beer and sets it on the table. Elbows resting on his knees, Diego asks quietly, "What now?"

"We need a plan for when everything goes to shit." Guillermo rolls his head sideways. "Do you remember our agreement?"

His xenobot doesn't meet his eye. "Are you asking if I remember you trying to perform a lobotomy on me?" Bending his can top back and forth, it springs free with a clink. He sighs and turns to Guillermo. "We've been over this. You have no idea what that surgery will do to me."

He's right. Guillermo knows he's right. But Alejandro's glowing pink face burns in his mind. What exactly does a future under the stallion's leadership hold? His talk of obedience and a firm hand doesn't sit well with Guillermo. He won't allow the Cerebrum particles to be abused, and judging by Alejandro's attempts at pacifying him, the stallion knows it. "Carlos could assist."

"Oh, now I feel much safer."

"Enough, Diego. If anything goes wrong, I'll stop the procedure at once, but you promised to revisit this amnesia after the investigation on MS275. It's time. Locked away in your memories is a clue, something that we can use to bring Terra Nova to its knees. If I'm right and Alejandro is working with them, do you think he'll wait around for you to regain your memories on your own?"

Diego pulls his knees up to his chin. "No."

"Then we have to do something."

He turns to Guillermo. "I want to be awake for this."

Stunned, Guillermo barks a laugh and slaps Diego's back. "Now, that's the spirit."

Diego lies on the ground on the shop floor. Guillermo sets to work sterilizing the space while Carlos sits back on his heels and sharpens his blades with undue diligence. Staring up at the ceiling, Diego snaps, "I think the table saw is quite sharp enough." Carlos smiles.

Guillermo injects Diego with as much sedative and painkiller as the xenobot can safely take—he thinks. Carlos makes an incision near the base of Diego's skull. Inside, blood, veins, and tissue snake through a complex network of wiring. Carlos bends close, unbothered by the blood, mesmerized by a light that pulsates outward. The power cell.

"This is the precursor to the Cerebrum particles, isn't it?"

"Yes. Come on, let's be quick about this." Guillermo looks at Diego, eyes still open and staring at the ceiling. "How are you doing so far, Diego?"

"I'm fine. Let's get this over with."

Guillermo turns to Carlos. "What are his vitals?"

"Within normal limits." Carlos threads a lighted scope into the opening. "There's a fluid buildup. Could be causing the amnesia." A glance toward Guillermo for confirmation.

"Maybe. Aspirate it." Carlos removes the fluid. Guillermo watches Diego carefully. "How does that feel, Diego?"

"I don't feel anything." The tube worms deeper. Diego freezes, then convulses.

"Diego?" The xenobot's limbs slacken. Guillermo turns to Carlos. "Something's wrong."

"His blood pressure's dropping," Carlos responds indifferently. He continues to aspirate as Diego's lips turn blue.

Pressing two fingers into the xenobot's clammy skin, Guillermo detects a dangerously weak pulse. "Stop! He's going into shock." The guardian pushes Carlos roughly aside, scanning for the root cause. "There, he's bleeding." He injects Diego with a vasopressor and throws a blanket over him. Diego should be able to self-repair from a little blood loss, so the fact that his body is reacting this way means Carlos hit on a critical region of the neural network. "Do what you can to stop the bleeding, then close him up."

"We don't know if the fluid buildup was the source of his amnesia. We should continue with the procedure."

"No. We're done here."

Uneasy, Guillermo observes as Carlos, full of bitterness, does as he's told. Diego was right: something's definitely wrong with the young new xenobot. Where Inés and Diego are motivated by empathy, this bot is moved only by curiosity. Guillermo pushed too hard and too fast with Carlos, determined as he was to see Juan reanimated. His temple spasms twice, and he rubs his forehead. ¡Qué tonto! The only way to know what went wrong is to inspect the power cell, and something tells him Carlos won't be amenable to that. Carlos finishes retrieving the scope and seals up Diego's skull, then strips his gloves and cap and turns to Guillermo.

"Don't involve me in another one of these pointless exercises. This was a waste of time. I see now why Juan still sleeps. You are completely incapable of seeing things through when they get hard, aren't you?" Carlos stalks away into his room, the privacy shield sealing behind him.

Stunned, Guillermo shakes his head and bends toward his patient. "Diego? Can you hear me?" The xenobot coughs and struggles into a seated position. "¡Oh, gracias a Dios! How do you feel?"

"Light-headed, but fine otherwise. What happened?"

"You went into shock, so we aborted the surgery." Guillermo hesitates. "Do you . . . remember anything?" Diego shakes his head, then winces. The guardian slumps back against the wall. "I'm sorry, Diego. You were right. You were both right. This was a waste of time. I'm glad you weren't seriously hurt."

"No, just mildly hurt."

"What did I miss?"

Guillermo looks up into Wright's accursed glowing eyes and flinches. "Detective! How did you get in?"

Wright ignores him, dropping to the floor at Diego's side. She helps him to his feet and, spotting the bandages at the base of his skull, turns those hellcat eyes on Guillermo. "You did the surgery." Weary, Guillermo just nods. He can't take any more of these accusatory confrontations. The detective plants her fists on her thighs and leans close. "You never learn, do you?"

"It's okay, Anna. I let him do it."

Wright whips around and faces Diego. "It's not okay. Just because you built them, doesn't give you license to toy with them. This bot is every much a person as I am." The detective grabs Diego's skins from the floor and tosses them to him. "Come on. Let's get out of here. While you two were playing ER doctor, I was working the case. We've got some leads to follow." Diego follows her into the lift, sparing one last look at Guillermo. The doors seal, and the guardian shuts his eyes against the anguish in his xenobot's soft green eyes.

CHAPTER TWENTY FOUR

MARILINA

"GOOD MORNING, DR. CHAMORRO." The ship's AI announces its presence into the darkness of Marilina's room in a voice as coarse as sandpaper of the lowest grit. "Shift change is in thirty minutes. You have time before your work begins to join the others from your shift in the mess hall."

"Thank you, Mirai, but I'm not hungry." The doctor worms her fingers into her soft pillow with a content smile (her tough, Coalition-issued pillow tucked away under the bed), dreams of Alejandro still fresh in her memory. She wishes he'd given her a concrete timeline for when they'd see each other next, but this entire mission is an exercise in patience. All she knows for now is that the new Coalition leader always makes good on his word.

She pulls back the sheets and climbs down from her cot. Her bunkmate's cot is empty, so Okumu must already be off to breakfast. Marilina tugs her sheets firmly back into place and slips into form-fitting medical skins, then ties her short hair back into a neat bun and steps into the hall. The sound of the others chatting over a shared meal floats toward her from the mess hall. Turning left, she walks down the long hallway to the medical bay in the starship's rear, boots ringing with each step.

"Howdy, Doctor." The admiral's clear blue eyes look down at her. "I'd like a word with you, if you don't mind."

She follows him back down the hall against a tide of crewmembers heading up to the flight deck. He leads her through the middeck to the hallway on the other side, just outside the barracks, and draws himself up with a smile that makes her nervous. Is this about the pillows? Her neck and shoulders wind into knots.

"I just wanted to say congratulations."

Well, this is unexpected. "For what?"

"The vote. I know we had our disagreements, but the decision is made. Earth's orphans are moving forward, and so should we. I'm happy for you, Marilina." He offers his hand formally.

Such a strong leader. The doctor smiles and shakes his hand. "Thank you, Jack. That means a lot. Alejandro has big plans for our little colony, you know."

The smile the admiral wears strains. "I bet he does. One thing at a time. Let's focus on getting there in one piece. How is your first time flying going?"

She relaxes. "The first week has been surprisingly smooth. You were right: the real thing *is* more fun. I'm nervous about this wormhole, though."

"Want to know a secret?" He leans close as they fall into step, a hint of crisp pine wafting her way. "I am too."

Marilina spends the better half of her morning taking inventory and reviewing the report left behind by the previous shift. The medical bay is cramped, but the Meridian are used to performing their duties along roadsides and in public spaces, rain or shine, so she doesn't mind. She sits under a portal window on a shelf cut into the wall and watches the stars drift past. From inside the ship, it feels like they're barely moving, but she overheard one of the officers say the *Rebirth* is traveling at an astonishing 3 million kilometers per hour. She rubs her mother's cross around her neck. Mami would want her to pray right about now. It wouldn't hurt, but what's a mere god to her when her ship is under the protection of Alejandro's Coalition?

A knock startles her out of contemplation.

"Come in," Marilina calls. For a second, she's sure it's the admiral grinning down at her, but the relaxed fit in those olive skins gives this crewmember away as his remarkably similar brother. The doctor hops down from her perch. "Henry, right?" He nods, sticking out his hand, and she shakes it stiffly. "Sorry if I was distracted. I'm not used to traveling like this."

The younger Monroe's laugh is so like the admiral's. A genuine sound full of warmth that infects anyone nearby. "You don't have to explain to me. I was in terraforming before this, and travel is the best part."

She only smiles. "How can I help you, Henry?"

The laughter in his eyes fades as he rubs the back of his neck. "Well, I'm here because I've, ah . . . been having a hard time with the flight." His gaze shifts away.

"How are you feeling?" Marilina silently notes his dilated eyes and sweat-streaked skins. While he reflects, she scans his temperature: 36.8°C.

"A lot of nausea. Sometimes a headache. I've been dizzy on and off."

She looks up from her wristband unit, where she takes notes. "On and off? How long have you been feeling this way?"

"Since shuttle launch." The poor man's ears darken into two sticks of guava paste. "I've been spending a lot of time in the barracks, to be honest."

The doctor's lips form a thin line. "You should have come sooner. Wait here." She pokes her head into a back room. Okumu is alone, wearing a VR headset, eyes unfocused. Marilina interrupts as gently as she can. "Keshi, I need scopolamine." The technician jerks out of a sim and sits up straight.

"Yes, Doctor."

Returning to the front of the medical bay, Marilina hands a patch to Henry. "Don't worry, flight sickness is normal and easily treated. Wear this behind your ear for up to three days. If your symptoms come back, come and see me."

The grin returns. "I'll try the patch. Thanks, Doctor."

She folds her hands at her waist. "You're welcome. I'm surprised the flight affected you this much. You have such a strong family history in space."

"I'm not usually this bad, but it's dangerous out there." Henry peels the sticker off the patch and slaps it to his neck.

"Ah. The wormhole, right? We won't even feel it. At least, that's what the officers keep saying." The doctor begins straightening up the bay.

"No, it's not that." He rubs his neck again. "Never mind. Thanks for the patch, Doc."

"I hope the rest of the flight goes more smoothly for you, Henry."

At 0550 ship time, Marilina scoots off her perch again and rolls her stiff shoulders. The first wave of the shift would converge on the mess hall in ten minutes, but she arrives to an empty kitchen. She tugs on the drawer marked **CHAMORRO,** and her eyes light up. Some of her favorite meals are listed on the ration packs. Her hand hovers over a packet of oxtail soup, Pilar's specialty. She plucks the package out of the row and closes the drawer with a snap.

The others file into the kitchen. Eager to be out of the way, the doctor heads to the small oven on the other side. She smiles at Henry as she carries her soup into the mess hall.

"Mind if we join you?" Two crewmembers tower over her.

Smiling up at them, the doctor slides down the bench. "Grab a seat while you can." The mess hall is tiny, with seating for no more than a dozen crewmembers. It isn't a place to linger.

"I recognize you. Dr. Chamorro, right? I'm Lee." Marilina accepts the handshake of this short, wiry-haired man.

Beside him, the second crewmember bows his head. "Marcus."

"Did you know each other before the mission?" She can guess the answer. These men are obviously from different stations.

Marcus shakes his head. "Nope. I'm from the Montréal station. Lee's from Melbourne."

Henry takes the seat across from Marilina and looks around the table. "So, what do you all think about the vote?"

Marcus hunches over his tray, but Lee grins and bends forward. "I can't wait to see what Martinho can do as leader. That's a man who knows how to get things done." Marcus grips his fork tightly.

"I don't know," Henry says. "Our mission never would've happened without Frank Roarke. I trust him."

Lee is whipped up into a fervor now. "That's the problem. If we always do things the way they were always done, nothing will ever change." He gulps coffee from a mug.

Marcus takes several long seconds to set his fork down. "Nothing needs to change. Not now. We were right on track before your boy showed up and stirred the pot. What's going to happen to the colony now that he's in charge? No one's talking about that. Are we just going to be stranded out there while he focuses on Earth?" He evades the doctor's gaze. "I didn't come all the way out here for nothing."

The debate suddenly feels personal. Marilina frowns. "You have nothing to be afraid of. None of you does. Alejandro vowed to oversee the safety of this crew as we establish the colony. He wants us to succeed. This vote doesn't mean the end for us. There's still so much uncertainty ahead. Let's focus on our mission and see what the future holds."

She finishes her soup in silence. The last time she ate oxtail soup was with her aunts, before they entered cryo. Alejandro showed her aging aunts so much care and respect, and he vowed too to help fulfill Marilina's lifelong duty to end the cryo program and reunite her family. Chin held high, she stands and carries her trash to the waste drawer. Alejandro will come through for her. For all of them.

FEBRUARY 4, 3041 | ONBOARD REBIRTH, JUPITER'S ORBIT

At the top of the landing, Marilina freezes, momentarily star-struck by panoramic windows. Their ship passes quite close to Jupiter, each of its stripes wider than the entire flight deck. Her breath catches in her throat. In all her time traveling with the Meridian, she never dreamed she would leave Earth's orbit. She thought she'd seen it all by now, but the colony has opened doors to a whole new future of possibilities.

Alone on the flight deck save for a handful of Coalition officers, the doctor sinks rigidly into a seat and soaks up the view. It's been over a week since she last peeked up here. So long as the ship is cruising below light speed, the civilians onboard are free to roam wherever they please, but with no real reason to be up here, she's stayed below deck. She had no idea that this view surpasses anything else on the ship.

Henry Monroe climbs the stairs to the flight deck and joins her, descending wordlessly into a seat beside her, and gazes out the windows with a look of longing. They ponder the planet, the solar system, and the universe in silence.

The planet-terraformer leans over and mutters, "I'm pretty nervous about this part."

She looks out of the windows. "The wormhole?" It's on her mind, too. She can't see it yet, but in her imagination it's like a centrifuge, and their ship is the rotor.

"Not that. I mean, not *just* that."

"What then?"

He rubs his neck, his words so quiet she can barely hear him over the soft hum of the HVAC. "This is where my dad died, you know? I can't help feeling like this is the end of the road for me, too."

Perplexed, Marilina straightens. "What happened to your father was an accident, Henry."

He glances over his shoulder at the empty seats surrounding them and shakes his head. "It was Terra Nova." The words chill her, but she maintains a stony expression. He raises an eyebrow at her. "You're going to tell me not to worry, aren't you? That Martinho will deal with them?"

"Yes." She closes her eyes, holding her breath. She's weary of this part.

Beside her, he fidgets. "Yeah, okay. I hope you're right, for everyone's sake."

Mirai materializes in front of them and interrupts their conversation, her blank smile so like that of the nuns of the doctor's childhood. "Good afternoon, crewmembers. We have entered Jupiter's orbit and are preparing to approach the wormhole. Be advised, you have thirty minutes to return to the flight deck and strap in. This ship cannot approach without all crewmembers safely buckled into their harnesses. Thank you for your cooperation."

Henry looks perfectly miserable beside Marilina, sweat forming on his brow and breath coming in rapid bursts. If he doesn't calm down, she'll be forced to delay their entry into the wormhole to treat him for a panic attack.

She leans close. "Please listen. I understand your fears, but you don't need to worry."

He settles back, face pallid. "Please don't say that Martinho is watching over me."

The doctor closes her eyes and breathes in slowly, letting his comment wash harmlessly over her. He's just overwhelmed. "Would you feel better if I said that those starships are?" As the *Rebirth* rounds a bend, an entire fleet of glistening, ivory Coalition ships comes into view just beyond one of Jupiter's many satellites, looking like Mami's bone china laid out for a dinner party. Opening his eyes, Henry's mouth falls open. "Our escort, if I'm not mistaken. Courtesy of Alejandro Martinho."

CHAPTER TWENTY FIVE

JACK

"ADMIRAL, YOU'RE GOING TO want to see this."

Jack strolls up to the cockpit and drops into the command seat beside his pilot, Colter Pruitt, still wiping sleep from his eyes. Just thirty minutes ago he'd been chasing Z's. Normally his shift wouldn't begin for another four hours, but the entire crew is strapping in for the wormhole.

"No way. He came through after all."

The holos above the flight deck show an escort of two dozen starships. With all of Martinho's talk of Earth, the admiral assumed that the Coalition's new leader would leave the *Rebirth* and its crew vulnerable to a Terra Nova attack. It's just as well—Dad's captor is many light years ahead of them, and they need to close that distance.

He opens a direct line to the fleet leader. "You ladies and fellas are looking sharp. Good to see you again, Admiral Ono."

"You're clear for entry, Admiral Monroe. We'll cover your rear."

"Copy." Jack tingles with equal parts excitement and dread. Attack or not, it's time to get moving. A cursory review of the flight log indicates all systems are ready. He enters the authorization code that reactivates the engines, glancing at his pilot. "Any news?"

"Nope. It was a peaceful ride. Crew got a kick out of the views." Pruitt doesn't share the admiral's fresh-faced perkiness, but he's wearing an eager smile. The pilot's helmet rises up from his collar and clicks into place over a thick mop of curls, leaving the visor open.

Jack flashes an easy smile in return, activating his own helmet with his retinal implants. "Nice. Let's get moving, then. Mirai, anything to be concerned about up ahead?"

"Good afternoon, Admiral." The ship's AI materializes in front of him, hovering over the control panels in a paper-thin body and sleek, dark hair that fans out over her shoulders. Like most ship AIs, she's quiet, serious, and devoid of anything close to a personality. Nothing like Guillermo's bots. "We have a clear path to the wormhole, but there is no guarantee of safety once inside."

Thanks for stating the obvious. The admiral calls over the military comm line to his flight engineers. "Chandra, are we about ready to rock and roll?"

"All clear, Admiral." Prickly. Even with the Coalition's escort, his crew is tense with the possibility of an ambush.

Turning to his pilot with a gloved hand hovering over his visor, ready to lock it in place, Jack says, "I'm ready if you are."

Pruitt hoots. "Let's do this!"

Mirai vanishes from the cockpit, reappearing as a ten-foot-tall flickering holoform on the flight deck. Her final warning to the crew is delivered in a monotone. "All crewmembers, please remain seated with your harnesses properly fastened until instructed otherwise. We are about to reach light speed and will be entering the wormhole in two hours. Significant turbulence can be expected on entry. The estimated flight time through the wormhole is approximately eighteen hours. Your cooperation is appreciated."

A green light overhead indicates that all passengers are accounted for. The admiral throttles the engines to life, and the starship rumbles as its speed climbs to ten percent of light speed, then twenty. Right now they're cruising along an arc inside Jupiter's gravitational field, but the engines catapult them into a graceful swing towards the wormhole. Jack's stomach lurches.

"Whew!" Pruitt shouts into their private line. "Nicely done, Admiral."

Jack grins, but he keeps an eye on the Coalition's fleet, spread out in a defensive sweep behind the *Rebirth*. His palms are sweating inside his gloves. Once they're inside the wormhole, those starships will retreat back to Earth's orbit. If Terra Nova is coming for them, now is the time.

The wormhole towers placidly ahead, a powerful vacuum of swirling mist. Its gaping maw waits to swallow their ship into oblivion. Teeth clenched, he reminds himself that dozens of unmanned cargo ships made it safely to the other side and back before theirs. It doesn't stop all five of his senses from screaming at him to turn back. Back to home, to safety, to everyone and everything he's ever known and loved.

It's just a touch late for that.

They careen towards the wormhole at searing speeds, the surrounding stars turning to white streaks. Their starship enters light speed at the lip of the opening and shoots forward. All at once they're inside, engulfed in pitch black darkness. He can't believe it. They're safe. No ambush.

The ship rattles.

The admiral's gaze shoots down to the control panels, searching for the source of the quake. Phew: the automated shields are still activated, and even if those fail, thermal blankets will protect against impact with interstellar dust particles at hypervelocity. He watches debris hurtling past with sweat tickling his eyes.

"Admiral, we have a problem." Jack's senior navigator, Jorge Romero, speaks into the military line. "There's an obstruction ahead." The admiral can't see a thing through the unnerving darkness outside, but the holos show an asteroid caught in the wormhole, this one so big that, unlike its smaller counterparts, it survived the wormhole's oppressive gravitational force. The blockade is directly in their path.

Jack swiftly calls the ship AI's attention to the problem. "Mirai, route an emergency path to avoid that obstruction."

Mirai appears in front of him with a distressed look on her normally mild face. "Request denied, Admiral. All simulations indicate unfavorable outcomes if we detour from our current path."

He stares at her, heart railing against his ribs. "There's an unfavorable outcome barreling towards us right now. Reroute us!"

"Request denied, Admiral," Mirai repeats in her infuriating monotone. Unbelievable.

"What are we going to do, Jack?" Pruitt asks in a tight voice.

The admiral watches the obstruction on the screens. They're headed right for a collision, and he has to do something, or they're all going to die. Deep breath. If Mirai won't help, he'll do it himself. He knows what he's doing.

Following his instincts, he calls out, "Brace yourselves!" over the common line, where the whole crew can hear. Throwing out three decades of training, Jack takes manual control of the ship. The *Rebirth* creaks and moans as it lurches down at a sharp angle, directly into the asteroid's slipstream. The massive starship isn't rated for this kind of maneuver, but it has the desired effect. Their ship narrowly avoids a collision.

Alerts spring up on his holos. Some of the largest debris is breaking through their shields.

Mirai stares down at Jack with emptiness in her opaque eyes. "Return command of the ship to me, Admiral Monroe." He ignores her. They haven't cleared the obstruction yet. The asteroid is directly above the ship.

"Pull up, Jack!" Pruitt cries.

Chandra's plea echoes Pruitt's. "Admiral, I really don't recommend manual operation at our current velocity!"

Jack grits his teeth and ignores all of them, keeping his eyes glued on his holos. He trusts the *Rebirth*, and he trusts himself. The ship takes more damage from debris, tripping new alerts. He's counting on that damn asteroid to move faster, but he's bought the ship all the time it has. The admiral takes a breath and counts to ten, then yanks upward on the controls, steering the ship back onto its flight path. Heart racing, he turns the ship back over to automated navigation. Incredibly, there's no collision. He exhales shakily.

Beside him, sweat gleams on Pruitt's face. "I haven't seen you fly this brazenly since you got your second star." The pair burst into exultant laughter. They survived.

The rest of the trip through the wormhole is a lot less eventful. Through the starship's windows, a deep, dark pit glares back at them. Jack keeps his eyes trained on the holos. He's relying on the ship's sensors to pick up any new obstructions. Beside him, Pruitt keeps watch on the ship's internal functions for critical malfunctions while they fly at light speed. It's high-stress, hyper-focused work. He and Pruitt barely speak for hours.

Once the initial wave of anxiety subsides, Jack begins to relax. Larger debris hurtles past in a flash of white, drawing his attention. These aren't asteroids . . . they're destroyed ships. Could these be the missing cargo shipments that never made it to Zomenos? His pulse spikes. He straightens, eyes narrowing. This is it, what Terra Nova thought was worth killing Dad over.

"Take a sample from one of these foreign objects, Mirai."

"What is that about?" Pruitt asks.

Mirai deploys three webs. The first two miss, but the third makes contact. The admiral turns to his pilot with a satisfied grin. "What if that debris is actually Coalition hardware?"

Comprehension dawns on Pruitt's face. His cheeks split into a smirk to mirror Jack's. "Nice thinking. Looks like you got one."

"Prepare a full workup on that debris," the admiral tells Mirai once she finishes hauling their catch aboard. Her report should be able to trace the wreckage to the exact mission it went missing from.

Jack gets a call on the military line while he waits. "Admiral, it's Officer Chandra. Preliminary diagnostics of the damage we took during entry into the wormhole are complete." Chandra sounds, if possible, more unpleasant than usual.

"Thank you, Officer. Go ahead."

The engineer's response is crisp with rebuke. "The right wing took all the damage. It's premature to say for certain, but all other parts of the ship appear fully operational."

The admiral relaxes. Structurally, the wings are the ship's most vulnerable—and dispensable—parts. "Thanks, Chandra. That's better than it could have been."

"I expected worse," the officer replies stiffly.

Chandra can shove his thinly veiled criticism. He'd be dead if it weren't for Jack. "Once we're clear of the wormhole, you and Hoffman can take an orbiter out for inspection of the wing. That will be all, Officer."

The admiral returns his attention to the debris. "Let's see what we've got," he mutters to himself. To Mirai, he says, "Status update, please."

"My analysis was inconclusive." A holo pops up between him and Pruitt with a pearly sapphire breakdown of the metals comprising the ship. "I am unable to match this debris to any known alloys."

Sigh. That doesn't make any sense. If it's not Coalition hardware, then whose is it, and why was Terra Nova bent on hiding it? He chews on this while the ship speeds on.

After almost exactly eighteen hours of flight time inside the wormhole, a gap widens ahead. For the first time, light is visible from the other side. Jack pokes Pruitt, who dozed off. Jerking upright, the pilot whoops. The end of the wormhole is in sight.

The starship rockets out of the wormhole and into a new star system. A shock of stars greets them, nearly blinding Jack after the sightless flight. He dims his visor until the light becomes tolerable. This is it. His birthright. The first person to command a ship through this system was his own father, and, for less than ideal reasons, they're both here together for the first time. The admiral clenches his fists inside his gloves. They're close now. Most of the light ahead comes directly from the system's star, nearly twice the size of the Sun they left behind. The nearest planet in the system looms close, an icy white marble frozen completely solid. Jack exhales and crumples back into his seat with ecstasy.

"Welcome to the kin system," Mirai announces pleasantly to the crew. "You may remove your harnesses."

Once the ship slows to a safe velocity, the admiral clears his engineers to take an orbiter out. He isn't enthusiastic about the delay. They'll burn an incredible amount of antimatter to reach cruising speed again, but there's no avoiding it. He needs to know the extent of the damage taken in that wormhole. An ice planet, dubbed Petra by Coalition astronomers, winks and twinkles as the ship floats by.

While he waits, an encrypted message comes through from Roarke. At the sight of the sender's name, he dives into the message. Coordinates. Dad's co-ordinates—or Roarke's best prediction, anyway. The former Coalition leader came through one last time. The admiral hops up and strides over to the navigators' station, where his officers work in silence. Jack claps his lead navigator on the shoulder.

"Got a few minutes, Romero?"

"What can I do for you, Admiral?"

"We need to modify the flight path for the final leg of the journey."

Romero frowns and folds his hands on the console. "Yes, sir. What's wrong with the current flight path?"

"Another ship came through the wormhole ahead of us. The Coalition thinks it's headed for the colony. We have orders to follow and capture. I've routed our new landing site to you."

"Well, this might pose a challenge." Romero opens Roarke's file attachment, and an incomprehensible explosion of lines, charts, and projections overlay one another. The officer launches into an explanation, highlighting different lines for comparison and walking Jack through the calculations. It's total gibberish.

The admiral stops Romero midstream. "What's the problem? In plain Eng-lish, if you don't mind."

"The problem is that these coordinates place our new landing site 5 kilo-meters due west of the colony."

"Why is that a problem?" The officer points, and suddenly Jack understands. "The mountain range. The *Rebirth* won't be able to cross that terrain." Relieved that the admiral is following along, Romero nods, but Jack only shrugs. "Set it up. We'll just have to hike it." He's got no choice. This is where the Cerebrum particles predict Dad's most likely location to be. Now that those particles have fallen to Martinho, Jack won't get another chance at this. As for the crew, well, that's what basic training is for. He can tell Romero hates this, but the officer has the good sense to simply nod.

"Yes, sir."

Mirai interrupts. "Admiral, the orbiter has docked with your officers onboard. They are entering the airlock now."

Jack snaps to attention. If Chandra and Hoffman haven't found any critical damage, they need to be on their way immediately. "Fantastic. Thank you, Mirai." He doesn't have time to get comfortable. His two mission specialists return from their inspection, Hoffman grinning proudly, but Chandra wearing a hefty scowl. "How did it go?"

Chandra's voice is like a string wrenched taut. "It was a cursory damage assessment at best, but from what we saw, the main vessel sustained no extensive damage."

The admiral wants to grin, but he keeps his reaction neutral. "That's great news. Did you have any trouble accessing the panels?"

"Everything was verified with the borescope."

The ship might still have internal damage, but it must be pretty minor if his engineers didn't find anything. Relaxing, Jack says, "This sounds like the best-case scenario." He turns to Pruitt, who has busied himself with the controls but kept an ear cocked toward the conversation. "Romero should have routed you an updated flight path. Let's get this mission back on schedule."

"We got lucky, Admiral," Chandra growls.

Jack stills, glancing over his shoulder. He made the right call, and he's not about to defend himself to an engineer. All that matters is that they're heading safely for the colony, and Dad.

MAY 2, 3041 | ONBOARD REBIRTH, THE KIN SYSTEM

The final leg of the journey passes in relative calm. One day, it's there: planet Zomenos, the size of a pinhead. Jack darts to the tall windows on the left. The planet has a thick, swirling atmosphere like the one rumored to have once enveloped Earth.

"Mira, there she is!" Gabriella and Henry are climbing the stairs to the flight deck. His stepmom jogs over and hugs him. "What do you think?"

The admiral laughs and kisses the top of her head. "I'm ready to see it for myself." He still hasn't told them about Dad, but they've got time before they make landfall. With the crew united on the flight deck for landing, it's time to bring his family up to speed. "There's something you two should know. Guillermo came through for us. I have Dad's coordinates. He's alive, and he's here. That's why we're here now. We're going to find him." The shock on their faces mirrors the way he still feels.

Henry finds his voice first. "Alive? That's great news!"

Gabriella sinks into the command seat. "I can't believe it. I didn't want to get my hopes up that he was still out here somewhere, but . . . the colony? How?"

Jack shakes his head. "I'm not sure I understand it either. We're touching down near where Roarke thinks he'll be. I'll keep you posted."

They're ready for the descent. On his right, Pruitt begins the systems check while the rest of the crew trickles onto the flight deck. Up close, a rich ocean of violet water covers most of the exoplanet's surface. Sparkling white landmasses lie between the swirling oceans. Even though it's nothing like docking at the Ring, the admiral gets the *Rebirth* onto the ground without so much as a bump. He assembles with his officers in the airlock. The sooner they unload, the sooner they can start exploring. He leaves Chandra with orders to stay onboard and oversee the civilians until the area is secured.

Jack hovers at the front of the airlock, just inside the hatch. "Mirai, we're ready to head out. Throw up a bubble, please." Through the windows, the surrounding sky flashes white as a translucent dome goes up, protecting the crew from any non-human life forms that might be lurking beyond the bubble.

Once the perimeter is secure, the admiral hops down from the hatch and lands in thick grass of a rich, dark blue. He's stunned. The ground is alive with long blades rippling in a light breeze. Holding his breath, he does something he's wanted to do for years: he takes off his helmet and breathes in. The warm air is seasoned with salt and peat.

His officers jump down behind him and spread out. Remembering himself, Jack springs to his feet. With practiced deftness, he checks the laser cannon clipped to his wristband unit. A cursory scan of the area immediately surrounding the ship indicates no other life forms are present. He relaxes.

With the landing site clear, the rest of the crew begin filing out of the ship. The admiral approaches the edge of the dome and gapes up. His arms fall to his sides. Their ship is nestled in the shadow of a soaring ridge of mountains. Incredible. Looking around, he can't help but notice there's no sign of another ship. He checks his wristband unit for thermal activity, but there's nothing outside the bubble. He sighs. Of course, it wouldn't be that easy. Where did that purple-eyed girl run off to with his father, then?

Jack puts some distance between him and his officers, trotting to Henry's side. "What do you think, little bro?" He claps Henry on the back, wearing a broad grin. "Huge mountains, tall grass, beautiful beaches?"

His brother looks dazed. A lopsided smile touches his lips. "The guild could never replicate this," he mutters. Abruptly, he shivers, and his body stiffens. He looks at Jack. "Did you feel that?"

The admiral is nonplussed. "No. What's up? You look like you've seen a ghost."

Henry shakes himself, embarrassed. "Nothing." He smiles. "This is the first day of the rest of our lives, you know that?"

"That's right."

Jack puts his arm around his brother and looks out at the mountain peaks again. There's a long road ahead of them before they find Dad and reach the colony, but he knows one thing for sure. "We're not orphans anymore."

PART II

PORTAL

CHAPTER TWENTY SIX

ANNA

F LARE IS THE WORST of it.

Solar flare, shine, party glow—these are all street names for the opiate that sweeps the stations in the wake of Martinho's new regime. A knockoff of the longevity injections strictly regulated by the Coalition, flare sells in alleyways and behind Zero Gs on every station. Users love its versatility: snort it, inject it, sniff it, or just smoke it. They claim it's just like GLOW, but it comes with intense feelings of easy euphoria and a fun-sounding climax during sex that you won't get from an ordinary longevity shot. The only problem is that, unlike the real thing, a flare crash (they call that a flame out) has a kickback like a rocket, and long-term abuse leads to altered personality disorders, hallucinations, violent tendencies, and painful abscesses that erupt and flake all over the arms and legs.

Turns out it's the skinless who inherit the world.

It's dusk now, and a lot can hide in the shadows. Detective Wright's cruiser idles outside a small patisserie named Valerie's. A little girl in pigtails waits outside holding a pastry oozing custard, powdered sugar and chocolate between sticky fingers. A skinless emerges from the alley, grabbing her by the arm and snarling in her face. Hungry, they're always hungry. The girl screams, but the skinless doesn't notice. It reaches for the pastry, moaning in a language too far removed from English to be intelligible. Anna stops the hovercraft and flings open her door, but Diego grabs her arm.

"What are you doing?"

She whips around and faces him, a long set of braids flying with her. "You see the junkie, don't you? I'm stopping it." They have bigger fish to fry, but she's not going to let that addict hurt an innocent girl.

"What's the point?" Diego calls after her, but she's already running down the street. True, skinless have overrun the streets, but she's still an officer, and she's got to do something, even if the Coalition itself has turned a blind eye to the problem. Thumbing the safety from her laser cannon, she takes aim with a steady arm.

Blast!

A narrow, purple beam streaks out of the end of the detective's wristband and sears the junkie's biceps with a blackened welt. The skinless shrieks, releasing the girl, who stumbles to her feet and sprints in the other direction with her pigtails bouncing behind her. Good.

Anna strides up to the creature. "Get out of here before I call this in."

She's never been this close to one before. The wretched thing might have been an ordinary white lady with dark hair and brown eyes once. Human. This disgusting animal crawling at her feet now has gray, darkly veined skin that hangs loosely from weak bones. Stinking flesh oozes pus where the laser burned her. Back hunched, she skitters crab-like toward the detective on all fours. It's hungry, it can't be reasoned with, and it isn't afraid of her.

The skinless lunges for the detective, spit dribbling down its chin. Anna raises her laser cannon, but four more approach from behind an abandoned warehouse across the street. Behind them, a dozen more pairs of eyes emerge from the shadows.

"Shit."

The detective backs away, but the nearest one grabs her arm and throws back its head, baring yellow, cracked teeth. Anna's lip curls at its rancid breath. From behind her, a laser blasts. She turns and sees Diego.

"Head for the cruiser. I'll cover for you." A double-barreled cannon is strapped to his shoulder. He fires off three more rounds in the direction of the approaching hoard. Shrieks fill the air.

She dives for the hovercraft waiting on the curb, and the doors fly open. "Get in!" Diego jumps inside and they take off. The xenobot fires several more rounds, ensuring that the junkies don't follow. At her flat, the detective puts the hovercraft in park and closes her eyes. They can't keep this up.

"I warned you not to try that," Diego says gently.

Her eyes spring open. "That girl is alive because of us." No thanks to Martinho's Coalition. Things were bad with Roarke, but Anna always had a sense he was trying to do right by Earth's orphans. Not anymore. The newscasters don't even cover the skinless anymore. She raises her chin. "I'd do it again."

She expects a lecture, but Diego only smiles. "And I'd have the escape car waiting."

The detective rolls her eyes and plants the palm of her hand on his face, pushing him away. "Let's get upstairs. We need to plan our next move."

The flat is the first place they visit untouched by Martinho's regime. Anna curls up on a squat couch, lights a jimmy, and sighs. Diego sits stiffly in the old blue armchair to her right.

"You think we're ready?" he asks.

"You know the answer to that." With the press of a button, holos bloom inside her living room of Guardian Bernard, her estate, her groundskeepers, and her known associates. "Hugo is your supervisor. He'll meet you outside the estate tonight and escort you onto the premises, and you should be able to make your way from there. I'll be with you the entire time."

"I know."

It's taken months to pull this operation off, but the stage is set and its star actor has been rehearsing his lines day and night. If Diego succeeds in infiltrating Bernard's staff, they should be able to find *something* linking her to Kojo Osei and Terra Nova, enough for Guardian Nuñez to step in. Assuming the old man answers her call. They haven't spoken since the surgery all those months ago, but Diego is confident that Nuñez is still monitoring Martinho and biding his time until he can pop the lid off this Juan's ice coffin. Anna shakes her head. She can't imagine the kind of love that drives this guardian to work that hard for his man. She's certainly never felt it. The detective steps close to a still shot of Bernard and Martinho together, taken on the day of his ascension to Coalition leader. She laces her fingers together and tucks them under her chin. "We just need to get her talking. Once we do, something tells me she's going to have a lot to say."

MAY 2, 3041 | COLOSSI INFINITI, EARTH'S ORBIT

"Are you sure this is a good idea?" Diego asks, not for the first time. He sinks deeper into a winged velvet armchair, fidgeting in his new skins.

Anna glances up at him from the floor. "Sit still. Of course not—that's why it'll work." Earth leers at them through her office window, casting its shadow over Diego's uneasy form. She'd rather do this at her flat, but she has more resources at the Ring. Crouching at Diego's feet, she tugs his skins down and covers his ankles. In the groundskeeping trade, the skins fit looser. The detective stands up and takes a step back. Arms crossed, she evaluates the xenobot's appearance with a critical eye. He won't get far if he can't pass for a human servant.

"It'll work," she repeats, dropping onto a ruby red leather sectional against the wall. Arquette called her plan to match her shiny new office's furniture with her eyes "grotesque." The memory makes her smile.

Diego rubs his hands together. He's a little too excited about this next part for Anna's comfort. "All I need is a vial of your blood to maintain the connection between us."

The detective wrinkles her nose and digs her fingers into the leather. "I draw the line at sharing needles."

"If you'd rather do it the hard way, I can biopsy your cerebral cortex to establish the neural link. That's what Guillermo did, but I figured you'd rather just hand over a few milliliters of blood."

Anna glares at him. "Alright, alright. Don't be so melodramatic." She crosses her legs in the chair and rolls up her skinsleeve, studying every move as Diego unwraps a needle and points it at her. It hovers over her forearm, and she yanks back.

The xenobot raises his eyebrows. "Are we doing this or not?"

"I don't know. Have you ever done this before?" She rubs her arms together.

"Of course not." He winks. "That's why it'll work."

Diego arrives at Guardian Bernard's estate and meets Hugo, a typical Frenchman with brown hair shorn low, a square jaw and dark stubble. He is head groundskeeper of the entire estate, he tells Diego proudly, and he expects his newest staff member to maintain the reputation that Hugo and his men have worked hard for. A tour of the property follows, with strict instructions never to enter the actual dwellings. Then Diego is left to himself.

Even though they're linked, Anna can't actually communicate with the xenobot. Boots kicked up on her desk, she unwraps a bean burrito and waits. This operation could take hours or days. Cheese oozes from the sides after her first bite. On the Marseille station, Diego succeeds in circumventing the Bernard estate's security and breaking into the guardian's living quarters.

"Good work," the detective remarks through half-chewed shreds of tortilla.

Seeing the events unfold through Diego's green eyes is like watching a low-budget film, with limited colors and pixelated vistas. It never occurred to her that his view of the world is this simplistic.

There's nothing in the office but a long steel desk. Anna stifles a groan. For some reason, he lingers. Her eyes narrow. What's he thinking? He sits at the desk and rifles through drawers until he finds a small chip tucked away between the folds of an antique briefcase. Dumping it out, he plugs it into his wristband unit.

"Access denied," it reads.

"Nice try, Diego," the detective mutters. She sighs, leather creaking as she leans back. The wristband unit's small screen flickers, and suddenly he's in. Holos leap out, revealing news articles and photos.

Anna folds her hands behind her head and smirks. Diego can hack anything.

There's a photo of a tall woman with Bernard's straight nose, thick eyebrows, and wispy hair, but she wears the sight-enhancing goggles of the bunker days on Earth. Now that's one old photo. Her look-alike is receiving an award of some kind. The header reads, "Noelle Bernard wins Pioneer Award for revolutionary new technology."

The detective shoves her wrapper aside and runs a search on Noelle. Her research confirms what's on the chip: the Bernards invented a technology that converts natural gas to protein. Anna scratches her head and keeps reading. Noelle catapulted the Bernard name, joining the bourgeoisie, but nothing ever came of her technology. The detective pivots her search to the family's company, Plant Matters. It was hugely successful, selling their product at a steep markup. They didn't sell very much, but they had the market cornered. Anna's eyes narrow. So, the Bernards built their wealth through a monopoly. That could be useful.

"What about Osei?" she mutters. They need something from *this* era that they can use to squeeze a confession out of Victoria, not Noelle. It's useless, of course. Diego can't hear her.

The xenobot freezes, then. Voices down the hall grow louder. He scrambles, putting everything back into place.

"Get out of there, Diego." None of this will matter if he gets caught. He squeezes into the closet between two towering stacks of boxes and waits. The voices are right outside the room now.

To his supreme luck, no one enters, and the voices dim. The detective sighs with relief. He needs to get out of there and return to the grounds before Hugo notices his absence. Diego must be thinking the same thing. Exiting quietly, he creeps toward the grounds and escapes the building unseen. He rounds a corner and comes face to face with Hugo.

"I told you. No one enters the house." The neural link dies.

"Damn it."

Anna leans back in her chair and waits for the neural link to return. It requires constant effort from Diego to maintain, so he could've just lost concentration in the excitement. The minutes stretch on languidly.

She stands. There's nothing for it. She'll have to extract Diego herself. There's no telling what Bernard will do with one of Nuñez's xenobots trespassing on her property, but the detective doesn't want to find out. Rounding the desk, she throws back the door and nearly bowls over Sergeant Arquette.

"Can we talk?"

Well, this is frustrating. "In a bit of a hurry, Sergeant."

The old boar regards her with an expression she doesn't like. "I would be too if I were you."

Eyes closed, she exhales. Inside, she's squirming. "It's Diego, sir. He might be in real trouble. I need to go after him."

His mustache twerks. "That won't be necessary, Wright."

The sergeant steps aside just as Diego rounds the corner to the offices.

Anna gapes. "How did you . . ." With a glance at Arquette, she corrects herself. "What are you doing here?"

"My office, please." The pair follow him down the hall and sit across from him. "You're a good detective, Wright, but even good detectives can be dismissed."

"I'd say I'm a *great* detective."

The mustache bristles. "You show up when you feel like it; you only work the cases that suit your own ends; and you're disrespectful, careless, and outright dangerous to your fellow officers."

"Woah," she exclaims. "I'm never careless."

Arquette's small, beady eyes quake with intensity. "To summarize, you're a liability, Wright, and I can't ignore that."

The detective leans against the wall behind her and kicks her boots up onto the desk. "Idle threats aren't your style, Sergeant."

A vein works in the sergeant's temple. "No, they're not." He leans forward and shoves her boots off his desk.

"Hey!" She loses her balance and throws her arms wide.

"You're both gathering your things and leaving for the Helsinki station," Arquette continues as if she hasn't spoken. "I've already arranged transport. I'll escort you to your pods. Guardian van Leeuwen will meet you on the ground on the Helsinki station and show you to your accommodations."

A thousand questions explode in Anna's mind. The first one she vocalizes is: "We don't get our own hovercraft?"

Her CO stands and leans forward, looming over her with an iron grip on his desk. "Hovercrafts are a privilege for those who can follow orders. Or were you planning another trip to the Marseille station?"

Grimace. "You knew?"

The sergeant relaxes. "Of course I knew. I sent a team to extract the xenobot with as little attention as possible. Something you seem incapable of doing."

She crosses her arms. "The Frenchman."

Nodding, Arquette pulls up a holo of the Helsinki station. The coastal city center is surrounded by large swaths of open nature and farmland. The detective waits without enthusiasm for the sergeant to explain. "Helsinki's crops are failing, and its guardian can't figure out what's changed. I need you to look into it."

Diego nods and stands. "Of course. Thank you, Sergeant. We'll get on it right away." He turns to Anna expectantly.

Remaining seated, she says, "Really, Sergeant? Since when do Coalition detectives care about crop failures?"

Arquette rises slowly to his feet and spreads his hands across the small desk between them. "Don't be a goddamn fool, Anna," he whispers. "Open your eyes and look around. It's not just the Coalition that's changing. Martinho's men are everywhere."

"What, his 'Skeleton' crew?" Snort. "I'm the lead detective of this whole division. What could they possibly do to me?"

The sergeant walks around the desk and stops in front of her. "He's watching us—and not just you. Even the guardians are lying low, avoiding attention. People are playing it safe, Detective. Going underground, acting above suspicion, and *keeping quiet*. If you want to stay safe, you'll do the same and investigate the damned crop failure like I told you to."

"Why don't we just listen to him, Anna?" Diego asks quietly.

The detective is livid. This turn of events proves that she and this xenobot are on to something here, something Bernard has gone to extreme lengths to hide. She wants more than anything to confront the guardian right now, but she's overruled. She leans back, keeping her boots firmly on the ground this time, and laces her fingers together. It won't pay to be hasty. Bide her time. "Helsinki it is." It's as good a place as any to plan their next move.

CHAPTER TWENTY SEVEN

ALEJANDRO

MAY 2, 3041 | COLOSSI INFINITI, EARTH'S ORBIT

LEADERSHIP IS A DIFFICULT thing. It demands unwavering conviction in the chosen one, but that's rarely enough. A leader must depend on their lieutenants to marshal the troops and hold the people in line. Alejandro steps close to the window and presses his hand to cold, reinforced glass. The sun in his direct line of sight brings that "solar flare" business to mind. He can't allow such things to test his leadership.

The Coalition leader sweeps a fluttering, translucent cape over his shoulder and flexes his wrists, checking the golden bands of the Cerebrum particles rotating in tight formation close to his skin. The opioid epidemic has, of course, nothing to do with him or his leadership, but he'll be blamed for it, regardless. Fists clenched, he tucks his hands between the folds of his cape. He hears the whispers of resentment. His guardians are responsible for placating the people, but this drug is proof of their failure.

A small matter to be handled in due time. Much larger events are already in motion that require his attention, including those that Frank Roarke sparked in his final moments as Coalition leader. A nerve works in Alejandro's temple. He still can't fathom why the old relic would authorize the launch of the *Rebirth* on the eve of his new leader's ascension. Faith in the colony has soared in recent months, and news of the starship's landing has rekindled hope for Zomenos. This mustn't be allowed to fester. Earth's orphans must understand and accept their future right here, inside the habitat his ground crews so meticulously prepared. He needs his guardians' obedience more than ever right now, and this time, the message must be clear.

Rustling behind him announces the arrival of his guardians. At last.

"Everyone is here," he observes without sentiment. In the old days, Frank Roarke never required complete attendance of his guardians at his meetings. That was the first step in losing his grip on the Coalition. Total compliance is non-negotiable. "Terrific. Let's begin."

The Coalition's highest leaders follow Alejandro down a spiral staircase to the lower level of the meeting hall in subdued silence. Black walls decorated in gold filigree echo with the click of boots on marbled tiles of evergreen. Fire crackles in a simulated fireplace in the center of the room. Armchairs and couches line the walls. To be sure, the room is quite garish, which is why Roarke never used it, but such ostentation mollifies these guardians. While the others find their seats, Alejandro stands in front of the fireplace and tosses his cape over his shoulder once more. It catches the light of the sun behind him, and several guardians stare at the wink of colors reflected back.

"Our time has come to decide what will be done with the crew of the *Rebirth*," he begins. "The starship exited the wormhole safely, and by now, many of you have heard of their smooth landing on planet Zomenos. The question of what we do with this highly skilled crew remains."

"Easy." Guillermo Nuñez speaks from an armchair to his right, still the only one among them to forgo anything approaching professional attire. "We allow the mission to proceed as planned. Listen, Alejandro. I know you're rooting for the habitat, but there's no reason not to have another option, no?"

Alejandro slides his twitching fingers deeper into his cape and strides back and forth in front of the crackling flames. He rests his gaze on the eccentric inventor responsible for the Cerebrum particles glowing on his own wrists. The man wears an easy smile, and he's well liked among his peers, especially those of the old guard. Alejandro has tried to neutralize Roarke's right-hand man, and the guardian of Guadalajara has never outright denied him, but Guillermo's lighthearted dismissal of his new leader's goals is, at best, insolent. Something must be done about him. Obedience is not optional.

"This is a new era for Earth's orphans," Alejandro continues as if Guillermo never spoke, "and I want to hasten our arrival at our final destination. The people are, as you know, restless, and our rations remain limited. Hedging our bets isn't practical anymore, if it ever was. A fuel depot on Zomenos would speed up Earth's restoration by as much as twenty percent, allowing completion of the project this year."

A murmur of interest sweeps the room, but Guillermo continues with his same tired argument. "We have our best scientists and engineers on that crew. Consigning them to mining wouldn't be fair to them after all they've done."

Samkelo Ngcobo's wrinkles fold over and over in a complex origami arrangement as he leans forward. "We can all learn from Guillermo's wisdom, Alejandro. I have a question of a practical nature. The planet Zomenos is light years away. In all the time since its discovery, we've sent just over a dozen cargo shipments there, and at great cost. How will mining this new planet be cost-effective?"

Alejandro closes his eyes. Obedience. He requires their obedience. Unthinking, unasking. The structure of debate that Roarke fostered among his guardians is suffocating. Yet, tolerance now will go a long way toward building the obedience that he expects. An olive branch, and one that proves his capability and all that they might accomplish if they are but to heed his demands. "I've already developed a solution to this very problem: portals. It's the same technology used in Leaping, but where Leaping gives motion to the subject, my portals are static devices that give motion to anything that passes through them. Allow me to demonstrate." He draws a handheld mirror from within the folds of his cape and hands it to Samkelo, then retrieves a second mirror and holds it high. Removing his wristband unit, he sets it on the glass. It disappears.

Samkelo sucks in his breath, bowing his head and staring at his hands. Alejandro's wristband unit rests on the glass surface of Samkelo's mirror. A small demonstration of his technology. Luiz is already scaling the portals for the grand transfer from Zomenos.

"It's time to choose," Alejandro declares. "All in favor of the colony?" Guillermo holds his hand up, as does Samkelo. No one else does. Alejandro nods without emotion. "And those in favor of the fuel depot?" Eighteen hands rise. His lip curls. "I'll inform the colonists."

Eighteen obedient guardians. As for the others, well, he'll have to come up with a solution for them.

MAY 2, 3041 | SÃO PAULO STATION, EARTH'S ORBIT

The young new leader of the Coalition returns home to the study. Sitting down and resting his feet on a plush, round ottoman, he closes his eyes with a rough sigh. Commanding the guardians is taxing in a way that being one of them was not. Did Frank Roarke feel so drained after these encounters with his leaders? Luiz's light step announces the arrival of his tea, which Alejandro accepts eagerly. Forget the Coalition. He must focus now on Earth.

He delights in using the Cerebrum particles to open a holograph with Maggie Barasa. The geologist has been quite busy undergoing her own leadership transformation, and these days she all but glows from the excitement of the resettlement effort. A small shuttle carrying two dozen hand-picked station dwellers—restorationists, each one—arrived on Earth earlier that day. With the arrival of the *Rebirth* on Zomenos, Alejandro must recapture the attention of his orphans, and there's no better way than to deliver news of Earth's revival. Maggie answers his call in wide-eyed panic, fit with tear-stricken cheeks.

Alejandro lurches out of the armchair and nearly spills his tea. "What's wrong, dearest Maggie?" Her usually radiant optimism is absent.

The geologist takes a ragged breath and wipes her cheeks. "It's the new arrivals. There was an accident on the shore."

He stills. Quietly, he says, "I thought the beaches were cordoned off."

"They are. We ordered the new arrivals to stay off the beach, but one of them slipped away and waded into the water. Her suit was too heavy for her. It pulled her down below the surface. She's dead, Alejandro."

"Dead," he repeats.

While the colonists enjoy rabid fandom, the poor choices of a single restorationist could unravel everything he's built. Word of this accident will shift hope in favor of the colony once it reaches the stations. That cannot happen. His gaze snaps to Maggie's still shaking face, and he notices now how her shaved head glistens with water. The geologist must have attempted to save the drowned woman herself. "Who else knows about this?"

Her wide eyes race back and forth. "Just Rocío and a few of the other arrivals."

A few. That's too many. Alejandro withholds a sigh forming in his chest and refocuses. "Rocío Valdez. One of your team members, if I recall correctly?" A nod. "What was she doing there?"

"Rocío was in charge of the group. I . . . left them with her. I'm so sorry, sir. I shouldn't have done that. I accept full responsibility." Her eyelashes are heavy with fresh tears.

Alejandro shakes his head. "Thank you, Maggie. That's enough crying, I think. Listen carefully. No one else must learn of this. Am I clear? No, not even João. Now, I want to speak with Rocío."

The shaking stops. "Alejandro, please. She's in no condition to meet. It's been a long day, for her most of all." Silence stretches between them until the geologist remembers herself and bows her head. In this too, obedience is a must. "Give me time to fetch her."

Maggie disappears, and he paces the study. This can't be happening. This *cannot* be happening. So much for his carefully laid out rules and regulations. Is anyone doing as he says down there?

Catching a glimpse of his own reflection in the gramophone, his dark eyes are small, panicked, and unimpressive; his hair disheveled; his cape askew. Small wonder no one takes his orders seriously. He grips the heavy antique and thrusts it to the ground, its ornate horn chipping the hardwood floors. For all his bluster, the relic remains largely undamaged, like the remnants of Roarke's Coalition and everything he stood for. Even now, Roarke's enduring legacy makes a mockery of Alejandro. Breathing hard, he stares at the instrument. Strength, he must show strength.

He Leaps.

MAY 2, 3041 | THE HABITAT, EARTH

The dome encasing the habitat is inches from Alejandro's face. Beyond, fuchsia and gold ribbon over a shoreline at low tide. Any closer, and he might have arrived on the very shores that swallowed up his deceased recruit. He must be more careful, and yet he can't stop grinning. No one, not Frank Roarke, not even Guillermo, has ever Leaped farther than the other stations in Earth's orbit. That Alejandro Martinho stands here now, on Earth, is testament to his control. He turns.

Wide-eyed, Maggie waits with the geologist Rocío Valdez in a secluded corner of the habitat. Rocío is a short woman with dark features and round cheeks. She reminds him abruptly of Marilina. How does the doctor fare in her own circumstances? Does she still love him, or has she, like so many of the others, been beguiled by notions of making a permanent home on that alien planet? Now isn't the time to ponder. He pushes her from his mind, focusing on the hapless woman in front of him.

"Rocío. I've come quite a long way to visit. Let's chat."

La tormenta has a long history, and as Alejandro watches Rocío struggle beneath the cloth, he understands why. Again and again, Maggie refills her jug and pours unfiltered ocean water down the selfish woman's throat. Helpless to stop it, Rocío soon passes out. And yet, she'll live, and none will be the wiser. Good. Let the woman know the suffering she has caused—not just to her unfortunate victim, but to all orphans. This woman's recklessness has the power to undo all their futures.

Hours later, Rocío awakens and, eyes widening with the recollection of her circumstances, screams silently against her cloth. Alejandro looks into Rocío's terrified eyes.

"Again."

CHAPTER TWENTY EIGHT

GUILLERMO

THE DOORS TO THE lift slide apart and the guardian steps inside. This is far from his first attempt at reasoning with Carlos, pero será el último. The Coalition's decision to reclassify the colony as a fuel depot will be the ruin of everything. Guillermo needs his xenobot on his side in order to confront Alejandro Martinho. The lift whizzes to the shop level and, skins stretching against his tight muscles, Guillermo steps out. He can't risk that meeting yet, not until Carlos agrees to have his chip repaired. Without that, the xenobot is without purpose, without remorse. This isn't the ethical robotics Guillermo pioneered.

This is a monster, and it must be stopped.

"The inventor returns." A rich, husky voice he doesn't recognize speaks from behind Carlos's privacy shield. Guillermo swivels to the right. Surprisingly, the shop has been restored to its original purpose, yet a bizarre collection of potted plants, loose papers, ceramic jars and plastic containers covers every surface. The guardian's eyes narrow at a blaze of scorch marks on his workbench. His head cocks toward the voice, expecting some trickery, but Carlos is totally unrecognizable. In place of Juan's long, bouncy curls; skinny arms; and long fingers of an artist; the xenobot now sports short, straight hair; paler skin; and a more muscular, more *manly* physique.

"¿Qué es esto?" Guillermo crosses his arms. "That's one hell of a transformation. What have you done to yourself, mijo?"

Carlos's lips—pale and thin, no longer Juan's supple and kissable ones—turn downward. "It's transfiguration, actually. I'm not Juan's body double anymore."

The old guardian stifles a chuckle. So, these are the lengths one will go for free will. Rubbing his face with both hands, he asks, "Well? Are you happy now?"

"Happiness is an irrelevant goal. You chase after it with every breath you take, and you fail utterly, daily." His xenobot strides past him to the bench.

Better to try and fail than never try at all, pendejo. But he didn't come here to debate his own happiness. Closing the distance between them in three strides, he says, "If your neural network were fully functional, you'd chase it too. Here, let me show you." Straightening, he opens a hologram displaying the schematics inside Carlos's chip. "Your neural network should have equipped you with the full range of human emotion: happiness, sadness, anger, jealousy—you get the point. You experience a limited range of these, but you're obviously falling short."

"You've explained this before." The xenobot picks up a warped plastic spoon and holds it up to the light, frowning.

Guillermo's voice hardens. "Yes, well, it hasn't sunk in, so I'm doing it again." He grips Carlos's muscular shoulder. "It's a simple fix. I can repair your power cell right here in about an hour. You'll retain all of your thoughts and memories, but you'll feel so much better."

"I doubt that." The xenobot shrugs Guillermo's hand away. "Aren't you paying attention? Your chip only limits my potential. Look at everything I can already do." Carlos points at a planter on the bench, a patchwork fusion of many plants. The guardian steps closer, a sharp fragrance slapping and stinging his eyes. He coughs.

"What's all this, Carlos?"

The xenobot smirks. "Test subjects. Couldn't risk botching the attempt on myself."

"Is this the outcome you wanted?" Languid branches reach for the ground.

Carlos steps between Guillermo and the planter. "Leave them alone. They need more water than I can justify with current restrictions. That's not all I can do either. Check this out." Stepping back against the far wall, he spreads his hands in front of him, a vortex forming between his splayed fingers. Some kind of energy siphon? The whirlpool expands, shooting directly at Guillermo's chest with a high-pitched whistle. He flinches, but Carlos disappears and reappears in front of him, catching the tornado and absorbing its blast. Sparks hit the ground, but Guillermo is unhurt. The xenobot faces Guillermo, grinning. "Cool, right?"

"Now I see where those scorch marks came from."

The smile fades. "I've gotten much better at controlling it."

A call comes through the guardian's implants. "Hold that thought. It's Diego." Carlos rolls his eyes, a hologram of Diego filling the shop. ¡Dios mío! Guillermo's first xenobot is a sight for sore eyes. He and Diego have had their share of battles, but Diego's green eyes, listless and defeated right now, express something Carlos thoroughly lacks. "¿Qué te pasa, Diego?"

He scratches his short-cropped dark curls. "Well, I made it through my first undercover operation, but then I was busted by the Coalition."

Guillermo tosses his head back, flicking his long hair to the side. Is that organization good for anything anymore? "Uff, that's awful. Lo siento. You've been working on that for months. What's the plan? Did you get anything on Bernard?"

"Yes, actually. A lot. Flight manifests from unregistered ships in and out of our system."

The guardian's breath comes in sharp gasps. "You don't mean . . ."

"I do. Terra Nova ships. Maybe the ones that gunned down Derek and I, although I can't be sure of that." Obviously frustrated, the xenobot rubs the back of his neck. "From what I can tell, they've been running their own operation through the wormhole, although I can't say what for."

A sigh. "I can guess: a fuel depot. The Coalition voted to pass Alejandro's movement, but I'll bet Terra Nova has been planning this for a lot longer." Rubbing his chin, Guillermo paces the length of the small shop. It sure sounds like Victoria is a player for the terrorist organization, but the link to Alejandro is shaky without her testimony. "Anything else?"

"Not really. If we apply the right pressure, she might give us more, but that's not possible right now."

Guillermo frowns. "Why not?"

"We've been reassigned. Anna and I are on the Helsinki station right now."

Helsinki? ¡Anda a la mierda! How are they going to get Victoria to flip with Sergeant Arquette sniffing at their heels?

Beside him, Carlos says, "I have an idea. It's just you and me now, Guillermo, but we can end this today."

Diego falls silent, anxious eyes flicking from one to the other. The guardian crosses his arms. "What do you mean?"

"Set a meet with Martinho. You create a diversion, and I'll disarm him. His plans will unravel without the Cerebrum particles."

Licking his lips, Guillermo says, "You're going to shoot him with your air rifle?"

"Maybe. I've got more than one trick up my sleeve."

The hologram flickers as Diego steps closer. "That might be our best plan for now. Anna and I are useless until the sergeant clears us to get moving off this rock again."

No bueno. Guillermo always planned for this confrontation, but if he green-lights this now, Carlos becomes a weaponized machine without a conscience.

The xenobot leans in with a knowing look. "I don't *need* your help or your consent on this, Guillermo. I've been watching Alejandro Martinho for months. Did you know about his failed resettlement team?"

Blink. "Failed? What are you talking about? The Coalition was briefed on that. The team is thriving on Earth."

"You were lied to." Carlos opens his hand, and a new hologram appears beside Diego of a woman wearing a hazmat suit and lying in a stretcher on a beach, face bloated with seawater. The image was captured from an odd, faraway angle. Carlos must have hacked the security footage of the habitat. He closes his hand, and the hologram disappears. "This can't continue like this. I can Leap to São Paulo right now if I choose, but this plan is more likely to succeed with your help."

If Alejandro is lying to the Coalition, that means he's desperate, and a desperate man is a vulnerable one. They have no choice but to exploit this. Guillermo throws up his hands. "Okay, okay. Diego, sit tight. I'll call you back with the results." He composes a message. There's just one thing that the Coalition leader would want badly enough from Guillermo to get him to clear his schedule: a new and improved version of the Cerebrum particles, one that integrates seamlessly with his organic mind. The same request Frank Roarke made of him on more than one occasion.

`Been thinking about your request. Still want those upgrades?`

The response is almost instantaneous. `My estate, one hour.`

"Here we go." Guillermo looks into Carlos's dark eyes. Unrecognizable, now. Will the xenobot come through for Earth's orphans, or will his callousness be the end of humanity?

MAY 2, 3041 | SÃO PAULO STATION, EARTH'S ORBIT

The home of the Coalition leader has changed. Gone are the rows of books, the record player, the antiques inherited from Sebastián Cruz. Alejandro's study is threadbare, with only an old leather armchair hinting at the origin of this place. Guillermo turns and smiles at the muffled thud of footsteps on thick wood. The young stallion will get an earful for always believing he knows better than his elders. His smile dies on his lips.

"Good afternoon, Guillermo. Are you impressed with my progress?"

Transformed, Alejandro glides into the room, slippers barely touching the ground, that cape of his trailing like the graceful wings of a raptor. How is the man levitating? This is beyond the simple flotation Roarke managed with the Cerebrum particles in his infamous seat. Wait, where are the nanoparticles? He sails closer, and Guillermo stumbles backward at dark irises flecked in writhing gold, alive, like the particles that used to be at the Coalition leader's wrists. His gaze sweeps the man, but the particles are noticeably absent. Alejandro has *absorbed* the particles into his flesh.

"How are you doing that?"

Alejandro's lip curls. "Oh, come now, Guillermo. Jealousy doesn't suit you."

"I'm not jealous. I just can't understand how the particles penetrated your skin." Guillermo can guess, but it doesn't really matter. Whatever his new leader has done is incredibly reckless and dangerous. "You're becoming like the skinless outside."

Golden irises spiral faster. "I am nothing like those wretched souls. I've learned to fuse my cells with the particles. Hardly the same as snorting illicit drugs."

"Yes, I can see that." Guillermo crosses his arms. Just keep him talking. "What do you need me for, then? Looks like you've got what you wanted. The particles have integrated into you."

Gold flares, making the old guardian squint. "A temporary solution. It's incredibly taxing to maintain this form." Alejandro glides closer. "I need something permanent. Your neural network, integrated seamlessly with my organic matter."

"You're asking a lot." Where is Carlos?

Eyes narrowing, Alejandro floats away. "Don't lie to me. I know about your xenobots. Clever technology." Behind them, an android appears in the doorway. Guillermo's heart drops. The android is holding Carlos, bound and gagged. The android dumps his xenobot unceremoniously on the floor between the two men. Alejandro thrusts his arms down, and Carlos levitates as if yanked upward by a string. The Coalition leader leans close to Guillermo and snarls, "You could have joined me. If you had, your precious gardens would be restored by this time next year, and the frozen would awaken to their new life in the habitat. Instead, you sneak this machine into my home behind my back?"

Alejandro clutches Carlos by the back of his neck with cold determination blazing behind his golden eyes. Guillermo freezes. The xenobot's new, dark eyes stare at his creator, wide and full of a fear he didn't believe possible. It's hard to say which of them is the man, and which the machine. With his other hand, Alejandro punctures the base of Carlos's skull. Blood spatters the floor as bone and metal alike crunch. Ripping out the xenobot's chip, he drops Carlos to the ground, unseeing eyes upturned toward Guillermo. The Coalition leader's slippers land lightly on the blood-streaked floor. He holds the chip close, turning it in his palm.

"Thank you, Guillermo. This will do."

¡Ten cuidado, hombre! With the power cell in hand, the old guardian is obsolete, and they both know it. Alejandro dives, arms out, and lunges for Guillermo, but Guillermo is faster. He drops into a roll, curls his fingers around Carlos's wrist, and Leaps.

CHAPTER TWENTY NINE

MARILINA

NEWS OF THEIR MISSION reclassification leaves Marilina hiking through a salt marsh alone. Most of her crew view her as an enemy and the source of their misfortune. Despite all the months they bunked together onboard the *Rebirth*, even Okumu can barely meet her eye. The doctor's boots squelch deep into spongy, peaty mud, but her footing is sure. She may be confused—sad, even—that the colony was reclassified as a fuel depot, but she won't jump to conclusions about Alejandro like the others without hearing his rationale. Up ahead, the mountain ridge wavers in and out of her field of view, its terrain uncertain.

Henry Monroe falls into step beside her. "You look like you're lost in thought."

The doctor smiles. "I was thinking of tomorrow's hike." She's grateful for his kindness where the others are distant, but she remains guarded.

He steps carefully through uneven soil beside her. "You're not worried about this reclassification?"

"Alejandro has his reasons."

Henry glances sideways at her. "What difference does it make? Mining is dangerous, hard labor. This isn't what we signed up for."

"All of this is dangerous and hard." Tall grass ripples ahead, like above-ground seaweed. "I see your point, Henry."

"Do you?" The terraformer stops in his tracks and studies her. "You know you're probably the one person who can change his mind, right?"

Ducking under low-hanging branches, she grabs Henry's hand and pulls him back. "Be careful. If you fall, you'll get a face full of mud." A tangle of roots waits just over the bend.

"Thanks." Their hands release.

"I'll think about it," she promises. But she's not sure. Alejandro knows how much this mission means to her, how important it is to reopen the cryo gardens. If the rest of the orphans resettle on Earth, what does that mean for her family? Would Alejandro really abandon her to a lonely fuel outpost? She runs her forefinger over Mami's cross and bites her lip. No, he promised he would come up with a way to remain in touch. Mami would tell her to have faith.

They break for lunch at the edge of a forest.

"Finally!" Henry exclaims. "I'm sick of mud. Want to join me and the ag unit for lunch?"

Marilina removes a pair of gloves slick with sweat and dirt and brushes long hair out of her eyes. "After my shift." She turns back and looks out at the wetlands in farewell.

The doctor maintains her post at a blue medical tent for the first half hour of their break. Most of the complaints are of tendonitis, twisted ankles, sunburn, and athlete's foot. Dr. Nuñez relieves her, and Marilina plods down a narrow path to a wonderfully flat and dry open field tucked in the shadow of the mountains, where the rest of the crew relaxes with their lunch. Puffy clouds roll overhead, offering shade from the relentless heat of this planet's star. A hush falls over the group as she approaches, but Henry jumps to his feet.

"I invited Dr. Chamorro to join us," he explains in a rush. Ignoring the mounting tension, she reaches inside her pack for her rations.

Henry leans close and mutters in her ear. "Messages from home are starting to come through to the wristband units."

"I see." Marilina shoots a look at the others, but they still pointedly avoid her gaze. "What's going on there?"

His gaze shifts to his boots, somewhere beneath the tall grass. "Addict tents are on the rise. Some new drug called flare. Lots of looting and hurting people. Sounds horrible, actually."

"That's awful," she says. "The Coalition isn't helping them?" She unwraps the banana leaves around a nacatamal and eats the hearty tamale quickly. Their break will end soon, and she certainly doesn't plan to enter the mountain range's uneven, rocky trails on an empty stomach.

Henry drops his voice. "We heard that Martinho has his own task force patrolling the streets."

"How is that a bad thing?"

"It's a 'shoot first, ask questions later' kind of thing. People are calling them his Skeletons."

The doctor sets the nacatamal down and laughs uneasily. Don't jump to conclusions. Alejandro is a compassionate man, a Meridian. He wouldn't condone violence . . . would he? "People will say anything," she says, but she resolves to get to the truth.

MAY 4, 3041 | THE MOUNTAIN PASS, ZOMENOS

Waking with every muscle on fire, Marilina pushes her blanket to the side and slips into her boots. Still wearing her sleepskins, she pulls back her tent flap and steps out into camp. The others are all still in their tents. She creeps past, careful not to disturb them. Tall blades of indigo grass tickle her ankles. They made camp high up along the winding path that cuts through the mountain range, in the shadow of a tall peak. The doctor approaches the mountain and grips its rocky side, steadying herself. Their system's star, Anima, is just visible, an orange spot nestled between two peaks. A thick layer of mist blankets the azure valley below. The sight fills her with a sense of majesty. She sits beneath the high peak and settles into a meditation that soothes her tired muscles.

By the time Marilina returns, breakfast is well underway. She declines, refilling her canteen with fresh water from a stream and heading to the medical tent. Light work is the best medicine for sore muscles. Her work continues to be straightforward, with just one interesting case of tree nut allergies sprouting a rash identical in color to the tall grass. The biggest surprise of the morning is that the former guardian Lucy Mérieux checks into the tent with the admiral.

"Good morning, Guardian," the doctor greets the woman automatically. "What can I do for you?" Rattled, Mérieux strides into the tent and tugs the curtains shut, then sits on the makeshift bench and crosses her arms.

Admiral Monroe rubs her arm. "She has food poisoning."

Marilina steps closer. "You ate the tree nuts yesterday?" The patient nods. Many of the others did too, to mild effect. Fortunately, the former guardian has no rash. The doctor swiftly takes her patient's vitals. Mostly normal, BP slightly elevated. She frowns. "What symptoms are you experiencing?"

Her fair skin turning pink, Mérieux grimaces. "I've been nauseous all morning. I've thrown up twice already."

"Nothing else? No pain? Cramps or diarrhea?"

The patient shakes her head. "Fortunately, no. I might be more tired than usual? Is that a symptom?"

Marilina leans against a folding table that holds her supplies and laces her fingers together. They're all more tired than usual after yesterday's hike. "It could be. Do you mind if I run some tests?"

"Please do."

Reaching into her kit, the doctor retrieves a lancet. "I just need a blood sample."

Mérieux holds out a small and uncalloused hand, and Marilina pricks a finger, rotating it as she squeezes. A single drop of blood wells up and falls onto a plastic slide that the doctor inserts into her wristband unit. Immediately, a holograph displays her patient's electrolyte and hormone levels, liver and kidney analytes, and an array of other useful information. Mérieux leans forward and pores over the results, but Marilina's trained eyes zero in on human chorionic gonadotropin, elevated at 50 mIU/ml.

Pulling up a stool, the doctor sits across from Mérieux and Monroe. The two strike an imposing pair. Seated across from the guardian, the slender woman is much taller. Would Alejandro be Coalition leader now if this woman, well-liked on her own station, had never left? It certainly would have made things a lot less complicated between them. "I have good news. You don't have food poisoning, Guardian Mérieux."

Closing his eyes, the admiral claps his hands together. "That's great."

Mérieux frowns. "What's wrong with me, then? Stomach bug?"

"No." The doctor pats her patient's hand with a smile. "You're pregnant."

Stiffening, Mérieux yanks her hand away. "That's not possible."

The admiral leans forward. "Lucy takes GLOW like the rest of us, Doctor."

A pause. "I'll run more tests."

The mystery pregnancy plagues Marilina's thoughts the rest of the way through the pass. No one can become pregnant while taking GLOW. The drug halts reproductive hormone release, but her tests suggest that drug uptake is slowed, and the usual indicators that the drug is working are absent or diminished. She is perplexed. There's nothing like this in the literature. Worse, if GLOW has stopped working for Mérieux, it can stop working for the others.

While the crew sets up camp for the evening, a message from Alejandro comes through on Marilina's wristband unit. Her heart soars. He can be there tonight? She isn't sure what that means. The distance between them makes a call impossible. His message includes a string of numbers: coordinates. The doctor copies them onto her map and locates the place, only a kilometer away. She arrives at a secluded clearing and gasps.

True to his word, Alejandro stands across from her. No shimmering outline, just real human flesh. She drops her arms and rushes to his side. He catches her, easily lifting her. They kiss under the light of twin moons.

"How did you get here?" Marilina breathes.

Alejandro sets her back on the forest floor and smiles. "Look inside your pack." Marilina pushes past her rations and extra skins, but there's hardly anything in there. Inside a zipped compartment, she finds a pocket mirror beside a potted cutting of sacuanjoche. The fragrance of its bright, yellow petals envelops her, intoxicating her with memories of home. "It's a two-way portal. I can visit you anytime, now, anywhere. As I promised."

She turns the glass over. "Can you hear everything I say and do with this?" Flushing, she remembers her conversations with Henry.

Headshake. "Don't worry, I'm not spying on you. Portaling works through the transfer of organic matter. The challenge lies in ensuring that I don't explode out of your pack."

"So, it's like a Leap." Well, that's a relief. Marilina is dazed by this new turn of events, but this doesn't change the reason she anxiously awaited this reunion. "I wasn't sure if you'd come at all, after I learned about the mission reclassification."

"Please don't take that personally. As Coalition leader, I must be prag-matic."

"And these Skeletons? That's you being pragmatic?"

A spark of gold flashes in his eyes. She blinks. "My task force is only doing the job the Coalition fails to do itself. We've been living in outer space for *fifty years*, Marilina, and for many, that's simply too long. The people are restless. I'm protecting them from themselves."

The doctor bites her lip. "I've heard otherwise."

Alejandro laughs. "What—that my task force is hurting innocent peo-ple? You would believe that, after all we've been through together?"

This is the same man who gently gripped Pilar's hand and supported her into her cryo pod. That's not a man who would mistreat his people. "Of course not." He strokes her hair, but she steps back stiffly. "But we're not together anymore, are we? You've condemned me and all the other colonists to the same fate as an MS275 miner."

He sighs. "You're angry. I don't blame you. You're a talented physician, Marilina. A Meridian. You are, in fact, the one person I truly consider my equal." He grips her shoulders lightly, pulling her into his arms. Uncertain, Marilina closes her eyes and thumbs her cross, comforted by his familiar scent of cedar. "I'm not abandoning you to a lonely existence on this planet," he whispers into her hair. "I actually have a favor to ask of you. Something very special."

She frowns. "Like what? I'm no miner. I'm not even a geologist. There's no reason for me to be here."

"I'm asking you to trust me. I will have a task for you very soon. It has to be you, my dear. You're the only one I can trust with something this important. You must follow my orders precisely." He steps back, searching her eyes. "Will you do that for me?"

Marilina presses her thumb into her cross until it hurts. Have faith. "I will."

Alejandro bends toward her and kisses her. They drop to the forest floor, and he removes her skins with his familiar tenderness. She gropes for his neck, but her fingers pause at a lump beneath his earlobe.

"There's something wrong with your implants," she whispers.

Lips trailing her throat and collarbone, he shakes his head. "Those aren't implants. They're a neural network." Her eyes widen, but she relaxes as he slides above her. They make love by the light of the twin moons, and afterward Marilina falls fast asleep in his arms. She awakens at dawn, but Alejandro is nowhere in sight.

CHAPTER THIRTY

JACK

THE WORD *PREGNANT* STICKS in Jack's mind worse than the dried mud on his once-pristine boots. He weaves through different groups settling in for dinner at the campsite, wearing an easy smile, but his stomach is doing air kicks. Just up the hill, a group from the developmental unit sits in a semi-circle playing a game of Black Holes. The admiral intends to be there for Lucy, so his attention can't be divided. The search for Dad needs to end fast.

Most of his officers are huddled together around a live fire in a group sim. He skirts the flames and keeps moving. Something like this can't be dispatched to just any officer. He could loop in Pruitt, but he scraps that idea. Jack needs this handled quietly, and Pruitt can turn into a blabbermouth with enough scotch in him. The last thing Dad needs is a lonely officer uncorking the Monroe family drama on a recorded message to their family back home on the stations. This is family business.

Having made up his mind, the admiral squares his jaw and rounds a thicket of trees and finds himself surrounded by green skins. His eyes find Henry's and, wordlessly, he nods. His brother jumps to his feet and excuses himself quickly. With a wave toward the others, Jack treads down the slope to wait for his brother. Henry catches up to him wearing a quizzical look.

"What's up? You look tense."

The admiral murmurs quietly in his brother's ear. "Plans have changed. I'm going to do a sweep, see if I can pick up Dad's trail. Are you in?" He steps back and searches Henry's eyes. His brother looks scared as hell, fidgeting and twisting the toe of his boot in the dirt.

"Oh." He doesn't meet Jack's gaze. "Of course. Where do we even start?"

Turning away, the admiral peers into the forest. "This is as good a place as any."

Henry turns two shades paler. "Why isn't military taking point on this?"

"I need someone I can trust." The admiral hesitates. Trust is a two-way street. He's bringing his kid brother in on a rescue operation, so he better come clean first. "It's Lucy. She's pregnant."

"Oh, wow. Congratulations?" A half-hearted attempt at a smile slips away, and they stare at each other for a long minute. "Okay. Well, at least we have the light of two full moons. I'm getting my own laser cannon, though."

As much as Jack hates that, he agrees. They take off into the forest, ducking under low branches and skipping over wild bramble, Henry chatting nervously the whole way. "I'm going to be a cool uncle. Beers and jimmies for the little guy while Mom and Dad are off-planet. Do you think Tío would give me his hovermoto?"

Spinning mid-stride, the admiral throws a hand out in front so he doesn't crash into a tree and frowns. "Guillermo will *never* give away Itza."

Shrugging, Henry grins. "I'm just saying, green is more my color. When did you two start trying, anyway? No judgment, but your timing sucks."

No kidding. Jack waits for Henry to pass through a narrow corridor between the trees and then falls back into step with him. "We weren't trying. Matter of fact, we're both still taking GLOW." Henry stumbles a few paces and Jack bumps into him. His brother's eyebrows disappear into his mop of sandy brown hair. "We never even talked about kids."

Henry pulls Jack into a one-armed hug. "One day we'll laugh about this."

"Thanks, Henry." Running his hands through his hair, the admiral steps back and looks around. "Wait, are you seeing this?" He points through the gap in the tree canopy. Some of the branches are bent, angling toward the ground. The brothers exchange a glance. These woods aren't empty. The purple-eyed girl must be close. "Come on."

They jog carefully downhill, following the light of the moons and dodging gnarly roots. At the bottom of the hill, the forest gives way to a clearing. Jack grinds to a halt, and Henry runs right into him.

"Sorry. Is that . . . ?"

"That's the orbiter from our ship." The small ship that Chandra and Hoffman took out to inspect the wing of the *Rebirth* now lies in the clearing, clearly lit by the full moons overhead. Its markings are all still there, confirming its identity, but that doesn't make any sense—they left that orbiter behind on the starship. *This* ship is ancient, even though the model number is from the latest VLT series. "What gives?"

Henry approaches the orbiter and wipes a streak of dirt from the panels. He holds his finger up. "It's been here a while, from the looks of it."

The admiral presses his palms into his eye sockets. Even if Dad's captor landed weeks ahead of the *Rebirth*, that doesn't explain why the orbiter in front of him looks like it hasn't breached the atmosphere in decades. A tug on his skins draws his attention.

Henry holds a finger to his lips and waves Jack down to the ground. Quick as a comet, the admiral drops into the dew-spotted grass beside him, straining his ears and searching for whatever has caught his brother's attention. Even in the moonlight, all he sees are endless branches.

Pointing, Henry whispers, "Tracks." Jack can't spot what the terraformer is looking at, but he trusts him. His brother rises in a low crouch, eyes trained on the ground. He steps several paces in a south-southeasterly direction. Following right behind, the admiral holds his laser cannon upright and pans continuously for threats. Henry freezes, nose high in the air, and turns to Jack. He mouths the words, *Do you smell that?*

Goosebumps snake up Jack's arms. He shakes his head and grips his cannon firmly.

Something flashes crimson red.

MAY 4, 3041 | THE FOREST, ZOMENOS

An idea strikes. If they're downwind of their target, they have an advantage. The admiral creeps past Henry and gestures for his brother to follow, setting his cannon to capture. They wait for what feels like an eternity, but Jack doesn't move a muscle. His breath comes smooth and even. That red blur could have been anything, but somehow he doesn't think so.

And then it moves again.

The admiral takes aim and fires three rounds. Polymer webs burst from the cannon in rapid succession and find their target. He leaps to his feet and streaks out from behind the brush, halting so suddenly that Henry careens into him. Jack catches his brother and heaves him upright.

"What in the known universe is that?"

Straightening, the admiral circles his catch. An enormous lizard, three meters long, is caught in his web. The reptile is bedecked in cherry red scales from head to tail—the flash of red in the forest. Its eyes follow Jack, like a predator stalking its prey. Big and just as colorful as the rest of it, those eyes have thin, cat-like slits for pupils. This creature didn't make any of the mission briefings, and the reason is obvious. This thing is *fast*, much too fast for the surveillance footage.

Whack! The ground quakes with a slam of that tail. The admiral flings out his arm and steadies himself against Henry, who looks just as startled and unprepared as Jack. Mission protocol states to do no harm to any wildlife encountered, but the Coalition obviously wasn't referring to an apex predator. Drawing itself up, the lizard's chest expands.

Fire erupts, lighting up the night sky with a crackling, violet light, but the webbing holds. The fire snuffs out, leaving no trace it was ever there. And then the lizard speaks in unmistakable English.

"Release me at once, Admiral Monroe, or you shall pay for your mistake with your life."

His name. This alien lifeform just spoke his name. Deathly white, Henry looks like he's about to pass out. Swallowing, Jack grips Henry's forearm and faces the lizard. One of them needs to keep it together. As soon as this beast spoke, its category advanced from *alien wildlife* to *intelligent being*. The admiral opts for diplomacy.

What the hell, right?

With an easy smile plastered on his face, he says, "You have me at a disadvantage. I don't know your name."

The creature leaps forward at staggering speed. Jack checks the safety on his cannon, setting it to stun, but stands his ground. Snarling, the lizard opens its powerful jaws wide. Jaws that could snap a man's neck clean in half. Two rows of very long, very sharp teeth (the rip-flesh-from-bone kind) clamp down to no effect. Nostrils rake against the web, stretching it taut, but it doesn't break.

Obviously, this alien reptile is a highly intelligent, extremely dangerous problem for the colony. The admiral's threat assessment escalates. It's probably been hunting them for days. If he hadn't caught it, it might have attacked at any moment. He raises his laser cannon. Time to eliminate this threat.

"Wait!" Henry throws his arms between Jack and his catch.

Glaring, the admiral lowers his cannon a few millimeters. "What?"

"You're not just going to kill it, are you?"

Unbelievable. Jack never would have brought a civilian along if he'd known how this night would go. Right now, his kid brother is a poor stand-in for an officer trained in close combat. "Now isn't the time to get soft, Henry. Step aside."

The alien unfurls to its full height, spreading a powerful pair of wings two meters wide on each side and capped in sharp talons, and soars above the brothers.

Damn. Didn't notice the wings.

"Release me," the lizard bellows in more of that exquisite English, "or I shall call my brethren here to do it for you. You won't like what happens if I do."

There's more of these things? The admiral weighs his options. Chances are pretty solid that this alien's reinforcements will arrive faster than any Coalition officer could. Jack is stuck with his brother as his sole backup, and if Henry passes out, that leaves them outnumbered.

"Do as he asks," Henry pleads.

With a look of disgust, the admiral drops his laser cannon to his side and retrieves a diamond knife from his boot. Approaching slowly, he keeps his hands visible.

"I'm going to release you." He can't believe he's talking to an alien. "Just stay back, alright?" The lizard returns to the ground, resting on its laurels, and Jack tears an opening through the tough web. With three quick strides back, he trains his laser cannon on the alien. It steps through, and Henry stumbles backwards at the look in those menacing snake eyes. For a long moment, all three of them stare at each other in frozen silence.

"Why are you following us?" Henry ventures.

"I owe you no explanation, creature," it hisses. "It is you who have trespassed on sacred land with your firebox. State your purpose here so I can decide whether to kill you."

Sacred, huh? This alien values the land as much as its life. Diplomacy *can* work. Following a hunch, the admiral lowers his laser cannon. "We want to build a home here, same as you."

The lizard bares its razor teeth again and inches closer. "If that is true, why do you siphon the lifeblood from this place?"

Jack exchanges a look of genuine surprise with Henry. "We've done no such thing."

"Liar," the beast bellows. The admiral gulps, but he holds his ground. "Cease these collections at once or I shall do so for you." It turns away.

Henry creeps forward. "Wait." It pauses, but doesn't face the brothers. Henry glances at Jack, who only shrugs, so he swallows and asks, "If we do as you ask, are we free to go?"

The beast is silent for a very long time. Then, it speaks. "Heed my command and protect these lands, and you'll come to no harm from me."

Eyes closed, a relieved smile spreads across Henry's face, but the admiral's mind races. How are they going to stop siphoning when it hasn't even begun? The beast steps forward and spreads its wings to their full capacity. The moons shift into view between the trees, and its left flank catches the light. Jack gapes at the beast's veined, sinuous skin. This is no lizard.

"That's a dragon." The word falls from his lips unthinkingly.

The beast faces him, staring with the eyes of an ancient alien race full of mysteries. "I haven't been called that in a long time. I prefer that you call me by my name, Pyrrhos. Until we meet again, Admiral Monroe."

Jack marches alongside Henry back to the campsite in silence. It takes all his self-discipline not to run headlong into camp and announce the presence of dragons to his crew. He steps carefully through the underbrush, suddenly seeing this forest through the eyes of Pyrrhos. The creature called it sacred land. Sacred how? With the mission reclassified to fuel collection, he doesn't see how they're supposed to protect the land. They're never going to find Dad with a literal dragon breathing down their necks.

"What do we tell the others, Jack?"

He presses forward. "Nothing."

"Are you sure about that?"

Stopping in his tracks, the admiral throws out his arm ahead of Henry. He turns to his brother. It's obvious that Henry is dying to tell someone. Nervous energy courses through him, making him dance on the balls of his feet and tap his fingers on his thighs. "We need to figure out what these collections refer to." Whatever they are, a dragon is holding them responsible. Jack hates being blamed for someone else's mess. "You heard Pyrrhos. If we put a stop to it, he'll leave us alone." He turns and continues on in the direction of the campsite.

Henry scrambles after him. "What was he talking about, Jack?"

Headshake. "I don't know yet. Look, I'll send a few of the officers out to investigate this lifeblood business. Until we know more, I need your absolute silence. Am I clear?"

Henry is taken aback. "Okay. Why all the secrecy?"

The admiral rests his head against the bark of a tree. "Because we're dealing with a dragon, Henry, a freaking real-life, fire-breathing, winged dragon, and the Coalition *cannot* find out about it until the threat is handled." God damn it. It goes against everything he believes in, but they're going to need help, and a lot of it.

CHAPTER THIRTY ONE

ANNA

THE GUARDIAN THAT WAITS for Anna and Diego just beyond the teleportation pods is a pale, forgettable sort of man. They're chasing crop failures on the farthest station from Colossi Infiniti instead of building leverage against Guardian Bernard. Peachy. The Finn bows deep and offers his hand to the detective, which she accepts. Play along and bide your time, Anna. The opportunity to escape from this remote station will present itself.

"Good day. I am Guardian van Leeuwen. I have waited so long to meet you, Detective. Please make yourself at home on my station." Diego inches forward, hand outstretched.

"This is my partner," Anna explains, eyes roaming over short, colorful buildings visible for dozens of kilometers. A touch of salt spices the fresh, crisp air that blows on her cheeks. "How can we help?" Might as well get this over with.

van Leeuwen bobs his head. "The agricultural unit is failing, and we've ruled out soil and water anomalies, so I fear that criminal activity may be behind this." The detective nearly snorts. What criminal would travel all this way? With what ships? The guardian's eyes, clearer than the nearby gulf water, intensify. "Grain and vegetables are our primary exports. Our station relies on its crops." He purses his lips. "Without them, my people face cryo."

"We'll help you, Guardian." Diego's green eyes shine, but the detective suppresses a sigh.

They are dumped at the mouth of a long gravel path that they follow to a brick cottage deep in the woodlands, far from the bustling coastal city center. As much as Anna hates to admit it, there couldn't be a better, more private location for a detective and her partner to maintain a covert base of operations right under the new Coalition leader's nose. If only they weren't bogged down with the station's problems.

The weather takes a nasty turn just after their arrival. Frigid air heavy with gulf mist pistol-whips the station. Shivering in her quilted armchair, Anna throws an itchy woolen blanket over her lap. "Why are we still pretending to investigate this crop business?"

Diego pores over a shimmering blue holo detailing members of the agricultural guild, cross-checking it with another holo of access points into the unit. His brow pinches in irritation. "Who is pretending? Sergeant Arquette wants us to figure this out." Evidently content to sift through tedious lists and reports (and not even wearing the thermal skins issued by the Coalition), he swipes two fingers in the air.

Anna rolls her eyes. Bots. "The atmosphere is thinning on this station. That's probably the source of your precious crop failure. Can we go?"

Guardian Nuñez appears in front of their useless simulated fire, cradling an unconscious Carlos. "Diego," he croaks, "I need your help." Diego drops to his knees and scurries forward, holos disappearing. Tossing her blanket aside, the detective leans forward and cups her chin in her hands. The baby xeno isn't unconscious—his spine has been ripped from the back of his head, and Nuñez is covered in a bloody mess of spinal matter and shredded steel. Anna never really liked the creepy xeno, but he didn't deserve this.

With one hand on Nuñez's back, Diego scans the carnage. "What happened, Guillermo?"

The guardian's eyes pinch shut. "Alejandro."

"Your ambush didn't take," Anna observes. So much for that plan. She looks at Carlos's mangled remains. "Is he dead?"

"Maybe. Alejandro took his power cell. I don't know if I can save him."

"*Took* his power cell? For what?"

Neither of them answers. Diego grips Nuñez's shoulder. "Let's get him to your shop."

"Are you crazy?" the guardian exclaims. "That's the first place the Skeletons will go."

"Your equipment could save Carlos's life. We have to take that risk."

A rare fear wages war behind Nuñez's honeyed eyes, but he nods. "As long as we scope the place out from a safe distance. If it's clear, we'll head inside. If not . . ."

"Let me worry about that," Diego says grimly. His eyes search Anna's. "I'll come back as soon as I can. Don't do anything rash while we're gone."

She flops back onto the armchair and spreads her hands. "How much trouble can I possibly get into on this dump of a station?"

"Anna."

The detective shoos them away. "Go. I'll be fine." They disappear, leaving her alone. "Wait here all by myself while you two have all the fun? Yeah, right."

MAY 6, 3041 | MARSEILLE STATION, EARTH'S ORBIT

A young maid escorts Anna into an open room gilded with vintage ceiling moldings. Long drapes of soft grays and beiges frame high windows. One hellishly expensive crystal chandelier hangs over an antique dining table holding a bouquet of white hydrangeas.

"Un café?"

"Yes, please."

The android exits, leaving the detective alone.

Growing restless, Anna rubs one end of the crisp white table linens between her thumb and middle finger. She's waited a long time for this showdown. This guardian needs to fear her enough to testify against Martinho. Even for Detective Wright, it's a tall order. Diego would've told her to keep working on the crop issue, but Carlos was their biggest weapon against Martinho, and the Coalition leader dispatched him like a rag doll. They need a win. This way, she'll be one step closer to ending this.

A rustle accompanies the soft click of a pair of heels. Anna turns with one hand on the mantle of a decorative fireplace and cocks an eyebrow. Guardian Bernard crosses the room and seats herself across the long table, rich emerald dresskins shimmering prettily. Thick dark curls are combed to one side in an absurd braid dotted with diamonds. She smooths her gown with a hand decorated with an heirloom ruby while the maid reenters with two tiny cups of espresso. The guardian sips with an air of polite curiosity.

"I've heard so much about you, Detective." A faint, lilting accent.

"Only good things. I'm sure of it." The detective follows Bernard's lead and sips coffee from the ridiculous little mug.

A magnanimous wave follows. "Please. How may I be of service to the Coalition?"

Anna sets down her coffee. "I am investigating Alejandro Martinho as the leader of the criminal organization known as Terra Nova. We know that, first as guardian and now as Coalition leader, Martinho infiltrated the Coalition with Terra Nova sympathizers such as Kojo Osei." She props one elbow up crookedly and laces her fingers together, giving Bernard a level look. "And we know that you are one of those sympathizers."

"The Marseille station stands with the others," Bernard says. "In fact, we made a generous donation to the Coalition very recently. You have surely heard of this, I suppose?"

"I have. I've also heard that you've given several speeches promoting Martinho's agenda recently."

The guardian chortles. "Didn't we vote him into leadership? We, the members of the Coalition, do as we are asked. Forgive me, but I don't see how that makes me a terrorist sympathizer." Her perfect nose wrinkles.

"You spoke as a character witness at Osei's trial, and you condemn the colonization of Zomenos in favor of a fuel depot. I know that you're running an unauthorized operation in and out of that star system. What else are you hiding, I wonder?" Bernard's laughter chokes off. Anna leans forward, resting her elbows on the table. Every muscle flexes, a trap begging to be sprung. Come on, little mouse. "All that I'm asking is that you tell us everything you know about Terra Nova—especially Martinho's role." The detective sinks back in her chair with an inviting wave of her hand. "If you do that, I can offer you complete immunity."

The guardian surveys Anna over a golden-rimmed mug, sipping lazily. "Why don't you come with me?"

Wrong-footed, the detective scrambles to recover. "I'm comfortable right here, thanks."

Her target only laughs pleasantly. "Oh, please. I insist."

Anna plays along and joins Bernard at the door. Why is her mouse so calm? The guardian leads at a frustratingly unhurried pace up a spiral staircase and out onto a balcony. Crystals hang from the ceiling, creating a pompous curtain of dancing lights. The estate is a sprawling expanse. Crystals, antiques, and fine accouterments are one thing, but it's clear from this vantage point that the Bernard wealth knows no bounds. The detective recoils. The guardian towers over her wearing an expectant smile, but Anna shrugs, refusing to give this woman the satisfaction of a reaction.

"It's a lovely view," she remarks dispassionately.

The faintest of creases mars the handsomely smooth skin of Bernard's forehead. No GLOW injections in prison, though. "There is no equal to this estate in all the stations," Bernard avows. A curious look follows. "Perhaps you don't understand." She nods to herself, adopting a patient expression. "Frank

Roarke was the most powerful man on all the stations, a beloved man of the people—until he was cast out. Alejandro Martinho is ruthless where Roarke was a pacifist. One day he too will run out of schemes. It is the Bernard name that is most respected on all the stations. Do you know why that is?

"It's because *wealth* is the *only* thing that matters.

"The Bernards prospered all through the Final War and the Underground Winter, and I reap the benefit of that now. No, I will not sell Alejandro's secrets to the Coalition. Look how easily Alejandro strips the Coalition of its power. You are nothing but an impotent reminder of an old way of life. Like Roarke, the Coalition runs only so long as the people are pleased with it. You would bribe me with the leadership's favor? Of all the people who might hold any power over Terra Nova, you are the weakest and most powerless of any of us."

Anna folds her arms and leans lightly against an ivory banister. "You're right." She offers a conciliatory nod. "The Coalition isn't powered by monetary wealth. Its power lies in law and justice. I'm not here to bribe you. I'm here to scare you." She unfolds her arms and steps closer. "Your wealth was built on favors curried for terrorists under the cover of darkness. I'm holding a candle up to that wealth so everyone can get a good, long look at it." She takes another step, pushing her face right up to Bernard's. The sweet scent of perfume nauseates her.

"Do you feel the fire yet? You should. You should be sweating from it. Truth always emerges in the light." Anna breathes hard. The two women glare at each other.

Breaking, the guardian casts her eyes away and steps backward. She looks disgusted. "What is this talk of candles and flames? What do you know of truth? You have nothing: no proof, no power. You scare me not at all. I am growing tired of listening to this. The maid will see you out." Bernard turns on her heel and stalks away.

"I have the testimonials and documentation to prove all of it."

The guardian freezes. "The Bernard name is well-respected," she says quietly, her back to the detective. "We kept thousands of people alive during the

Underground Winter. There is no documentation to the contrary, and *no one* would dare make such accusations against us."

"Are you willing to stake your freedom on that? You're no different from your ancestors." Anna flicks the crystals hanging from the ceiling carelessly. "The days of war and famine may be over, but you're still playing the same game. The Bernards' influence catapulted you to the top of the space era. Now you collect station taxes under the pretense that it all goes towards this secret nutrient supplementation process and spend your people's money on chandeliers and dresskins.

"That's embezzlement, by the way.

"I know what you're thinking. Martinho will flex his power, so the accusations of assisting Terra Nova won't stick. You can probably avoid a prison sentence for the embezzlement charges. But how well do you know the man you've staked your wealth on? How well does *anyone* really know Alejandro Martinho?" Another pluck of string, and lights bob and eddy on the ground.

For the first time, Bernard's scornful pretense slips. She opens her mouth but can't find the words to defend herself. Her face burns with either fury, fear, or both.

The detective looks her squarely in the eye. "Allow me to make myself perfectly clear. There are two options here. You can cooperate with this investigation, tell us everything you know about Martinho, and carry on as the disgustingly corrupt leader of this unsuspecting station. Or you can protect Martinho, lose your position in the Coalition and all of your assets, and join him in prison." Anna raises her chin. Step into the trap, little mouse.

MAY 7, 3041 | MARSEILLE STATION, EARTH'S ORBIT

An obnoxious beep awakens the detective. She flops over and, realizing through the fog of sleep that this is her emergency frequency, she sits bolt upright and accepts the incoming call, thoughts of sleep banished. A holo of a woman appears before her. Anna rubs her eyes.

It's Guardian Bernard.

"I'm ready to talk. Come at once." The call terminates.

Pushing the sheets back, she hastily slips into her skins. It was a big risk confronting the guardian head-on, and she was starting to worry the woman wouldn't testify. She darts out of the cramped hostel room, pausing to regain her footing on the dark landing and making her way by the light of a single orange night orb flickering at the end of the row. The detective hurries to her borrowed hovercraft—technically stolen—and flies down the dark, narrow streets to the Bernard estate.

Once again inside the lavish estate of the Bernard family, Anna's hair stands up in the back, her jacket hastily buttoned over her skins. The soft glow of night orbs suspended in the air casts shadows along the wall. This time, she gratefully accepts coffee when offered.

Bernard waits in the sitting room. Forearms resting on the table, her face comes into sharp relief in the glow of the orbs, eyes rimmed red and puffy. Her nose is colored deep pink. All the arrogance and grandeur that the detective remembers vanish. Anna barely conceals her surprise, but the guardian pays no notice.

"Alejandro knows."

A shiver snakes down the detective's spine. "What did you tell him?"

Lilting laughter bubbles up from Bernard. "You really don't know anything, do you?" She smiles sadly. "In that case, you might not live long. We're both out of time, I'm afraid."

Anna slams her hands on the table and speaks through clenched teeth. "Start making sense before I decide to leave."

The smile fades. "Relax. I didn't tell him anything. I didn't need to. Alejandro has a way of finding things out."

"Does he know we're meeting now?"

The guardian starts to shake her head but pauses. "Well, maybe. Anything is possible with him."

"Then you'd better get to the point." The detective leans back and folds her arms. "You have three minutes before I walk out of here."

"We're going to need a lot longer than that. Why don't I start from the beginning?"

A rush of excitement floods Anna's veins. She rests her forearms on the table. "When was that?"

Bernard reaches one hand outside of the glow of the orbs. It comes into view again, holding a jimmy. The detective arches an eyebrow. She assumed this woman to be above such habits. The maid lights the jimmy, and the guardian closes her eyes and breathes deeply. Exhale. "Do you remember the explosion on the Johannesburg station?"

Mention of the unsolved case makes Anna grind her teeth. "Everyone remembers."

"That was just one of many of Alejandro's schemes." Bernard smiles wistfully, putting the jimmy to her lips once more. Anna's heartbeat quickens. At last, a testimonial.

Settling deeper in her seat, Bernard holds the jimmy loosely in one hand. "Alejandro first came to me when I was a young guardian, perhaps twenty-five years ago? The Coalition had just been briefed on a set of habitable planets in distant galaxies that could serve as suitable replacements for Earth and presented proposals for their top contenders. Alejandro was furious. He spoke out against wasting station resources scouting these planets instead of restoring our true home. He was overruled, as you may have guessed."

"So, what was his plan?"

Bernard laughs and shakes her head. "He'll kill me after this, you understand?"

"I won't let that happen."

More laughter. "Yes, if you say so, Detective. He planned to ensure that Earth remained the priority and formed a group of operatives to oversee the task. He wanted my support."

"Terra Nova."

The guardian does a hit of jimmy and smiles. "Exactly."

Folding her arms, the detective studies Bernard through the flickering orb light. "What did Martinho need you to do?"

"At the time, I merely had to turn a blind eye to the activities of his operatives. In exchange, he assured me that Marseille would remain prosperous in times of drought."

"The water supply."

Bernard smirks. "Yes, he can be quite literal."

"You're saying that Martinho orchestrated the raid of the SS849 station?" Anna hardly dares to breathe. This is it. The moment it all started for her.

The explosion that killed Ma.

"Precisely."

Finally. After all these years, she can be sure. A slow, shaky breath escapes her. Noticing her hands trembling, she clenches her fists and tucks them into her lap.

Oblivious, Bernard continues with an air of boredom. "Alejandro claimed that for Earth to become the main priority, pressure needed to be applied. He targeted the water supply early on, one of our most precious resources. The objective was to instill respect and fear."

The detective lets out a low breath. "Smart choice. As far as we could tell, they disposed of nearly everything they stole during the raid. We couldn't trace the shipment." Her eyes narrow. "What else did you do for them?"

"Well, Alejandro's operatives needed approval to justify travel." Bernard waves her jimmy in loops through the air over and over again, hinting at the frequency of such requests. "It would draw too much attention if the requests were always routed through him, so I handled many of them. There were also occasions when his operatives required a safe haven. I was instructed to permit a temporary rest on Marseille without asking questions.

"Things changed after the Coalition selected Zomenos for colonization. Alejandro made more and more demands of his supporters. He asked that we become a voice for the restoration within our own stations, that we vote against colonization, and that we spread the idea that colonization was merely an agenda of self-aggrandizement. Since you darkened my doorstep, I took the liberty of finding out what he's up to now. You won't like it."

"Try me."

Smoke clouds the guardian's features. "Skeletons. Arrests of high-ranking Coalition officials. Waterboarding." Her hand shakes. "I never agreed to such unseemly displays of torture and violence. He's working on his most vicious feat to date. He isn't turning the colony into a long-term fuel depot. When the first blast is detonated on Zomenos, the colony will be destroyed. A tragic end to a noble effort. I suppose that as long as that colony remains a viable alternative to Earth, his rule can be challenged. The colonists will be honored in a public ceremony. It's all planned." Anna is, for a moment, speechless. "You understand that Alejandro will deny all of this, Detective."

"It doesn't matter what Martinho says at this point." Anna stands. "I have more than enough to warrant his arrest." She gives Bernard an appraising look. "I suggest you come with me. You're not safe here, and I need you to testify in person."

The woman sniffs. "Haven't you been paying attention? Martinho *knows* that you're investigating him. You can't protect me. We're the same now, you and I. Dead women selfishly fighting for air." She pushes her chair back. "The only difference is, I think you might just be crazy enough to keep going. I hope you succeed, Detective."

Bernard has no intention of getting caught. The detective lunges across the table for the guardian, but she blinks and her witness is gone. Her fist slams onto the table, and she looks around. She's alone.

Anna jogs outside into the cool night air, sucking in air. The grounds are sparsely lit by more night orbs, but the tall trees hide most of their light. She trudges back to the hovercraft, grass crunching loudly underfoot. Bernard's testimony pins Martinho as the leader of Terra Nova once and for all, but

Bernard isn't here to testify, and Anna can't tail a Leap. With one hand on the door of her vehicle, she pauses, head cocked.

"You can come out now."

She waits with her hand resting lightly on the door, back to her pursuer. A tall figure rushes towards her, shockingly fast and light on their feet. Its shadow looms above her. Drop into a crouch and spin, leg out. Her assailant loses his feet and falls. In the next instant, Anna is on top of him, chest pinned to the ground, arms twisted behind his back.

"Who are you?" she demands, cuffing him. Her attacker remains silent. The detective seizes him by the shirt and flips him bodily so she can take a good look at his face. Hooded black skins shroud dark eyes. His face is painted white, with two dark circles disguising the shape of his cheekbones and brow. "A Skeleton," she surmises. "You're too late."

He smiles. "Am I?" Anna frowns, her retort on her lips, but something crashes into her skull from behind. Her whole body slackens, and she falls forward, her conscious mind instantly papered over in blackness.

CHAPTER THIRTY TWO

GUILLERMO

CARLOS LIES UNMOVING ON the stones of Samkelo Ngcobo's enclosed patio, blood and sinew and shattered steel seeping from the back of his head onto a towel. Shade sails tucked between high plastered walls create a canopy of privacy. Perversely, this opportunity to repair the xenobot's faulty power cell is what Guillermo wanted all along, but, ¡chingados, not like this! He exchanges a glance with Diego beside him, and the elder xenobot nods. They must work quickly. It won't take Alejandro long to discover them.

Guillermo spares a glance at the man harboring the fugitives. "Thank you for your help, Sam."

"It is nothing, old friend. I only wish you had come to me sooner." Kneeling beside Guillermo and his robots, Samkelo exchanges the blood-soaked rag beneath Carlos's head for a fresh one. Sabe, pero he's been too wrapped up in Carlos and Juan to consider what the other guardians might think of Alejandro's regime. Most of the others have meekly accepted the stallion's rule, but like Guillermo, the guardian of Johannesburg is old enough to remember the pain of leaving Earth and its bunkers behind. Of course he'd have reservations about the pace of its repopulation. Samkelo tucks the corners of a heated blanket around the unconscious xenobot, studying Guillermo out of the corner of his eye. "You have been in this robotics game as long as I've known you. Was this Frank's plan?"

Rocking back on his heels, Guillermo mops sweat from his brow. He's grateful for the shade, but the humidity on this station is brutal. "No, xenobots were my vision. Un gran futuro nace. Power makes a man greedy, and these leaders of ours can't help but chase it. Sometimes I regret choosing this path." Diego's head whips around, but he continues working.

Sage humor bends the other guardian's lips. "Indeed. You've done something incredible here, and it takes great strength of constitution not to use it for personal gain. Have you given thought to what comes next?"

It's *all* Guillermo thinks about. "Dismantling Alejandro's regime?"

"I mean afterward. Who will lead us when he is gone? It can't be Frank Roarke. The people chose a fresh start, and they were cheated, but that doesn't change the fact that it's time for someone new to steer the Coalition. Someone they can trust." Samkelo pauses. "I think it should be you."

Guillermo laughs. Frank Roarke made him the same offer, once. Who would follow him now after all the mistakes he's made? His own station crawls with skinless while he hides from their Coalition's highest leader. "One step at a time, amigote. Hand me the drill."

Carlos's entire neural network was damaged, its intricate wiring shredded. The reinstallation is slow. It's not as simple as plugging in a new power cell. It must be completely rewired and re-grafted into the xenobot's tissue. It's highly sensitive, focused work. Guillermo now wishes he'd brought more sutures and rags, but they spared only enough time to grab a new power cell and a small toolkit from his shop. Samkelo hands him another towel.

The Sun rolls across the sky behind the high walls of Samkelo's estate with alarming speed. The temperature drops, prompting Diego to cast about for more blankets for the unconscious Carlos. Por supuesto, even a xenobot can catch a chill. Samkelo assists where he can, sometimes falling back and giving

Guillermo and Diego space while they consult on a difficult choice. As day turns to night, Samkelo joins Guillermo on the stone tiles and speaks quietly in his warm timbre.

"Present circumstances notwithstanding, I'm glad you're here now. The news that we were misled about the habitat fills me with dread. It is time to make our stand against Alejandro together."

Exhausted, Guillermo pats the old guardian on the shoulder. Right now, it's time for a nap. Alejandro will have to wait. As soon as the repairs are complete, Guillermo trudges inside to a long, black couch and closes his eyes. He dreams of levitation and blood—blood on his boots, blood soaking into wood, blood in gold-flecked irises.

"Memo, wake up. Carlos is awake."

Guillermo lurches to his feet, head swimming. Diego crouches at his side. Staring blankly at the unfamiliar white room with its silvery shades and antique lamps, he remembers that he's on Samkelo's estate and rushes back out onto the patio. Carlos sits up, rubbing the crown of his head. ¡Mil gracias, he's alive! Relief courses through Guillermo's veins. Eyes wild, Carlos spins at the crack of boots on stone, but visibly relaxes at the sight of his creator.

"I'm so glad to see you." He grips Guillermo's hand tightly in both of his. "Where are we? What happened? Last I remember, I was in Martinho's hands."

With Diego's help, Guillermo fills him in, studying the xenobot's reaction closely. Fear, relief, joy, and anger pass through his eyes in quick succession. Carlos has changed, alright. Time will tell whether it's a permanent fix resulting from the new power cell, or merely the shock of his near-death experience.

Samkelo joins them, a silken bathrobe wrapped around his skins, carrying a tray of food and wearing an austere smile. "A miraculous turn of events. You've once again proven that you're not to be underestimated, Guillermo." He stoops to his knees, offering fresh fruit to the xenobot.

Diego pulls Guillermo aside. "I'm glad Carlos is okay, but I'm starting to think that Anna isn't."

Speaking of someone not to be underestimated. Guillermo spreads his feet and crosses his arms, but softens. Diego has spent weeks in the detective's company, and they've obviously grown close. "What makes you say that?"

A hologram springs to life, displaying a series of unanswered messages from Diego to the detective. "It's not like her to go this long without checking in. And it's not just these messages." He pauses, staring at his boots. "We established a neural link. She's not on Helsinki. Help me find her?"

Guillermo's mouth hangs open, suspended. "Wow. I thought you hated being joined to a human."

Diego glares at him. "You never asked for my consent."

Shaking his head, Guillermo chuckles. It's only different because it's *her*. Ignoring this information for the time being, he says, "Okay. So you lost her, eh? No te preocupes, Diego. You've got nothing to worry about. She's a spitfire, but she'll be back." He settles into one of Samkelo's many richly made velvet armchairs.

The xenobot's mouth forms a thin line. "Can you take this seriously, please?" He takes a deep breath and doesn't meet Guillermo's gaze. "The link is dead, but I traced her last known location. She's on the Marseille station." Guillermo slaps his hands to his face. Of course that impatient woman ran off after Bernard without them. A pleading note in Diego's voice recaptures his attention. "I'm banned from the Marseille station after that undercover operation. I never ask you for anything, but I'm asking now. Will you help?"

Guillermo shakes his head. More than anything, he wishes he could bury the hatchet with his first xenobot, but Diego's timing is miserable. "This is a really, really bad idea. Alejandro is looking for us, and Carlos needs time to recover. We should lie low."

Diego looks disgusted. "You never back down from a challenge, Memo." Shaking his head firmly, like this is something he can just swish away, he steps close. Green eyes brim with a fire Guillermo's never seen before. "You're always talking about the importance of familia. Well, Anna is family to me, and she's in trouble. Help her."

So, Diego really does care about this woman. Guillermo tilts his head back and closes his eyes. The detective is a prickly one, but she always comes through for him, and she's looked after his xenobot all this time. If Alejandro's Skeletons are after her, she must be onto something on the Marseille station. Diego is right. She needs their help. Guillermo sweeps his hair out of his eyes and heads into the kitchen. It's still the middle of the night, yet Samkelo is seated at a long steel countertop sipping coffee. "I have another favor to ask, Sam. Something's wrong. Diego and I are going to check it out. I'm sorry to even ask this, but can Carlos stay with you until we return?"

Looking completely unsurprised, Samkelo strides across the kitchen and grips Guillermo's shoulders. "Of course, Guillermo. Take care. I'll monitor your xenobot's recovery. We'll decide what to do about Alejandro Martinho when you return."

MAY 7, 3041 | MARSEILLE STATION, EARTH'S ORBIT

They Leap. A Coalition hovercraft is parked outside the Bernard estate, and a quick check confirms that it's stolen. The detective is here, then. All the windows are dark inside the estate, and only the automated orbs light up as they pass. A sweep of the perimeter makes it pretty clear that the place is deserted, except for Wright's vehicle. Inside, there's not a soul to be found, but the ash from a jimmy looks recent. Muy extraño.

The guardian shrinks into the tall bushes and keeps a lookout. With the detective and her witness both missing, where does that leave their case against Alejandro? They might have to make some hard choices pretty soon. Diego crouches low on hands and knees and shoves his head under the hovercraft, searching for evidence—torn skins, scorch marks from a laser cannon—anything that might help them find the detective. Staying low, Guillermo thrusts his armband out and adds more light to the search. Diego cranes his neck, looking for anything at all with human bodily fluids that could be used to identify an assailant, but there's nothing there. His face falls.

"Venga," Guillermo calls. "Maybe we can find something out back."

Diego wriggles out from underneath the hovercraft and pushes himself back onto his haunches. His sigh tells the guardian what he already guessed: there's nothing here. Diego reaches for Guillermo's outstretched hand, but freezes. He points and Guillermo follows his gaze. A set of tracks leads away into the trees.

Guillermo shoots a look at the xenobot. "Those could just be the staff."

Shaking his head, Diego lowers his voice. "I worked here for a day, remember? Staff don't go out this way."

They follow the tracks with renewed determination. Guillermo lags behind as Diego weaves through the thick grove of trees. "Slow down. I can't keep up." With an impatient huff, the xenobot obeys. They circle the grounds a second time, coming to a stop near the rear entry. Diego beckons with one hand, and Guillermo squints at the ground. Their query is bleeding. Muttering to himself, the xenobot tugs on his short curls and spins away. He's spiraling.

"Don't get carried away," Guillermo says. "We don't know who that belongs to."

Diego composes himself, scraping dried blood with a thick leaf and running the sample through his wristband unit. "It's not Anna's blood." Guillermo's heart hammers while a hologram populates with the result. "Son of a bitch! I knew it."

A man's face appears with travel credentials stamped underneath: ESTAÇÃO SÃO PAULO.

CHAPTER THIRTY THREE

MARILINA

PREGNANCY IS AMONG THE most obvious signs of a GLOW failure, but dozens of other inconsistencies could point to another one. The medical team's orders are clear, and they are well-experienced for the task by now. Determining the scope of this medical mystery is simply a matter of time. Straight-backed and stoic, Marilina sweeps down the line.

Keshi Okumu is behind a wall of holographs. She looks up. "Good morning, Dr. Chamorro. I have yesterday's results."

"Let's take a look," Marilina says. Okumu pinches the air with two fingers and rotates her wrist. "Guardian Mérieux isn't the only one," the doctor observes quietly, pointing to the progesterone and estrogen levels of their female crewmembers. "The sex hormones in these women are the same as those of a woman too young for GLOW." Anyone sexually active is at risk of sharing the former guardian's predicament, then. Marilina looks at Okumu.

"That is true. Growth hormone and melatonin have also declined in these crewmembers since the shuttle launch."

"The entire endocrine system is affected then," the doctor murmurs to herself. She bends closer to the holographs and verifies the technician's report, absently fingering her mother's cross. Every crewmember shows the same trend. GLOW is failing, and the problem extends far beyond unwanted pregnancies. Marilina rubs her arms, but it hardly soothes her. Soon, they would all begin to age normally again, their internal organs at risk of a whole host of issues. Hardly news she's eager to deliver to a crew that already ostracizes her.

Eyes round, Okumu watches the doctor. "What should we do, Dr. Chamorro?"

But they aren't authorized to do anything more without notifying the unit leads. "Just keep running the tests," Marilina says. "Don't share these results with anyone else."

As the morning dwindles, the consequences of this GLOW failure dawn on her. She's been too busy to open her own test results yet, but it's unlikely that the drug is working for her. Could she be pregnant? Her breathing uneven and wafer-thin, she opens her wristband unit and scans her own results. No: her hormone levels are definitely outside of range for GLOW, but she's not pregnant. A shaky sigh traverses her chest. Fatima would call this a milagro, but Marilina knows better. She was simply lucky. Be more careful. Alejandro is navigating far too much—and behaving far too erratically—to be ready for fatherhood right now. The ordeal makes her wonder: is she prepared for whatever he has in store for her?

"Fruit?" Okumu holds out a small blue fruit the size of a peach and covered in hair, like a kiwi.

The doctor looks up in alarm. "Where did you get that?" The technician points into the forest. Dumbfounded, Marilina stares. "You ate untested food from the forest?"

"The foundation of our colony is discovery, Doctor."

This evokes a smile. "We don't have to be reckless about it, Keshi." After a moment's indecision, she holds out her hand and accepts the fruit. There is no higher power watching over her, but that's no reason not to indulge in small pleasures. She's aging normally now. Might as well enjoy it while she can. Besides, this is the most her technician has acknowledged her since the mission was reclassified. Biting right into the hairy skin and sweet, its tangy juice erupts as the supple fruit gives way easily with each bite. Juice dribbles unexpectedly down her chin, but she catches it in her cupped hand.

"Be careful," Okumu advises, pointing at her skins. "The juice stains."

MAY 7 , 3041 | THE COLONY, ZOMENOS

The colony becomes visible as the forest clears, an oasis itself within the dreamscapes of this planet that forces Marilina to reckon with the divine once more. Neat rows of farmland greet the crew with crops ready for harvest. Beyond lies a long, short building housing the dormitory and, on the corner, the infirmary where the doctor will spend most of her time. It is idyllic. The crew fans out and looks on in subdued silence.

Their arrival brings none of the excitement it should have. Everyone knows what it means to be assigned to fuel collection. The colony might be theirs, but they'll spend the rest of their days mining this planet under long, hard hours. A sudden sense of loss crushes Marilina's shoulders. This is supposed to be her home and Mami's, the prescribed salve to wounds festering in her family and in so many others across the stations. Henry was right. She could have tried harder to change Alejandro's mind, and it might be too late now.

Simple and unpainted, the dormitory reminds her of the adobo houses on the Guadalajara station. She treads slowly down the long halls until she finds her room and bends toward a retinal scanner. Soft blue light bathes her face. A lock clicks, and the door swings open.

The room is small and threadbare, but it's hers, and the sight fills her with cozy, warm feelings and whispered promises of home. A cot is set up on the left, a dresser and desk on the right. The doctor sets her pack down on the chair, tucking her skins neatly into the dresser and laying out her wristband unit and first aid kit on the desk. Carefully, she sets Alejandro's flowers on the desk, near the window. An island breeze wafts from its petals. It deserves to be planted in the full light of Anima, but the researchers would never allow it. She sits on the edge of her cot holding a photo of herself sitting next to her brother, taken before her trade assignment at age 14. Quique's wild curls make her smile.

The glint of her pocket mirror catches her eye. Her reflection comes as a shock. Her hair has grown long in the months since the shuttle launch and now kinks and curls in all directions as it always does when it grows long. It's time to trim it. She turns the mirror over. Alejandro knows that the crew will arrive at the colony today. Will he visit? Does she want him to?

No sooner than she thinks it, Alejandro appears across from her. Stunned, Marilina jumps to her feet and tucks the mirror inside her skinpockets. "You're here."

That rare smile she's missed so much spreads across his face. "Don't look so pleased." He scans the room, gaze lingering on the soft yellow petals of the sacuanjoche. "Your accommodations are sparse. Is there anything you need?"

Resentment boils over: her frustration at being stonewalled by the crew, her confusion over Alejandro's intentions, and her impatience with his vagueness. "I don't need special treatment. What I need—what my crew needs—is the colony reinstated. We've built something wonderful here, Alejandro." She flushes, breathing hard. Not once since that day in the sandpits with Quique, when Papi sat her down and explained her future to her, has she raised her voice. She's always done her duty, thinking of herself last, and she's had it. If there really is a divine hand at work on this planet, she has earned the right to enjoy its creations.

"I see." Alejandro studies her for a long moment. "That's not possible."

Cooling off, Marilina closes the gap between them and takes his hands. This man responds to reason. "Of course it is. We've only just arrived. Reinstate the colony, please. The crew would be thrilled to resume what we've prepared so hard to do. This colony is the home we always wanted."

That golden spark she's seen before returns to his eyes, prompting an involuntary shiver from the doctor. Something's changed about him, and it runs deeper than those strange eyes. She's not sure exactly what, but she barely recognizes the man she once loved, who protected her with an entire fleet of starships. Does he remember his promises to her? He continues as if she hasn't spoken. "It's not possible because the drilling is already well underway."

Marilina shivers. "How can that be? The Coalition has only ever authorized colonization efforts here leading up to our mission."

Head cocked, his eyes glitter in an unnervingly stiff fashion. "There are channels outside of the Coalition for those with enough vision to pursue them. I never limit myself. Frank Roarke fostered a healthy spirit of debate among his guardians. Personally, I think they ask far too many questions of their leader."

Too many questions? Henry's words come back to her in a rush: *It's a 'shoot first, ask questions later' kind of thing. People are calling them his Skeletons.* She steps backward. It's true, then. The man she loves has turned away from the principles of the Meridian and embraced cruelty instead. Logic and reasoning were abandoned long ago. He will certainly never see the majesty of this planet.

Alejandro turns toward the desk and sits. "We're on the same side, dearest. We always have been. I want to return home, the same as you."

Marilina stiffens. "The colony is my home now."

With one leg crossed over the other, he rests his hands idly on his knee and gives her a patient look. "Zomenos is a poor imitation of Earth. You needed something to focus on after Quique passed, and I understood that. Look at how marvelously you've recovered! It's time to accept the *real* future of Earth's orphans. Come. This isn't a social call. I want to show you my plans." He reaches for her hand, but she jerks away.

"The drill site, you mean? I won't be a part of that."

Alejandro falls very still, eyes lingering on her hand, wrenched away from his. He straightens in his chair and fixes her with chilling eyes. Marilina flinches at that gaze, bereft of the kindness she's so used to. There's no trace of the rare smile she knows so well.

"What exactly do you mean?"

With a shuddering breath, the doctor raises her gaze to those golden eyes. They want different things, yes, but it's clear to her now that he'll never allow the colony to succeed. He views Zomenos as an obstacle to his grand plans and believes himself justified in dimming its light, but he's lost control. Marilina senses that she's on hazardous ground, but she throws caution to the wind. "I mean that this was a mistake. You should leave. I'm sorry, Alejandro."

The Coalition leader's left cheek twitches just below his eye. He takes in the sight of her: back straight, hands folded, head held high. Resolute and unyielding. His expression disconcertingly calm, he reaches deliberately into his skinpocket and retrieves a black pocket square. "You may not believe this later, but I'm very sorry too." Standing, he towers over the doctor. "I cared so deeply for you. I thought we understood one another." He frowns. "I was mistaken. I'm sorry for that." His expression twists into a hateful, vile look, and Marilina tenses, suddenly afraid. "You aren't the only one who misplaced their trust. I shared so much with you. For that, I can't allow you to leave."

Marilina leaps to her feet. The desk sways, and the vase falls to the floor. In one swift movement, Alejandro advances and crushes the palm of his hand holding the pocket square over her mouth. Her eyes widen, but he pins her with his other arm and prevents her escape. She rails against him and cries out. His pocket square only muffles her words.

"Don't struggle," he says in a cool tone. "This isn't how I want to remember you."

Tugging harder, she throws all her strength into wrenching free. Alejandro is much bigger than her, however, and at her continued resistance, he scowls and places his free hand over her right shoulder. With a grunt, he yanks hard. *Pop.* Marilina cries out again into the handkerchief and slumps against him.

"There, see? This is far more dignified." More pressure on the handkerchief cuts off her air.

Unable to breathe, Marilina bites down instinctively on Alejandro's hand with her failing strength. Iron floods her mouth. He jerks his hand free with a clipped yelp, and air rushes into Marilina's lungs. Sucking in a deep breath, she feels her head clear and formulates an escape strategy. Seizing her moment of opportunity, she twists side to side and pumps her arms outward in quick succession. Still reeling from her bite, Alejandro loses his grip. She stumbles free. The doctor spins and drives the palm of her hand up into her assailant's nose. He lurches forward, blood on his face and hands. Now! Marilina darts forward, hands curling around the doorknob, but it doesn't turn, and she thumps bodily against the door. She fumbles for the scanner but, in doing so, she smears his blood everywhere. The door remains locked. Panicking, the doctor desperately wipes the scanner clear.

Alejandro lunges at her and pins her to the ground, knocking the air out of her lungs. Dimly, she recognizes a potent island breeze embracing her. Her flowers were crushed by her fall. He presses his forearm into her throat, and terror clouds her thoughts. Fat, bloody dewdrops fall from his nose and spatter her face and skins. His face is covered in blood, his eyes bulging. Marilina sputters and struggles, limbs flailing wildly.

"Not this time," he snarls, trapping her free arm with his.

"Alejandro, *please*," she gasps, tears stinging at her eyes. He can't do this. He can't, he can't, he can't. The grip around her throat tightens. Marilina wheezes and coughs violently. Her strength weakens, then fails altogether. The last thing she remembers is Alejandro's blood-streaked, black-and-gold eyes over hers.

CHAPTER THIRTY FOUR

JACK

Lucy leads the way north to a riverbank, holding hands with Jack. His restless eyes rove the countryside. It's only slightly safer inside the colony's dome than out, where that fire-breathing dragon and its threats lie in wait. Long blades of dark blue grass ripple in the breeze, catching the light of Anima. It's a cloudless day, and a beautiful one. Lucy turns and winks, and despite himself, he grins back. Right now, before the Coalition's drilling directives come through, they can still pretend the colony can exist like this forever.

Past her thick braid, a stream climbs higher up into the mountain peaks in the distance, defying gravity like the wormhole that led them here. Their first waterfall. Downstream, a dark streak below the water's surface catches his eye. The water ripples and breaks, and a fish leaps into the air. It wriggles, suspended for one magical moment. A spray of clear water glistens in the daylight.

This can't last. Ever since he learned about Pyrrhos, the admiral feels like his back is against the wall, caught between loyalty to his beloved Coalition, however faraway, and the demands of an alien that can snuff out their little colony anytime it wants.

Laughing, Lucy splashes Jack. "Come on, the river's not that deep here. Let's go for a swim."

He shrugs. "Okay, but you better keep up." She wades out ahead of him, quick as a shooting star. The whole time, the admiral keeps his eyes peeled for an update from his officers on their search. They've got to settle the matter swiftly. This whole siphoning business is costing him precious hours that could be spent searching for Dad. Catching up to Lucy, he ducks underwater and swims to the bottom. Schools of fish zigzag past him through the clear water. He stares, thunderstruck, noticing their weird lips and shrunken fins. Pictures of fish from Earth were probably saved in holos somewhere on the stations, but he's never seen one. The riverbed is coated in big, smooth stones that reflect the morning sunlight in ribbons and streaks. Deep underwater, the river is a rich curtain of velvet. The sensory experience is overwhelming with his mind preoccupied, so Jack pushes off a stone and swims back up, breaking the surface with a splash.

Beaming, Lucy resurfaces at his side. "It's so warm!" His stomach is in knots, but he smiles back. It's starting to sink in that Dad's trail might be cold yet again, and without Roarke's help, nothing the admiral does will make a difference.

Toweling off for lunch, a message comes through from Pruitt. `Got something.` Jack's stomach somersaults. Finally. He nudges Lucy, and she follows him away from the riverbank, where they can talk without the rush of water. The last thing he wants is to shatter this crazy beautiful illusion she has of the world they're in, but he swore to himself he'd loop her in if Pruitt found anything, and they could really use a guardian for this. They step quietly into the trees, shaded from the noon daylight.

"There's something you need to know. I got a tip about an unauthorized drill site near the colony, so I sent a few of the men to check it out."

With drops of water clinging to her bare shoulders and collarbone, Lucy half gasps and half laughs. "You're kidding." He shakes his head, so she does a quick scan of their surroundings. The others have yet to discover their spot. "Okay. What's it doing here?"

"No clue, but I combed through all the old mission files, and there's no record of it with the Coalition." Jack tosses his towel over his shoulders and pats water out of his ears.

Pulling her dripping braid away from her damp skin, she cocks her head. "You think this is Terra Nova's doing."

"Has to be."

"Okay. What do you plan on doing with it?"

The admiral hesitates. What *can* they do? Pyrrhos wants the drilling to stop. A promise is a promise, but this one risks Jack's entire career. "I don't know yet. Now that we're on fuel collection, it seems like the Coalition won't want it destroyed."

Lucy's big eyes sharpen. "But if it *is* Terra Nova, that raises a lot of questions about Alejandro's allegiances." He nods. This is exactly why he wanted her in on this. Decommissioning this drill puts the colonists in Martinho's crosshairs. If an admiral is going to accuse the Coalition's leader of cavorting with terrorists, he better have a guardian to back him. Lucy rests her head against a tree and closes her eyes for a moment, but they spring open. "You waited to tell me this. Why?"

Suddenly nervous, Jack musses his hair. Nothing gets past her. "Well, you know, what with the baby on the way . . ."

"You didn't want me to worry."

"Yeah. You've got enough on your plate."

Her eyes narrow. "Let me decide when I've had enough. Deal?"

"Deal." Got off easy on that one. He pulls her into a hug. "Pruitt is standing by with an update. If it's not too much for you, I was hoping you'd join in." Lucy scoffs and shoves him playfully, and he makes the call.

A holo appears of Pruitt and Hoffman side by side. Pruitt's wide stance tells Jack the officer is calm and collected, but Hoffman is obviously agitated. With another glance in Lucy's direction, the admiral speaks first. "You two were gone awhile. Find anything good?"

Pruitt says, "Sorry about the wait. There's a drill here alright, but it's really well-hidden. Hoffman busted out some cool gadgets to find it."

Lucy's eyes are trained on Hoffman. "So, not Coalition issue then?"

The engineer shakes his head and licks his lips nervously. "Definitely not. Most of it's completely unregistered, which is bizarre because, well, it all should've been listed on the flight manifests going into this region, shouldn't it?"

The admiral exchanges a glance with Lucy. Hoffman's report only confirms what Jack's own cursory analysis led him to suspect. There's nothing for it at this point but to say what they're thinking out loud. "Anything to suggest we're dealing with Terra Nova?"

Hoffman's jaw drops as his eyes fall to the ground. "I didn't think of that. Maybe?"

"It would explain why none of the materials are registered," Pruitt amends carefully. "Can't say for certain, unless there's a head badge you all know about that we can look for."

"But it's definitely human technology?" Jack asks. Lucy's gaze could cut steel, but he avoids her eye. It can't hurt to be thorough after his encounter with Pyrrhos.

Pruitt shrugs. "Yeah, I'd be comfortable with that assessment."

Lucy shakes her head. "Terra Nova couldn't possibly have enough antimatter to pull this off without insider resources. They would have had help from someone in the Coalition. Maybe even a guardian." Jack grinds his teeth. He's pretty sure he knows which guardian, but he keeps his thoughts to himself. She plants her feet wide and looks at Hoffman. "Can you dismantle it?"

Hesitating, the admiral runs his hands through his hair. Pyrrhos's orders were to remove the drill, but Jack doesn't take orders from an alien, even an alien dragon. "Wait. Let's tread lightly with this. We can't be seen as making a unilateral decision here. If there's a mole on our crew—and the smart money says there must be—then they'll be reporting on our activity."

"Then we find them first." Lucy's eyes smolder with outrage.

Jack shakes his head. "We run this up the chain and leave it to the Coalition to decide. Keep watch over it for now. If anyone shows up, I want to know about it."

Pruitt's brow twitches. "Sure, I can do that." Sooner or later, whoever built this thing will come back for it, and when they do, Jack needs to know about it. As for Pyrrhos, well, as long as the drill is offline, it should be enough to leave them be.

MAY 7, 3041 | THE COLONY, ZOMENOS

Another flash of red streaks across the window. Lucy left for the dining hall with the others twenty minutes ago, so the admiral is alone. Against his better judgment, he leaps to his feet and jogs into the forest, away from the safety of the dome, pausing at the sight of familiar violet firelight. Pyrrhos emerges from the trees, lumbering high over Jack. Crackling firelight reflects in amber eyes. The dragon rests on its hind legs with its wings tucked out of sight, holding its head high in an almost stately way. The admiral shakes the urge to bow before the beast. It growls its perfect English.

"You have not fulfilled my request."

Back arched, Jack summons a smile. "Hello to you, too. We're working on it. I sent my men out to deal with the problem, but they only just arrived this morning."

Pyrrhos rears high and drops to all fours, long talons clawing into dirt. The ground quakes with his anger. "You must move more quickly."

Jack frowns, peering at the dragon, and notices belatedly that Pyrrhos's breath is labored, and he squints like he's in pain. The admiral takes a stab in the dark. "Does this 'lifeblood' have some kind of effect on you?"

A long tail whips the ground, but Jack waits. Eyes narrowed with suspicion, Pyrrhos says, "Siphoning it weakens me, yes. I am a shepherd of the land. Its pain is my pain."

"So, you have something at stake here." And the admiral has leverage.

Pyrrhos bows his head. "I am at your mercy, it would seem."

They can't destroy the drill now. Whoever went to the lengths to install it would have sent someone to protect their investment. Obviously, these dragons would never condone a fuel depot on this land, regardless of where it came from or its purpose. Yet even though the drill wasn't cleared for installation ahead of time, the fact remains that the crew is under orders to collect fuel for Martinho's regime. This puts the colonists at the heart of a conflict between an alien race and a corrupt Coalition.

Jack clasps his hands behind his back. After the way the Coalition bungled Dad's mission and subsequent investigation, he's not terribly sympathetic. Besides, a crew is a family. Ultimately, the admiral's responsibility isn't to the Coalition. It's to them, and they're in danger as long as this dragon views them as a threat. His leverage won't mean much if Pyrrhos sends his cronies after the colony. "That drill was planted without my prior knowledge or approval. Consider it gone." To hell with Martinho.

Eyes still narrowed, Pyrrhos leaps for the admiral so quickly that Jack doesn't even have time to blink. The beast towers over him, reptilian eyes boring into its prey. "Do not betray me, Jack Monroe. It will be the last thing you do."

The admiral holds his ground and nods. Satisfied, the dragon spreads its wings and launches into the night sky. When Pyrrhos is far from sight, Jack lets out a shaky breath. He heads back to the colony, unable to shake the feeling that he's about to bring a supernova down on his crew.

CHAPTER THIRTY FIVE

ANNA

A NIGHTCLUB RAGES INSIDE the detective's skull. What the hell happened? She tries to rub her head, but her arms are bound behind her. A hard tug tightens a rope against her wrists, but she breathes a sigh of relief. Handcuffs are harder to escape. Hazy memories swim through her mind. Bernard's testimony, the escape, and the Skeleton that clubbed Anna on the way out. Jerky roils up from her stomach. Eyes watering, she rolls miserably onto her side in case she hurls. Something soft brushes against her. She opens her eyes and sees—

Nothing.

Pulse spiking, Anna blinks. Her surgically enhanced eyes adjust to the darkness a second later, and the room slowly takes shape around her. It's not a room, not even close. With colossal effort, the detective lurches upright and looks around.

She's lying on a pile of bodies.

Shit.

Anna heaves herself forward. This is the worst goddamn day of her life. Well, second worst—the bomb that blinded her and killed Ma sucked, too. She rolls down the human graveyard, grimacing the whole way, and smacks down hard on smooth stone. Turning her head, she spots another body rolling after her fast. She grunts and rolls to the side. Propping herself up high, she takes a good look at the soft, fleshy person she'd woken up next to. Recognition sets in. Oh, fuck. It's van Leeuwen.

More bile burns her throat, and this time, she doesn't keep it down.

Enough. Breath heavy and ragged, she rolls onto her back and contemplates her predicament. Stalactites or stalagmites—whichever—dangle from the ceiling by the thousands. A cave, then. Beneath her, the cave floor is smooth rock, worn down by years of dripping water. She could be anywhere, but a Skeleton would have dispatched her on their home turf, so she must be on São Paulo. She's gotta get out of here and find Bernard. Wavering, her gaze flicks to the guardian on her left. Should she do something about van Leeuwen? The Finn was nice to her, and the idea of leaving him behind puts the taste of curdled milk in her mouth. A quick glance at her own feet tells her what she's already guessed: she's bound at the ankles too. Well, she's no use to him in her condition, and she's not getting far like this.

The stench of the bodies nearest her is a big clue that they aren't recent. Looks like her captors left her here for dead. Cowards. She supposes that this is where all the Skeletons' victims end up. Anna sets to work wriggling along the cave floor. It's slow progress. She stares bitterly up at the long, sharp daggers hanging down from the ceiling. A fat lot of good they're doing her way up there.

Fuming, she worms her way steadily through the cave. Bernard has to testify against Martinho, but the only problem is, she doesn't want to be found. It's unlikely that the guardian got herself trapped here . . . wherever "here" is. Bernard can Leap, ropes or not. If it were Anna, she'd have Leaped as far away as humanly possible. Nuñez and Diego better have had better luck repairing Carlos, or they're all screwed. After well over an hour, a woman moans.

She can't believe it. Bernard is here after all.

Reinvigorated, the detective continues her crawl. The Skeletons may have gotten the jump on Bernard at her estate, but if she comes to before she's arrested, she'll never be found. Anna grits her teeth and wriggles forward on her belly.

Anna stops. The woman ahead is dressed down in blue Coalition skins, not the long dresskins Bernard loves so much. This person's hair is shorter than Bernard's, and a lot darker. The detective quickly loses heart. This is just some station-dweller that got on the wrong side of a Skeleton. Well, at least there's a set of low-hanging daggers up ahead. Anna pushes on. With any luck, one of those crystals will be sharp enough to cut rope.

Arriving at her target, the detective flops onto her back and drags her bonds over a long, skinny dagger. She cuts her hand at once. "Shit!" Tongue between her teeth, she drives harder, keeping her movements short and precise. The rope starts to give.

Crack. The icicle cleaves in two.

"Great," she mutters. "Now what?"

About 10 or 20 kilometers away, the Skeleton victim stirs. "Is someone there?"

Sigh. What does she look like, some kind of hero? "I'm here, but I don't think I'll be much help." Then, to Anna's amazement, the other woman stumbles to her feet and turns to her. "They didn't tie you up?"

"Who?" The stranger looks every bit as confused as Anna feels. She's a small thing, alright. Hardly worth killing. No wonder the Skeletons didn't bother to bind her hands or feet. The little woman steps forward, and suddenly her full condition becomes clear. Eyes widening, Anna's detective brain analyzes the sight before her. This woman has been through a ringer: face smeared in blood, throat purpled all over (choked by someone with big hands), arm clutched to her side (dislocated shoulder, probably). Through all that blood, this woman stares at the detective with every bit as much curiosity in her eyes as Anna feels.

"Your eyes," the stranger croaks. "Who did that to you?"

"Don't take this the wrong way, but I'd be more worried about whoever did that to you."

The woman looks unafraid. "He won't be back. He thinks I'm dead."

Snort. "You should be."

"Yes, you're probably right. It was a miracle." Anna notes the way she rubs her thumb over a cross around her neck as she says it. "Where are we?"

"Not sure. My guess is São Paulo, though." Eyes bulge, but the stranger keeps her thoughts to herself. Joining Anna, she bends close, and the detective can't help but flinch at being so close to someone so disfigured. The woman reaches past Anna for the broken dagger and breaks Anna's binds with it. Finally, but unexpectedly free, the detective lurches forward with a gasp. The stranger gestures to her own arm, the dislocated one.

"Will you return the favor? I can't set it myself. I tried."

With a grunt, Anna grabs the bad arm and yanks on it, popping the arm back into place. The detective bows as an involuntary whimper escapes her new companion. "Good as new." She sticks out her chin. "So, who did this to you?"

The woman's laugh is thick with scorn. "You'd never believe me if I told you. What about you?"

Shrugging, Anna rubs her wrists. "The Skeleton crew. They'll *wish* they're skeletons when I'm through with them."

"What are they like?" Sudden urgency blooms in the woman's voice.

"Cowardly assholes, that's what." The detective pauses, narrowing her eyes at the woman. "You've never seen them before?" Her new friend shakes her head. But that's impossible. There are Skeletons on every station, walking around in broad daylight, harassing innocent people left and right. The only people who could possibly miss them are the—wait. Anna peers closer at the woman's skins. They're Coalition issue, alright, but they have a shiny purple emblem at the collar and silver trim. She whistles. "You're a colonist." The woman nods. "I think you missed your flight."

"No, I made it to the colony. I was portaled to this place by . . ." She bites her lip and fumbles with a cross around her neck ". . . by Alejandro Martinho."

Anna barks a laugh, but a haunted look in the woman's eyes chokes off her amusement. She's telling the truth, or thinks she is, anyway. The detective holds her hand out to her small companion. "You got a name?"

The woman accepts her hand. "Dr. Chamorro."

"Detective Wright." A fresh idea blooms. If Chamorro portaled into this cave, then she can portal out. Can she take them straight to Martinho? He knew about Carlos the first time, but he's not expecting a rematch anytime soon. They're not going to get this kind of advantage twice. She sticks her chin out. "Martinho roughed you up pretty good. Kinda looks like he left you for dead."

"Yes."

"How does that make you feel?"

Chamorro grips that cross around her neck again and swallows, turning away. In a very small, but very clear voice, she says, "It makes me want to return the favor."

"Good." Anna spins and faces the cave walls. That just leaves one big question unanswered. "This portal of yours. Does it travel both ways?"

"I can take us to him, if that's what you're suggesting. There's no way of knowing we're coming. He's at the colony, Detective."

"To detonate it. Right." The look of plain shock on the doctor's face makes Anna raise her eyebrow. "You didn't know?" Chamorro shakes her head. "Don't worry, he won't get that far. You might have to face him again. You good with that?"

The doctor lets go of the cross around her neck and straightens. "I think I need to see whatever happens next."

Anna grins, and she can tell her eyes are glowing again from the way Chamorro fidgets. "Let's get out of here, then. I've got someone I need to find first. Someone who can help us both get our revenge."

CHAPTER THIRTY SIX

ALEJANDRO

MAY 8, 3041 | THE MOUNTAIN PASS, ZOMENOS

I**T'S MIDNIGHT. A BREEZE** flits in and out of the drill site, cooling Alejandro's cheeks. He lifts his face to it, its clarity a welcome respite from a day of difficult decisions. His Marilina was to be the one to herald in this victory. Her betrayal means it must be he who sees this project through to its completion, and that does not come without consequences. Eyes closed, he withdraws a breath, releasing its weight from his chest. A process that takes many weeks must now be resolved this night.

Behind him, a jaunty crunch of leaves announces Kevem's arrival. Turning, Alejandro sees Pagu tread silently beside him. He smiles. At last, someone he can count on. "Welcome, my friends. We must make haste. The time has come to claim our rewards and leave this place once and for all."

Kevem grins. "You got it, boss." His platinum hair catches the faint light of the waning moon. Its partner is absent from the sky, and the cloud cover ensures that it's considerably darker tonight than on previous visits to this place. So, even the moons must go it alone when the time comes. All the better. A cover of darkness will ensure their privacy, and their success.

"Your will shall be done, sir." Pagu bows, her curtain of dark, springy hair spilling over her shoulder. Sycophants, both of them, yet they remain among his most ruthlessly clever operatives, and the closest things to friends Alejandro can say he's ever known on this strange and twisted journey. Oh, the journey it has been.

"Tell me, how is the recovery coming along?"

Pagu turns her palm upward and throws up a holo. "You'll be pleased, sir. Our stores are already filled to 10% capacity."

A nerve works in Alejandro's temple. "Just ten."

The woman's gaze flicks to Kevem, whose face is, as it so often is, slack with incomprehension. Pagu licks her lips. It must surely be taxing to work so closely with the dim-witted man, but she's never once complained, and Kevem does have his uses. "Yes, sir. There was interference, presumably from the colonists. We can certainly make up the difference. We haven't yet employed the hydraulic system."

A flick of the wrist. "Yes, I know about that." Alejandro steps forward and gazes up at the magnificent drill rig, a result of years of careful planning and Kevem's own ingenuity. It was no small feat to smuggle the rig into this star system undetected, conceal it, and assemble it before the colonists ever arrived, but one must never underestimate the determination of Terra Nova. Alejandro himself never ceases to be amazed at what this pair can accomplish behind the Coalition's back. Their plans won't be undone by a few colonists' haphazard attempt at dismantling their equipment. Alejandro folds his hands under his chin. It won't do to underestimate them either. Marilina is proof of that. May her god have mercy on her. "The colonists are proving resistant to the drilling. We may encounter difficulties from them."

"Understood. I'll see to it that the colonists aren't a problem for us any longer." Pagu's eyes, two black pools of ink, don't blink.

Brow pinched between forefinger and thumb, Alejandro says, "Please, Pagu. We've talked about this many times before." He has no doubt that she can accomplish it. Dispatching a crew of less than a hundred people, most of them unsuspecting civilians, could be done in a night. True, without Marilina, his own dwindling tolerance for the colonists wears thin, but the Coalition remains compliant, and he intends to ensure that they remain that way. Premature termination of the colony would be disastrous for his campaign for Earth. It must appear an unfortunate accident, brought on by the colonists themselves. The woman's singular aptitude for assassination has proven, at times, useful, but she's never cared for subtlety or diplomacy. "No harm can come to the colonists before the recovery is complete." With Pagu, one can never be too explicit. SS849 taught him that.

Kevem glances at Pagu, yet when she remains silent, he says, "We have more than mere hydraulics at our disposal, sir. Compressed air would deliver more pressure and speed up the recovery." Chastised, Pagu clasps her hands behind her back and casts her gaze meekly down at crystalline soil, white as lily pads.

Another breeze buffeting his firmly set shoulders, Alejandro turns his smile on Kevem. Yes, the pair of them complement each other perfectly. "Do that, please. We have mere hours left before daybreak. The recovery must be complete by morning."

"All hail the pale blue dot," they chorus.

MAY 8, 3041 | THE MOUNTAIN PASS, ZOMENOS

It is but a matter of time until the drill is functional once more, and the peaceful rush of the river nearby is quickly drowned out. The drill site is full of the raucous screech of machines, but the result will be more rewarding than the temporary peace of this exoplanet. The chaos invites memories of the orphanage, of squealing children running with abandon, of complacent nuns that did nothing to curtail such wanton rebellion. What a waste. Orbs light up the site, but Terra Nova's instructions are clear: draw as little attention as possible. Overhead, their cloud cover holds steady.

At nearly two in the morning, Luiz arrives with close to a hundred more operatives. Relief, smoother and sweeter than a black cup of cafezinho, courses through Alejandro's veins. The android's ingress means that the new portal on São Paulo is online and ready to receive the first batch of ore. Alejandro steps close to the container. Pale moonlight reflects off clear, sparkling crystal streaked in violet. The minerals on this planet are of incredibly high grade, higher than anything they've collected from the mines below Mars or Enceladus. A relatively straightforward refining process from this container alone will produce more energy than the stations use in a year.

"You are close to attaining your vision, sir." Luiz stares down at the containers between them.

Alejandro's lip curls. "Indeed. Thank you for your attention to the portal. The final piece of this puzzle is in place." Luiz nods. Turning away from the containers, the Coalition leader gazes out at his team, singing merrily. Many of these operatives have been at his side since his earliest days at the orphanage. Feckless youths without the strength of mind or body to improve their own circumstances, let alone those of their fellows. Even then, Alejandro recognized that Earth's orphans were in need of firm guidance, and that the price of such guidance is absolute obedience. Terra Nova will always remain his single greatest achievement, a beacon of unquestioning compliance. Through it, he will shepherd these lost little orphans home.

"We've cleared many hurdles on the path to this day, you and I, Luiz. It embarrasses me to admit that when Guardian Nuñez surprised me with that xenobot, and again when his detective squirreled away that weak-willed deserter Victoria's testimony, I thought we'd reached the end." Unsurprising though it is to learn just how infirm Victoria's constitution really is, he'd nevertheless hoped that their long-standing alliance would buy her silence. A nerve works in his temple. "I should have known I could rely on you to trim back such unseemly loose ends."

Luiz nods. "It is my pleasure to serve."

Across the gaping ditch before them, Terra Nova works merrily, shouting orders over the squall of the machines and hauling containers onto hovercrafts for transport through the portal. Alejandro's gaze flits to the android. "What is it that makes humans so prone to such short-sighted, self-centered, ungrateful choices? I offered Guillermo exactly what he's always wanted. Marilina, too. What is it about our pathetic minds that twists us away from loyalty, from obedience, from our promises to each other?"

Luiz shakes his head. "That's not for me to say. A newer model, perhaps one of these xenobots, may have an answer."

A smile. "*I* am the final model, Luiz."

And it's time to make use of his upgrades. A peculiar thing happened when Alejandro joined with the xenobot's neural network. Something akin to memories—or perhaps merely just programming—flooded his brain. Scattered, broken fragments, they were, many of them incomprehensible. Yet within them, there were useful bits of information, among them a way of turning air into a weapon. The tactic is not dissimilar to the levitation he mastered early on in his ownership of the Cerebrum particles, and in this case, such a clever manipulation could make the difference in this recovery.

Stepping forward, Alejandro approaches the drill site, where a probe has been inserted to speed up recovery. It's still only at thirty percent. "Remember this moment, Luiz. Tonight, we make history." Feet lifting from the ground, he hovers above the drill and angles his open palms down. A controlled stream of air pulls from the atmosphere, forming a vortex between his hands. With careful patience, he draws in more current until his weapon is a meter wide. Then he takes aim.

CHAPTER THIRTY SEVEN

GUILLERMO

THE FILE ON THEIR Skeleton is light. Paulo Oliveira is fifty-eight years old, under 180 centimeters tall and a sprightly 70 kilos. Brown hair and eyes. No identifying marks, scars, or tattoos. No prior convictions either. No one said this would be easy, but damn if it isn't nerve-wracking to be on São Paulo when Alejandro is already looking for them. ¿Qué se le va a hacer? Diego is determined to find Detective Wright, así que it's the least Guillermo can do to help.

The pair pay their suspect's flat a visit, but there's no one there. Searching the small unit, they find the Brasileño's cloud access point, and Diego hacks into it with ease. Oliveira's reminders are frustratingly lacking in details: dinner with Miya last weekend, a dentist appointment, a morning conference call. Guillermo thumbs through the man's contacts looking for Miya. He punches the woman's address into his wristband unit and hurries out of the flat, but no one answers the door at her apartment. Another dead-end.

Guillermo and Diego wander down the road to the Ribeira de Iguape River and sit on a bench. "It can't be a coincidence that a Skeleton was at the Bernard estate at the same time as Anna," Diego says. He rests his elbows on his knees, staring into the murky brown water with a brooding stitch between his shoulders. "What could Wright have found on Marseille that was worth targeting her? And where is Bernard now?" Guillermo doesn't answer. He wishes he could take his hovermoto out to clear his head right about now. A chill breeze whips through his light skins, but the temperature automatically adjusts. They blend right in here, and most station dwellers pay them no attention, but before long they are joined by a wizened elderly woman with long gray hair and yellowed teeth.

"São mexicanos?"

Guillermo winks. "But of course." Her accent is thick, but her mind is sharp.

She nods shrewdly, her bedraggled hair fluttering in the breeze. "Do you miss Mexico? I miss São Paulo—the real city, before the war, with the salt of the ocean, suntans, and colorful birds."

An indulgent smile. "The only memories I have of Earth are of the bunkers."

The woman spits. "The São Paulo of old was much like this place, only it's been many years since it was this nice." She brandishes a thin, frail arm. "War turns everything to ash."

Diego watches her with interest. Few people can say they remember an Earth without bunkers. "It must have been nice to earn an upgrade."

She smiles then, revealing a gap between her front teeth, and looks fondly out at the river. "We used to play in the caves, you know."

The guardian frowns. "Caves?"

"Yes, the caves underground," the old woman repeats. "You don't know about the caves?" She straightens proudly and looks sideways at Diego with another of her crooked smiles. "My parents always hated those caves. It's a wonderful place for a child to get lost, you know. Youth is a dangerous thing, my little garoto."

His restless mind had begun to wander, but this jolts him back to the present. "¡Híjole! What did you say?"

The old woman glowers at his suddenly rude disposition. "I said that youth is dangerous. Don't be so sensitive," she croons, taking his hand in both of her shriveled ones.

Guillermo pulls away, heart hammering with excitement. A cave would be the perfect place to hide a captive. "No. You said a child could get lost in the caves. How big are these caves, exactly?"

"Oh, the caves are several kilometers long each. It's a *big* river, can't you see?"

Diego catches on. "Where is the nearest cave?"

"The Caverna Santana is just up the road. Follow the river. Don't get lost now, my garotos!"

The old woman cackles behind them as they take off sprinting along the riverbank. Guillermo runs as fast as his legs will carry him. The detective has been missing for nearly twenty-four hours, so if the Skeletons have her, the chances of her safe return are dwindling fast. They can't let the Skeletons win. Setting aside whatever intelligence the detective stumbled into, Diego obviously has feelings for the woman. Man and xenobot tear along pavement at reckless speeds, but Guillermo doesn't care. He whips around a couple locked in an embrace knee-deep in the wild grass that grows along the river. They run for 2 or 3 kilometers before he spots what the old woman described: an enormous cave that bores into the mountainside and disappears beyond the river. It's an awfully public and conspicuous place to stow a hostage. The far more likely explanation is that this is where someone might dispose of a body. Don't think like that. She's alive. She has to be. He takes a deep breath and rushes on, the cave swallowing him up.

They plunge into near-darkness. Guillermo skids to a halt, fumbling with his pocket orb. Light clicks on, and he waits for his eyes to adjust to the orange glow. Cool, damp air clings to his skin, carrying a musty aroma. The entryway to the cave has a domed ceiling, but as they continue deeper below ground, the cave opens into a labyrinth of passageways and corridors. This pinche search could take days.

The guardian's heart sinks. "Mierda." The sound carries surprisingly far. He covers his mouth. The detective's captors could be down here with her.

They begin the tedious process of searching the tunnel. Guillermo doesn't carry much with him, but Diego sears a mark into the walls of the passageways they clear with a laser cannon. They move quickly, pausing just long enough in each corridor to convince themselves that there's no evidence of recent human occupation.

One hour passes, then two. Guillermo grows weary. Thoughts of stopping cross his mind many times, but each time he presses on. If the detective is still alive, she doesn't have time for him to rest. If she isn't—he grimly reminds himself again and again—he needs to find her and the brutes responsible for her death before the evidence vanishes. For Diego. So, he pushes on, searching everywhere, his legs screaming for rest while his mind races with possibilities. Just as the guardian considers calling the search off, voices ping off the cave walls ahead. He turns toward Diego, who nods, and they tear off after the sounds, the light of their orb bouncing ahead of them. This is it. They have to be prepared for whatever they find. Guillermo thumbs the safety off his own laser cannon. They round a bend and stumble across two women.

¡Mira! It's the detective.

Diego skids past him and collides with Wright. "Oh, thank goodness. I was so worried." He pulls her into a crushing hug, but she doesn't protest. The guardian smiles to himself.

Wright only laughs. "Thanks for bringing reinforcements, Diego. Have I ever told you that you make a good detective?"

The ladies' story is unbelievable. The young doctor traveling with the detective looks worse than the time Guillermo went topside on Earth and lost control of his hovercraft going over the Vólcan de Colima—*while* it was erupting. So, this is what Alejandro is capable of. Puede caminar como un hombre, pero es un demonio. The doctor doesn't speak much, but the look of iron determination that she wears says she's tougher than she seems.

Back outside in the daylight, Guillermo crosses his legs on a patch of grass and stares up at the detective. "So, Alejandro figured out how to extend the

Leap beyond the controller." The stallion is full of surprises. "And now he wants to suck all the juice out of that planet and blow the colony and all those people with it?"

Wright nods, those glowing eyes on fire. "That's the gist." She plants her feet wide. "Here's what I'm thinking. Dr. Chamorro here can get us onto the planet with that portal of hers. We surprise Martinho with a rematch with Carlos. He'll never see us coming."

Guillermo shakes his head. "What about Victoria? Even if we take out Alejandro, we need her testimony to seal this case."

She shrugs. "She Leaped. Could be anywhere by now. We're better off getting whoever is helping him on the colony to flip."

"Whoever is with him now is in this deep. They won't flip, no matter what we offer. Victoria already went on record. We need her."

The detective knows he's right, but she crosses her arms. "Facts are facts. She's long gone, and I have no idea where to.

Guillermo leans back in the grass. "I do." The piggyback Leap is something he's floated with Roarke many times, but no one's ever attempted it. Could be dangerous. Fatal, even. But in all the time he's spent on the stations, this is the first time he's felt close to moving on, to rebuilding a home, to Juan. They just need to find their witness first. "Let me worry about that. I'll take you to Carlos, but after that you're on your own. I'm going after Victoria."

MAY 8, 3041 | SS849, SATURN'S ORBIT

Piggybacking lands the guardian in the middle of the wetlands. A biting wind thrashes the air, rendering the thermal regulator of his skins useless. His muscles tauten reflexively against the numbing squall. It'll be mere minutes before frostbite sets in. He squints at his surroundings in the receding artificial station light. With a shock, he realizes that this station is completely devoid of the

Sun's warm rays. Victoria Bernard Leaped out of the Earth sector entirely, and piggybacking after her blindly might now cost Guillermo his life.

He pitches his head back and casts his gaze skyward, searching anxiously for the familiar golden star, but falls backwards with a startled cry: the unmistakable arc of Saturn's icy rings looms close. He's on Enceladus. Damn it, Victoria. Mopping his brow with the back of a shaking hand, he closes his eyes and takes a deep, calming breath. Settling on the ground to think, his hands meet slick permafrost. He pushes himself back up onto his knees. Immediately beyond his location, richly colored moss of burgundy and green stretches across a long, flat plain.

Rubbing his frozen hands together, he stumbles to his feet and closes his eyes. There are just a few precious minutes left before these punishing temperatures cause him permanent damage. If he's going to get out of here alive, he needs to focus. Concentrating, he grasps for the one person on this station he might be able to trust. The merciless gusts vanish, allowing some measure of warmth to creep back into his skin.

Lei Du's office light is still on, despite the late hour. Back to the door, the guardian asks, "What are you doing back here so late, Campbell?" She turns, and her next words die on her lips. "Guillermo? What in the universe are you doing here?"

He steps forward and bows his head. "It's good to see you again, Lei."

"Did you Leap all the way to this sector from the Guadalajara station?" Du marvels, bustling around her desk and taking a closer look at him. If memory serves, she's a short, squat woman with sharp eyes and a sharper tongue.

"From São Paulo, actually," he replies grimly. "Lei, this isn't a social visit."

"Clearly." She leans against her desk, her frown lingering on his inadequate gear. "What's this about, then?"

Groaning, he buckles into a stiff, wooden chair. "I'm looking for Victoria Bernard. She's a witness in a highly classified investigation, and she's on the run."

Du studies him with hands clasped lightly before her. "Victoria has everything she could want on the Marseille station." The prickly guardian always loved the work on SS849, but her position never earned her the same wealth and influence as the other guardians, and her words are grizzled with resentment. "Why would she run, and why here of all places?"

Shrug. "I assume she thought she could disappear into anonymity here."

The woman's expression is unreadable. Hands resting on either side of the desk, she shakes her head. "Victoria wouldn't flee her home unless the circumstances were extraordinary. What aren't you telling me?"

A barking laugh escapes Guillermo, but inside he's squirming. Everything rides on Du helping him now. "I've missed you, Lei. You've always been able to cut right through the pretense, haven't you?"

The knuckles on her hands are white from clenching. "Don't make me ask twice."

"Cálmate, relax. I can't tell you much, but it involves Alejandro."

The woman's mouth hovers open. "Wow, really? Why didn't you say so sooner? Alejandro has been making fools of the Coalition from the beginning. How can I help?"

Sighing, the tension leaves Guillermo's shoulders. He still has allies in the Coalition after all. "Thanks, Lei. Like I said, this is all classified. All I can tell you is that Victoria Leaped here two days ago. The Coalition would be deeply indebted to you for helping figure out where she is now."

Her eyes narrow. "How could you possibly know that she Leaped here?"

"I piggybacked."

Forehead creasing, Du leans forward and whispers, "How?"

"Never mind that. We need to find Victoria."

This earns him a glare. "Fine. Hold onto your secrets, Guillermo." She taps her bottom lip. "A transport shuttle arrived yesterday with new recruits. If I were her, I'd join up with them there." A hologram opens, displaying a glowing roster of names.

Guillermo stands and joins her. "I don't see her on there."

"She could be using a false name," Du persists, eyes glued to the list.

"Well, unless you propose knocking down the door of every woman on the list, that doesn't help us." He drums his fingers on her desk. "Why don't I take a trip to the barracks and see if anyone knows anything there?"

Du's head jerks upward. She snorts. "The barracks? You? If someone is harboring a fugitive, they aren't going to talk to you or me."

"What do you suggest, then?" Guillermo snaps.

"I suggest that you get some rest and let me handle it," she retorts. "My men will look into it."

Headshake. "No way. I don't want anyone else involved."

"Those recruits will be more willing to talk to my men," she says. "Besides, you're exhausted, and you came to me for my help. Campbell is sharp as a tack. He'll find her."

He can't just fall back and let some SS849 miner do his job for him, but Du is right. He's been pushing through a fog of exhaustion ever since the encounter with Alejandro. It can't last. "Fair enough," he admits. "Let's see what he can find out."

"Done." Du strides briskly to the door. "Let's find him and get you settled. You should find the visitor's suite to your liking." She holds the door open for him, waiting.

"Lei, I can't stay in the visitor's suite. It's too conspicuous. Victoria thinks she's safe here, but she'll Leap again the moment she thinks she's being followed."

The resignation in his voice stops Du from arguing. "Then you'll have to stay in the men's barracks like everyone else. Campbell can take you there." She appraises him again with a harsh look. "You'll need warmer skins. Damn it, Guillermo—this is the tundra. What were you thinking, chasing a blind Leap?"

Guillermo steps past her and turns. "I was thinking that the future of every orphan depends on me bringing Victoria in to the Coalition."

CHAPTER THIRTY EIGHT

MARILINA

MAY 8, 3041 | THE MOUNTAIN PASS, ZOMENOS

T HE DOCTOR STEPS OUT of the portal and back onto the sparkling white soil of the colony. To her left, Detective Wright releases her grip on her shoulder. On her right, the two robots stare straight ahead. The mirror portal like burning coal to her, she pockets it quickly. Ever since she awoke in that cave, she's dreaded this moment, but she faces it with the courage of Mami, Papi, Quique, and all the other Chamorros behind her. Mami is the reason she's still alive: moments before she lost consciousness, she slipped her fingers through her leather necklace and loosened Alejandro's grip around her neck. For the first time in her life, evidence of a higher power emanates with clarity. She rubs her cross and whispers a silent prayer for strength.

Dropping to a crouch and heading for the cover of the mountainside, the detective beckons Marilina to her side. The doctor swallows and joins her, clapping her palms over her ears. Why didn't they think to bring earplugs for this deafening noise? The group divides, and the two robots duck into a thicket of trees. Just around the face of the mountain, a chasm many kilometers deep splits the ground. A massive steel rig towers over the crater, with hundreds of workers surrounding it. This must be Terra Nova. Marilina stares, wide eyed, at the events unfolding.

So, this is what Alejandro planned all along. One great cache of ore stowed safely through the portal, then the colony can be destroyed. He said that she was the only person he could trust with this. Did he intend for her to die with the others? She'll never know the truth now. How naive of her to believe that their feeble commonalities made them the same. He is no Meridian. A true Meridian would never commit genocide.

The detective taps her shoulder, drawing Marilina's attention back to the present moment. Wright points urgently up at the sky. It's too loud to speak, so she mimes the question, "He can fly?" The doctor gapes up at the sky, and there he is, the man she once loved. Hovering far above the drill site with his new cape fluttering behind, he pummels the crater below with gusts of air that seem to come from his own hands. Even from this distance, his dark eyes glint with shavings of gold. Seeing him now paralyzes her. She remembers his hands around her throat, and she claws at her neck, gasping.

A strong pair of hands takes hold of her shoulders and shakes her, hard. Lightheaded, the doctor refocuses on two glowing red eyes in front of her. Marilina shrugs away the detective's hands and mimes, "Thank you."

Wright studies her for a moment, then leans close. The acrid scent of a jimmy lingers on her breath. She shouts into Marilina's ear, "You sure you want to go through with this? The bots and I can take it from here. No need for you to see him."

Alejandro used her to plant his portal in the heart of the colony. Without her, his operatives would've had to smuggle it onto the planet through more traditional—and much slower—channels. The doctor is complicit in this crime, whether she likes it or not, whether he tried to kill her afterward or not. His success now would be the end of the colony, and the death of all these people. She won't let him go through with it, and she won't stand by and allow anyone else to finish this for her. Marilina stands from her crouch. "I want to do this."

A moment of silence passes between the two women. Then, Wright nods. "Okay." She signals Diego through the trees, and the two robots circle back around the drill site. The detective turns to Marilina. "You've got ten minutes. Go get him, Doc."

MAY 8, 3041 | THE MOUNTAIN PASS, ZOMENOS

Focusing on maintaining her cool composure, Marilina steps out from behind the face of the mountain and evenly through supple soil. Heads turn as she approaches the drill site, and, recognizing her, some of Alejandro's operatives shout, but none approach. She is his, and he is hers. Terra Nova won't interfere.

The commotion reaches the Coalition leader, and his gold-streaked eyes turn on her, chilling her to the bone. "Welcome back, Marilina. I'm embarrassed to admit that I wasn't expecting you."

"No," she says. He soars gently to the ground. One by one, the operatives surrounding them cease their work and watch with naked curiosity. Even the drilling stops. They are enveloped in total silence. Alejandro closes the gap between them, pausing just inches away from the doctor. "I can protect myself."

"Clearly not." With his forefinger, he strokes her cheek. The hairs on her arms stand on end. Be brave, Mari. He studies her, his motions languid and robotic. What has happened to him that he's changed so drastically since gaining power? "Where is the detective, if you don't mind my asking?"

Marilina swallows. "Not here." So, he guessed about Wright. He doesn't know about Nuñez's robots, however. This will work.

Nine more minutes.

A deep, mirthless laugh emerges from within the black chambers of his heart. "Even for you, that's quite childish." Turning his back to her, he calls loudly, "Detective? You can come out." He turns back to the doctor, evidently content to wait for the detective to present herself. "Why have you returned, dearest?"

"I came back for you."

Annoyance tightens his face. "Enough. You can't stop what's about to happen. You'll die here with the rest of them. Is that what you want?" Marilina's heart soars. Alejandro has no idea she's working with Guardian Nuñez. The plan just might work.

Seven minutes.

Arranging her expression into one of careful deliberation, she says, "I have more faith than that. You should have finished me off in the dormitory. Detective Wright saved my life, and she can save this colony."

"I'll deal with that detective," he snaps. Apparently, he's more than willing to believe Marilina's survival to be Wright's doing. He turns his back on her. "Last chance, Detective." He's losing patience. Keep him distracted. Remembering the caves, inspiration suddenly strikes.

Five minutes.

"Those caves," Marilina says, drawing his attention once more. "They're filled with corpses." She presses her eyes closed against the memories that well up of bone crunching underfoot. Pushing them down, she continues. "Old corpses. They've been there for years." The smile returns to his lips again. He knows exactly where she's going with this, and he *wants* her to ask. "How long have you been hiding bodies there, Alejandro?" She steels herself for his answer.

He's close. Too close. As close as he was in the dormitory, when . . . She swallows. Get a grip, Mari. Spiced cologne reaches her nostrils. That smell was everywhere when he was choking her, but so were her flowers. Chin high, the doctor holds her ground.

"Since I took over the restoration project, dearest." He grips her hand, and a whimper escapes her shaking lips. Just two more minutes. "Restoration enlistment plummeted in the years since the Moscow bunker failed. The Coalition felt safer orbiting Earth than working toward its recovery. People started to question whether we even needed to restore the planet anymore. If the last bunker was ruined, was it even safe for the ground crews anymore? I took measures to quiet those who spoke out against the restoration. It was working for a while."

"Until the wormhole was discovered."

"Yes." A hateful look sweeps over Alejandro's face. "I despised Commander Monroe for his discovery. A pity he was never found. I would dearly love to see the look on his face when this colony is detonated. Ah, Pagu. Thank you." Marilina whirls around and sees Detective Wright being dragged through the dirt by a slight woman in all-black skins with dark, springy hair and darker eyes. The operative has Wright's arm pinned effortlessly behind her. The detective squirms, but Pagu appears cool, collected, in control.

One minute.

Marilina faces Alejandro, mind racing. "The admiral believes you had his father killed."

He shrugs, the languid robotic look returning to his eyes. "I wish I had." His grip on her hand tightens, but his eyes are on the detective. "You are quite a nuisance, Detective. It's fitting that you will die here with the others."

"Just doing my job." The doctor's heart pounds. Hold on for a little longer. The detective's face twists so that only Marilina can see, and one red eye winks.

A hand falls on her shoulder. "It's alright, Dr. Chamorro." Green eyes look into hers. "Your work here is done." Alejandro's grip on her hand releases. Her head spinning, she sees a gust of air blast him violently back. Guardian Nuñez's robot hovers overhead. A tornado forms a kilometer away, terrifyingly close, and engulfs Alejandro, battering his cape with holes and tossing him brutally through a whirlpool at well over 100 kilometers per hour. No one could survive that. Marilina closes her eyes and sighs, leaning shakily against Diego for support. She did it. The colony is safe.

"I don't think so." Pagu shoves the detective into the ground, pressing her boot into Wright's face, and deftly spins a laser cannon into place, its barrel trained unwaveringly between Marilina's eyes. A second operative with a shock of short silver hair joins Pagu, his own cannon pointing at Diego. The woman's gaze flicks up to the sky, where Carlos remains focused on controlling his tornado. She looks down at the detective. "Call off the xenobot, or the doctor dies."

CHAPTER THIRTY NINE

JACK

MAY 9, 3041 | THE COLONY, ZOMENOS

THE ADMIRAL'S EMERGENCY LINE goes berserk. It can't be morning yet, can it? His chest heaves with persisting dreams of a purple-eyed girl flying away with Dad. He shakes it off. Now's not the time. Eyes closed, he checks the name of the caller with his implants: Officer Pruitt. Jack bolts upright and throws the covers off. Pruitt would only reach out if there were activity at the drill site. Beside Jack, Lucy stirs.

Pruitt's holoform lights up the small cottage with a blue glow. Blonde curls hang low over wild eyes. Crouching low, the officer hides from someone—or something, the admiral reminds himself. He hasn't told his officers about the dragons yet, and he doesn't intend to, not until this investigation is resolved. The colonists have enough on their minds. Knowledge of an alien race making demands of their crew would start a panic. He's got to come to the crew with solutions in hand.

The admiral wipes his eyes. "Hey, Colter. What's going on?" Lucy sits up and crawls forward, all trace of sleep vanishing from her eyes.

His reply comes in a whisper. "We've got activity. There was a bit of a commotion about an hour ago, and a bunch of people showed up out of nowhere. They can't all be colonists, Admiral. There's too many of them. I'd put the number in the dozens." Pruitt's eyes are unfocused, watching something in the distance. "What should we do?"

"Don't engage." Jack bounds to his feet and rifles through his drawers, pulling out the first pair of skins he finds and poking his head through. Lucy does the same. Terra Nova must have sent another ship through the wormhole, but he can't see how. Admiral Ono has the entrance well guarded. Or is Ono part of this coup as well? He rakes his fingers through his hair. It doesn't make any sense. Another possibility occurs to him: the purple-eyed girl could be working with this group. Chances are, he'll find Dad at the drill site. He fixes a grim look on the expectant officer. "We're coming to you."

"Hold on." Pruitt throws up a hand. "Something's up. I think they're arguing."

Exchanging a glance with Lucy, the admiral says, "We'll be there right away. Stay sharp." Ending the call, he turns. "This is our chance."

Lucy nods, lips forming a thin, determined line. "If Terra Nova is on this planet, we can end this tonight."

Through a window behind them, bright moonlight washes the floor. Jack crosses the small, open room to her, determination shining in her dark eyes. "What happens if it *is* Terra Nova?"

"Then we bring the Coalition down on Alejandro. We still have good people among the guardians: Nuñez, Kapadia, van Leeuwen, Ngcobo." The former guardian winds her long, sleep-crushed hair into a braid with deft fingers and cups Jack's cheeks. Fire dances in her eyes. "If we do this right, we'll finally come out from under the interference of terrorists."

The admiral rubs her palms between his hands. "Agreed. How do you want to play this? You want to come with?" Pregnancy or not, he's not about to try to dissuade her.

To his surprise, she shakes her head. "I'll drop you off, but we need to get ahead of this. I'll come back here and put feelers out with the other guardians. Ping me when you're ready to return."

A weight lifts from his chest. If this rendezvous goes sideways, the last thing he needs is to worry about her safety. "You got it." He grips her forearm, and she Leaps.

MAY 9, 3041 | THE MOUNTAIN PASS, ZOMENOS

In the space of an instant, the admiral arrives at Pruitt's side. The officer's eyes widen. He's probably never witnessed a Leap before. Lucy departs with a brief kiss, and Pruitt waves him down. Jack huddles beside Hoffman in the low brush under the mountain pass. It's later than he thought. Dawn is only an hour or two away. Bright orbs light the pass.

Following Pruitt's gaze, the admiral zeroes in on a flat, massive clearing just around a bend. A well-hidden drilling rig sits in the center of the clearing, 4 meters tall, its triangular base covering a gargantuan region. He can't believe it. Pyrrhos was right: this is a serious piece of machinery, and it's already up and running. His jaw clenches. Terra Nova made suckers of them all, but it's the colonists who will be forced to answer Pyrrhos for it.

Screams draw Jack's gaze to the base of the rig. A swirling tornado tears up dirt, sucking in equipment and even some of these unauthorized operatives. High above, a body floats in the sky, just visible. A swift scan of the admiral's wristband unit for warnings comes up blank. How is that possible? His researchers put together a supercomputer predictive ensemble to prevent catastrophes like this. He draws his officers' attention to the weather formation with a two-fingered wrist flick, and Hoffman immediately fires off an alert back to the colony.

In the heart of a crater, a skirmish has broken out. Squinting, the admiral scans for that shock of purple hair, but Dad's captor isn't visible from this vantage point. He doesn't think twice, sprinting toward the rig with Pruitt close on his heels. It's damn near impossible to guess who is friend and who is enemy. They fly across the ground on light feet, but a dark man being held at gunpoint nevertheless turns at their step. Jack locks eyes with Diego and, stumbling, lurches forward. It's *not possible* for Diego to be here, but his eyes aren't playing tricks. Stunned, the admiral nudges Pruitt. "We've got a hostage at 2 o'clock. He's a friendly."

"Copy." The officer hefts his laser cannon to eye level and fires two rounds without breaking stride. The operative holding Diego captive drops to the ground unmoving. Grinning, the robot rushes forward, disarms his captor, and bounces back up with his new weapon trained on the operative.

Charging into the heart of the skirmish with a surge of adrenaline, Jack spots a woman in black skins single-handedly pinning Detective Wright under her boot and holding Dr. Chamorro at gunpoint. Questions multiplying at a dizzying rate, the admiral aims his laser cannon and fires, blasting the weapon out of the woman's hands. The operative yelps, wringing her hands, and Chamorro responds with an impressive sweep of her leg. The woman thumps bodily onto the ground beside the detective. Freed, Wright dives on top of her aggressor.

Beneath her, the woman laughs, giving Jack the willies. Terra Nova attracts the most disturbing people. "He told me you would come for me. I've been waiting for you for a long time, Anna. How are the eyes?"

The detective freezes. "It was you?"

The woman twists and smiles up at Wright with ice in her eyes to match her tone. "Who else? You're lucky your mother isn't here to see this. Thirty years to plan your revenge and you still never saw me coming." Seizing on the detective's momentary shock, the operative drives her palm into Wright's nose and shatters it with a crunch.

Jack grabs the woman's shoulders and yanks her away from the detective, but Chamorro steps between them and pistol whips the operative with her own laser cannon. "Don't touch my friend." The doctor helps Wright to her feet. "Come here, Detective. I can set that for you."

With two fingers pressed to the operative's neck, the admiral says, "She's out cold." Chamorro pinches the detective's nose between two fingers. Yesterday, this was his gentle doctor. Today, she's a Terra Nova fighting baddie? His head just might explode. "Where did you learn to fight like that, Marilina?"

Wright grimaces, but Chamorro's fingers jerk and reset the nose in a single, clean movement. The doctor's cheeks split into the biggest smile that Jack's ever seen on her. "The Meridian aren't helpless, Admiral."

Across the crater, the tornado suddenly and violently dissipates. The body above comes crashing to the ground. No—two bodies, each trying to strangle the other. Straining his eyes, Jack spots Alejandro Martinho, unmistakable in his long cape and weird, brassy eyes. His opponent gropes for the Coalition leader's neck, and cherry red blood spurts everywhere.

"No way." The admiral spins to the others, voice cracking. "What's he doing here?"

Chamorro bows her head. "Alejandro built a portal. He's been using it to travel to the colony." She points. An archway of glass looms over the drill site.

Slack-jawed, the only response Jack can think of is, "Slick."

A red flash streaks overhead. Chamorro's eyes turn round as orbiters, but the admiral's heart leaps into his throat. Things are about to get complicated. A violet firebolt shoots down from the sky and spirals straight toward them. If they don't get out of the way, they'll be engulfed in its flames.

Pruitt seems to be thinking along the same lines. "Hey!" he shouts, waving madly.

Wright takes off sprinting and tugs Diego and the doctor to the ground. Jack and his officers grip the unconscious operatives and drag them away from the drill rig. The firebolt reaches the drill, bursting into a hundred smaller bolts that rain out in every direction. The admiral throws out his arm and catches Pruitt in the chest, digging in his heels and narrowly avoiding the spray. His breath comes in shallow gasps. That was way, way too close.

The red flash crash-lands between Jack and the others and skids to a stop. Straightening, Pyrrhos rounds on the admiral with a glare that reflects the crackling fire. "You said you would end the damage to my lands, Admiral Monroe."

Pruitt thumbs his laser cannon. "Heads up, Jack."

"Hold your fire, Officer!" Jack shouts. Pruitt backpedals, confusion etched across his face. To Pyrrhos, Jack calmly answers, "We were working on it. You beat us to it."

The dragon whips the ground with its tail so hard that the admiral loses his footing. Pyrrhos leans close, eyes level with Jack's. "You weren't," he thunders. "I feel every one of its thundering vibrations. You would have destroyed these lands had I not intervened. You have failed to meet my demands."

The admiral scrambles to respond, to convey the layers of betrayal unfolding here to this furious alien. "These aren't my men, and that isn't our drill. There are others, people like me, who are trying to use this planet for their own ends. We're not with them, and we want to stop them, same as you."

"Liar."

Swallowing, Jack says, "I'm telling the truth." He jerks his thumb in the direction of the two men still scrambling on the ground. "That man there with the golden eyes is responsible for all of this. We're trying to end this, for good."

Pyrrhos's gaze flits from Jack to Martinho. His reptilian eyes flutter, like he's been drugged. If the dragon believes the admiral, he never has the chance to say so. Instead, the crimson beast quivers and collapses to the ground. Jack exchanges a look with Pruitt.

"Is it dead?" the officer asks, edging around the body in a generous arc. He keeps his laser cannon trained on the dragon, just in case.

"Pyrrhos!"

Three more streaks of color arc through the night sky, lit up by glowing firelight, and two more aliens land on either side of the fallen dragon. Pruitt leaps backward. The first bends to Pyrrhos' side and pushes its snout into his.

The second crouches low and faces the men, back arched, poised to strike. It bellows deafeningly, a forked tongue whipping out.

Pruitt trains his laser cannon on this second creature, but Jack's gaze is snared by the third. A mere golden blur, the third and biggest of these beasts aims straight for Martinho. The man grappling with the Coalition leader springs away, suspended in the air.

"Carlos!" Diego cries.

The golden dragon crashes onto the ground with Alejandro Martinho pinned beneath. Incredibly, he's alive, and cries out, but a clap of thunder drowns his voice. Paralyzed, Jack watches a bolt of lightning arc down from the sky and strike Martinho squarely in the chest. The Coalition leader shakes with the impact and falls limp. The golden dragon launches into the sky and disappears. His companions lift Pyrrhos, spread their wings, and take off after him.

CHAPTER FORTY

ANNA

MAY 9, 3041 | THE MOUNTAIN PASS, ZOMENOS

IT'S DARK. TOO DARK. Somewhere along the way, the tornado must have swallowed up the orbs lighting up the drill site. This planet's star is only just peeking over the horizon. Anna turns to Diego, his green eyes flickering with firelight. *They got him!* Stunned, she smiles, and he smiles, and then he's hugging her, but she's too happy to care that he's hugging her, and the loony night disappears into the warm folds of his skins.

A small shadow dashes from the detective's side into the crater, where Alejandro Martinho lies unmoving. The slight doctor bends over Martinho, presumably checking for life. If he's alive, then he belongs to the detective. Military is close behind, swiftly setting up a perimeter while Chamorro works. Just visible in the distance, Carlos stirs and walks slowly back from the trees.

"Wait here. I'll do a sweep," Diego says. "Some of those operatives might still be armed and ready to try something."

"Okay. Take Carlos with you." There's only one operative Anna cares about. Eyes narrowing to slits, she calls, "That Pagu woman is mine. Don't let her out of your sight." The terrorist was probably just trying to distract the detective, but if she had anything to do with Ma's death, she won't get off easy. Anna hangs back (there's too much smoke to safely follow) but Diego takes off, stumbling through debris from the ruined drill rig. Between the firestorm and the twister, this place is a disaster.

Left alone, the detective is reminded that this all began in the dark, and that she's loathed it ever since. There was a lot of time to kill waiting for Ma on that freighter, too. A teenager then, Anna passed the time by leafing through the catalog for the military. She planned on enlisting, just like Dad. Ma sure hated that. Maybe the point was for Ma to hate it. But then, Anna hated that freighter and begged not to be dragged to the edge of the Solar System in it.

Each day of Ma's assignment began with Anna memorizing the requirements of each rank, making silent promises to herself of attaining the highest laurels. She was going to complete the application as soon as they got back from Enceladus. That day, the day the freighter rumbled, she waited outside the mess hall while Ma "interrogated" someone in their room. The explosion rocked the ship, and Anna lurched and fell forward, coming down hard on her palms. She never even heard the blast. People were shouting, but Anna couldn't see. Panic consumed her. She can't see—why can't she see? They found her shaking, crawling on the floor, crying Ma's name, weak, helpless, and blind.

"Anna?" The detective jerks. There's no freighter and no Ma, but she can see, and as usual, that means she's looking right into Diego's concerned eyes. "The area is secure, and Chamorro says Martinho is alive . . . Are you okay?"

"Never better." Anna stares at the impossibly tall archway behind them. "Creepy," she mutters, but it's the only way to bring Martinho and his goons in to the Coalition. Turning, she clocks a weird look on Diego's face. "What?"

Diego takes a hesitant step forward. "There's something I've been meaning to tell you." He's looking at his feet. For such a sophisticated xenobot, he sure does embrace a lot of silly human behaviors.

She crosses her arms. "Spit it out. As soon as Monroe's men give the signal, we're heading in."

"Of course. The thing is, when you took off by yourself, I was angry, but when you didn't answer, I got worried. I kept track of you with the neural link, so I'd know you were safe."

The detective cocks an eyebrow. "Yeah? Here's a piece of advice. Stalking is a criminal offense. Stay out of my head if you don't want to share a cell with Martinho on 433 Eros." Monroe waves them over, so she gives Diego's hand a tug. "That's our cue. Time to roll."

He still wears that weird expression, but Carlos catches up to them, so he falls silent, taking a deep breath and nodding. "Okay. Let's go."

MAY 9, 3041 | THE MOUNTAIN PASS, ZOMENOS

With the xenobots in tow, Anna traipses down into the crater. The fumes of burned metal choke off her air. She protects her mouth and nose in the crook of her elbow. Around them, Terra Nova stirs, but the officers keep their laser cannons primed and ready, and the unarmed operatives fall back, watching. Martinho lies on the ground near the rig with his skins ripped open, revealing a white lightning bolt scar over the criminal mastermind's rib cage.

"Cool." The detective's gaze flicks to Monroe. "Remind me again, what were those things?"

The admiral returns a steady, impassive look. "Dragons."

Hands on her hips, she nods. "Right." She supposes she ought to be more concerned for the colonists' safety, but that problem feels very distant compared to this one. She juts her chin toward her unconscious perp. "Is he going to make it to trial?"

The doctor stands, wiping tears from her cheeks. "He's alive. That's all I can say for certain."

What? No, no, no. Anna's jaw tightens. "I can't prop up a vegetable before a tribunal, Doc."

Monroe steps forward. "We know. I've granted Chamorro a temporary leave from the colony to assist with the transfer to the facilities at the Ring."

The slight woman bows her head. "Those physicians have never seen anything like this, and no one's ever treated a man that's part machine. I'd like to be there to oversee his treatment."

The detective gives Chamorro a long look. The woman is an enigma. The doctor was beaten and bruised, inside and out, but she got her justice, and if it were Anna, she'd high-tail it out of here. Something is holding Chamorro back. Fingernails digging into her waist, the detective asks, "You want to help him. Why?"

Soft brown eyes flit up and meet her gaze. A breeze flutters her hair. The doctor's actually sort of pretty, in her own plain way. "It's not about helping him. Like you said, he needs to stand trial." Her gaze returns to the man on the ground, and she rubs that cross of hers again. "He has a lot to answer for." Anna cocks her head and shrugs. This isn't the vengeance either of them was hoping for, but they're going to have to make it work.

"Okay," the detective says. "Looks like you and I are working together a little while longer, Doc. You got a stretcher?" Chamorro nods, bending over her medical bag and retrieving a long rod. It unfurls and snaps straight. Anna turns to Diego and Carlos. "Mind helping?" The xenobots lift Martinho onto the stretcher. At first blush, it seems like a flimsy piece of fabric, but the doctor taps a code into her wristband unit and the stretcher goes taut, hovering in the air.

Anna steps to Monroe's side, watching Terra Nova look on in silence. "I'm not sure about this. The evidence is on our side, but we lost our key witness, and I'm not optimistic about flipping these disciples."

"You'll think of something, Detective. Can I ask a favor?"

At this, the detective raises her eyebrows. What could the admiral want from her? He reaches into his pack and hands her something smooth and crystalline. Metal. She turns it over in her hands. "What's this?"

"Debris we passed inside the wormhole. We ran an analysis, but it's not a known alloy."

Anna holds it up, watching the way it glints in the weak firelight. "What do you want me to do with it?"

Monroe angles his chin and speaks directly into her ear without the others overhearing. "Guillermo told me about Diego's amnesia. Maybe this will jog his memory."

"Of the commander's attacker, you mean." The detective pockets the metal and nods. It's probably worthless—Diego's memory didn't recover after days of poring over that wreckage, but that doesn't mean anything. "I take it you never found our young abductor."

"No. We found a ship in the forest, but . . . Well, it was a dead-end."

Sigh. The admiral knows better than she does that this case has gone cold, but to be fair, they've solved a lot of cold cases in the last few days. Why stop now? She glances at Monroe's officers, eyes darting in every direction. "Are you three going to be okay alone?"

Monroe follows her gaze, staring up out of the crater. "I think so. We've got dragons on our side, remember, Red Eyes?"

Anna grins and nods. "Good man. Carlos can stay and help cover you. Try to keep this colony in one piece until the Coalition can round up the rest of Terra Nova."

She scrambles to the top of the crater and takes a long look at the scene: the ocean of trees just beyond the drill site, the mountain ridge that disappears into the sky, the star cresting the horizon. If they all play their parts right, this will be home one day. Mm-hmm. What would that be like? Diego and the doctor join her, the stretcher carrying Martinho hovering between them. "Okay, Doc. I'm counting on you to save this prick's life so I can punch him in the face."

Chamorro smiles. "I'll do what I can."

Monroe's officers escort them to the portal, keeping Terra Nova at bay. Not so fast. The detective stalks right up to Pagu and that silver fox that attacked her and Diego. "You two are with us." Diego cuffs them, and they pass through the archway. Anna steps up to the arches and pauses. The glass catches the light of dawn, reflecting in prisms. For a man bent on burning this place to the ground, Martinho sure made something eerily beautiful out of it. She shakes her head and steps through.

CHAPTER FORTY ONE

GUILLERMO

FIVE DAYS PASS IN an uneasy limbo. Guillermo now dresses in the fashion of the station: a lined and insulated pair of blue and black skins and sturdy waterproof boots to prevent frostbite in these extreme temperatures. Gracias Señor por estos milagros. Aware that he has a recognizable face—especially to Victoria—he grows out his beard and disguises his identity with a vanity AI interface named Tara. He raises an eyebrow when Du offers it to him.

"Don't look at me. It's the fashion," she says. He doesn't argue. The detective is counting on him to secure their key witness for Martinho's trial, and Guillermo doesn't plan on letting her down.

To pass the time, he takes up work alongside Campbell and his partner Martinez at a water treatment plant. Guillermo sits at a control board, poring over endless holograms of meter readings. The job isn't difficult, and he can almost forget the problems in Earth's orbit. Out here, solar flare, Skeletons, and deadly coups are distant problems. Besides, the water treatment plant is warm. Head cradled between his hands, he loses himself in a wall of numbers.

He's been tasked with monitoring final contaminant levels in the water tanks prior to shipment. Enceladus is the orphans' sole source of drinking water, so impurities are heavily scrutinized. A message from Du makes him jump.

`We've found her. Meet me at once.`

¡Al fin llegan buenas noticias! Tingling with anticipation, he stands.

Martinez glances up mildly. "Going somewhere?"

Guillermo pauses. He doesn't want to pique the curiosity of the other operators, but there's no avoiding it. Nothing interesting ever happens around here, and they would welcome a distraction from the steady scrawl of numbers. He leans into the inevitable, arranging his expression into one of urgent fear. "My mother is in the hospital. Accident on MS275."

Readings forgotten, Martinez looks him fully in the face. "That's awful, Rodrigo," he says, calling Guillermo by the moniker he's assumed. He appears genuinely sympathetic. "Go ahead. I can take over here."

"Thanks," Guillermo replies with a grateful smile. In another lifetime, he'd stay and buy this nice guy a few cervezas. He rushes out of the room, curious heads turning in his direction, and ducks into an empty corridor. Out of sight, he Leaps to SS849's guardian's office.

"Took you long enough," Du observes.

"So? Where is she?"

The guardian taps her wristband unit and produces a holomap of SS849. Formerly known as 2906-TV$_{16}$, the Saturnian trojan-turned-mining-outpost is a tiny asteroid, sparsely terraformed, and home to fewer than 1,000 orphans at any point in time. "Victoria is in the lower north quadrant." She points. "It took a while to find her because, well, that's the last place I expected her to be."

He tilts his head in her direction. "Why is that?"

"It's low-income housing," Du explains. "It's laid out as a shared living space. Everyone gets a bunk, a towel, a few pairs of skins, and a toothbrush. The kitchens and toilets are threadbare."

Remembering Martinez's sympathetic eyes, Guillermo clucks. "These are good people. Can't you do better?"

The guardian's eyes are stony. "We put people to work on SS849 instead of banishing them to cryo."

Her words cut like steel on a lathe, but this is no time for a pissing contest. He changes tack. "So, you think this is where Victoria is hiding?"

"I do. She's going by the name Vivian Bertram." Du taps her armband, and a woman's face replaces the map. Guillermo blinks. The old woman here has short, wiry, gray hair and wrinkled, mottled leather for a face, but the longer he stares, the more Victoria Bernard emerges from beneath the façade. The eyes, cheekbones, and lips are unmistakably hers. Muy bien, Victoria. Fascinated, he studies the mask for a long time.

"Tara did an incredible job with her." It occurs to him that Tara must have been the inspiration for Carlos's own transformation. He meets Du's eyes. "Let's go get her."

She nods, but she doesn't move. "I'll admit that I'm impressed with you, Guillermo."

He tenses in surprise. "You're not one for idle flattery."

"It's not idle. I got a call yesterday from Sam. He asked me about you."

Alarmed, Guillermo straightens and plants his hands on his hips. He never told Samkelo where he was going after retrieving Carlos from the Johannesburg station. "You told him that I'm here?"

"I said we're working together. He didn't pry." Du studies him with those sharp eyes of hers. "He wanted to know if I'd back you as Coalition leader."

This again. Guillermo closes his eyes. Obviamente, Samkelo is anxious as to what will happen when the news of Alejandro's arrest breaks, and he's in a rush to settle the matter of leadership and show stability. Guillermo still isn't sure. The robotics guild will investigate Carlos as soon as Alejandro is behind bars, and that could raise doubts about Guillermo. Earth's orphans deserve better. "What did you say?"

She raises an eyebrow. "I told him that I don't want anything else to do with the Coalition and its corrupt guardians." Her expression softens. "But if we must have a leader, I'd follow you."

Wow. A shaky breath follows. He didn't realize how much her answer would mean to him. Throat dry, he replies, "I didn't ask for that."

"I didn't ask to be dragged into your mess, either. You're the right man for this, Guillermo."

Now, that's just not true. "Thank you, Lei." The tension between them dissipates.

Du nods to herself. "Campbell is in the lower north quadrant right now. Let's see if he has eyes on her." She pauses, sending a message to Campbell over her wristband comms. His answer is almost immediate. "He's in position."

"Well, I can't let Campbell take all the credit, can I?" The two of them Leap in unison.

MAY 13, 3041 | SS849, SATURN'S ORBIT

They arrive at the very public kitchens. Muy inteligente, Victoria. Very smart, indeed. Guillermo looks around, registering his surroundings. Du wasn't kidding—this place is scummy. He avoids touching anything as he separates from the station's guardian and ambles between short tables. Campbell sits in the far corner, drinking coffee from a mug stained with the coffee rings of countless diners before him. With deliberate eye contact, the miner tilts his head a few inches. Guillermo follows his gaze.

There she is, a few meters away. Primped and proper Victoria, guardian of the Marseille station and heiress to the Bernard estate, disguising herself as an ordinary old woman. Guillermo bites his lip hard, closing his eyes and tossing his head back. It was all worth it: the blind Leap of faith, the deadly tundra, Du's saucy attitude, and the endless hours of pretending to give a shit about water impurities. Their star witness is ready to take the stand.

He tenses, but in this room full of people, Victoria hasn't noticed his arrival. She keeps to herself, looking out the window at the ice moons Titan and Rhea. Water spouts from a polar jet stream just visible on Enceladus's surface below. At this angle, Saturn's rings form a thin band around the gas giant. A plate sits untouched in front of her, stacked with pancakes and vegan sausages and eggs. She sips coffee. Even in this disguise, on a barren miner's station, her poised elegance sets her apart from the station workers, and none approach her. Guillermo advances warily, his movement unhurried, even arbitrary. He sits down beside her and places his hand over hers.

"It's over, Victoria."

Milky eyes widen as his grip tightens. "Guillermo? Let me go!" she shouts in an old woman's croak, feigning innocence.

"I can't." He gazes at her without a shred of remorse. "You owe it to every single person in this room to return to Colossi Infiniti and testify before a tribunal."

Glaring, Victoria struggles impotently. "The detective has everything she needs from me. I don't owe these people or the Coalition anything." She wails again, her shock of frizzy gray hair whipping from side to side.

"Your duty is far from over. It's time for you to publicly testify against Alejandro."

Victoria stills, then laughs. "You miserable fool. It's not just him. All of Terra Nova knows my face. If I am to testify, I will die that very same night. You don't know them like I do, Guillermo. They will find me."

"We'll protect you."

Her laugh rises to a shriek, and the act draws a crowd. It's time to leave. He turns and locks eyes with Du. In all the commotion, he hadn't noticed her or Campbell approach.

"Don't worry about these workers, Guillermo. We'll get this sorted."

The miner turns and shouts, "This is official business, folks. Back to your meals, please."

Guillermo speaks fast over the relentless howls beside him. "Thank you, Lei, for everything. We'll set the Coalition back on track once the dust settles on this trial. This station won't be forgotten. That's a promise."

"I don't need any more empty promises, Guillermo. Take care of Alejandro, and then take charge."

Chuckle. "You got it, Lei."

CHAPTER FORTY TWO

JACK

TIME STARTS TO LOSE meaning. The aftermath of Terra Nova's incursion on the planet consumes the initial hours after the detective's departure. Once the remaining terrorists are rounded up and sent through the portal, the colonists find themselves lacking clear direction. The Coalition rescinds the order for the fuel depot within days of Martinho's arrest, but no further orders are issued, and that leaves the colonists adrift on a faraway planet without a purpose. Worse, news of dragons slingshots through the colony. Angry, derisive remarks fly, especially about their suddenly meager-looking dome. Uncertainty climbs.

That morning, the admiral follows the dirt path that cuts through knee-high grass out to the farm. This, at least, is something he can focus on. Resting his forearms on the gate, he waves at his younger brother and, grinning, Henry waves back. With any luck, the farm will have live animals in the coming weeks. Jack's gaze flits to the sky. Will their alien friends pose an issue for their livestock? A call pulls him from his musing. Guillermo has finally reached out!

Stepping away from the gate, the admiral takes the call with all the nervous energy of a new recruit on their first day of basic training.

"I am so glad to see you, Memo."

"Same to you, mijo."

His uncle sports a fresh cut with a fade on one side. He's found himself a pair of new, tight-fitting skins with a low V revealing a few peeping chest hairs. Jack shakes his head and grins. He could never pull that style off, but Guillermo looks sharp. The guardian's holo inches closer with a little giddy-up in his step.

"Tell me you have our orders."

Guillermo freezes and hangs his head. "I do, but you're not going to like it."

Under the shade of a thick canopy of leaves, the admiral leans against a tree and crosses his arms. "Don't make me guess." He can take it. Whatever happens next, anything beats this miserable waiting game.

His uncle nods. "Dale. The good news is that your crew is clear to proceed with your original mission: establish the colony on the exoplanet Zomenos and catalog the living species in the surrounding area."

Blink. "Fantastic. Why wouldn't I like that?"

Rubbing his hands together, Guillermo bounces on the balls of his feet. "Because future missions to Zomenos are on hold until the Coalition is convinced of the continued health and safety of your crew."

"What does that mean?" A nerve works in Jack's temple. That's hardly any better than their previous consignment to fuel collection.

"GLOW, for starters."

Eyes closed, the admiral drags his fingers through his hair. Well, that explains the radio silence from the Coalition all these weeks. He grinds his teeth, but freezes. GLOW won't save his molars if he cracks a tooth. None of this is the Coalition's fault. Why would anyone give up the lifespan and health benefits of the longevity shot for a planet they've never seen? Yet the fact that he has zero control over this cranks his gears. "I can't do anything about that until my Meridian-trained head physician returns."

Holoform flickering in a ray of light that surges through the branches, Guillermo bows. "Pos sí. Tienes razón. I have good news for you there. Alejandro is awake."

"No way!" Jack pumps his fist. "Why didn't you lead with that? Is the trial date set?" That dragon's attack was scary, deserved or not. The fate of his former leader should be determined by a tribunal, not an alien.

"It'll be soon. No one wants this dragged out. I'd guess a few more weeks." A pause stretches. "Anyway, it's not just GLOW, Jack. Those aliens are a problem."

"You mean the dragons."

Guillermo scoffs. "Me vale. Call them whatever you want. What are you doing about them? I won't lie to you. The Coalition has deep objections against continued missions with hostile forces on that planet."

"They aren't hostile." Those dragons were here first, and if it weren't for Terra Nova, they never would've attacked . . . in theory. With the way things ended between Jack and Pyrrhos, it's hard to know for sure. "I'd like to enter into negotiations."

"Negotiations." His uncle stares at him. "With dragons. Jack, have you lost your mind?"

The admiral puts on his easy smile. "My mind is perfectly fine. Just trust me, Tío. Let me handle this. You have the final say, don't you?"

Guillermo crosses his arms and stamps his foot. "Nothing's decided yet. I'm still just a guardian, same as everyone else."

"I do get the news here. Coalition leader? When were you going to tell me?"

"There's nothing to say, yet. It's pending internal review of my xenobots. You're asking me to stick my neck out for you so you can try to reason with aliens. Have I got that right?"

"Please just trust me on this, Tío," Jack repeats. Of course, even if these creatures agree to a truce, there's still the matter of convincing his crew to stay. He looks out at the colony from his shaded spot. His cottage is directly across from the farm, and beside it, the dormitory, prepared to accommodate two more missions. Right now, most of its rooms are empty, and they'll stay that way if his crew demands to return. A bridge to cross another day.

"Okay, okay. Mira, there's one more thing I want to ask you before I get back to the Ring. What has Lucy decided?"

The admiral's fingers twitch at his sides. Great question. Lucy volunteered to lead the charge in fully dismantling the drill rig and restoring the land, and she's risen to the occasion impressively. Their exchanges have been brief these last two weeks, mostly early morning goodbye kisses and an occasional late-night romp. He hasn't been able to bring himself to ask whether she wants to be a mother. "I don't know yet. She says she needs time."

Guillermo chuckles. "Okay, I won't pry. Just let me know if I'm going to be an uncle again."

"What about *my* dad? Has Diego come up with anything?"

His uncle's face falls. "I'm sorry, Jack. The sample you gave the detective didn't change anything. It's a good idea, though. Want me to take a look?"

Sigh. Dead-ends everywhere they look. What difference does it make? The admiral can't bring himself to give up, though. With all of Terra Nova locked away awaiting trial, Dad deserves to be found. "Sure, Guillermo. Anything could help."

MAY 20, 3041 | THE COLONY, ZOMENOS

On his way back from the farm, the admiral stops by the colony's border and checks in with the morning patrol. Teams of two, one of which is always an officer of the military, man the perimeter day and night. As he approaches now, Jack wears his brightest smile, aware that Pruitt is probably still seething over the events at the drill site. The officer made his anger known at the time, but Jack dodged his questions. Just visible at this distance, the dome forms a clear shield that ricochets back daylight at certain angles. The mountain range where Terra Nova was taken down looms in the distance.

"Morning, Admiral." Grass swishes against Jack's ankles as he joins Pruitt and looks up at the mountain. Nothing like this exists on the Montréal station. One day, he'll be safe enough to attempt to scale it. Pruitt glances sideways at him. "Can we talk?" Jack follows Pruitt out of earshot of the developmental unit officer. Pruitt takes a steadying breath and squares up to him. "Are you going to tell me what in the universe happened to Martinho? I mean no disrespect, but you put Brian and I in the line of fire, and we deserve to know."

The admiral tucks his hands into his skinpockets. "I don't know." It's a lame answer, and it makes him cringe, but it's true. He's never seen that golden dragon before, and no one really knows what happened to Martinho.

"Right." Obviously frustrated, Pruitt shakes his head and begins pacing. "That alien knew your name, Jack."

"It did."

The officer pauses nose-to-nose with his CO. "You knew those things were coming here, didn't you?"

Jack takes Pruitt's attitude in stride. Hand on the officer's shoulder, he says, "Not necessarily. I thought the threat to you was minimal. If I thought the information pertinent to your assignment, I would have told you."

Pruitt stares back, his voice dropping to a whisper. "Look. I trust you with my life, Admiral. You've earned that. But Brian? These civvies?" He shakes his head. "They're talking, and they want answers."

Jack's chest heaves with a deep breath. "I know. They'll get them. I can't bring my crew open-ended problems without solutions, Colter. If you want in, I could use your help. I spoke with Guardian Nuñez about it today, and we have the green light to engage the dragons. If I set up a meet, can I count on you for backup?" It's a big ask, but Pruitt said it himself: Jack's earned it.

Pruitt blows air out of the side of his mouth, but he nods. "Yes, sir."

The weight momentarily lifted from his shoulders, the admiral returns to his cottage and calls a meeting with the unit leads. Before he does anything else, he'll need the support of his leaders. Fortunately, all three of them recognize the danger of ignoring the alien race, and his plan is approved within minutes. Eager for lunch, Darnell and Gabriella head for the door, but Jack catches up to Lucy and steers her away.

It's a day of difficult conversations, apparently.

"Hey, listen, I know you're busy with the drill site, but can we talk?"

Lucy scoots onto the small table in the center of the cottage and swings her legs. "You want to know if I'm planning to keep the baby."

A nervous laugh peals from Jack, high and nasal. "Am I being that obvious?"

She rolls her eyes. "Come on. I know you. You're dying to ask."

Arms planted on her shoulders, he shrugs. "Okay. So?"

"*Okay, so?*" Lucy mocks him, but she smiles. "I'd keep it. If it's healthy, that is."

A wide grin splits his cheeks. "Really? What changed your mind?"

"You, obviously. You coordinated Alejandro's arrest, put down a terrorist incursion, and saved the colony from the threat of aliens. I wouldn't do it with anyone else."

Jack laughs. "I had a lot of help, including yours. This is great, Lucy!" He ropes her into a hug, kissing her cheeks over and over. Amazing. He's going to be a father.

CHAPTER FORTY THREE

MARILINA

MAY 25, 3041 | THE COLONY, ZOMENOS

MINUTES PASS. THE DOCTOR hovers outside the locked door to her dormitory room, frozen before the retinal scanner. The first step to gaining some semblance of normalcy is reclaiming the room on the other side of that door. Marilina swallows. She can still taste the cedar of his cologne. There was blood everywhere. It must be a dried smear by now. The blood on the other side of that door had prevented her escape.

Breathing hard, Marilina doubles back three steps and rubs her numb fingers together to get them to stop shaking. She can't do it, can't return to the place where she was almost murdered. Hot tears warm her cheeks, and the doctor races down the hall. It's too much. She thought she could handle it, thought she'd even moved past it, but she's been surviving on a cocktail of shock and adrenaline for weeks, and now that she's slowed down, it's all catching up with her. Double doors burst open, her vision turning white in the light of Anima, and Marilina runs headfirst into something. She tumbles, her fall cushioned by crisp blades of grass.

"Whoa, easy!"

With a blink, Henry's face swims into view. She must have run right into him. Cool air buffets the heat rising up the doctor's neck. Scrambling to her hands and knees, Marilina stammers, "I'm so sorry. Did I hurt you?"

"I'm fine. Are you?" Clear blue eyes that match the cloudless sky above frown down at her. He offers her his hand and pulls her firmly back to her feet, but she's still shaking. That frown deepens. "What's wrong?"

Rubbing her arms, she looks away. "I can't go back there."

Henry's gaze follows hers up the stairs and back into the dormitory. "Oh, right. It happened in your room, didn't it?"

Don't think about the blood, Mari. She nods, her gaze rooted to the ground.

Taking a step back, he peers up at the dormitory building. "There are lots of empty rooms in there," he points out. "We just have to talk to engineering about finding you a different one. Maybe a south-facing room," he adds, eyes roving to the side of the building.

Curiosity tugs the corners of her lips into a trepid smile. "Why south?"

Henry grins. "Oh, I just like watching the river." The doctor turns and faces south with him. Anima casts its rays onto sparkling violet ripples. "Large bodies of water like this are unheard of on the stations. Even the smallest streams and lakes take years of terraforming. It's really special to see water flow from a naturally occurring body, you know?"

A breeze carries the clean scent of the river their way, and with it, memories of sacuanjoche. It occurs to Marilina that she's stopped shaking. This colony might be where she was almost murdered, but it's also where she experienced true friendship. Her crew is full of people like Henry, who have tried to show her small kindnesses ever since she was recruited to this mission. Alejandro can't be allowed to poison this, too. The doctor can have a family here: she's earned it. Hands clasped behind her back, she only nods.

"South-facing, it is."

MAY 28, 3041 | THE COLONY, ZOMENOS

It takes time, but Marilina gradually settles back into the colony. She returns to her work at the infirmary, wondering often if Alejandro will make a full recovery. The last she saw him, he was awake, but he mostly stared up at the ceiling and ignored his doctors. The white lightning bolt scar on his chest is hot to the touch, but it remains free of exudates or abscesses, and cultures repeatedly return negative results. His injuries seem to be of a (she cringes at the thought) *supernatural* nature rather than a physical one. She never would have believed that science could fail to explain something like this, but the milagros are stacking up on this planet. Either way, his injuries are beyond even her skill. She suspects that with his neural network destroyed, the Cerebrum particles are the only thing keeping him alive. The Coalition ordered their removal, but the doctor advocated on his behalf. No one, not even Alejandro, fully understands how he fused with the particles in the first place. Extracting them safely is out of the question. There is no point in saving his life only to kill him in surgery. Enough people have died already.

He is, at last, someone else's concern now.

With her return through the portal approved, the doctor's primary patient in those early days of the colony is Lucy Mérieux. That morning, the former guardian arrives bright and early for her ultrasound appointment. After Marilina's brief return to emergency medicine—with an unprecedented case of an alien assault on a cyborg—obstetrics feels quite out of the doctor's wheelhouse, but she carefully seals such thoughts behind a veiled smile. Future missions will carry more physicians with them, and she can soon defer such an ordinary thing as a fetus to the experts.

"Good morning, Lucy. Any changes since last week?"

"Not health-wise, but I feel very different?" Mérieux steps onto a scale, and Keshi Okumu takes her vitals.

Marilina looks up from her patient's chart. "Everything's going to feel different for a while. How so?"

Mérieux's forehead creases over, accepting a blanket and gown from Okumu. "This is probably going to sound silly, but I feel . . . *good*. Out-of-control good. Euphoric. Like a flare high or something."

"Sounds awful." The doctor laughs, and Admiral Monroe joins in.

Mérieux continues to frown. "This might be unrelated, but I'm also having really vivid dreams."

Folding her arms, Marilina raises an eyebrow. "Alright. Why don't you get changed so we can take a look at this baby, then?" The doctor withdraws, and on her return, gestures for Mérieux to have a seat on the cot. With the admiral's support, she climbs onto the bench. Marilina presses a transducer against her patient's belly and rolls it around. A holograph appears between the three of them, showing the baby in three dimensions. The beginnings of a full head of hair, fingers and toes are visible.

"Congratulations, you two. It's a girl."

The baby curls its fingers into two tight little fists and turns away. A young girl's voice fills Marilina's head. *Away. Must sleep.* No one else seems to have heard. How strange.

The admiral grins. "She's already got her mother's spunk."

A jolt passes through the doctor's hand. With a yelp, she drops the transducer back on the cart. The soon-to-be parents stare at her as she rubs her hand.

"Something wrong?" Mérieux asks.

Marilina hesitates. Don't get the patient worked up. "No. I'm sorry. We can try again next time." Something that feels like it comes from outside of her makes her add, "The baby needs her rest." Why did she say that? Uneasy, she rubs her cross.

Mérieux exchanges a look with the admiral.

"Alright, no problem," he says. He squeezes her hand, but Marilina feels his eyes on her as she discards the sleeve on the transducer and hands the patient a cloth. "We'll be back next week," he repeats.

When the pair is out of earshot, Okumu steps around the cot and leans close. "Are you okay, Doctor?"

Marilina glances out of the doorway, but they're long gone. She shakes her head and rubs her hand. "This is going to sound weird, but that baby *spoke*, and then it burned me." She shrugs and smiles, handing the technician the patient's gown. "I'm losing my mind, aren't I?"

Okumu wears a solemn look. "You're not losing your mind, Doctor. Crazier things have happened here already, haven't they?" She sweeps the bedding from the cot and heads for the laundry room. Marilina stares after her, rubbing her hand.

MAY 28, 3041 | THE COLONY, ZOMENOS

Later that afternoon, the admiral finds Marilina alone in the infirmary catching up on her case reports. Outside her office window, Anima hangs low in the sky. She looks down at her wristband unit, startled by the hour. With how few patients there are, she should have left hours ago, but the morning's events tug unhelpfully in her periphery.

"Is everything okay with you?" the admiral asks. "You looked like you saw a ghost earlier."

The doctor thinks again about the little girl's voice she thought she'd heard. It's impossible, obviously. There are no children in the colony, and no matter what Okumu thinks, the child growing inside Mérieux can't be the source. Marilina shrugs and smiles.

"My ears were playing tricks on me." She shuts down the holographs in front of her. A task for tomorrow.

"Alright," he says. To Marilina's relief, he changes the subject. "There's something I've been meaning to ask."

Marilina sets her bag down near the exit and returns, pulling up a chair across from him. "Let me guess. You want to know if GLOW is working yet." Word of the Coalition's decision spread quickly through the colony. The doctor senses that the others have been dying to ask her opinion, but were instructed not to.

"I just want good news for my crew. We're all eager for the missions to be reinstated."

She is too. Her family will remain in cryo if the colony is aborted. What then? Will they all be sent to Earth, Alejandro's vision to be fulfilled after all? After everything she's been through, such a fate is too bleak to contemplate. "I'm optimistic," she answers truthfully. "It's too soon to say for certain, but our most recent tests are trending in the right direction. I'm monitoring it closely."

The admiral visibly relaxes. "That's the best news I've heard in a long time."

Marilina looks out the window into the field, sighs, and grins. A rush of contentment courses through her. The colony is just beginning to hit its stride. Everything's going to be okay. No, everything's *wonderful*.

Shivering, the doctor meets the admiral's gaze. Maybe she's losing her mind, after all. With a shaky attempt at another smile, she says, "Isn't it?"

CHAPTER FORTY FOUR

ANNA

A SCREECHING CACOPHONY ECHOES through the chambers of the Hall of Orphans as the audience takes their seats. The detective drops into a chair between Guardian Nuñez and Diego. The xenobot smiles, full of nervous jitters, and squeezes her hand. She squeezes back, but her eyes are on Alejandro Martinho, led down the aisle in plain gray skins by two armed guards. He should be shaking in his boots, but he stares straight ahead with his back arched and shoulders squared. Anna faces forward. He's not scared yet, but he will be. She closes her eyes, breathes in, and smiles. Today's the day, Ma.

The stands flash and twinkle, populating with the holos of dozens of Earth's orphans. There must be orphans from every station on the tribunal, maybe even a few colonists. Behind them, the rows are full. Guardian Osei's trial was well attended, but the audience today numbers in the thousands. A hooded judge takes the bench, and it begins.

"Detective Wright, please come to the stand." Nuñez prods her. Time for her performance. Boots clack on steel as the detective strides to the witness stand. "Walk us through your investigation. What was your involvement?"

Leaning back on a rock-hard bench, the detective closes her eyes. She's rehearsed this a bunch of times. Take your time and keep your cool. "I was brought on by Frank Roarke when he was still Coalition leader. My job was to investigate a missing person in relation to lost shipments to the colony on the planet Zomenos. I worked with Guardian Nuñez and later, his robot Diego, to investigate several possible leads. Those leads all traced to the work of a large criminal syndicate that calls itself Terra Nova. We prosecuted the former guardian, Kojo Osei, on the basis of his work with the syndicate. We now believe Alejandro Martinho to be the leader of the organization."

Thousands of pairs of eyes watch Anna in silence, with emotions ranging from shock to anger to fear, but across from her, Martinho catches her attention with a small smile. Her eyes narrow. Men like that have never known fear. This is all a game to him. Well, he doesn't know it yet, but he's lost. Martinho has so much to answer for. The detective settles back on the unyielding bench and refocuses on the judge, who speaks in their usual low growl of genderless anonymity.

"Thank you, Detective. The prosecution has charged Alejandro Martinho and his associates with racketeering under the alleged organization known as Terra Nova. What first led you to suspect Martinho?"

Cool air blasts the witness stand, sending a shiver through Anna. Her gaze flicks once again to the defendant across from her. "It was clear from the very beginning that Terra Nova had allies within the Coalition. Their broadcast implicated the restorationists as possible allies, too. Diego and I suspected that a guardian was leading Terra Nova itself, and Martinho's positioning as the restoration leader felt too convenient."

Nodding, the judge withdraws in their high chair, a silent indication that the prosecution may proceed. Taking his cue, Nuñez leaps forward. "You've gathered a lot of evidence for this case, Detective. Dígame: give us the highlights."

Smirk. "With pleasure. You'll hear from two guardians today who have agreed to testify against Martinho and his associates. Both of these guardians allied themselves with Terra Nova to undermine Frank Roarke's colonization efforts and funnel resources to Earth. We also have a direct admission of guilt in the raid of SS849 from one Patricia Ferreira, and the testimony of two witnesses assaulted by Terra Nova operatives, myself being one of them." Resting her elbows on the back of the bench, she expands on each one in turn. Still, Martinho remains unruffled, those gold-speckled eyes of his scintillating in the low light. He can't possibly deflect all these charges. Why's he so smug? High up in the stands, the tribunal looks on in silence.

The defense rises. "Detective, you mentioned the raid of SS849 earlier. Mae Wright was onboard that freight ship, wasn't she? Your mother."

"That's right."

"Can you honestly say that your decisions leading up to this trial were never impacted by her tragic death? Or that Miss Ferreira's admission of guilt, off-record, wasn't coerced by a woman with a vendetta?"

Anna rolls her eyes and glares, but she knew all along that the defense would use Ma against her. "Every living orphan has been impacted, directly or indirectly, by the crimes of this syndicate. If we had to wait for an objective lead to take this investigation on, we'd never close this case. Ferreira is guilty. I didn't coerce anything out of her. She offered that information up freely."

Whispers travel like the wind through the halls. Dismissed, the detective returns to the prosecutor's bench. Nuñez spares her a conciliatory smile, but she can see his jaw clench. Thanks to her, he's got to regain their edge. He quickly calls Kojo Osei to the stand, but the defense only gains more ground. Racketeering charges can be slippery: the burden of pinning individual charges against members of the syndicate falls on the prosecution, and it has to be clear that those members weren't acting alone. In this case, Osei's testimony falls short of convincing the tribunal that he was actually working with Terra Nova and not just Martinho. Anna slumps back in her seat. This isn't good.

In a surprising move, the defense calls Magadaline Barasa to the stand. Unable to believe her luck, the detective drives her heels into the floor and stares. The geologist's holo flickers to life, and the defense coaches her through a glowing testimony in favor of Martinho's strong leadership, quick instincts, and successful track record as a restorationist. Anna clenches her fist under the steel desk in front of her and swaps glares with Nuñez. It's hard to prosecute a saint. Patience, she reminds herself. The defense apparently has no idea what it has just done.

Rubbing his hands together, Nuñez struts forward. "Miss Barasa, you've been a part of the restoration since the beginning, right? Did anything change when Alejandro took over?"

"Absolutely. He was wise, always exploring new paths. He led us to new technologies that sped up the restoration. It was incredible." Fortunately, the detective has had a few conversations with the geologist herself, and a helpful tip from Guardian Bernard led to an interesting discovery that Nuñez can now exploit.

Nuñez says, "Of course. How would you describe his temperament?"

At this, Barasa shrinks, glancing in Martinho's direction. Anna smiles. They've got her cornered. "Guardian Martinho dislikes failure."

"Nobody likes that." Nuñez bounces on the balls of his feet. "Was there ever a time when you were afraid of him?"

The geologist's gaze flicks this time to the judge—as if that can save her. "Yes."

"Explain."

Squirming delightfully, Magadaline Barasa delivers a disturbing account of exactly what Martinho's displeasure looks like, painting a grisly picture of her time on Earth. Nuñez steers her expertly. The more she attempts to gloss over or withhold the worst details, the greater the tribunal's outrage.

"Thank you for sharing, Miss Barasa. It sounds like that was difficult to talk about. Did you know anyone by the name Rocío Valdez?"

Her face scrunches. "Yes."

"Tell us what happened to her, please. Take your time."

Barasa's account of the waterboarding of Rocío Valdez by her own hand sends a ripple of outrage through the hall, and the tribunal's sympathy for either her or Martinho evaporates.

The detective whispers in Diego's ear. "There. We've done it. Now Bernard just has to play her part."

As Magadaline Barasa exits, Victoria Bernard takes her place. The guardian has been cloistered away from everyone but her guards and the prosecution for weeks, and it's taken a toll. Like Martinho, she arrives in plainskins, but Bernard lacks his unflappable confidence. She shrinks on the witness stand and avoids his unnerving gaze.

Nuñez steps between them. "I'll cut to the chase, Victoria, since your testimony is already on record. As the defense helpfully reminded us, the crimes committed by Alejandro Martinho and his associates weren't necessarily connected in any way to Terra Nova. So, in your experience, was this the case or not?"

Bernard leans forward and speaks in a voice chapped by fear. "Oh, yes. Every individual I worked with was an associate of Terra Nova, including Miss Ferreira. It was the cornerstone of our agreement. I didn't otherwise engage in dealings with him."

The court adjourns that evening on quaking ground. Barasa and Bernard delivered Martinho right into the prosecution's hands, and he's not slithering out of them this time.

JUNE 14, 3041 | COLOSSI INFINITI, EARTH'S ORBIT

The trial continues for two more weeks. With so much evidence to go through, and so many players involved, it drags on, but none of the other witnesses' testimonies are as shocking as Magadaline Barasa's. It's obvious which way the tribunal leans. That's why it's surprising when Anna receives word that Alejandro Martinho himself plans to take the stand.

She stares at Nuñez with a flat look. "It's suicide."

"I don't know about that, Detective." Agitated, he paces the dark steel of her office floor. "He's going to attempt to humanize himself again. It's the only way to turn this back in his favor."

"He won't. It'll only backfire."

Nuñez shakes his head firmly. "We can't take that chance. Where are you with la doctora?"

Anna closes her eyes. "I promised her that she wouldn't have to do it." Dr. Chamorro returned to the colony weeks ago under the unequivocal agreement that she would *not* take the stand. Shielding the doctor is the least the detective can do—after what Martinho did to her, asking Chamorro to sit directly across from her abuser and recount the gory details feels dirty. "Why don't I take the stand again? I know her story backwards and forwards."

The guardian cocks an eyebrow. "That's not the same as a personal account. Ya sabes. I shouldn't have to tell you. Get the doctor to take the stand. This might all come down to her."

Easy for him to say, but Anna makes the call. The doctor's holo fills her office, looking surprised and vigilant.

"Hello, Detective. I didn't expect to hear from you again."

"I didn't expect to call. I'll be brief: Martinho is taking the stand in his own defense. We need your testimony."

A startled gasp escapes Chamorro's lips. "You said you wouldn't."

"Martinho's decision changes things. You can do this, Doctor. You're tough as nails. I hate to ask, but Nuñez thinks we're going to lose without you. Do you want that?"

Chamorro bites her lip. Poor thing. The bruises on her throat have only just healed. When she left, they were still a sickly green. None of that changes the fact that her abuser might walk free if she doesn't do something. "It's okay, Detective. What do you need me to say?"

A few hours later, Anna is back at that painfully firm prosecutor's bench. She's not exactly convinced that Chamorro will show. The woman's PTSD is obvious. Martinho's own testimony is smooth as butter, and he easily deflects

Nuñez's attempts at turning the tide in their favor. There's a reason this man was able to weasel the Coalition right out of Frank Roarke's willing fingers. He's as charismatic as they come. Damn him.

When the time comes for Chamorro to take the stand, the detective bows her head and holds her breath. Come on, Doc. It's now or never.

A holo of Dr. Chamorro springs to life, and Anna finally releases her breath. The doctor came through after all. Nuñez bulls forward eagerly, and Chamorro launches into her story with careful, deliberate words.

"I met Alejandro when he was still a guardian. I believed him to share many of the same values that I did. We're both former Meridian, and most of us join out of a love for our people. He was kind to me at first and passionate about Earth's restoration. I thought he was very rational. I even believed in the restoration myself. It wasn't until after he became Coalition leader that I noticed how . . . unstable he really was." Chamorro stares down at her hands, clenched into fists in her lap. She pauses, taking measured breaths, and looks up into Anna's eyes. The detective nods. You've got this, Doc.

"Alejandro made repeated promises that Terra Nova would never hurt me, but he wouldn't answer when I asked how he could know that. I attributed that to the arrogance of inexperience, but it was all part of his ruse. He later asked for my help, planting a portal device on me to take, unknowingly, to the colony, which he used to travel there. I learned afterward that he'd sent many ships to the colony before then. Terra Nova was on the planet before the colonists were, building their drill for their own purposes. He planned to use me to coordinate the transfer of the planet's minerals to the stations. When I denied him, he assaulted me."

Nuñez grips the stand in front of Chamorro's holo. "Thank you, Doctor." He glances at the judge. "The rest of Chamorro's testimony is in her file. I see no reason to question her further."

"Agreed."

Attempts at cross-examination are poorly received by the tribunal. The court adjourns to await a decision. Outside, Anna waits with Diego, but she's too nervous. Escaping into the atrium, she whisks a jimmy from the inner folds of her pockets.

"This is it, Diego. Everything we've worked for comes down to this moment." She studies him over the smoke trailing from her jimmy. "What do you plan on doing after this is all over?"

Diego smiles. He's fidgety today, but everyone is. "I wanted to ask you about that. I like working with you, Anna."

She returns the smile. "Yeah, you're alright." Blowing a ring of smoke, she juts her chin toward him. "So, you think you want to stay on with the Coalition? You'd have to deal with Arquette, but you could do worse."

The xenobot stuffs his hands in his skinpockets. "Actually, what I'm trying to say is, I want to be with you."

Shrug. "I got that. I'll put you down as my partner."

"You're going to make me spell it out, aren't you?" He shakes his head and laughs, looking *really* nervous. Glancing in both directions, he says, "Anna, I love you."

The detective's heart ricochets against her chest like rounds from a laser cannon. Love? She's never loved anything. "Oh. Sorry, I guess I completely misread that." She pauses, and he waits, those green eyes in rapture, as if she's the only thing that matters in the world. Is that love? Maybe. "Look, I don't do 'love.' I don't even usually do 'like.'"

His frown cuts her unexpectedly. "Yes, you do. You love your mother."

"Yeah? You want to end up like her?" Anna presses her back into the wall and closes her eyes, jimmy to her lips. It's not helping as much as it usually does.

A long silence stretches between them. He nods. "Okay. Forget I said anything." He stares at his boots for a moment. "We should probably get back, shouldn't we?"

Their conversation plays on a loop in Anna's head as they head back into the hall. *Love?* No. No way. She's only recently gotten used to the idea of trusting anyone but herself. Love is levels ahead of that. When he isn't looking, she steals a glance. Why did Nuñez have to make these xenobots so ridiculously emotive, anyway? He should have done a better job. If a xenobot can fall in love with her, it's faulty.

The judge speaks into the weighty silence. "The tribunal has reached its decision. Alejandro Martinho and his associates are found guilty of racketeering under the criminal organization Terra Nova. The charges include assault, murder, kidnapping, arson, bribery, extortion, fraud, and money laundering. Its members are sentenced to one hundred years in prison."

"We did it!" Nuñez hoots and grips Anna's slack shoulders. Dazed, she grins and hugs Diego, but he flinches, and they quickly withdraw. He'll get past this.

They won. They *actually* won.

CHAPTER FORTY FIVE

ALEJANDRO

AT THE END OF a long walkway lies a set of double doors. Those doors open just twice daily, once in the morning and once in the evening. Each time, a guard steps through, boots reverberating on steel. The guard inspects the prisoner's cell thoroughly. Inmates may request digital media such as e-books and music, but they may not have physical books or records. Few personal effects are allowed. Alejandro's cell is at the far end of the walkway, on the other side of a heavy door with a small window. Interaction with other inmates is disallowed. Visitors are disallowed.

Why should that disturb him? He's been alone before. Even at the orphanage, surrounded by children, and even as he attained power and influence, he's always felt acutely alone. It never mattered. People themselves aren't the antidote to loneliness. It is connection—to be seen and felt and understood—that makes the difference, and Alejandro has felt that precisely once in his entire life.

Today is an exception. Today, he is expecting a very special call.

The ring of boots on the steel platform comes to a stop, and he sits up.

"You have five minutes."

Alejandro's heart quickens. "Thank you, Raul." The air before him darkens to blue, and a holograph appears of Marilina Chamorro. The physician looks well. Her hair once again defies gravity in short, loose curls; her cheeks are supple and rosy; and her eyes are devoid of the fear he's come to expect in them. He smiles. She doesn't. "Marilina. This brings me much joy."

The doctor studies him with something bordering on apathy. So, she's guarded. That's wise. She was always an astute learner. "I can't say the same. What do you want? I thought you weren't allowed visitors."

"I am a man of persuasion." He steps closer. "I'm sorry. The neural network I used was defective. It sharpened my prefrontal cortex but dimmed my limbic system. Too late, I realized the implications." Forgetting for a moment that she is merely a holograph, he reaches for her hand. His fingers grasp air. "I never meant you any harm, and I'm ashamed to admit I made the greatest mistake of my life."

Marilina grips her wooden cross, ever round her neck, and says nothing.

His gaze drifts to the floor. She doesn't believe him. Why should she? The neural network unleashed a coldness deep inside him that he didn't believe possible. Which is real: the man he thought himself to be, or the man who strangled the woman he loves?

"That's all?"

Hope sings in his heart at the curiosity in her voice. "What else is there?"

Laughter, high and light. "Alejandro, you tried to destroy the colony. You had van Leeuwen assassinated, Detective Wright kidnapped, and you diverted every available resource to your own ends. Apologizing to me won't make a difference."

A flick of the wrist. "The colony, still? I know you, Marilina, now better than ever. You're not this simple-minded. In fact, you're every bit as ruthless as I am, when the right pressure is applied." For a second time, he reaches unthinkingly, this time to stroke her hair. She, too, forgets the distance between them and backs stiffly but swiftly out of reach.

A curiously sad smile overtakes her features, and she shakes her head. "I'm sorry for you too, then. I'm happy here, Alejandro. I have friends. I have hope. I'll have my family soon, too, but you have none of that. One hundred years is a long time to be alone. I'll inform the Coalition of this lapse. Don't call me again, please."

Her holograph fades, leaving behind nothing but the faint, periwinkle impression of her eyes, her nose. He sits on the cot, and it creaks loudly.

"Sorry, sir. I hope it was worth it."

The platform beyond his cell rings again with the thud of boots. His gaze flicks to the ground beside his door, where Raul left his dinner tray. Alejandro retrieves it, sitting at his desk. He spoons mashed potato into his mouth and chews, despite the fact that the food on the tray is already pulverized into moist sand. The dish has no spice, hardly any vegetable spread, and just a dash of salt. Spice, sauce, texture—these are what give rise to culture, to society. Without culture, what is mankind beyond a mutation from other primates?

What is he without mankind?

AUGUST 15, 3041 | 433 EROS, EARTH'S ORBIT

A light beyond the small window, his portal to the outside world, draws Alejandro's attention. There is no light beyond his cell. Most of the cell blocks on this barren asteroid are physically adjoined. His is not. The maximum security cell was installed at the top of a skyscraper (if it can be called such, given the asteroid's mercurial atmosphere) and can only be reached by a singular lift. All these weeks later, he recalls the ride quite well. From such a distance, and without opportunity to view the penitentiary below, light outside his window is unheard of.

Alejandro rises and approaches the door, where he waits. Minutes pass. Then, the unmistakable *swish* of the double doors at the end of the hall accompanies the thud of boots. It's not Raul. It's the middle of the day. The ringing comes to a stop outside his cell door.

"Morning, Sunshine." A face appears in the window of his cell. Detective Wright's bionic eyes radiate warmly out at him.

He turns away. "What can I do for you, Detective?"

Out of the corner of his eye, the detective plants her hands on her hips. "What's the matter? Am I not as fun as the doctor?" So, Marilina lived up to her word and reported Raul's indiscretion to his superiors. "She told me about her visit. That's the last time that'll happen." Alejandro grimaces, and Wright smiles. Such white teeth. There's nothing so white in this whole, poorly lit cell, and their brightness irritates his eyes.

"Don't you have other cases to solve, Detective?" he grumbles. "Or do you only ever think of yourself and your immediate loved ones? A pity you don't have two mothers, or I'd gladly dispatch another."

"I might," she retorts in a singsong voice. Voice lowered, she leans close. "Tell me why, and I'll leave you to your own devices."

His eyebrows knit in exasperation. "Why, what?" Those puerile red eyes only watch him. "Why did I form Terra Nova and have your mother killed?" She nods, and his laughter follows, dry and low. "Someone as simple as you could never understand."

"Try me."

Alejandro closes his eyes and rests his head against unblemished steel. "When the fate of humanity falls to men like Frank Roarke, men like me will always rise to prevent the demise of civilization."

"Ah. So you're a hero."

Tittering, he opens his eyes. "Are you?" He settles against the wall. "As I said before, I don't expect you to understand."

The detective crosses her arms. "But you're not part of that civilization anymore. Was it worth it?"

"The colony will fail. Not today. Maybe not a year from now. But it *will* fail, just as Earth failed, just as the stations are crumbling now, as all civilizations must. History repeats itself. You'd paint me a villain, wouldn't you? Yes, well, perhaps it is villainous, scandalous even, to imagine a brave new future and to be bold enough to chase it when others can't or won't."

This iteration of mankind is the weakest. The bunkers induced a psychological trauma in those of the old guard. Nuñez and Ngcobo and their ilk. It left them reaching in desperation for small comforts that only compounded the systems of inequity that led to Earth's demise. This colony of theirs is precisely that: a small-minded attempt at starting over somewhere new. Alejandro's vision was on a grander scale. To bend Mars, Enceladus, and yes, even Zomenos, to the singular task of restoring Earth. Yet, his orphans couldn't see past their precious colony. A pity. They'll learn the error of their ways in time.

A fragrant aroma of citrus draws him from his reverie. Smoke curls from the detective's mouth. His nose wrinkles. "Leave me. I prefer silence to your depraved company."

"I've been called worse." Eyes closed, Detective Wright sucks on the stick protruding from her lips and blows more smoke into his cell. "I'll go. You'll die alone, but I've still got people." She cocks her head. "How about that," she mutters. Refocusing on Alejandro, she flicks ash into his cell and waves cheerily. "Later, Al!"

Disgusting habit.

Alejandro bends to the task of scrubbing the ash from his neat floors. If he never sees the detective again—never sees *anyone* again—it won't be soon enough.

CHAPTER FORTY SIX

GUILLERMO

REACHING INTO A CABINET, Guillermo collects four glasses. He pours horchata from a pitcher, and feeling festive, rummages through a drawer for cinnamon sticks. Glasses loaded onto a metal tray, the guardian carries them into the living area, resisting a surging temptation to pirouette and spill all of it. Tomorrow, the cryo gardens close. Tonight, they celebrate.

"I hope you're thirsty."

Diego takes a glass. "Mm, spicy." Beside him, Carlos sits with his hands in his lap and watches. Cada uno es demasiado serio. Xenobots or not, they need to learn how to party.

"Go on," Guillermo says. "You'll like it." Juan loves horchata, but the guardian keeps that to himself. Setting down the tray, he slurps from his glass and uses his implants to search for some music. The walls rumble with the bass of robotón. He smacks his lips. Now, that's more like it. "Listen, Carlos, I have a favor to ask you."

Carlos downs his drink with a smile. He's grown more tolerant of his creator's music ever since his neural network was repaired. "What is it?"

Guillermo squats beside him. "My nephew found something strange in that wormhole. Go on, Diego, show him." Diego obediently retrieves the scrap metal and hands it to Carlos. "It's not a known alloy. Can you analyze it?"

"Sure. You think it's Terra Nova?"

"Exactly." Guillermo still can't believe that after every Terra Nova operative was rounded up, nothing in any of their testimonies and none of the evidence adds up to Derek's location. Did the commander make it to the planet or not? Who took him? It's driving Guillermo crazy, so he can't imagine how Jack feels. He can't even look into the admiral's eyes, azul celeste como el cielo, without seeing Derek.

Diego watches the guardian carefully. "Can we talk upstairs?"

The shop has been neglected. Guillermo needs another project, but he just isn't feeling the itch right now. The thought of Juan's eyes opening has him bouncing off the walls with excitement. For now, he sweeps dust from the workbench and sits. Soon. Diego grabs a chair from against the wall and pulls it close.

"I never properly thanked you for helping track down Anna."

Legs crossed, Guillermo looks up at Diego with his hands folded over his knee. "She never really needed our help."

"Maybe not, but I'm glad we were there." the xenobot says simply. "There was a time when nothing mattered to you but Juan, you know."

Guillermo sighs, staring at a scorch mark on the floor. One of Carlos's. So, this is what Diego wants to discuss. "In a lot of ways, that's still true." He shakes his head. "Carlos never really would've replaced Juan, and you deserve better than what I've shown you. You xenobots are your own person. Alejandro reversed my method when he became more machine than man, and it got him nowhere." Looking up, he sees Diego wiping his eyes. It makes Guillermo's own eyes sting.

Sniffling, Diego presses his palms into his eyelids. "I guess I always thought of you as selfish, but you're in love, and that's what you do when you love someone. Right?"

"Maybe I was." Guillermo swallows and angles his head to one side. "I'm not perfect, Diego, but I'm learning. When this all began, I didn't know if robots really felt complex emotion. Now I do." He taps his fingers on his knees. "Does the detective know how you feel?"

Diego flushes deep crimson. "She doesn't feel the same way."

"How do you know?"

"She rejected me, okay? Threatened me, actually."

The guardian pulls his knee up higher and shrugs. "Are you sure that's what she was doing?" Diego's mouth falls open with a fresh protest on his lips, but Guillermo holds up his hand. "Mira. You know the detective better than I do, but if she doesn't have feelings for you then why has she kept you around this long?" He picks up his glass, long forgotten, and finishes his horchata. "Pues, all I'm saying is that people don't always say what they mean. Try again."

Diego shakes his head. "I made a fool of myself. I won't make that mistake twice."

Chuckling, Guillermo waves his hand around his shop. "You're in good company, mijo. That's what love does to a man." He tilts his glass toward his xenobot in salute. "Don't let your ego get in the way of your own happiness. ¡Vámonos! Do you want her or not?"

SEPTEMBER 1, 3041 | GUADALAJARA STATION, EARTH'S ORBIT

All around, hundreds of people crowd into the cryo gardens, its creeping vine receding from their intrusion. It's the fullest Guillermo's ever seen it. Beside him, Carlos peers down at Juan's chinos suaves with more than a little curiosity.

The detective stands at Diego's side, watching in silence as Guillermo inspects the valves on the pod. After fifty years, this thing better not bust open during shuttle launch and kill his partner. Every one of these pods will be loaded onto one of the Coalition's unmanned freight ships for the long voyage to Zomenos. Guillermo will be waiting when Juan opens his eyes.

"We did it, mi cariño," the guardian whispers. "Everyone played their part well, and now it's your turn. Pórtate bien, and don't do anything I wouldn't do on that ship." Wink. "I'll be waiting for you in a few months."

"You know he can't hear you, right?" the detective mutters. Diego nudges her in the ribs.

Samkelo's booming voice interrupts. "Hello, Guillermo."

Rising, Guillermo slaps his back and grins. "Sam! I can't believe you came all the way for this."

Samkelo folds his hands over his gut. "We were promised this day would come when you were first made into a guardian. Do you remember?"

Oh, he remembers. "I made a lot of promises back then." Guillermo chuckles and rubs Carlos's shoulders. "Some worked out better than others. You remember the detective, don't you? Detective Wright, this is Guardian Ngcobo."

"How could I forget?" Samkelo graciously bows. Wright shakes Samkelo's hand. Apparently nervous, the xenobots clam up in Samkelo's austere presence, making Guillermo smile. "I bring news. That's partly the reason I traveled here."

Guillermo's stomach flips. Samkelo can only be referring to his review for Coalition leader. He licks his lips and summons a smile. "Come on, Sam. You're not going to embarrass me in front of my guests, are you?"

"I wouldn't dream of it." Samkelo inclines his head. "The Coalition has completed its review. The robotics guild was thoroughly impressed with your neural network. They've even gone so far as to recommend immediate, widespread adoption. They want to see more of your ingenuity, old friend. We'd like to formally offer you the position of leader."

Guillermo staggers back into Diego. "Neta. Wow. Thanks, Sam."

The position comes with its own challenges. For all their differences, Frank and Alejandro both lusted for the power of the Cerebrum particles, and now Alejandro will wear his for life. Will the same greed overcome Guillermo? He glances at the pods being loaded onto the transport shuttle. He was willing to let Carlos die if it meant he would see Juan's face sooner. Is he any better than his predecessors, after everything he put his xenobots through?

He is. He knows he is. It isn't the temptation itself that ruins a good leader. It's their choices. Guillermo has made mistakes, de seguro, but with his xenobots' help, he's accomplished what neither Frank nor Alejandro could. The people are united for the first time in years. He can do this. No—he *should* do this.

"I accept."

Wright steps forward, hand outstretched in exaggerated formality. "Congratulations, Nuñez. I guess I ought to start showing you more respect."

Grinning, he takes her hand. "Don't strain yourself, Detective."

CHAPTER FORTY SEVEN

MARILINA

KNEELING IN FRONT OF her cot with fingers laced, Marilina bends her head. Prayer never came easily to her before. Mami's cross is cupped between her hands, filling her senses with a grounding, spiritual scent of frankincense and myrrh. Lines of concentration crease her forehead as she grasps for the words to Fatima's prayer to the Virgen. Please, bring them home safely.

She gasps. What will her parents say when they learn of Quique's death, or her involvement with Alejandro? They'll understand, won't they? They have to. The blame can't fall to her. Marilina has done her duty to them, and it's time they acknowledge all that she's accomplished here. Tucking her cross hastily beneath the folds of her skins, she stands.

The doctor wanders through an open field toward the square alone. A breeze flits past, refreshing on her cheeks. Her skin feels softer and smoother now. GLOW must be taking effect in her once more. It's a major relief. GLOW was a key factor in the Coalition's decision to send the cryo pods to the colony. Soon, all of Earth's orphans will follow. The sky above shifts to the color of surgical steel, threatening rain. The seasons are beginning to turn. She rubs her hands together against the brisk wind.

Under the shade of an arching, gnarled tree, Henry reclines in the crook of its enormous root. Another member of the agricultural unit, Eve, and several officers form a semi-circle around him. Marilina heads toward them. A game of Black Holes is about to start. She's only recently learned the rules, but she's gotten quite good.

"Listen up, guys." Henry speaks seriously. "Astronauts are wild. Claim a trick by laying your card down over it first. Anyone who tries to claim a trick after it is taken is in the hole. Anyone who can't follow suit and can't play an astronaut is in the hole. Play an asteroid to get out of the hole. If you're out of asteroid cards, draw from the deck. If you trump with a wormhole card, you get double points."

"Yeah, yeah," Officer Pruitt interrupts. "We all know the rules."

The admiral produces a deck of cards and shuffles deftly. "We can use my deck." Marilina settles in between the two brothers while he deals out one card to each of them, face up. Card games are a favorite pastime among the crew, and they're a welcome change of pace from the anomalies the doctor faces in the infirmary. "Looks like I'm dealer," Admiral Monroe pronounces matter-of-factly as he deals the final card to himself. An astronaut lays face up in front of him, trumping the other cards. All the better for Marilina: she's well positioned to gain points and take an early lead.

"How did you find the Zomenos edition?" Eve exclaims, admiring the shimmering silver and purple deck. The wind blows her vibrant red hair into her eyes and sends waves rippling through the tall grass. Smoke pipes from the chimney atop the kitchens across the square. The units take turns at kitchen duty, and tonight the developmental unit has threatened (or promised, as the doctor chooses to think) a spicy affair. Fragrant onion and garlic waft their way. Dinner will be ready soon.

He shrugs, shuffling and dealing out the first hand. "I'm an admiral."

Pruitt glances in his direction. "I thought the meeting went well today." He sorts through the cards in his hand. "I bid two."

The admiral inspects his hand. "I thought so too. The Coalition is putting a lot of trust in us, after everything that's happened." He tips his head toward the doctor. "We have Marilina to thank for monitoring GLOW so thoroughly. Let's just hope the dragons keep their word."

Rumors of their alien neighbors have injected a certain amount of tension into the colony, but Marilina feels none of it. She's already faced the most dangerous man alive and survived. She just can't muster up the same fear of these dragons, not even after treating Alejandro's injuries herself. They protected the colony from him, intentionally or not. The doctor scans her cards. "Pass. Thanks, Jack. I hope so, too. The truce was their idea, wasn't it?"

Brow furrowed, Henry stares at his cards for a while. "Pass," he says finally.

"I pass too," Eve pronounces with an unhappy slump in her shoulders. Elbows on her knees, she kicks out her feet comfortably in front of her and looks at the others. "How do we know we can trust them?"

"I'll take your bid," Admiral Monroe tells Pruitt. He throws down a card with ten purple moons and turns to Eve. "It's fair to be skeptical," he adds, "but a truce is more prudent than a war."

With a flourish, Pruitt lays down a card with twelve moons. "Ha!" he interjects. "I'll take this round, thanks."

Marilina stares at all those moons. "Not so fast. That's a lot of points." She lays down a three of moons, confusing the others. Pruitt still leads the round with his twelve, but she's betting on herself.

Ignoring her, the officer regards the brothers. "Well, if we're going to coexist with dragons, they should come out of hiding." A perfectly fair point, if Marilina had a say. She doesn't, so she remains silent. She has faith in the unit leads to sort this truce out.

Henry stares at the cards in his hand for a long time. "You'll feel better once you meet them. It sounds crazy, but being able to put a face to them helps." He sighs and lays down a card with seven blue orbiters, making everyone groan. He has failed to follow suit.

"Already?" Marilina raises her eyebrows. It's only the second round.

"Aww, Henry," Eve tuts.

Henry answers heavily. "I know. I'm in the hole."

"Why did that dragon attack Martinho, then?" Eve's voice is shrill with anxiety.

"Alejandro got what he deserved," Marilina declares quietly. He can say whatever he likes, blame everything on that neural network, but she doesn't believe him. It will be a long time before she forgets his hands around her throat, or the crazed look in his eyes while he attempted to end her life. He was found guilty by a tribunal. He doesn't get to rewrite his own narrative, now.

Eve glances sideways at the doctor, but the pile of cards accumulating in front of her is irresistible. Henry starts to chime in, but she slaps down an eight of moons and pitches an astronaut on top of it in quick succession. Marilina is faster, slipping her own purple astronaut in beneath Eve's.

"What!" Eve exclaims, leaping to her feet. Her outrage curdles, giving way to despair. "Now I'm in the hole, too!" she wails, casting an injured look at Marilina. "I can't believe you would waste an astronaut on the second round!"

The doctor collects the cards before her with an impish grin. "Doesn't look like a waste to me."

Pruitt sighs. "What were you saying, Henry?"

Henry watches as Marilina lays down the first card of the next round: six ringed Saturns in orange. Drawing from the deck, he replies, "If that dragon hadn't intervened, its friend would've died. The way I see it, it was just looking out for its own. You would've done the same. The drill site was never sanctioned, so there's no reason to escalate things between us." He huffs. "No good. I'm still in the hole. You're up, Eve."

"Well you and the admiral would know what's best," Eve muses. "You've spent the most time with those dragons." She glares acid at Marilina as she draws a card from the deck. "Yes!" she hoots, tossing a newly drawn asteroid onto the pile. "Out of the hole!"

"We'll know more once I get a chance to meet with Pyrrhos," Admiral Monroe promises. He sighs as Pruitt lays down another twelve. "You're loaded with those, aren't you?" he gripes. The doctor swoops in with an astronaut to win the round.

"Maybe I am," Pruitt says, unabashed. Marilina collects three more rounds in quick succession. The mood steadily sours with each hand. The night sky darkens to a deep indigo and twin moons rise, glowing brightly amidst the stars. The air is heavy with curry, and Marilina's stomach rumbles.

"Why don't we call it, eh?" Henry suggests with a glance at Eve silently fuming beside him.

The doctor would be happy to oblige, but Eve objects testily. "No. Last round. We're seeing this through." She may be losing, but Marilina rather admires her commitment.

The admiral pulls an asteroid card from the deck after being in the hole for two rounds. "Well at least I didn't end the game in the hole." Pruitt plays his last card with nine blue orbiters on it.

The doctor smiles apologetically at Eve. "If I'm not mistaken, I believe I've won." She brandishes a wormhole card, claiming the round indisputably and doubling her point total. She beams into the shocked silence. Yes, she's rather pleased that the colony will continue after all.

CHAPTER FORTY EIGHT

JACK

The dome stretches overhead, the single greatest protection the colonists have from outside forces. The admiral tilts his head back, tracing its glassy arc out of sight. It's not the first time he's stepped foot beyond its protection, but it feels much crazier now that he knows everything waiting beyond. Nothing he can do about that. Their truce is on the other side, waiting to be finalized.

Henry glances sideways at him. "So? Are you ready to be a dad?"

Fingers running through his hair, the admiral wades through the grass. The white boots of the military are streaked unrecognizably blue, so he's swapped his for a practical set of black ones. There's a lot to get used to on this planet, but grass stains weren't even on his radar. "I hope so. I just wish I were half the man Dad is."

Wherever he is.

"Come on. When are you going to stop idolizing him?"

Jack halts in his tracks. "I don't do that." Caustic skepticism in his brother's eyes draws a self-conscious grin from the admiral. "Okay, maybe a little. But Dad wasn't around much. He's the pilot that discovered Zomenos, and he's larger than life, you know?"

"That doesn't mean he was a great father, or that he's better than you."

Jack shrugs. Henry will never understand. They share the same parents, but Henry was too young when their biological mother died to remember her, and he never really tried to follow in Dad's footsteps. He has no idea how lucky he is to just exist, as himself, without expectations. The admiral pulls his jacket snug against a headwind. Dad's bomber jacket. He notices Henry noticing.

"Sometimes his legacy feels like a noose around my neck." His gut twists. It's disrespectful to think it, let alone speak the words.

Henry rounds on him. "See? That's what I'm talking about. You have every right to want to step outside of his shadow, and you've done it!" He paces backwards and spins like a top, arms outstretched. "Look around. Dad may have discovered this place, but you put in the work to get us here. People look up to you. Hell, Colter would follow you to the edge of the universe. Shove the guilt and just be proud of yourself, geez."

Exhaling shakily, Jack ducks under a branch and stares straight ahead. No guilt. He tests the waters. "My kid will grow up knowing her parents. That's something we could never say."

"Exactly." Henry glances at him. "You're going to keep looking for him, aren't you?"

The admiral keeps his eyes glued ahead. "I have to."

Nudge. Jack turns, but Henry points at the sky. A red blur shoots through the trees. Is this an ambush? Unsure what to expect, the admiral tenses, but Pyrrhos flies past and lands in a clearing up ahead. The brothers take up a jog. Rows of fiery red scales shine like rubies along the dragon's sleek neck, chest, and tail. The spikes that frame its face look sharper, its meaty chest and legs more muscular. There's no questioning it. This dragon is at its prime.

"Pyrrhos," Jack exclaims. "You're okay. That's a relief." His own words take him by surprise, but it's true: these aliens never deserved to come to harm by Terra Nova's hand.

The dragon inclines its spiked head. "My brethren saw to my healing." There is a pause. "I am sorry that Brontos attacked your kin. He acted out of fear. He has been disciplined."

It will be a long time before the admiral forgets the scar Martinho bore. Dr. Chamorro thinks he'll wear it for the rest of his life. He'll live, but that dragon put him in a coma for over a week. Nothing like that can happen again. Ever. His *and* Dad's reputations are on the line. "Right. Well, that's why we're here. To set the terms of this truce."

Pyrrhos growls, "What are your demands?"

The admiral exchanges a glance with his brother. Does Pyrrhos speak for the others? Intuitively, Jack knows the answer. One leader can always recognize another. "We need your assurance that no harm will come to our colony at your . . . talons. In exchange, we agree to keep the peace on our end."

"And if the terms are violated?"

Heels clicked together, the admiral tucks his hands behind his back. "I would ask that you allow us to discipline our own as we see fit."

"Why would we agree to such a thing? We know nothing of your laws or your punishments. My kind would not respond well to undue leniency for violators."

"You didn't show us that courtesy when it was your dragon doing the violating."

The dragon's tail lashes the ground, but he bows his head. "I propose a counteroffer. Should the terms be violated, the offender will be handled by their own kind, but the punishment must be approved by the opposing party."

"Sounds good to me. If we're agreed, then I have a favor to ask of you."

Those sharp, glassy eyes narrow to slits. "What might that be?"

Jack draws himself up. "My people want to meet you. All of you, or as many of you that will come. They have only my word to go on that you mean us no harm."

Pyrrhos regards him in silence. "That won't pose any issue. Assemble your kin on the open grass at dawn."

SEPTEMBER 20, 3041 | THE COLONY, ZOMENOS

News of the dragons' arrival zips through the colony like a laser beam. By sundown, every single crewmember has been alerted to the impending visit. The entire crew rises before dawn and, some still wearing their sleepskins, waits on the grassy field just beyond the dome. For a while, nothing happens. Then a shadow passes overhead.

"Look," someone calls out.

A streak of light plunges towards the crowd at supersonic speed. Jack clocks it at an impressive 3 thousand kilometers per hour. As it grows closer, swirling colors become visible: red, yellow, green, and white. They break apart and four imposing dragons appear. Long, tapered wings flap powerfully, light glinting from sinewy folds. The dragons crest the horizon, and the admiral's chest tightens. They really are magical. The fleet nears the crew on the ground, and the tension returns.

A white dragon breaks away from the others, spiraling toward Jack. It lands at a heart-stopping speed, breaking ground without so much as a bump. Glistening white scales cover a lithe body much smaller than Pyrrhos's. Up close, the alien is crowned in two short horns. Jack steps forward, but the dragon slithers up to Lucy instead, watching her with deep violet eyes like the oceans themselves.

"You are the Lissae?" It speaks in a haunting, otherworldly voice. Pale and speechless, Lucy only stares. The dragon steps closer. "You create life for your clan."

"Well, yes. How could you possibly know that?"

The dragon bows its head, revealing a row of long barbs along its spine. "I can feel its magic." Head whipping toward Jack, Lucy silently forms the word, *Magic?* He's just as wrong-footed as she is, but he's wary of saying too much just now. This dragon may be much smaller than Pyrrhos, but the admiral gets the distinct impression that this one is deadlier. Truce or not, he's got deep misgivings about how near it stands to Lucy. He angles his body, positioning himself subtly between the dragon and his partner. "You must take great care. The young can be careless with their magic, and manipulation of life energy can come at great cost. We can help you."

"Aisa." His words cracking like a whip, Pyrrhos lands beside them. A wordless understanding passes between the two dragons. Jack feels correct in his initial assessment that Pyrrhos is their leader, but Aisa inspires a primal fear in him that Pyrrhos's presence does nothing to alleviate. To Jack, he says, "Aisa speaks truth, but as usual, she omits. We have felt the babe's presence for weeks. Longer, if you count her time double."

The admiral stares at Pyrrhos. "Time double?"

"Yes. The babe, grown. That her time double exists here, now, can only mean that our magic will thrive with you here."

Magic. We're talking about real-life magic, not capes and card tricks. Jack is bursting with questions, but the crew mills about nearby. Now isn't the time for his answers. He fires off his most pressing question. "Where is her time double now?"

"She came through the sky, as you did, in one of those fireboxes. It landed in the forest near where we first met. The time double is gone now." A heady wave of realization crushes Jack: Dad, the purple-eyed girl, the ancient version of their orbiter that crash-landed in the forest. Dizzy, Jack spins to Lucy.

"The future. The purple-eyed girl is from the future, and she's our daughter." If Dad is with her, then he's alive.

The matter apparently settled, Pyrrhos steps past Jack and addresses the crowd. "We are the protectors to Pelypso," he intones. "We bid you welcome to these sacred lands."

CHAPTER FORTY NINE

ANNA

I F ONLY SHE COULD disappear. Leap away, like a guardian. Or just die. Anything is better than this. The detective waits with feet spread and arms crossed. There are people everywhere—hundreds of them. The rows beyond the stage burst with Earth's orphans, and they're all here to see her.

She'd rather fight a skinless.

Anna has visited this station a few times in her recent past, but she's never lingered. Nuñez chose one of the big-and-fancies to hold her ceremony in. She doesn't see why. There's nothing here for her and no one to give a damn about her. She can tell that flare never really took off on this station. Maybe that's Nuñez's doing too, maybe not, but it gives the otherwise modest station a huge edge over most of the others in the wake of Martinho's regime.

Her new leader delivers a nice speech from the podium in front of her. He talks about cleverness and ingenuity and perseverance. How fearless it was of the detective to confront a guardian on her own. How determined she was to build her case against Martinho. How the rising stakes never deterred her from doing the right thing. He doesn't talk at all about how the Coalition barred her from doing all those things.

Cowards.

Nuñez finishes his little speech and turns to her with a smile. This is the part where Anna graciously accepts a glass plaque and shouts pretty words of encouragement for the crowd below. She rubs her knuckles and glances at Diego, sitting beside her.

"Do I have to?"

Diego rolls his eyes and nudges her. "Get over there."

Anna bows her head and strides, awkward as the first time she tried a jimmy, to the podium. Her boots stick to slick steel and she trips, arms flailing. The crowd looks on in silence. It takes an eternity to reach the podium. Nuñez shakes her hands with both of his and hands her the award.

"Congratulations, Detective," the Coalition leader murmurs. "Enjoy your day."

Oh—there really is a plaque. It's heavy. What do they expect her to do with this thing, club a Skeleton and run? The old boar offered her a promotion along with the plaque, but she turned it down. She's already head detective. Anything beyond that just means a bigger desk and an even bigger waistline. No, thanks. She belongs in the field. Ma must have understood that about her, and that's why she hated the thought of her kid joining the military. Anna is a born detective, and she's not backing down just because Terra Nova is gone.

Nuñez turns away from the podium, gesturing for her to take the stage. The detective approaches and the whispers cut out. An orb hovers overhead, too bright. The floor is hers. She peeks in Diego's direction one more time, and he winks at her. He's beaming, that little boy scout.

One deep breath, and she speaks clearly into the hush. "This award is meaningless." Fresh whispers launch. She shakes her head. "I'm no hero. I'm just keeping a promise I made to someone. Now I want you to make a promise to yourselves. Promise that you'll take control of your own destinies. Turn the stations around. You don't need a guardian to do it for you. Don't let fear of Terra Nova or Skeletons hold you back, and don't turn your backs on the skinless, either. Just look out for each other, and work together, damn it. Do you think you can do that?" Diego catches her eye, grinning and blinking and wiping his cheeks. She looks away, shaking her head. "Otherwise, none of this matters." Anna brandishes her plaque high into the silence that follows and stalks off stage without a second glance.

No one else is behind the building, so that's where the detective goes for her hit of jimmy. The party is still going on inside, but she's had enough. One leg is kicked against the wall behind her. Leaning back against cool steel, she closes her eyes and breathes in deeply. There's a chill in the air, but Anna likes it. It tickles her into action, reminds her that there's more work to be done. Her vengeance is earned, but every day new arrests pour into the Coalition. She won't rest until every one of Martinho's Skeletons is behind bars. The door swings open and someone steps outside. Anna tosses her head back and sighs. She'd rather be alone. When she looks down, Diego is there.

"Oh, it's you."

"I figured I'd find you here." Oh no. He's got that odd expression again. His curly hair has grown long, masking his eyebrows. Those green eyes of his shine under the light of the orbs drifting nearby. He steps close, and she tenses. "You were talking about your mother in there, weren't you? You call for her in your sleep sometimes, you know."

Anna rolls her eyes. "Yep. You figured me out." She lifts her jimmy to her lips, but Diego catches her wrist.

"You're a hypocrite. You know that?"

Sigh. Why can't he leave her be? "What are you talking about, Diego?"

"Back there, you said 'work together,' but you do everything alone, Anna." She launches into a protest, but he stops her. "You definitely can, you just don't have to."

Uneasy, she only shrugs. "Yeah, I know that."

"Do you?" Diego cocks an eyebrow. Releasing her wrist and wringing his hands instead, he turns away. "If you haven't noticed, I've been at your side this whole time. I'm starting to think I'm wasting my time here."

Anna opens her mouth, but there's no easy retort for this one. Her shoulders sag. "What do you want me to say? I'm sorry, Diego. I've been on my own for a long time. I like it that way."

"Bullshit." He spins around. "Just admit it. You like having me around."

Anna laughs. "Don't be such a—"

"Bot?"

"I was going to say baby."

They stare at each other. A foreign impulse surges through Anna, and she's reaching for Diego's skins, jimmy falling to the ground, and pulling him toward her. Suddenly they're kissing. His lips on her mouth, his hair between her fingers, his heart thumping against hers—a real heart, as real as any human's, and moreso than her own eyes and implants. Her urge startles her as much as it does him, and they break away, breath coming in gasps. Diego steps back several paces and stares at her.

"What are you doing?" she asks.

"Just making sure I'm not dreaming."

Anna laughs and, stamping out her jimmy, takes his hand. "Okay. Definitely not a bot."

SEPTEMBER 29, 3041 | MONTRÉAL STATION, EARTH'S ORBIT

They return to a party just beginning to thin out. Anna leads the way, dodging as many of the bureaucrats as she can before they can try to convince her to accept the promotion or some other nonsense. They find Nuñez waiting for them near the stage. The Coalition leader wears a smart set of caramel-colored skins for the occasion, and his hair is slicked to the side. He nods at her.

"Felicitaciones, Detective."

Anna crosses her arms and leans against the wall. "Thanks. You didn't have to put all this together for me."

Nuñez winks. "It was no trouble, you know that." He lowers his voice. "I have another reason I wanted to see you two."

Anna drops her arms to her sides and scowls. "What now? Another one of your schemes?"

"Is that any way to talk to your new leader?" He chuckles. "I have something to show you both." He reaches into his pocketskins and retrieves the admiral's precious debris.

"Oh, right. It's just junk. What are you so excited about?"

His voice is nearly a whisper. "I know, so I had Carlos take a look." He turns over his palm, and a holo appears. He angles his body to conceal its contents from anyone nearby. "This shrapnel didn't come from the site of your wreckage, Diego. It didn't come from anywhere in this star system. It was in the wormhole, and I think there's more of it."

Anna crosses her arms. "Are you saying . . . ?" she trails off. It's too outlandish to say out loud, but if that scrap of metal didn't come from here, it had to come from somewhere. Nuñez claps his hands together.

"¡Órale! This alloy came from Zomenos."

ACKNOWLEDGEMENTS

I took my time with this book, and it passed through many hands to get to where it is today. First and foremost, thanks goes to the amazing KH. You deliver encouragement, feedback, support, and compassion, sometimes before I even realize I need it. Thank you for laughing at the silly things and for enjoying heaps of sushi with me.

Thanks always to my family and friends—confused though you may be about this path of mine—for supporting it anyway. Thanks to Abbey, Matt, and members of the Heise and Lakdawala labs for being the earliest sounding boards for this book, and to Dad for researching Kickstarter like it was his job. Thanks also to Grandma and Janet for supplying me with many of the tales that formed my early writing. A special thank you to Mom. Thank you for carrying Nicaragua to Miami with you, for the bedtime Goosebumps stories, and for the long summers in the library. I am undeniably a writer because of you, and this book is The Orphan Race because of you.

A round of applause please for my beta readers, the unsung heroes who tolerated this book in its tender youth and helped me spot its weaknesses: Abbey, Clancy, Alan, Kayla, CZ, Eric, Lisa, Adam, Chris, and KH. My gratitude is just as long for those professionals who helped develop this author's first book for publication: Sophie Playle, Alex Dawning, and Write! Pittsburgh. This book has traveled through its own wormhole, and I no longer recognize it. I mean that in the very best way.

Mil gracias to my Kickstarter backers for taking a chance on my wild ideas of sci-fi. We created something truly unique together: adamnemo42, Jessica Packard, Chris Flanagan, Rebecca ONeill, Chloe Koon, Andrew Aguirre, Stephen Jones, Lauren ODonnell, Daniel Martinez, Lisa Florida, Sarah Maya,

Laurel Kartchner, Megan Freeman, Taylor Eddens, Abbey Castillo, fayljlj, Patrick Dolan, Jay Vornhagen, Allison Culley, Seema Lakdawala, Michael Jones, Meshia, Mayrajones, Matthew Jones, Jacob Benedict, Paul, Samantha, biotteau jean-paul, R.S. Kellogg, Dominic Hilsbos, Dawn C., Andrea Matamoros, Jonathan, and Chandler Pope-Lewis.

ABOUT THE AUTHOR

Jenny Jones is a generalist—that is, someone with a curious mind for many things and expertise in a cherished few. She is Nicaraguan-American and cultivated an early interest in writing in sunny Miami, Florida. Her passions often take her places she never thought she'd go, and her love of science took her to Chapel Hill, NC, receiving her Ph.D. in Microbiology and Immunology and publishing research on herpesviruses, mosquito-borne viruses, and respiratory viruses. To many, she is simply a virologist, but she embraces the moniker Renaissance Femme to celebrate a generalist's approach to life. She resides in Pittsburgh, Pennsylvania with her partner (a fellow generalist), an unwieldy collection of instruments and paintbrushes, and their mischievous cat.

CONNECT WITH JENNY:

Website: https://jennyjonesphd.com
Instagram: @jennyjonesbooks